D0924376

the **Girl**

in the

Cardboard Box

Endorsements

In this page-turner, Daly introduces us to a "feral child" raised in a box who becomes involved in the lives of others with confining "boxes" of secrets in their own lives. The foster parents have their own hidden guilts that come to light in ever-increasing tension. I read this in one sitting because I had to find out, along with these people, how such situations could ever be redeemed. A well-researched book of hope.

—**Latayne Scott**, award-winning author of over two dozen books, including *Conspiracy of Truth* and *Protecting Your Child from Predators.*

I can usually tell if a book is going to be good within two or three chapters. With *The Girl in the Cardboard Box,* I knew after the first page. This isn't my kind of book, which should tell you something, because I was riveted. Jane Daly's writing is tight, evocative, and in places quite lyrical. Plus she tells a story that captivates. This is one you'll be talking about.

James L. Rubart, Christy Hall of Fame author

You'll be drawn into this special story immediately! Hayley and Jazzmine and Girl, a trio of unique people from the start. A story that says you don't have to be perfect for God to love and work through you.

—**Angela Breidenbach**, Christian Authors Network president and bestselling author, AngelaBreidenbach.com

In *The Girl in the Cardboard Box*, Jane Daly has given readers an engaging and inspiring story of redemption and forgiveness, reminding us that even the most dire of human troubles can be transformed through God's love and strength. Hayley and Jason have experienced the worst nightmare imaginable, and—like many couple—they have turned inward in their grief. They have sought explanations from human sources, and buried their own guilt in a mountain of blame and defensiveness. Yet just as their future seems the most hopeless, the light of God finds its way in through the cracks of their lives. Their story serves as a promise that in His gift of forgiveness, we can find our own hearts changed toward others, no matter what has happened in the past.

—**Ramona Richards**, author, *Murder in the Family* and *Burying Daisy Doe*

The *Girl*

in the

Cardboard Box

Jane S. Daly

PUBLISHING THE POSITIVE
Plymouth, Massachusetts

Copyright Notice

The Girl in the Cardboard Box

Cover and Interior Design: Derinda Babcock
Editor(s): Mel Hughes, Deb Haggerty
Author Represented By: Credo Communications LLC

PUBLISHED BY: Elk Lake Publishing, Inc., 35 Dogwood Drive, Plymouth, MA 02360, 2021

Library Cataloging Data

Names: Daly, Jane S. (Jane S. Daly)

The Girl in the Cardboard Box /Jane S. Daly

310 p. 23cm × 15cm (9in × 6 in.)

ISBN-13: 978-1-64949-244-9 (paperback) | 978-1-64949-245-6 (trade paperback) | 978-1-64949-246-3 (e-book)

Key Words: feral children; foster care; grief; forgiveness; guilt; emotional abuse; redemption

Library of Congress Control Number: 2021940965 Fiction

DEDICATION

To all the women who've lost a child – there is hope

ACKNOWLEDGMENTS

A huge hug to my hubby, Mike, for being the best encourager during the many times I was tempted to quit. Remember, "I just want to play with my sister."

My writing tribe, Inspire Christian Writers, Oregon Christian Writers, West Coast Christian Writers, and my Fire Pit Crew. You have taught me, encouraged me, coached me, and never let me quit. Thank you.

Mel Hughes, it was fun to work with your editing style. Your comments made me laugh, which is so needed during the grueling process of editing. I appreciate your help in making Zola better. Thanks!

Robin Jones Gunn—your keynote at 2017 OCW Summer Conference was like a baseball bat to the head—in a good way. I will never again put my hand in another woman's wash bucket.

Mom, you've been gone three years, but I still hear you ask me every day at dinner, "Did you get any writing done today?" I miss you every single day.

Thank you to the team at Elk Lake Publishing—you are awesome. Thanks for all the help you've given me to make this novel even better.

CHAPTER 1

The girl huddled under the stiff blanket, making herself as small as possible. Words exploded over her head. Mama's voice, loud. A man, yelling.

The familiar sound of a slap. More yelling.

After a few minutes, she raised herself a tiny bit and peeked through a slit in the box. Scary men with guns and shiny stars on their shirts ran toward her box. Mama had said to never talk to them.

One of them grabbed Mama and threw her to the ground. Mama screamed.

The girl scrunched back down, pulling the blanket over her head. She shoved her thumb in her mouth and squeezed her eyes shut until the yelling stopped.

Sunlight crept through the corners of the cardboard box. The girl put one eye up to the slit. Where was Mama? She whimpered, remembering the night before.

With a tentative push on the side of the box, she crawled out and stood. The grass wet her bare feet as she crept along the row of makeshift tents and boxes. No one stirred.

Her stomach rumbled. Mama didn't bring any food home last night.

She tiptoed to where the lady with no teeth slept. Sometimes she gave her something to eat.

A half-eaten sandwich lay in a battered shopping cart. The girl shoved away a mangy cat who also eyed the food and devoured the sandwich in two bites. She wandered outside the camp's edge and squatted by a tree to relieve herself.

The girl returned to her box, sitting in the sun, waiting for Mama to come back.

The summer sun beat down on the tents and makeshift houses when the homeless camp stirred to life. Sounds swirled around the girl as she scooted backward, farther into the box.

"Don't talk to no one," Mama had said. "Do you hear me, girl? No sound from you, or else." Mama always slapped her face as a reminder.

A sudden commotion at the far end of the camp sent her scurrying under the blanket. She shivered despite the heat inside the box.

More loud man voices. Hands clawing on the box. Then she tumbled out onto the hard ground.

"Oh, my word. It's a kid."

CHAPTER 2

Hayley Montgomery wiped the sweat off her forehead with a clean, white towel. She checked her Fitbit for the time of her five-mile run. A little over forty-three minutes. Dodging the one sprinkler had slowed her down. Tomorrow she'd be back on track.

After downing half a bottle of spring water, she counted ten almonds from the can, laying them in a line on the black marble countertop. She popped one in her mouth, making sure to chew completely before starting on the next.

Her cell phone vibrated with an incoming call from Jazzmine, the social worker.

"Hi, Jazz." The social worker's nickname rolled off her tongue.

"Hi, honey. I'm sorry to do this to you on such short notice. Especially since you've barely recovered from your last fostering experience."

Hayley grimaced. Parting with those two precious kids had been difficult. They needed a stable home with a mother who took good care of them.

Like you? The thought hit like a sucker punch.

Jazzmine's words came through a thick wall of grief. "I have an emergency placement, and you and Jason were the first ones I thought of."

Hayley bit her lip. She and Jason had agreed to discuss in advance whether they would take on another foster child.

Her eyes locked on a piece of pink fluff peeking out from under the subzero refrigerator. With the phone still to her ear, she bent and yanked the piece of fabric free. It was the missing ear from Pinky the stuffed elephant. How long had it been there and how had it worked its way out from under the front of the fridge?

Hayley held the scrap to her nose, breathing in what was left of her daughter's scent. Tears sprang to her eyes as she remembered how Cynthia wouldn't go anywhere without Pinky. Now Pinky lay in a box along with a few of her daughter's favorite clothes.

Get a grip, Lee. Your counselor said to face your grief and learn a 'new normal.' She'd done what the counselor said. At least, it's what she told herself.

She struggled to focus on her conversation with Jazzmine.

"Emergency? How so?" Hayley fiddled with the almonds, arranging them in a circle with Pinky's ear in the center.

"I'm not even sure how to describe her. Have you ever heard of a feral child?"

Hayley swept the nuts into a pile. "You mean, like a feral cat?" Her mind jumped to a story she'd read about a boy raised by wolves. Would this kid be like the one described in the book?

"Not exactly. She was found in a homeless camp living in a cardboard box. There hasn't been time to do a thorough evaluation."

"Oh my gosh! How terrible!" Hayley's stomach tightened. How could she deal with something so serious as a feral child? "I don't know, Jazz. Sounds pretty intense." What would Jason say?

Jazzmine's sigh echoed through the phone. "Please, Hayley. With your degree in child psychology, you're the most capable of caring for her."

Guilt clutched her throat. She hadn't been capable of caring for her own daughter, let alone some wild child. On the other hand, maybe this would help atone for her sins. She'd deal with Jason when he got home. Maybe.

"Fine. What's her name?"

"I don't know. She doesn't talk."

The girl bit her lip to keep from crying. Mama said don't make no noise or the bad people will stomp on you with their boots. This lady didn't wear boots. She was clean, and she smelled nice. Her skin was dark like hers, and her hair was short, like the policeman who grabbed her with his big hands.

"We're going for a ride in my car," the lady said. "I'm taking you to a nice lady's house to stay. Her name is Miss Hayley."

The words rolled over her without a foothold. *House, nice lady, Hayley.* Her brain had no reference point.

"I sure wish you could tell me your name," the dark lady said.

Girl. That's what Mama called her.

Shut up, girl. Hide, girl. Go with this man, girl.

The lady urged her to a car, opened the back door, and lifted her into a seat. The girl opened her mouth and howled as the lady put the straps over her arms. She stiffened and pushed the lady's chest. Arms flailing and feet kicking, she fought the lady's attempts to restrain her until her strength gave out. Tears poured down her face as the straps pinned her to the seat.

Sweat formed on Jazzmine's face as she fought to strap the little girl into the car seat.

"Stop struggling, sweetie." With a sigh of relief, Jazz fastened the last buckle. Straightening up, she wiped her forehead with the back of one hand.

"Whew, you are a feisty one." Now if she could only get her to stop wailing.

Jazzmine pulled the vile blanket out of the paper bag containing everything in the box where the girl was found.

She used two fingers to hand the blanket to the girl. Jazzmine gagged as the girl buried her face in it.

"Hayley will have her hands full, that's for darn sure." Jazzmine climbed into her ancient Honda and prayed the car would start.

The car coughed before reluctantly coming to life. She navigated the one-way streets of downtown Sacramento, chugging up the on-ramp to the freeway. The girl's wailing reduced to hiccups. Jazz looked over the seat to see the girl sleeping with her head tilted to one side.

What's your name, little one? Where's your mama? Thoughts tumbled around in Jazzmine's head. Surely this kid had folks somewhere. How had she come to be abandoned in a homeless camp? All Jazzmine's brood had at least come with a name. Even the ones she hadn't given birth to. She smiled, thinking of the best time of her day, when she walked through the front door of her house. No, slash that. Her *home*. The place she and Zeke and those five boys did life together. They didn't have a lot, not like Hayley with her family money. What they had you couldn't put a price on.

A glance in the rear-view mirror reassured her the girl still slept.

Jazzmine shuddered, remembering how they'd needed three people to hold her down to do a physical exam. By now, she should be used to seeing evidence of sexual abuse in a child of her age. Moms pimping their kids out in exchange for drugs, some as young as two years old. According to the doctor, this girl was approximately four.

No name, no speech, and already abused. Yup, Hayley would have her hands full.

Hayley paced before the window. Four steps to the right, four steps to the left. From her vantage point, she could focus on the driveway for Jazzmine's arrival.

One-two-three-four. Two-two-three-four. Three-two-three-four. At twenty laps, she sank down on the window seat, hands clenched in her lap, imagining Jason's anger. He'd be furious when he found out she'd committed to another foster kid without discussing it first. Plus, she'd lied to Jazz. unable to say no. Besides, this little girl needed her. And Hayley needed the child. Maybe this one would get her back into God's favor.

Her cell phone vibrated on the antique table near the top of the stairs. *Please don't let it be him.*

She crossed the landing in four quick strides. Not him, but almost as bad.

"Hi, Mother."

"How did you know it was me?"

"You ask the same thing every time, Mother."

"Why can't you have a house phone like every normal person?"

"You called me to criticize my lack of a house phone?"

Her mother sighed. Not a good sign. "No, Hayley. I called to ask you to lunch today at Scott's Seafood. Don't say no. We haven't had a nice chat for a long while."

More guilt. How did her mother manage to convey disapproval with a mere tone of voice?

"I can't today, Mother. I'm waiting for the social worker to bring a new placement." Hayley held her breath, waiting for the inevitable argument.

"Can't you ask her to reschedule? Isn't your own mother more important than some—"

Hayley cut her off before guilt overcame her. "I'm sorry, Mother. She's already on her way."

"Hayley, dear. When are you going to stop this foster nonsense? You must put the past behind you. It's time to have another baby."

"You act like Cynthia never existed." Hayley forced down her anger. She shouldn't try to fight with her mom. She'd never win.

"Now, you know that isn't true. The time for grieving is over. You need to move on. I'm sure Jason would agree with me."

I'm sure he would. With both against her, Hayley wouldn't stand a chance. She needed more time. More time to earn forgiveness. More time for redemption. Her perfect mother wouldn't understand.

"Gotta go, Mother. The social worker is pulling into the driveway." Hayley disconnected before her mother could respond to the lie. She tugged at the waistband of her white linen shorts. Did they feel a teensy bit snug? Should she have dressed less formally? Her mother's voice echoed in her brain. *Yoga pants are not acceptable clothing to wear every day.*

Hayley snatched the band holding her ponytail, pulled it off and shook her hair around her shoulders. Maybe having her hair down would be less intimidating to the child.

Cell phone in hand, she walked back to the window, biting her lips as she peered out. The phone vibrated against her palm with a text.

ZOLA: Hey neighbor. Bringing over a new recipe.

Hayley smiled for the first time since she'd rolled out of bed, picturing her kooky neighbor, Zola.

HAYLEY: Can it wait? Jazz bringing a new placement.

ZOLA: Right on. UR going to (heart) it. Gluten free vegan raw banana cream pie.

Hayley grimaced.

HAYLEY: Sounds...awesome.

ZOLA: It is!

Several smileys followed. Zola had too much time on her hands.

Hayley thought about her mother's comment. Should she and Jason have another baby now? What if the same thing happened again? Would God punish her twice for the same sin? With Jason pushing from one side, and Mother pulling from the other, Hayley knew she'd eventually cave and do what everyone else wanted her to do. She always did.

The rattling sound of a car pulling into the driveway changed the direction of her thoughts. Jazzmine really needed to have her car serviced. The car chugged to a stop and sputtered to silence.

Nerves like barbed wire shot through Hayley's arms, leaving her tingly. What would this child be like?

Hayley dashed across the landing, down the curved staircase, and pulled open the front door. She reached the last step of the porch as Jazzmine rounded the car.

"Hi ya. You ready for this, Mama?" Jazzmine greeted her with a quick hug. "Before I get her out of the car, here's the 4-1-1." Jazz handed her a manila folder. "Doctor's exam, approximate age. She's scheduled for an in-depth evaluation day after tomorrow. Info is in there." She pointed to the folder. "You know the drill by now, right?"

Hayley nodded.

"You talked to Jason? He's okay with this?" Jazz spoke over her shoulder as she opened the back door on the passenger side of the car.

"Sure," Hayley responded. At least she hoped so. Maybe. After he calmed down.

"Good. Let me get her out of the car. And sweetie, be prepared for anything."

With that cryptic remark, Jazzmine pulled the car door open wide and leaned in to unbuckle the car seat. Hayley strained to see around Jazzmine's back.

Nothing could have prepared her for the sulfur-like smell assaulting her nose before she had a chance to see the tiny girl with tousled brown hair. She wore a shapeless dress and ballet flats one size too big. Her arms and legs were covered with red dots. Some of them had been scratched open, the blood dried to a dull rust color.

The girl held a blanket which might have once been blue, stiff with dirt. Hayley couldn't tell if the stench wafted from the girl or the blanket.

Jazz released the last buckle and leaned toward the girl to lift her out. The girl wiggled out of Jazzmine's grasp like buttered corn and jumped from the car. After ditching the shoes, she darted across the broad expanse of lawn toward a neighbor's house.

Hayley dashed after her, wishing she'd worn her Adidas rather than low-heeled sandals now sinking into the soft grass. She found the girl huddled beneath the shrubs under Zola's kitchen window.

As she bent down, the sharp smell of urine filled the air. A small puddle formed in the dirt under the girl.

Hayley rested her weight on her haunches. Speaking with a soothing voice, she kept her hands in full view.

"Come on, little girl. Let's go to my house. Are you hungry? I have peanut butter and jelly. Most kids love PB&J sandwiches. Will you come with me?"

Hayley heard Jazz behind her, huffing with the effort of the fifty-yard dash across the grass.

Without looking up or acknowledging Jazz, Hayley focused on the girl.

"Let's go get some food, okay?" She held out her hand. Without making eye contact, she stood.

"You're the child whisperer." Jazzmine shook her head.

With her attention focused on the girl, Hayley didn't respond. She straightened, turned partially away, holding out her hand.

"Come on. Let's go to my house. Let's go get some food."

She glanced around and stepped out of the bushes. Hayley sauntered toward her front door, occasionally looking back to see if the girl followed.

Jazzmine took up the rear of their little procession.

The front door of Hayley's house stood open. She stopped at the bottom step of the red brick porch.

"Are you okay?" Hayley asked the girl.

No response.

"Let's go inside. I'll make you a peanut butter and jelly sandwich."

Hayley mounted the steps.

"I'll go grab her things," Jazzmine said. "Be right there."

The two made their way through the massive front door, down the wood-lined hallway, to the back of the house where the kitchen looked out over a park-like yard. The girl's feet left damp prints on the wood floor.

How soon could she get the girl out of her wet clothes? Hayley made a mental note to mop the hallway before Jason got home.

She watched the girl out of the corner of her eye as she pulled the makings for a sandwich from the cupboard. The girl seemed entranced by the view from the French doors.

Hayley kept up a soft monologue while she assembled the sandwich.

"Outside is our back yard. If it isn't too hot later, we can go outside and play. Do you see the swings and slide? They're fun. Do you know how to swim? We also have a pool. It's small but enough to get wet. Do you have a swimsuit?" Hayley cut the sandwich into four pieces.

The girl seemed frozen, until Hayley set the sandwich on the kitchen table. Quick as lightening, the girl snatched one piece off the plate and shoved the whole thing in her mouth.

"No, no! One bite at a time." Hayley grabbed the girl's arm and with the other hand, dug the partially eaten sandwich out of her mouth.

Jazzmine entered the kitchen. "I see you two are getting acquainted." She grinned, white teeth against dark skin.

"Thanks for the warning." With a grimace, Hayley wiped the gummy mess onto the plate and held it out of the girl's reach.

The girl started to howl.

"One bite at a time," Hayley repeated, setting one child-sized piece on the plate at a time. The girl snatched the morsel off the plate and shoved it into her mouth. Hayley continued with one piece until the sandwich was history.

All the while, Jazzmine filled her in on the details. "I'm sorry to spring this on you. The girl was found in a homeless camp. We have no idea where her mom is. One of the officers who as at the camp reached out to me. Unfortunately, the county facility is full. All my parents already have placements." Jazzmine rubbed a hand over her head. "I'm glad you and Jason were available. I figured, with your degree, you'd be able to handle her for a few days."

Hayley kept her eyes on the girl in case Jazz could read the guilt in them.

"Anyway, I'll work on a more permanent solution when I get back to my office." Jazzmine stood. "I'm gonna shove off now." She reached for Hayley and gave her a quick hug. "Don't forget to read the file. There isn't much, and it's heartbreaking."

Hayley nodded. Too many kids were used as human currency for their parents' drug addiction.

Jazz continued, "In the meantime, I'll be praying for you." She strode across the kitchen toward the door. "And text me anytime, day or night." From the entry, she called back, "Let me know what you want to name her."

Hayley watched the girl pace through the kitchen, touching everything. The marble countertop, decorative chicken near the refrigerator, ruffling the leaves on a plant sitting on a stand in the corner. The girl circled the kitchen three times before Hayley stopped her.

"Hey, little girl, let's go up to your room, okay?" Hayley held out her hand, as if approaching a scared kitten. The girl looked at Hayley's hand, and looked away. Hayley gasped as she caught a glimpse of the girl's eyes. They were the shade of emerald green called heliodor, a combination of green and yellow. The same shade as Cynthia's. Grief grabbed her neck like a noose, squeezing her breath out. How was it possible this little girl had eyes exactly the same as her own daughter? Was this another one of God's reminders she'd never be forgiven?

Images of Cynthia, running toward her, hands outstretched. Of Cynthia, playing make-believe. "Look at me, Mommy. I'm a princess." Her tear-filled eyes, crying over a broken toy.

A grunt from the girl brought her back to the present. Hayley shoved the grief down into the hollow place in her heart, took the girl's hand, and led her out of the kitchen.

The living room's ceiling stretched to the second floor with a balcony overlooking the entire downstairs. The stairs hugged one side of the living room.

As they ascended, Hayley spoke in a whisper the entire way.

"You'll like your bedroom. It's pink and blue. It used to be my little girl's room. She's gone now." Hayley swallowed against the noose. "There's a princess bed too."

They stopped inside the bedroom. The soft pink walls glowed from the afternoon sunlight. Blue teddy bears danced around the walls under the ceiling. Pink and blue teddy bear curtains framed two long windows.

"What do you think?" Hayley asked, stooping down to the girl's level.

The girl didn't move or respond, as if she waited for someone to give her a command.

Hayley moved to the bed and sat. She patted the spot next to her. "Come sit here."

Eyes down, the girl shuffled to Hayley and stopped in front of her.

"What are we going to call you, little girl?" Hayley inhaled and winced at the smell.

This child needed a bath and a clean set of clothes. Hayley walked to the adjoining bathroom and knelt next to the tub. After turning on the water and adjusting it to a comfortable temperature, she stood and turned back toward the bedroom. The girl walked on the balls of her feet around the room, touching first the dresser, the curtains, and the stuffed animals on the shelf. What was the child thinking as she made the circuit again and again?

"Come on, let's get into the tub." She moved toward the girl, who seemed to not hear her. "Come on, tub time," Hayley repeated with a sing-song lilt.

When the girl circled around past the door, Hayley took her arm and gently pulled her into the bathroom, closing the door behind them. Hayley stood facing her, and grasped the too-big dress, pulling it up over her head.

A sudden screech from the child sent chills up her spine. Like a wild animal, the girl shrieked and ran back and forth in the tiny bathroom, crashing into the walls on either side.

CHAPTER 3

Jazzmine closed the heavy wood door of the Montgomery home. Why did Hayley want to take on the county's throwaway kids? She seemed to have it all. For sure she didn't need the money. If Jazzmine had a home like this, well, she would sit by the pool sipping cold margaritas while a maid cleaned and cooked. If only.

"I shoulda been born rich instead of beautiful," Jazzmine muttered to herself as she surveyed the homes along the area called the Fabulous Forties. These places must be worth a cool mil or more.

"C'mon, Rusty, let's go back to the office." She patted the hood of her faded Honda and climbed in, hoping the air conditioning would choose another day to die.

Guilt stabbed her at leaving Hayley with such a difficult placement. Sometimes her job sucked. All she wanted to do was dash home and gather her brood of five into a hug and never let them go. What was wrong with people anyway—to conceive their babies into horror?

She'd seen tiny kids burned with cigarettes, just for fun. Broken fingers, arms, and more bruises than were ever found on all five of her kids put together.

Before backing out of the driveway, Jazzmine dug in her purse and pulled out her cell. She hit the first on the list of favorites and waited for the call to connect.

"That you, baby?" The familiar timbre of her husband's voice always brought a smile to her face.

"Yeah. I wanted to hear you say you love me."

"I love you to the moon and back." Ezekiel paused. "What's going on? Another tough placement?"

"Yup." Jazzmine adjusted down the volume on the radio. "This little one doesn't even have a name."

"Seriously? How's that even possible?"

"We can't find her mama. The police found her in a homeless camp downtown living in a box."

She heard Zeke's sigh through the phone. "What are you gonna name her?"

Jazzmine was quiet for a long beat. "I think I'm gonna let the foster parents choose her name."

Zeke's laugh came all the way from his belly. "Bet she'll have some millennial name like Opal or Tiffany."

Jazzmine laughed. "Or Olivia."

"Isabella," Zeke countered.

"Charlotte."

"Sophie."

"Stop, Zeke, you're killing me. Besides, this is simply an emergency placement with a great foster mom."

"I know, baby. Just needed to hear you laugh."

She was blessed to have this man. "Call the house and make sure Marcus starts supper. And remind him no screen time until all the chores are done."

"You got it. Jerome won't be home tonight. He's spending the night with a friend."

Jazzmine's stomach tightened. "It better not be with his hooligan friend, Sam. Every time he stays there, he comes home with a new swear word."

"Gotta go, baby. I'm heading into a meeting."

Great job deflecting, Zeke. Something she'd need to deal with tonight. For now, back to the office to see how many more parents had screwed up their kids in the past two hours.

Hayley stepped back, her calves against the back of the outside of the tub. Raw fear rippled through her. The girl lunged at her, nearly knocking her into the water. Hayley grabbed the girl in a bear hug, squeezing hard enough to keep her from being a human ping pong ball, but not enough to hurt.

The girl's heart pounded a staccato against Hayley's thighs. "Shh, little one. I'm not going to hurt you. Shh."

After a few moments, the girl shuddered a sigh, and her limbs relaxed. Hayley squatted, using her forefinger to lift the girl's chin. Their eyes connected. "I'm not going to hurt you. We're going to take a bath."

Hayley put her hands on either side of the girl's waist, and gently tugged down her panties. The girl whimpered but stayed still.

"Here you go, all ready for your bath." Hayley lifted her into the water. The girl's legs locked. "It's okay, you can sit."

The girl climbed back out of the tub, water dripping from her legs. Hayley repeated the process with the same result.

Sighing, Hayley said, "How about we go in together, okay?" Hayley stripped down to her bra and underwear and climbed into the bathtub. She reached over the edge and lifted the girl back into the water. Holding her in her arms, Hayley sank down until she sat in the tub.

"See? Not so bad. Now you try. Sit."

The girl eyed her warily and sat. Her fingers danced across the water's surface. She raised her hands and watched the water drip off.

"Why do I get the feeling you've never had a real bath before?" Usually the kids she'd fostered wanted to bathe every day, sometimes twice. Once they had the feeling of being clean, they couldn't get enough of it.

Hayley glanced at the puddle of water on the bathroom floor and reminded herself to mop up the mess before Jason got home.

She showed the girl how to use the soap and washcloth, keeping up a constant patter. "We need to find a name. You remind me of my college roommate, Shannon. She was dark-skinned like you with a mane of uncontrollable hair. Shannon is such a big name for a little girl. How about Shannie? My friend's mama used to call her Shannie."

Hayley jumped when the girl uttered a word. "Mama."

"That's right, Shannie. My friend's mama. Do you know where your mama is?"

"Mama." Shannie whimpered, dipped her face into the water, and took a drink.

"No, honey, don't drink the bath water. Yucky."

Wonder if she'll let me wash her hair? Sure needed it. Hayley talked the entire time as she lowered Shannie's head back to wet her hair. Did she imagine it, or did Shannie smile when Hayley rubbed her head with baby shampoo?

When they finished their bath, the water had changed to a dingy brown. Hayley should be used to it by now but sitting in the dirty water gave her the willies. She climbed out of the tub and lifted out the girl. After drying herself and Shannie, Hayley dug through the paper bag holding the girl's things. She found a spare pair of panties, another shapeless dress, and a stiff blanket. The girl lunged before Hayley could toss the blanket aside. She held it to her face while Hayley slipped clean clothes on her. When she was dressed, the girl curled up on the floor and fell asleep with the blanket over her head.

"Poor little thing. You must be exhausted from your eventful day." What must the tiny girl think, yanked from a homeless camp by police, forced to endure a physical exam, and now under a stranger's roof. With a last glance, Hayley headed across the hall to the master bedroom.

This used to be her favorite room in the sixty-plus-year-old house. Muted gray walls with darker gray accents gave a calm vibe. The bed pillows brightened the room with splashes of poppy and rose. Now she was reminded of the arguments she and Jason seemed to have almost weekly. He'd blow up, she'd cry and beg him to forgive her. He'd refuse to speak to her and go to bed with his back turned.

She shuddered, thinking of the fight they'd have when he returned home from his business trip and found out she'd taken in another foster child.

Hayley changed into dry running shorts and a clean tee shirt. She went about mopping the bathroom floor with a spare towel and retrieved the cleanser from a locked cupboard in the hall. Returning to the bathroom, she scrubbed the ring out of the tub, drying it with another towel. She gathered the wet towels in her arms, intending to drop them in the washing machine. First, she set them on the carpet, gently tugging the nasty blanket from the girl's grip. She replaced it with a clean quilt. Grabbing the blanket with two fingers, she scooped up the wet towels and headed to the laundry room.

After checking to see if Shannie still slept, she ran downstairs and did a quick mop of the entry and kitchen to remove all traces of urine-soaked footsteps. The plate with the sandwich crumbs accused her from the sink. She glanced over her shoulder, half expecting Jason to walk through the door, finger pointing. The plate went in the dishwasher. The door closed with a satisfying click. Nothing out of place, everything tidy.

Hayley took an apple from the fridge, munching as she returned upstairs to check on Shannie. With a start, she saw the empty place on the carpet where the girl had fallen asleep. A knife thrust in her gut. Deja vu. She shouldn't have left her alone.

Hayley raced back down the stairs. The front door was closed, locked, as she'd left it. A dark cloud of dread followed her as she ran to the French doors in the family room. If Shannie had gotten outside ... how could she have been so careless? Her mind replayed the last time she'd been distracted. She shoved down the memory. Focus, Lee. Focus on the present.

The French doors were also closed, the safety lock at the top still engaged.

Hayley bent over and took a couple of deep breaths, resting her hands on her thighs. Where could Shannie be? If not outside, maybe somewhere in the house.

A quick search of the kitchen, dining room, and living room revealed no trace of the little girl. She shot back up the stairs, calling in a sing-song voice, "Shannie? Where are you?"

Hayley paused outside each of the three upstairs bedrooms. A slight rustle pulled her into the pink bedroom.

"Shannie? Are you in here?"

A whimper, then silence.

Hayley stooped to search under the bed. "There you are. I wondered where you'd gotten to." Profound relief left her weak as she sank into a crouch.

Shannie was curled up into a tiny ball, as close to the wall as she could get. Hayley held out her hand. "Come on, sweetie. Let's get something to eat, okay?"

The word *eat* got Shannie's attention. At least the child understood speech, even if she couldn't, or wouldn't, talk.

Shannie scooted out from under the bed, leaving the quilt behind. Hand in hand, they descended the stairs into the kitchen.

Her tummy hurt. This wasn't home. What would this woman do to her? Would it be as bad as before—with those men? Mama said it would be okay, but it wasn't. Afterward, Mama would cry and fall asleep.

Where was Mama? This lady smelled good and she smiled a lot. She had food. That was good. Would Mama be able to find her here?

Hayley dropped Shannie's hand when they entered the kitchen.

"I have some toys in this bottom drawer. Do you want to play with them?"

The child stared down at her feet as she started her route around the room, touching each thing as she walked past. Hayley pulled open the drawer and gathered a plastic zip lock bag of Legos and another bag with tiny plastic dolls. She opened the bag of Legos and spilled them onto the table with a clatter. Shannie didn't react, seeming not to notice.

"Here you go, sweetie. Would you rather play with the dolls? Maybe you don't like Legos." She repeated the process, pulling another bag open and spilling the contents onto the table.

Round and round Shannie went.

The doorbell rang. A quick double knock followed.

"Sounds like Zola," she said, recognizing her neighbor's distinctive arrival.

She strode through the kitchen and the entry, pulling open the front door.

"Hi, neighbor." Zola swept past, hands full of plastic containers. She left a scent of sweet cinnamon in her wake on her way to the kitchen. "Some homemade goodies for you and your new charge."

Zola skidded to a stop at the kitchen entrance. Hayley practically bowled into her.

"What in the world?" Zola said, watching Shannie circle around the room on tip toes. As soon as she noticed Zola, she skittered behind a potted plant in the corner and curled into a ball.

Hayley pushed past her. "Zola, this is Shannie, my foster daughter."

Zola's voice dropped to a whisper. "What's wrong with her?"

Hayley took the containers from her hands. "Ever heard the term 'feral child'?"

Zola shook her head, the long hoop earrings swaying against her neck.

Hayley took a deep breath. "I haven't had an opportunity to do any research. What I've gathered from her file is she's basically been living in a homeless camp. In a cardboard box."

Zola gasped. "That's so wrong. Poor dear."

"No one knows how long she's been on her own."

"Where's her mother?"

Hayley shrugged. "No one knows her whereabouts, either."

Zola sank onto a stool and rested her chin on her hands. "Un-stinking-believable."

"Tell me about it." Hayley opened one of the containers. "What did you bring me today?"

Hayley wrinkled her nose at the contents. Zola's creations were hit or miss. Some days she made something so good, Hayley would beg her for more. Unfortunately, Zola never repeated any recipe. She claimed it violated her artistic nature. Today's creation resembled potting soil.

"I told you," Zola said, grabbing the plastic bowl. "Gluten free, vegan, raw banana cream pie. With chocolate." Zola stood and headed to the silverware drawer. She pulled out two spoons. "You're gonna love this."

If Zola's creation tasted anything like it looked, Hayley doubted it. She took the spoon her friend handed her and took a tentative bite.

"Oh. My. Goodness. This is amazing."

Zola smiled with satisfaction. "Told ya." She helped herself to a spoonful.

Before Hayley could take another bite, Shannie leapt up, hurled herself across the room, and grabbed the plastic container. She dug her hand into the mixture and shoved a huge amount into her mouth, smearing chocolate and banana over her face. Hayley lunged for her, but Shannie was quicker. She held the bowl out of reach and shot out of the kitchen.

"Oh my gosh! Shannie—no!" Hayley dashed after her as Zola's laughter echoed behind her.

Shannie streaked through the downstairs, shoveling handfuls of pie into her already full mouth. She dodged Hayley's attempts to grab her like Tim Tebow streaking toward the end zone.

After several tries, Hayley finally captured her at the foot of the stairs.

"Oh, no you don't," Hayley murmured. By now the bowl was empty. Hayley led Shannie back to the kitchen. "Let's get you cleaned up."

Zola chuckled. "I've got to admit I've never seen anything like that before."

Hayley wetted some paper towels and attempted to clean off the mess on Shannie's face.

"Good grief," Hayley said through gritted teeth.

A moment later, Shannie's stomach rumbled loud enough for both women to hear. Shannie vomited, spewing gluten free, vegan, raw banana pie down the front of Hayley's shirt.

Hayley burst into tears.

CHAPTER 4

Jazzmine sat at her computer, ear buds firmly in place. Soft music drowned out the cacophony of Love's Family Foster Agency. If only she could have a real office with a door to keep the noisy distractions to a bare minimum. Jazzmine glanced at the firmly closed door of her boss and sighed. *Some day.*

She searched again through the computer list of children reported missing in the past thirty days. Still nothing about a mixed-race female, three to five years old. What kind of mother wouldn't report her child had gone missing? Druggies, alcoholics, mentally unstable women, uncaring about the kids they'd brought into the world, that's who.

Jazzmine thought of Zeke and her brood and the hugs and sloppy kisses she'd receive when she got home. What she lived for. What she'd die for.

With a start, Jazz began a new search for women who were reported dead in the past thirty days. Her fingers flew over the keyboard, hoping to find an answer to the child's mother, yet hoping she was wrong.

Shannie scuttled under the table, knees hugged to her chest.

Hayley pressed a paper towel to her face as Zola gathered Hayley into a motherly hug.

"There, there," she murmured.

"Don't. You'll get your blouse—"

"It'll wash. Just a little *shmutz*." Zola rubbed Hayley's back.

"What am I going to do?" Hayley asked as her sobs slowed.

Zola held her at arm's length. "Right now, you're going to go upstairs and jump in the shower. I'll watch the little girl."

Hayley nodded, tears still dripping down her cheeks. "Thanks." Hayley wiped the worst of the mess off her shirt. "You'd make a great foster mom, you know."

Zola's laugh came from deep inside. "And have to deal with all this? No thank you."

Hayley's mouth turned up into a slight smile. "Right."

Thirty minutes later, Hayley entered the kitchen to observe Zola create something from the contents of the refrigerator. Her stomach dropped. Bits of lettuce littered the floor around Zola's feet. Carrots lay on the counter, alongside stalks of celery. The smell of chopped onions filled the kitchen. Hayley would have to clean up the minute Zola returned home.

Shannie huddled under the table, her face and hands clean.

"What are you making?" *Please let it be something normal.*

Zola turned around. "Didn't hear you come in." She turned back to the counter. "Nice big salad for you, light on the dressing. I found a cooked chicken breast in the freezer." The microwave dinged. "I heated it up. Do you want some on your salad?"

Hayley nodded.

Zola turned and smiled, waving a hand toward Shannie. "I'll cut some in small pieces."

Hayley sank down on a chair at the kitchen table. "You're a great neighbor, you know that? And a good friend." *My only friend.*

They couldn't have been more different. Zola hid her girth under shapeless dresses and plus-size tops. She wore her gray-and brown-streaked hair long and loose. Birkenstock sandals finished off the Earth Mother look.

Hayley tugged her wet blond hair into a neat ponytail. If only she could be more free-flowing like Zola. Instead of stressing over how quickly she could whip her kitchen back into perfection.

"Aw, tsk. Now I'm gonna blush." Zola carried the plate of salad over to the table and set it down in front of her. "Here, you eat. You look done in. I'll feed your girl."

Zola retrieved the chicken from the chopping board and brought it to the table.

"You'll need to set one bite at a time in front of her," Hayley instructed. "She has food issues."

"Got it," Zola answered, taking one piece, blowing to cool it. She took one piece in her fingers, set it on a plate, then leaned down and set the plate on the floor. Shannie grabbed the bite and shoved the chicken in her mouth.

"One piece at a time, *vild kind*," Zola drawled. When she was satisfied Shannie had chewed at least once and she'd swallowed the morsel, Zola placed another on the plate.

Hayley dug into the salad. Had she eaten anything since the almonds after her run? At least she wouldn't have to worry about gaining any weight from the bite of Zola's pie.

After she'd eaten and Shannie had been fed, Zola returned home. Hayley managed to wrestle the child into the tub again. After dressing Shannie in a spare nightgown, Hayley tucked her into the princess bed.

Hayley reached out a hand to stroke Shannie's hair. Shannie shrank back, scooting away.

Hayley sighed. "Let me read you a story." She pulled a book onto her lap, back against the white headboard.

"This one is called *Good Night Moon*." As Hayley read, Shannie's eyes drooped lower until she appeared to be asleep. Hayley eased herself off the bed. She turned off the bedside lamp, leaving the bottom night light on. The room was bathed in a soft pink glow—like her own childhood bedroom had been. Sometimes when Jason stayed out of town on one of his business trips, Hayley slept here.

Thinking of Jason's return tomorrow, Hayley went downstairs to do a quick pass through the house. Each door and window was locked. In the kitchen, she inspected the granite countertop to be sure there were no crumbs. The glass she'd used earlier went into the dishwasher. Jason would be satisfied.

Upstairs in the room they used as an office, Hayley booted up the computer, pulled a pad of paper from the desk drawer, and used a mechanical pencil to start a list.

Things to work on with Shannie:
1. Potty training
2. Eating slowly
3. Using utensils
4. Dressing herself
5. Talking???

Who was she kidding? The list would be irrelevant if she couldn't earn Shannie's trust.

She'd glanced at Shannie's file, discouraged by the smattering of information there. She read and reread the words, especially the part about evidence of sexual abuse.

Warped. Sick. *Obscene.*

Then again ... which was worse, using your child to satisfy your addiction, or letting your sweet girl die because of your negligence?

Would God ever forgive her? Could she forgive herself? Perhaps, if she could give this child the love and attention she deserved. Hayley would earn Shannie's trust. God would look upon her with favor again. Jason would back off, and life would go back to the way it was before the nightmare of Cynthia's death.

Hayley pushed the list aside, intent on burying the overwhelming grief by ordering some new kid's clothes. Amazon yielded a plethora of styles of shorts, tops, and sun dresses. Perfect for the blistering Sacramento summer. Jammies, undies, and two swimsuits went into her cart. Satisfied she'd thought of everything, she checked out, using the one credit card Jason knew nothing about.

She cleared the cache memory on the computer and shut it down.

Her phone chirped as she pushed the chair back. A text from Zola.

ZOLA: Doing okay?

HAYLEY: Yeah. Shannie's asleep and I'm going to watch some mindless TV.

ZOLA: Good for you. Hang in there. You're doing a good thing.

HAYLEY: You should think about it - fostering.

ZOLA: And get barfed on? I don't think so. :-) Besides, Sol and I are too old. Best left to you young ones.

HAYLEY :-) night.

Hayley stood and stretched, then walked across the hall to peek in on Shannie. She lay on her side, thumb in her mouth. Hayley headed back downstairs. A tub of mocha almond fudge ice cream taunted her from the freezer. She mentally calculated the number of calories she'd consumed during the day before retrieving a spoon, a small bowl, and the ice cream. Upstairs, Hayley undressed quickly, sank onto the bed, with the remote in one hand, spoon in the other. The bowl of ice cream held securely between her knees.

Her phone chirped again. This time from Jason.

JASON: Hey babe. Miss you.

HAYLEY: Me too. Home tomorrow?

JASON: Yup around 2:00.

HAYLEY: early.

JASON: Yeah thot we could spend the afternoon together.

A shiver of anxiety slid up her spine.

HAYLEY: Can't. Got an emergency placement today.

A full minute and a half passed before Jason responded.

JASON: We'll discuss it when I get home.

HAYLEY: Love you.

No response. She'd blown it again. They'd agreed to discuss whether they'd accept another foster placement. Why hadn't she told Jazzmine "no?" Because maybe, just maybe, this would be the time she'd finally have absolution.

CHAPTER 5

Hayley's phone pinged at five thirty the next morning. Eyes closed, she snaked her hand over the nightstand until she found the annoying device. Her heart leaped, then clenched. Was it Jason? Maybe he'd answered her last night and the text had been delayed. Was he still angry? If so, how would he respond when he got home later? The sun had barely peeked over the horizon and dread already weighed heavy.

JAZZMINE: Sorry for the last minute. Appt w/ psychologist at 9 today. Did you name her?

Good grief. Didn't the woman ever sleep? Barely light and she'd texted.

Hayley struggled to a sitting position, wiped the sleep from her eyes and composed a response.

HAYLEY: I named her Shannie.

JAZZMINE: Cute! :-) Thx. I'll check in later.

Hayley swung her legs over the side of the bed. Her feet sank into the plush carpet. She crossed the bedroom and headed out the door to check on Shannie.

Shannie wasn't in the bed.

On rubbery legs, Hayley hurried across the room to the closet. Empty, except for a few taped boxes of Cynthia's things. Baby clothes, toys, cherished items too precious to donate.

Where could Shannie be? Hayley squatted to peer under the bed, breathing a sigh of relief. Shannie slept, curled on her side, blanket completely covering her.

With a smile, Hayley tiptoed out of the room, and down the hall to the office. She did a Google search for neglected, abused, and feral children.

"A feral child is a human child who has lived away from human contact from a very young age, and has little or no experience of human care, loving or social behavior, and, crucially, of human language. Feral children are confined by humans (often parents), brought up by animals, or live in the wild in isolation."

Stunned, she shoved away from the computer. Shannie wasn't what she would consider feral. She'd at least had human contact and hadn't been confined. What had this poor child experienced in her short life? Sexual abuse, little or no love, living in a box in a homeless camp. Hayley shuddered. So different from her own upbringing. This would be a huge challenge, and she'd need help. Who—besides Jazzmine— could walk beside her on this journey?

Hayley started a mental checklist. Jason was always busy working, and he hardly noticed the previous foster child placements. None of her college or childhood friends contacted her anymore. Jason had kept her busy with his to-do lists, discouraging any outside socializing. He'd wanted her to devote her time to himself and Cynthia. She'd gone along, wanting to—needing to—keep him happy.

Mother was off the list. Her sister, Hannah, was too self-centered. Basically, she had Jazzmine and Zola. She'd figure things out. She always did.

Hayley showered and dressed in yoga pants and a workout shirt. She'd drop Shannie off at the psychologist's office and squeeze in a quick workout—the price to pay for the ice cream binge the night before.

"Come on, sleepyhead." A scrawny leg appeared from under the bed as Hayley gently urged Shannie from her safe place. "We need to get you dressed and fed."

At the mention of food, Shannie slid out from under the bed.

Hayley wrinkled her nose at the ammonia smell of urine emanating from the girl. Good thing she'd put potty training as number one on her list, if potty training was even possible. *Sigh.*

She retrieved a protein bar from the dresser and held it out. Before Shannie could snatch it out of her hand, Hayley pulled it back.

"First, we go potty." Hayley led the way to the bathroom, Shannie close on her heels, squealing.

Hayley quickly stripped off the wet nightie and panties. Shannie climbed into the bathtub and lunged for the treat.

"No bath this morning, sweet girl." She pulled Shannie out of the tub and set her on the toilet. Shannie squirmed off.

"You need to go potty." Hayley set her back on the toilet. "Stay there. Once I hear tinkling, you can have a bite." Hayley broke off a piece of the bar. She placed the remainder on the counter. Shannie's eyes shifted from Hayley to the bar and back.

Hayley raised an eyebrow. "Don't even think about it."

Shannie continued to lunge for Hayley's hand, but she held it out of reach. After a few seconds, tinkling in the toilet was enough for Hayley to release the piece of bar and give it to Shannie.

"Good girl. That's what we want."

Shannie stuffed the piece into her mouth. Before Hayley could reach for the toilet tissue, Shannie jumped off the seat and grabbed the rest of the bar from the counter. She shoved the bar, wrapping and all into her mouth.

"Aaaack! No!" Hayley lunged, but Shannie was quicker. She raced out the door, ran through the bedroom, and dove under the bed.

Hayley wiped the sweat off her forehead with a tissue from the glove box. Wrestling a wriggling child into a car seat was not her idea of a good way to start the trip downtown to see the psychologist. A glance in the rearview mirror assured her Shannie wasn't any worse for her resistance. Showing up with a bruised little girl would only complicate matters.

Before pulling out of the garage, she checked her phone again. No text from Jason. At least he'd be home today. Would it help, or make things worse?

He'd done some parenting things with the two kids they'd fostered. A little pool time with them, a few games of Uno. In reality, he didn't get it—her need to make things right. Absolution for Cynthia's death.

What if she hadn't gone to get a bottle of water? What if they'd stayed inside that morning? What if ...

A shriek from the back seat jarred her back to the present.

"What is it?" Hayley glanced over the back seat. The smell of poop filled the car. Thank goodness she'd had presence of mind to put Shannie in a pull-up before they left the house.

Shannie squirmed in the car seat, pulling against the straps.

"I know, sweetie. We'll get you cleaned up when we get to the doctor's office." Hayley sighed. This would be a very long day.

Shannie dozed in her car seat as Hayley pulled into the garage. Jason's BMW sat in its usual spot. She felt a flush of pleasure, followed by a jolt of panic. Jason was home early. There'd been no time to shower after forty minutes on the spin bike and five sets of arm exercises. A quick swipe of lipstick and a dusting of powder removed the shine from her nose and cheeks. She pulled the band from the ponytail and fluffed her hair with her fingers. Taking a deep inhale, she held it for a count of ten, and released it through pursed lips.

Time to wrestle Shannie out of her car seat and into the house. Shannie put up no resistance as Hayley unbuckled her. She tumbled into Hayley's arms like a limp helium balloon. Maybe she'd be able to get Shannie down for a nap before Jason could react.

After closing the back door of the SUV, she shifted the child's weight to one hip. Using a free hand to open the door into the house, she stepped lightly into the kitchen. Jason sat at the table, an open bag of chips in front of him. He tapped his laptop, staring at the screen.

"Hi." Hayley spoke softly, tentatively. "How was your trip?"

"Brutal." Jason didn't look up.

Hayley moved toward the doorway toward the living room.

"Is this the kid?" Jason glanced up and reached for a handful of chips.

"Yes. Her name is Shannon. I call her Shannie."

"Skinny." Jason pushed back his chair and stood. He leaned toward her, arms outstretched for a hug.

Shannie stirred in Hayley's arms, and came fully awake. Her eyes shot to Jason's six-foot two frame, took in his red hair and beard, and she shrieked.

She wriggled out of Hayley's grasp and shot into the living room, all the while uttering ear-piercing shrieks. Hayley started after her, but Jason detained her with a hand on her arm, pulling her back.

"What in the world was that?"

Hayley's stomach clenched. "Have you ever heard of a feral child?"

"Feral? Like a feral cat?"

Hayley nodded.

"You've got to be kidding me. You're the foster mom to a feral child?" Jason shook his head. "This is crazy. She's crazy. And you're crazy for taking this on."

"She's not actually—"

"Send her back." Jason sat back down at the table. "And take a shower."

She was dismissed.

Hayley found Shannie behind the living room sofa. How the child wedged herself in such a tiny space was beyond amazing. "Come on, baby girl. Let's go upstairs."

No amount of coaxing could get the child to budge. Hayley glanced toward the kitchen. Jason's attention focused on something on his laptop. Holding her breath, she slipped into the pantry and grabbed a package of goldfish crackers.

Armed with a fistful of goldfish, she held her hand out of reach. "Come on, Shannie. Let's go."

Inch by inch, Shannie scooted forward until at last her entire body slid out from behind the sofa. Hayley held her palm open so Shannie could grab as many fish as she could fit in her tiny fist. These went right into her mouth.

Thirty minutes later, Hayley had changed Shannie's diaper, washed her face and hands, and tucked her into the bed for a nap.

"Time for a little rest, sweet girl." Hayley pulled down the blackout shades. A thin strip of sunlight sneaked along each side of the shade, gently illuminating the bedroom. Shannie's eyes were already drooping when Hayley tiptoed out the door. Would she find her under the bed again when nap time was over?

Hayley climbed in the shower. With the water pounding down over her head, she let tears fall. Jason's anger was her fault. How long would it last this time? Would he make her send Shannie back into the system? Jazz would be disappointed. How could she keep everyone happy, including herself? And God. Would he ever be happy with her again, or would her entire life be spent trying not to disappoint everyone. And failing.

Later, Hayley padded down the stairs, Shannie on her heels.

Slowing as she reached the bottom of the stairs, she stopped before fully committing herself to enter the room.

Jason sprawled on the living room sofa, engrossed in the CNN talking heads. Hayley sensed Shannie's tension when Jason came into view.

"Shh, it's okay. That's Jason and he's not going to hurt you." *At least not physically.*

Jason glanced up. "When's dinner?"

"I'm going to fix it now." Hayley hurried into the kitchen before Shannie could react and Jason could respond.

Hayley set to work, sautéing salmon fillets, careful not to overcook them. Jason hated overcooked food. Shannie sat on the kitchen floor in front of the bottom drawer where Hayley kept plastic food containers and their lids. Out of the corner of her eye, Hayley noticed Shannie took each one out of the drawer, set it on the floor, repeating the process in reverse.

Satisfied the child had something to keep her occupied, Hayley took out two plates and spread lettuce over each one. She added slices of avocado around the edges, adding halved baby tomatoes to create the artistic flair Jason loved. While the salmon cooked, she put some homemade macaroni and cheese in the microwave.

How soon could she get Shannie to eat at the table like a normal kid? With Jason home, this would be dicey, having to feed her under the table, bit by bit. If she didn't watch, Shannie would grab every bit of food in sight, shove it down, and vomit it back up. Jason would flip out.

Hayley walked to the kitchen entrance. "Dinner's ready."

Jason stood and clicked off the television. "Smells good. Salmon?"

"Salmon salad." Hayley turned back in time to see Shannie heading for the stove.

"No!" She dashed over as Shannie reached for the skillet. Shannie shrieked and dove under the table.

"Good grief, Lee. Are we going to have to deal with this chaos all during dinner?"

Hayley tamped down a feeling of panic. "It'll be fine. Sit down. Please."

With a heavy sigh, he sank down in one of the wooden chairs. Hayley dished a piece of salmon onto one of the salads and brought it to him. With a wary eye, she watched for any chance Shannie might decide to dart out from under the table and try to grab Jason's food. That would be a train wreck for sure.

After Hayley dished out her salmon salad and set it at her place, she retrieved the mac and cheese and brought it the table. Spooning up a small bit, Hayley blew on it and held the spoon under the table. Shannie grabbed the spoon and used her fingers to shove the food into her mouth.

35

Jason had eaten half of his salad before Hayley had a bite of hers.

"I've been thinking," he said, laying down his fork.

Her breath caught. Any time he started the conversation this way, it meant something bad.

"I think we ought to sell this place and move."

"Move?" She loved this house. It had been built in an era when no two houses were the same. Hayley adored the nooks and crannies, the wooden stair railing, the deep windows. "Move where?"

"Maybe to Rocklin. Or El Dorado Hills. Get a brand-new place. Bigger." He took a huge bite of salmon.

Hayley pictured a soulless McMansion, devoid of mature trees. A desert in the middle of suburbia.

"Why?" It was the only word she could force out through the knot of tears in her throat.

"Look around." Jason gestured with his fork. "This place is ancient. The pool needs to be resurfaced. We'll probably need a new roof next year. It's a lot of upkeep. We'll have to dip into your trust fund to get the trees trimmed."

Her trust fund. Right. She'd inherit it at thirty. In two years, there would be an annual income more than replacing Jason's salary.

"With a bigger place, I could work from home."

"Work from home?" Hayley echoed. What would she do with him home all day? Directing her steps, giving her even more lists of things to do.

Jason leaned back in his chair. "Whatever. Anyway, with a bigger place, we'd have more bedrooms. We need to talk about having another kid."

"You've been talking to my mother."

Red blotches crept up Jason's neck. He shifted in his chair. "I talk to your mom. Sometimes."

Maybe he had a point. They should move away from this place. Somewhere fresh. Some place where she wouldn't constantly be reminded of her incompetence as a mother. Where she wouldn't pass the place on the street where she cradled her daughter's limp body as she …

"Anyway, I talked to a realtor. We should be able to get about nine hundred K for this place."

Hayley's skin burned. "You've already talked to a realtor? We haven't even discussed this yet."

"We're talking now."

"Oh my gosh, Jason." Tears formed behind Hayley's eyes.

"Don't get your panties in a knot. I didn't sign a contract or anything. Sheesh."

Shannie took that moment to shriek her displeasure over not having any more to eat. Jason shoved back his chair.

"I can't handle this. I'm going to watch the game." He stood and stomped toward the door. Over his shoulder, he said, "Talk to Jazzmine about sending her back. We don't need this right now."

Hayley retrieved a sippy cup and filled it with milk. Shannie sprang out from under the table and lunged for Hayley's uneaten salmon. Hayley distracted her with the milk. Shannie grabbed the cup and tipped it up, milk dribbling out the corners of her mouth.

Hayley slumped in her chair. Maybe she should 'send her back.' She was in over her head. What made her think she could help this little victim? She thought about the list she'd made. Things she wanted to accomplish to help Shannie get along with people in real life. Shannie would be better off with someone who had more experience. A woman who didn't let her daughter run into the street.

CHAPTER 6

Jazzmine side-stepped three bikes, a skateboard, and a soccer ball heading from the car up the walkway to the house. The front door flew open and a dark streak of lightning passed, knocking her off balance.

"Hey!" Jazzmine shouted, righting herself and glaring at the offender.

"Sorry, Mom." Her oldest son skidded to a stop on the bare lawn and grinned.

Before she could scold him, he hopped on the skateboard and rolled down the sidewalk.

"That boy'll be the death of me," she said with a smile.

She stepped through the front door, closed it, and leaned against it with a sigh of contentment. The delicious smell of something cooking set her stomach growling.

"That you, baby?"

Jazzmine smiled at the sight of Zeke as he walked out of the kitchen, wearing an apron and carrying a pair of salad tongs. The barest hint of stubble darkened his cheeks. Sweat beaded on his bare head, evidence of the kitchen's warmth. He'd changed out of his work slacks into athletic shorts and a tee shirt.

Jazzmine moved toward him, dropping the heavy briefcase, and leaned into his chest. "Something smells awfully good."

Zeke's voice rumbled against her ear as his arms wrapped around her.

"The kids' favorite. Homemade mac and cheese with hot dogs."

"Cut up in itty bitty pieces?" Though the answer was obvious, she wanted more of the comfort of his voice.

"Mmmhmm. Hard day?"

"Good guess."

"Go get washed up. Supper in ten. I'll round up the prisoners."

Jazzmine pulled away. "One of them escaped out the front door."

Zeke shook the salad tongs. "I told the boy supper would be ready soon."

Jazzmine shrugged and headed down the hall to their bedroom.

Five expectant faces looked up when Jazzmine entered the kitchen ten minutes later wearing a pair of comfy shorts and an oversized tee shirt. Zeke brought a steaming casserole dish and set it on the table. He followed with a green salad, heaped with fresh veggies, and a basket of bread. Kito reached toward the bread.

"Uh-uh. You know the rules." Jazzmine frowned at the boy. "First we say grace. Then we wait to be served."

"Let's pray." Zeke took her hand and Hosea's.

After the prayer, chaos reigned as everyone clamored to be served next. During the fraction of a moment before the ensuing chaos, Jazzmine smiled at her husband.

"Good job, baby. Again."

Before he could answer, several boys spoke at once. There were calls for seconds, small arguments, and some good-natured shoving.

"He got more than me!"

"No, I didn't. You always say that."

"It's not fair!"

Jazzmine set her fork down with a satisfied sigh. "Before you ruffians run off, let's have some civilized conversation. Who has something to tell about today?"

The boys appeared to think for a moment. Two hands shot up.

"Yes, Marcus?"

"I didn't get sent to the principal's office today."

Jazzmine bit her lips to keep from smiling. "Very good, Marcus. You didn't have school today."

Marcus sent her a cheeky grin.

"Okay, how about you, Jerome?"

"Me and Jamal jumped off the diving board today."

Jazzmine glanced toward Zeke.

"My sister came over and took them to the community pool so I could get a couple hours of work done."

"Great! Your sister is awesome. The correct way to say it, Marcus, is, 'Jamal and I jumped off the diving board.'"

"And I wasn't scared," added Jamal.

Looking around at their little brood, Jazzmine's heart filled with pride. Sometimes she had a hard time remembering which ones she'd given birth to, and which had come broken and scared. After Marcus, no more pregnancies. The official diagnosis, polycystic ovarian syndrome. Because of her job at Love's, adoption made the most sense. Jerome was three when he came to them. Too young to remember the woman who'd lost parental rights due to neglect.

Jamal and Kito were fondly named 'the twins,' because they arrived at practically the same time and were only a few months apart. Since coming to live with them, they'd been inseparable.

Later came their miracle, little Hosea. Born from her and Zeke. They were quite the family. Loud, raucous, sometimes annoying. Always delightful.

"Can we go now?" Marcus stood, shivering with pent-up energy.

Zeke's voice was firm. "Sit back down and ask the proper way."

"May I be excused?"

"And me?

"Me too?"

All five spoke at once.

Zeke nodded as the boys scraped their chairs back and grabbed their plates.

"Not so fast. Jamal and Kito, it's your turn for dishes." Zeke placed a big hand on each of their shoulders, pointing them toward the sink.

"Can I go outside, Mommy?" Hosea's liquid brown eyes pleaded.

"Sure thing, little man. Stay in the front yard until I come out, okay?" She worried more about him than the others. Maybe someday, he'd grow up and be big like Zeke. At five years old, he seemed to favor her side of the family. Small boned, short stature, skinny. And gentle as a kitten.

After checking to be sure the two boys were on cleanup duty, she headed outside.

She grabbed a webbed lawn chair out of the garage and opened it up on the driveway. From her vantage point she could see up and down the street. Marcus, Jerome, and some neighborhood kids played a game on their bikes, using a rolled-up newspaper to tag each other.

A few minutes later, Zeke appeared and handed her a frosty glass of iced tea.

"Thanks, baby." Jazzmine smiled. "You know you're my hero, right?"

Zeke laughed as he pulled out another lawn chair. "What's on your mind?"

"Now why would you think anything is on my mind?" She put one hand on her chest with raised eyebrows.

Zeke chuckled. "C'mon, baby. I know you're worried about somethin'."

Jazzmine sighed. "Oh, all right." She took several sips of the tea and set the plastic tumbler on the concrete. "I'm worried about ... one of my clients."

"Go on."

Jazzmine bit her lip, needing to talk, but still needing to maintain client confidentiality. "I called one of my foster parents for a difficult emergency placement."

"Miss Priss?"

Jazzmine playfully slapped his arm. "Stop. People can't help it if they're raised as Sacramento royalty. Besides, you aren't supposed to know about my clients."

They were quiet for a moment. Jazz couldn't help thinking how different her childhood had been from Hayley's, who seemed to have it all. Money, beauty, and two parents who were still married. And probably a trip to Disneyland every year, too.

"Anyway, I'm wondering if this placement will be her undoing."

Zeke leaned back in his chair and wrapped his arm around her shoulder. He leaned in, his breath warm against her ear. "Sometimes we need to be undone in order to be redone."

Late afternoon sun filtered through the trees, casting their shadows over the back yard. Hayley slouched in the cushioned lounge chair, watching Shannie roam from dandelion to dandelion. She crouched down, picked one, smelled the flower, and tossed it away before moving to the next one. How did Shannie totally absorb herself in a task? Hayley hadn't been able to concentrate on any one thing since Cynthia had been ... after more than a year, she still couldn't form the word 'killed.' An ugly word, far too ugly for the blonde-haired, green-eyed cherub who was her baby.

When Cynthia died, was that when Jason had begun controlling every move? Or had he started long before and Hayley hadn't noticed? Her entire life had been going with the flow, doing what everyone expected. Mom, Dad, teachers, and now Jason.

The one bit of rebellion to the status quo was her insistence on doing foster care. Her stomach clenched, remembering last night's argument.

Jason had slammed his fist on the bathroom counter.

"We agreed to talk about whether or not we would take in another foster kid, remember?"

"I know. I'm sorry. It's, well, Jazzmine—"

"Now you do what a social worker says over your husband?" His face, inches away, darkened.

"N-no. But—"

He'd pulled out the big guns. "If you hadn't let Cynthia play in the front, we wouldn't be in this situation. This pretend family you're trying to make out of, what? Other people's cast-offs?"

Hayley gulped. "How long are you going to blame me for Cynthia's d-death?" her voice shook.

Jason's finger stabbed against her chest. "I don't know. Maybe until we have another baby, and you prove you're capable of taking care of her." He pointed toward the bedroom where Shannie slept. "In the meantime, get rid of her. I have too much going on at work to come home to chaos and a wife who's overwhelmed."

Hayley squirmed on the lounge chair, remembering how he'd gone to bed with his back turned. How had they ended up so far from where they'd started?

They'd met in college. Not her type at all. She'd always gone for the intellectual types, men studying law, medicine, accounting. Someone Mother and Daddy would approve of. Jason was a struggling entrepreneur, never sure if he'd be able to pay his rent, let alone support a wife.

He'd relentlessly pursued her, making her feel like a princess. When Hayley invited him home from college to Sacramento to meet her parents, he'd managed to thaw Mother's icy demeanor.

Looking back, maybe he loved the idea of her more than herself. Jason was an orphan and an only child. His parents had died tragically in a car accident when he was sixteen. He adored Mother, and the feeling was mutual.

Hayley turned her gaze to Shannie. Where would this child end up? Back with a homeless mother, or forever lost in the foster system? Would she ever be able to talk, to function in society? What would Hayley's part be in Shannie's long-term progress? Very small, if Jason had his way. At least he'd signed the foster agreement before stomping off to bed. Only because she assured him Shannie would be with them for a short time.

Today had begun well. Shannie tinkled in the toilet this morning. Breakfast of toast and scrambled eggs went smoothly, even though she still refused to sit at the table, preferring to be underneath.

And after stony silence, Jason had left early to go to his downtown office. Usually Hayley would beg him to talk. Lately, it was too much effort.

The distinctive ring tone of the cell phone disrupted Hayley's train of thought.

"Hello, Mother."

"Hayley, dear, I'm going to stop by this afternoon after my board meeting."

Hayley's hackles rose. Mother never asked if this was a good time, or if she was busy. Her call always came across as an official pronouncement.

"I'm not sure—"

"I'll be there around four o'clock. I have something to discuss with you."

Great. "Discuss" usually meant lecture. What would it be this time—the baby lecture, the trust fund lecture, or the Jason lecture? She'd have to get Shannie down for a nap before Mother arrived.

"Fine, Mother. I'll see you when you get here," disconnecting before she could find another button to push. Mother had button-pushing down to a science. *Wonder if they gave PhDs to controlling mothers?*

Hayley did a mental inventory of the house. A quick spot-mop of the entry after Shannie went to sleep. The downstairs bathroom probably needed to be checked as well. Jason had a habit of leaving the seat up. Mother would surely notice the sin.

Speaking of sins, she'd need to change out of her yoga pants and into a pair of linen shorts. And an appropriate top, of course. A cursory glance at her toes showed the need for a pedicure. Looked like closed-toed shoes today.

If Hayley wanted to get a snack fixed and Shannie fed, they'd better get moving. Hayley heaved herself out of her comfy chair. "C'mon, Shannie. Let's go inside."

Shannie continued the quest to discover every dandelion in the backyard lawn. Had Jason asked her to call the landscapers? Probably. One more thing to tick him off.

"Shannie. Let's go."

No response.

Hayley's impatience grew. She marched over to the child and grabbed her upper arm, pulling Shannie to a standing position. Shannie howled and let her legs collapse. Hayley stumbled and barely caught herself before she fell.

The howling continued as Hayley dragged Shannie across the lawn to the patio.

"We have to go inside now." Hayley struggled for breath as Shannie pulled the opposite direction. Hayley finally picked her up and carried her, flailing, to the French doors and into the kitchen. Hayley set her on the floor.

The patience Hayley had learned dealing with out-of-control foster kids snapped when Shannie lunged for the door.

"No!" She moved to block Shannie's second lunge toward the glass in the French door. "You'll get hurt." Shannie threw herself against Hayley, screaming like she'd been burned. The hairs on the back of Hayley's neck tingled. Demon possessed? The thought swept through her mind, recalling the video in college about demon possession in some African countries.

Hayley dropped to the floor and gathered the hysterical child in her arms.

"I'm sorry, sweet girl. I'm sorry." Hayley murmured soothing words and sounds until Shannie gradually relaxed. "I shouldn't have grabbed you. I'm so, so sorry."

Hayley rested her chin on Shannie's curly brown hair. Guilt snaked a hand around her throat. She knew the rules: no grabbing or hitting a foster child. No hint of child abuse, or the child went back into the system, and her foster license would be revoked. For once, Hayley was relieved Shannie couldn't talk.

What had caused her to snap? Must have been the call from Mother. Or Jason's pressure to give her foster daughter back. Or Shannie's overwhelming needs. Hayley shivered a little and her heart beat rapidly in her chest. Should she try to be a better daughter, wife, and foster-mother? Haley shivered again and bit her lower lip. If so, *how?*

After a tear-filled snack, Shannie fell asleep. Hayley swept her hair out of her face with the back of one hand and used the bottom of her tee shirt to wipe the sweat off her forehead. She pulled the door to the pink bedroom partially closed and headed to the master bedroom to freshen up and change clothes.

The doorbell rang. A quick glance at the digital clock on the nightstand showed two o'clock. Her stomach sank. Mother had arrived.

CHAPTER 7

Mother's low-heeled pumps clicked on the tile entry floor as she swept into the room. Her lips tightened into a straight line. Hayley ran a hand down the front of her shirt, tugging it straight. Looking down, she waited for Mother's criticism.

"You look terrible." Mother sank gracefully onto the sofa and crossed one tanned leg over the other. A smooth linen sheath wouldn't dare wrinkle on Deborah Van Maren. Never Debbie or Debs. Always Deborah.

"I'm sorry. Crazy morning. Shannie—"

Mother put a hand up. "I didn't come here to discuss your feral child. I understand your need to get over Cynthia's passing. However, carrying on this way isn't healthy. Look at yourself." She waved French-tipped fingers at Hayley's stained tee. "Is this the way you present yourself to Jason?"

"Of course not." Hayley felt the heat of the white lie. Didn't she try to spread on a little makeup before he got home? He liked to see her in a dress, so she'd slip into a skirt and blouse. At least she did prior to Shannie.

"Very good. You wouldn't want Jason's attention to wander. That's what happens when a woman doesn't keep herself up." Mother pointed a finger. "Especially when you're trying to have another baby."

"We're not—"

"Your father and I are having a little get-together on Saturday night and we want you and Jason to be there. Your sister and Keith will be announcing their engagement."

Hayley mentally rolled her eyes. "So, they're finally going to stop shacking up?"

"Don't be vulgar. Hannah is doing the right thing by getting Keith to marry her. She's not getting any younger. And neither are you."

"Wh-what?" Hayley straightened her spine, leaning forward with a frown. "What do you mean?"

Mother sighed. "Your trust, my dear."

"What about my trust?" At thirty, she'd take full control over the funds in the trust Mother and Daddy set up after Gramps died. Hayley didn't pay much attention. Last time she checked, the balance totaled somewhere around seven million. Jason kept detailed records of their finances. She couldn't care less about the details, as long as the money grew.

"Daddy and I have briefly discussed changing your trust."

Hayley's shook her head. "Wait. Why?"

Mother ran a hand down her perfectly straight hair. "We feel it might be inappropriate to give you access to such a large amount of money, especially when you and Jason have no one to leave it to."

"What difference should it make?" Her parents were going to blackmail her into having another baby? *No money until you produce an heir.* Were they back in Biblical times where women had no value unless they could bear children?

Mother reached over and patted her knee. "You know as well as I do Jason isn't used to having that kind of money. He might spend it recklessly."

"Is this about having another baby? Or about Jason?" Hayley shoved the lid down on the rage threatening to erupt, unaccustomed to feeling such a strong emotion. Why couldn't she be like her sister for once, and tell Mother to go to ...

Mother stood in one smooth movement. "I'll expect to see you Saturday to help celebrate your sister's engagement."

Hayley and Hannah used to talk several times a week. Until Jason. Her sister hated him, refusing to come over when Jason was around, and eventually stopped visiting altogether. Jason said it was for the best, that Hannah wasn't a good influence.

Hayley's head reeled. Attending some huge society party at her parents' house sounded dreadful. "Mother, respite care for Shannie on such short notice might be difficult."

"You'll find someone. Daddy and I will see you Saturday at six-thirty." Mother rose gracefully. Gliding to the door, Mother delivered her final shot. "Please dress appropriately."

Hayley's sister, Hannah, sidled up in the spacious living room of their parents' home.

"Having fun, dear sis?" Hannah gulped down the rest of the glass of champagne, snagging another from a passing waiter.

"Sure. Fun." She glanced at her sister. Hannah stared across the room, eyes narrowed. Hayley's eyes roved over the room to see where Hannah's gaze had locked.

"Who is *that*?" Hannah hissed. She glared at her fiancé, cozied up to a petite blonde.

"Daddy's new physician's assistant, Kiersten."

Hannah gulped down half the champagne and turned back to Hayley.

"Well, she better not get any ideas about 'assisting' my boyfriend."

Hayley hid a smile. "You mean, fiancé?"

Hannah's eyes filled with tears. "Oh, Sis, I'm scared I'm making a huge mistake."

Hayley grabbed Hannah's arm and dragged her through the kitchen and out the doors to the patio. A few guests stood or sat around the pool. The fountain in the middle of the water changed colors from blue to red to green.

Hayley watched the display for a moment, her arm around her sister's waist. Hannah rested her head on Hayley's shoulder. "Remember how we used to swim under the fountain, pretending we were dolphins?" Hannah's wistful voice took her back to when they were kids. Simpler times.

Or were they? Mother's constant nagging about behavior, proper dress, manners. Classes in deportment and entertaining. No wonder Hannah had rebelled. Hayley admired her little sister for escaping the control. She'd never been brave enough, strong enough.

Hannah's voice brought her back. "You've always been so sure of yourself, Lee. You and Jason, engaged, married, having a baby." Hannah gasped. "I'm sorry!"

Hayley led Hannah over to a small grouping of chairs. "It's fine. C'mon, let's sit." They settled themselves on the plush outdoor cushions. Hannah leaned back with a sigh.

"It's just, well, since Keith and I have been living together, I've been able to overlook some of his ... flaws. Once we're married ..." Hannah's voice trailed off. She finished her champagne and set the glass on a nearby table.

"Flaws?" Hayley had always assumed Hannah was blissfully happy. Keith was tall, hot, and a successful pharmaceutical sales rep. They were always headed to someplace exotic, usually on his company's expense account as a perk for reaching sales numbers. At least, that's what Mother always bragged about.

Hannah waved a dismissive hand. "Like Daddy's PA, Kiersten," saying the woman's name with sarcastic venom.

"He hasn't cheated on you, has he?" Hayley leaned forward, eyes glued on Hannah's face.

Hannah laughed, an ugly sound. "Not that I've been able to catch him at."

"Have you talked to him?"

Hannah shrugged. "He slides out of the conversation like butter on hot corn. After that, he swoops me off to someplace romantic, and I let it go."

"Oh, Hannah Banana, I'm sorry."

Hayley's use of her sister's childhood nickname must have struck a chord. Brittle Hannah returned. "It's been too long, dear sister, since we've talked. We must do this again soon." Hannah stood, looking down at Hayley's upturned face. "If your Jason will let you off the leash, that is."

The parting shot pierced Hayley's heart. Just like old times. Hannah had always shown jealousy with barbs. A chill swept over the patio. Hayley rubbed cold hands up and down even colder arms. Was she on Jason's leash?

They'd had a huge fight when Hayley tried to explain how difficult it had been to find someone to watch Shannie for the evening. He said if she had talked to him about whether to agree to Jazzmine's emergency placement, she wouldn't be in this situation. Jason was right. They'd made an agreement early in their marriage to make big decisions together.

She'd let her husband down and paid the price. Hayley stood and walked across the patio and into the house. Conversations swirled around, mingling with the soft background music of a string quartet. Clinking of glasses and bursts of laughter filled the huge foyer. Everyone seemed to be having a good time. When had this type of party lost its appeal? Hayley longed to be home, snuggled in her bedroom with a good book and a glass of frosty iced tea.

"Where have you been?" Jason grabbed her arm the minute Hayley stepped into the house. "I've been looking all over for you."

Hayley's stomach shrank to the size of a raisin. "I was talking to my sister. Outside."

"Don't disappear like that. People are asking about you. 'Where's your pretty wife?' It's embarrassing when I don't know where you are."

Hayley pulled against Jason's grip. "I'm sorry. I didn't mean to worry you."

Jason abruptly changed gears. "Who's the guy talking with your dad?"

Hayley glanced around the room, her gaze settling on her father, deep in conversation with a thirtyish man in a sport coat and khakis. "My dad's CPA, Brian Rafferty."

Jason tightened his grip on her arm, pulling her toward Daddy. "I need you to introduce me. I've heard he helped my buddy's company go public. Chad and I want to do the same thing. We'll make millions."

Hayley let Jason drag her across the room. If he and his partner wanted to do something, no one could stop them.

"There's my beautiful girl." Her father broke off his conversation when they approached. He put his arm around her shoulders and squeezed. "Brian, this is my oldest daughter Hayley, and her husband, Jason."

Hayley always thought of her father as the handsomest man in any room. Ten years older than Mother, he was now in his early sixties. His thick hair had gone completely white, and he wore it slightly long. Not because of preference. He was always "too busy" to get a haircut. Mother constantly nagged him but somehow, he'd managed to fend her off.

Brian extended his hand, first to her, then to Jason. "I've heard lots about you." He smiled into her eyes. Hayley took in his light brown hair, trimmed with military precision. He wore a navy sport coat over a white silk tee and designer jeans. Jason could never pull off the same look.

"All good, I hope?" she replied, smiling. Jason nudged her arm. She stepped into her charm school training. "Brian, Daddy tells me you've helped some start-ups with their initial public offering."

Brian glanced at Daddy and back. "That's right."

Jason's voice was almost too friendly. "I'd like to talk to you about that sometime. My partner and I—"

Daddy laughed and clapped Jason on the shoulder. "Not now, my boy. This is a party. No time for business talk."

Jason looked ready to argue but didn't dare in front of Daddy. "Right. Sorry. Maybe we can connect later?"

"Absolutely." Brian took a step back. "I'm going to refresh my drink."

"Ah, there you are." Daddy turned Hannah, who stopped on her way to the bar. "It's the girl of the evening herself. Come give your father a kiss."

Hayley sagged with relief. The conversation was over.

Later, in the car on the way home, Jason wouldn't let it go.

"I can't believe your father cut me off." He slammed his hand on the steering wheel.

"You can always call Daddy's office and get Brian's contact info."

"That's not the point, Hayley. The point is, your dad treated me like some sort of ..." His voice trailed off. "He embarrassed me in front of his CPA. Besides, I didn't like the way the guy looked at you."

Hayley tried to change the subject. "Since when did you and Chad decide to go public?"

"We've talked about going IPO for a couple of months. Or selling."

"Why haven't you brought it up before? With me, I mean. Didn't we agree to make major decisions together?"

Jason barked out a laugh. "Like you did with this feral kid?"

"Shannie isn't feral." This wasn't the direction she wanted to go. "My mother stopped by yesterday."

"Oh yeah? What did she want this time?"

"She threatened to change my trust." The words were out before she could stop them.

Jason hit the brakes to avoid a cat running across the road. "What kind of change?" His voice was sharp as a steel blade.

Hayley shrank down in the seat as Jason accelerated. "She mentioned she and Daddy could change the date I could take over my portion of the trust from thirty to maybe older."

"And why would they do that?"

Hayley shrank even further. "She wants us to have another baby."

Jason smiled. "Well that's something we can take care of. Tonight."

Not the romantic approach she wanted.

CHAPTER 8

Jazzmine smiled as she pulled into Hayley's driveway. The smell of fresh-mowed grass seeped through Rusty's window. The lawns in this neighborhood always seemed greener than in her tract home subdivision. How did they do it? Was there some secret ingredient only rich people knew about?

Could be because five active boys never played football in these front yards?

Jazz climbed out of the car, slamming the door to make sure it stayed closed. Time to have Zeke check the latch. Again. She approached the front door with one more appreciative look at the neighboring homes.

Jazzmine rang the bell, then did a double take. The woman who answered the door resembled Hayley. The unwashed hair and vomit-dampened shirt threw her off.

"Hi-ya. What happened to you, mama?" She pushed past Hayley into the house, turning to look her up and down.

Hayley closed the door and leaned against it. "A better question would be 'what didn't happen.'"

Jazzmine pursed her lips. "Really?"

Hayley nodded. "You have no idea."

"Come on, girlfriend. Let's talk." Jazzmine grabbed her hand, pulling Hayley toward the kitchen. Shannie sat on the floor under the table, shoving handfuls of dry cereal into her mouth.

Hayley leaned down and took the box away, ignoring Shannie's wail. "Sorry. She must have grabbed the box when I let you in."

Jazzmine headed toward the cupboard where Hayley kept the coffee with the easy familiarity of someone who'd been there often. "I'll make coffee. You sit." She pointed to one of the wooden chairs.

Hayley sank down with a sigh, burying her face in her hands. "Crazy morning. She was out of control today. I thought I was making progress ..." Her shrug said it all.

Jazzmine made sure there was enough water in the Keurig machine. After inserting a pod, she pressed the button to brew. She repeated the process, bringing both cups to the table.

"Tell me what's going on, sweetie."

Hayley's words tumbled out. "I made a list. First potty training. I set her on the toilet this morning. Bribed her with M & Ms. It worked with Cyn—" Hayley gulped. "It worked before. She jumped off the potty, looked right at me, and pooped on the floor."

Jazzmine choked on her sip of coffee. The situation would be hilarious if Hayley didn't look so tragic. "It's a good thing, honey."

Hayley's head pivoted up. "What?"

"The fact she knew you were trying to get her to do something, and her rebellion shows she understands. It's progress."

Hayley wrapped her fingers around the mug of coffee. "I don't know—"

Jazzmine glanced at her watch. She had five more welfare checks to do before the end of day. "Let's go through some paperwork."

By the time Jazzmine completed her report, they'd finished the coffee. Jazzmine stood and walked to the sink to rinse out her cup. "Look, sweetie, you're doing fine. Keep doing what you're doing, and it'll all work out."

Jazz returned to the table and laid her hand on Hayley's shoulder. "Between your care and the occupational therapy, she's going to thrive. You'll see. In the meantime, I'm still searching for a more permanent placement. I know I told you this would only be a few days. However, we have a larger caseload than usual."

Shannie took advantage of the moment to wiggle out from under the table.

"Well, hi, little girl. Did you come out to say hello?" Jazzmine squatted down. "You take good care of your foster mommy, okay?"

Jazzmine stood and moved toward the door. Her head whipped around as colorful pieces of mashed up cereal spewed from Shannie's mouth and onto the floor. Jazzmine winced. "Sorry, sweetie. I'd love to stay and help. I've gotta dash. I emailed you the therapy schedule. Someone will be by tomorrow to start home therapy."

A twinge of guilt shot through her as she headed toward the front door.

By the time Jason turned down the street leading to his home, he'd worked himself up into a cold fury. His partner, Chad, had gotten on his last nerve. Always badgering him about numbers, numbers, numbers.

"We need to make a decision, bro," Chad had said.

Jason's lips tightened, remembering. *I'm not your bro. I don't even like you.* Yes, they needed to decide if or when they could sell the business. Or buy another company. Whatever. What they did with the business wouldn't matter once Hayley got her hands on her trust money. Unless Deborah decided to manipulate the trust.

His mind fishtailed over the possibility that everything he'd waited for would disappear. If only Hayley would stop this foster stuff. At first, he'd agreed to try it, merely to get her to stop crying over Cynthia. He had to admit, fostering gave him points with his clients.

"Yeah, the wife and I are foster parents. It's the least we can do, with all we've been blessed with."

He'd relished the smiles and pats on the back. "What a wonderful thing you're doing." Comments like those had made fostering worthwhile. Until now.

Why this kid? Hadn't Jazzmine said the placement would only be a few days? He gritted his teeth. Time to go home and let Hayley know it was time to quit.

Hayley turned on her plush mattress toward the window. A sliver of light slashed the blackness of the master bedroom. Jason's even breathing behind her indicated he slept. They'd had yet another argument. Hoping not to disturb him, Hayley tiptoed out of the bedroom. She stepped silently over the plush carpet to where the child slept in her daughter's old bedroom. No surprise, Shannie wasn't in the bed. She hunkered down to peer under the bed. The faint glow from the night light revealed Shannie hadn't crept under the bed either.

She sat back on her haunches, head hanging between her knees.

Where could Shannie be this time? A cursory glance in the bathroom showed no sign of the little girl. With a backward glance at the open master bedroom door, she crept down the stairs, avoiding the squeaky one.

Shannie wasn't behind the couch or under the coffee table. Hayley's bare feet barely made a sound as she tiptoed into the kitchen. She was sure she'd closed the pantry door, yet it hung open several inches. Her fingers searched for the switch in the darkness. The light revealed Shannie, asleep on the pantry floor, a box of crackers by her side. Crumbs mixed with thrown-up crackers lay in a hardening pool next to her cheek.

"Oh, sweetie, what did you do?" Shannie didn't stir as Hayley lifted her, turned and carried her back up the stairs. She was weightless in Hayley's arms, light as a hummingbird. Hayley tucked her in bed, smoothing the child's hair back from her face. She kissed her on the forehead and returned downstairs to clean up the mess before Jason woke up the next morning.

As she scrubbed the mess with a wad of wet paper towels, she thought back to what her sister said. How could Hannah ignore when Keith might be cheating on her? Jason would never cheat. They'd made vows to each other. Maybe that was the difference. Hannah and Keith weren't married, hadn't made the commitment.

Mother and Daddy were her example. Hayley vowed to never get divorced. Divorce would be unacceptable. She'd do whatever it took to make her marriage work.

Maybe now was the time to have another baby. She'd be better this time. She'd never be distracted, never let anything keep her from knowing exactly where her daughter was every moment. She'd leave her phone in the house when they went outside. They'd only play in the back yard, never in the front.

Hayley was a better person now. Lesson learned. Retribution taken.

Tears gathered in the corners of Hayley's eyes and slid down her cheeks. Sweet Cynthia. Her little body, broken in the street, struck by a passing car.

An eye for an eye. It was in the Bible. Maybe God's judgment was now completed, his revenge for her sin checked off in his book.

Hayley continued to scrub the floor long after it sparkled, remembering.

She'd met Johann as a junior at the University of California Santa Barbara. He'd been a foreign student from South Africa. She was entranced, first by his accent, and second by his old-world charm.

She'd fallen hard for him. They never talked about what would happen when he finished college and returned to his country. For the first time, Hayley learned how to make her own decisions and be herself. It was liberating to be free from everyone's expectations.

Hayley gave herself freely to Johann, and in return he gave her freedom. During those few months, Hayley laughed more, danced more, and loved more than she had ever done. She forgot what it was to have someone always looking over her shoulder, reminding her of the proper way to behave.

Glorious love.

Until Johann returned to South Africa. Without her. And without the baby she discovered she and Johann had made.

Hayley returned home after her junior year, empty and broken. She'd learned the hard way that rebellion had consequences. No one knew what she'd done. Except God. She'd taken the life of her baby, and he'd taken her daughter as payment.

CHAPTER 9

The familiar chaos of the office assaulted Jazzmine as she stepped through the door. Phones ringing, voices talking over each other, and the smell of burnt coffee. What was wrong with people, anyway? Drinking the last cup and putting the pot back on a hot burner. Sheesh.

Dodging through the maze of cubicles, Jazz reached her own space. Cubicle walls gave partial privacy. These were filled with pinned up photos of her kids and a few thank-you notes from former foster kids, now thriving adults. There were too few of those. Some days the endless cycle of yanking kids from their dysfunctional homes, placing them in the system, and then seeing those kids go back, pulled her into a funk.

Gloom would not suck her down today. There was too much to do. Her purse landed under the desk with a thump. The travel mug of coffee sat close by on the left of the metal desk, next to the list of "Things to do today." The chair creaked its familiar welcome as she sat to power up the computer. While waiting, Jazz reached for the phone to retrieve messages.

"Message one from an outside number: Ms. Washington, this is Lieutenant James Erby. Call me back at 916-579-2245. I have some news about the kid we found in the homeless camp."

Jazz replaced the receiver with a shaky hand. "News" usually meant bad. When was the last time she'd gotten good news? How would this affect Hayley?

Thoughts rolled around in her head, threatening a massive headache. With a sigh, she reached for the phone again. Better to get answers sooner rather than later.

She dialed the number she'd written down for Lieutenant Erby.

"Erby." He answered on the third ring, his voice clipped.

"Lt. Erby, this is Jazzmine Washington."

Papers shuffled in the background. "I'm glad you called. The homeless kid? The girl? I'm pretty sure we've found her mother."

Jazzmine's stomach dropped down to her Sketchers. "Oh?"

More rustling papers. "Her name is Barbara McNally, and she's currently held in Sac County lockup. She's been screaming about her baby. We thought she was strung out. After doing some digging, we found the kid's birth certificate and verified her identity. I thought you might like to know."

Jazzmine twisted the phone cord between her fingers. Whether good news or bad, time would tell.

The Sacramento County Recorder's Office hummed with activity as Jazzmine waited in line for her turn. Who would have thought a government office would be this busy on a Monday afternoon. With one eye on the slow-moving line, she checked her cell for any messages from home. She shouldn't be concerned. With Ezekiel working from home today, chaos would be kept to a bare minimum. Maybe she'd text him anyway. Just in case.

JAZZ: Everything okay there?

ZEKE: Sho nuff, Sugar. Worried?

JAZZ: Should I be

ZEKE: 6 men in one little house? I'd say so

Jazzmine smiled. She sure did love her man.

JAZZ: No broken bones, k?

ZEKE: :-)

Jazzmine slipped the cell back in her purse, moving to the counter. She took a business card out and handed the card to the clerk.

"I need to get a copy of a birth certificate."

"Over there." The clerk pointed to a bank of microfiche machines. Jazz knew the drill. Her search began with the girl's birth date, October 23, 2016. Little Shannon, or whatever her name, was almost five years old. How had her mother managed to hide her for so long? Had they always been homeless, or was there once a place they called home?

The date pulled up several possibilities. Jazzmine scrolled down until she found the mother's name, Barbara McNally. No father listed. There was an address. After five years, it probably wasn't valid. Not a lot of information. Low birth weight, no distinguishing birthmarks. At least she had a name.

Hayley struggled to open her eyes in the morning brightness. Jason stirred on the bed next to her.

"Good morning, beautiful." Jason reached over and pushed the hair from her face. "How about some coffee for your man?"

Hayley sat up and scrubbed a hand over her face. Coffee would help clear the cobwebs from her brain. She'd had a hard time falling asleep last night, after cleaning up Shannie's mess. Her dreams were filled with frightening images of car accidents and bloodied children.

"Sure. Be right back," she said with a thin smile.

A quick look into Shannie's room showed she was still asleep. Under the bed again.

Hayley hurried downstairs to the kitchen and filled the Keurig machine. She shouldn't keep Jason waiting.

Five minutes later, she carried two steaming cups up the stairs and into the master bedroom. Jason sat with his back against the headboard, laptop poised on his legs.

"Here you go." She set his cup on the nightstand.

"Thanks." Jason didn't look up from his computer. Hayley carried her mug into the bathroom and took a quick shower.

When she came back into the bedroom, Jason sat in the same spot, and his coffee looked untouched.

He glanced up and his eyes returned to the computer. "My coffee's cold."

"I'll nuke it for you." Hayley walked over to his side of the bed. Before she could reach for his cup, he grabbed her arm and pulled her toward him, planting a kiss on her lips.

"You're too good to me." He flashed her a smile, reminding her of when they'd first met.

She'd been a college senior, and he a struggling entrepreneur, five years older. They met at Starbucks near UC Santa Barbara. She did her homework there, and he used their free Wi-Fi, since he and his partner couldn't afford an office. After a few weeks of casual conversation, he asked her out.

She'd said no. After Johann and the abortion, she kept men at arm's length. She'd learned her lesson. Be the good girl.

Jason wouldn't leave her alone. At first, she'd been annoyed. He'd wait in Starbucks with her favorite drink, iced black tea. Her friends thought him sweet. Hayley thought him creepy.

He'd said his parents were dead, and he was an only child. He'd charmed his way into her heart and life.

Hayley's parents adored him, and for a wedding present, Daddy had given Jason a large sum of money to get his business off the ground. The investment was the push they needed to get their company to the next level. Now the business consumed him.

Hayley hurried down the stairs with Jason's coffee and shoved the mug in the microwave. She glanced around the kitchen to make sure nothing was out of place. The microwave dinged, and she pulled out the hot mug.

Back upstairs, she set the coffee down next to her husband.

Jason lifted his eyes long enough to acknowledge her. "Thanks."

"I'm going to go check on Shannie."

His face clouded. "Maybe you're already pregnant and we can stop with this foster thing."

Hayley shrugged.

Jason's attention returned to his laptop. As she walked out of the bedroom, she heard him say, "And your parents won't be tempted to change your trust."

Right. And you won't have to give up your dream of running your company remotely from a yacht as we sail around the world.

After Jason left for his office, Hayley coaxed Shannie into the tub to wash away the throw-up hardened to a crusty mess on her face and neck.

"Come on, sweet girl, let's get you clean so you can wear some of your new clothes."

Shannie loved the water. Hayley hoped to take her swimming later in the day. She had water wings and a floatie that would fit her perfectly.

After the bath, Hayley chose a flowered sun dress and white sandals. Shannie was docile enough to let Hayley dress her. Hayley made a mental note to get rid of the shipping box still in the back of her SUV. Jason would blow a gasket if he saw it.

"Let's put on your new shoes. Aren't they cute? They'll look wonderful with your dress." She pulled Shannie's foot toward her, working her toes into the sandals. With a squeal, Shannie yanked back her foot and took off running, out of the bedroom and down the stairs.

Hayley sat back on her haunches. "I guess you don't like the shoes."

She sprinted down the stairs and found Shannie behind the sofa. "Come on, sweetie. No shoes. I'll let you go barefoot." When Shannie didn't budge, Hayley resorted to the one thing she knew would work. Food bribe.

Hayley fed her tiny bites of apple dipped in peanut butter. The kid was a human funnel. She'd eat everything in the house if Hayley didn't watch her.

After breakfast, Hayley took Shannie outside to play. Although play wasn't how she'd describe Shannie's actions.

She seemed intent on picking every single dandelion from the grass. Maybe the occupational therapist would give Hayley some activities to help Shannie stay focused on something educational.

Her phone buzzed. A text from Zola.

ZOLA: How's the wild child today?

HAYLEY: Good. She's picking dandelions

ZOLA: Bring her to my house. Let's teach her to pull weeds

HAYLEY: :-) What r u cooking up today

ZOLA: Pizza with cauliflower crust

A smile worked its way up to her mouth.

HAYLEY: samples?

ZOLA: Sure thing, honey. Soon as I know it's edible

HAYLEY ;-)

She returned to watching Shannie. What a beautiful child. Those green eyes were amazing. If only she'd make eye contact more often. With her mocha skin, she could have her toes dipped in two or three different races.

Her phone buzzed again. This time a text from Hannah.

HANNAH: Can I call you?

HAYLEY: Sure.

Two seconds later, her phone rang. Hannah probably didn't even wait for Hayley's response.

"Hi, Sis. What's up?" She tucked one leg under her on the lounge chair and settled back.

"Hi. Say, I was wondering. Did I say anything ... inappropriate at Mother and Dad's party?"

Inappropriate? Hannah always said something inappropriate. What did she have in mind?

"Um, I don't think so. We talked about why you were hesitant to marry Kevin."

"Oh, okay."

"Speaking of which, you never did announce your engagement. You are engaged, aren't you?"

Hannah was silent for a few moments. "Kinda sorta."

Hayley laughed. "Either you are, or you aren't. Which is it?"

"I don't know. I want things to stay the way they are. All this pressure to get engaged. You know Mother will plan some God-awful wedding. She'll invite five hundred people."

"It'll be epic, for sure."

Hayley pictured her sister shrugging.

"I wish we could stay living together."

"Is this because of Kevin cheating on you?" Hayley watched as Shannie squatted down by the fence, picking flowered weed after flowered weed. She jumped when her sister responded.

"Kevin doesn't cheat on me! Why would you say something so mean?"

"At the party you said—"

"I did not. You're jealous because Kevin treats me like a person instead of a slave."

Hannah's words hit hard, taking her breath away.

"I-I have to go." Hayley disconnected and tossed her phone on a nearby table.

She wanted to be a good wife, no matter what. Hadn't her mother said her husband's needs came first? A wife's role was to be submissive. It was in the Bible. No matter if the romance disappeared somewhere between "I do" and "My coffee's cold."

Hayley squared her shoulders. The one thing she wouldn't do would be to give in to sending Shannie back into the system. She was determined to love the child whose mother had callously abandoned her in a homeless camp. She'd be the best mother ever, the mother Cynthia deserved, but didn't have. All because of God's punishment for the murder of her baby. So what if the abortion activists said a fetus wasn't really a human. Hayley knew the truth. Hadn't she heard enough sermons about the beginning of life? Selfishly, she'd chosen convenience over dealing with the consequences of her sin. All because she couldn't face the shame and disappointment from her parents.

And the thought they might withhold her trust money, leaving her to raise a baby on her own with no money and few job skills. This was her one chance to prove she could be a good mother. This poor abused child needed her. And she needed Shannie. For absolution. For proof she wasn't a monster.

If her parents changed the trust, so be it. She and Jason would figure out the finances. If Jason left her because she refused to give Shannie up, she'd figure out that scenario too. She'd show everyone, God included, she could be a good person, strong and capable.

The girl squatted on the grass, listening to the words the lady named Lee spoke in her phone. She sounded mad. No, not mad. Sad. Did the girl do something to make her sad? She'd be a good girl. Quiet and invisible.

Jazzmine stepped out of the county recorder's office and into the August heat. She paused to let the sun press through her cotton shirt. She dug through her purse until her fingers found her cell phone. No texts from home, no pressing emails. She was procrastinating, and she knew it. The easiest thing would be to call Hayley and give her an update. Jazzmine never did the easy thing. She smiled to herself. Mothering five boys was never easy.

She sighed. Rusty sat parked a few blocks away. The parking enforcement scooter had almost reached the expired meter when Jazzmine raced the last few feet to the car. She acknowledged the officer with a nod, climbed into Trusty Rusty, and fired him up.

Turning the car in the direction of the Fabulous Forties, Jazzmine formed the words she'd say to Hayley about what she'd discovered about the little girl named Shannie.

The ten minutes to Hayley's home passed in a blur. How should she break the news? Slowly, to let Hayley absorb the information. Or fast and sharp, like pulling out a five-year-old boy's tooth?

She still hadn't decided when she pulled into the driveway. Rusty chattered to a stop. *No more delay. Just do it.*

Jazzmine climbed out of the car, grabbed her purse, and marched to the front door. Sixty long seconds later, Hayley pulled open the door with a look of surprise.

"Is it time for a welfare check already?" She motioned Jazzmine inside. The air conditioning hit her with a blast of chilled air, a nice respite from the hot morning. "Come on into the kitchen. I was fixing some lunch for Shannie and me. You're welcome to join us."

Jazzmine followed Hayley. In the kitchen, her eyes were drawn to the little girl. Shannie sat on the floor by an open drawer, taking Tupperware lids out and putting them back. She wore an adorable flowered sundress. A pang of longing hit Jazzmine. Boys' clothes were so generic. She'd love to have a little girl to dress up like a princess. Zeke had drawn the line when she'd gotten pregnant with Hosea. Even though Hosea was a surprise, she couldn't imagine life without him.

Jazzmine crouched down on the child's level. "Look at you. Aren't you cute?"

"I still can't get her to wear shoes." Hayley busied herself chopping lettuce and arranging it on a plate. "Can you stay for lunch? I have plenty."

Jazzmine stood, dropping her purse on the granite-topped island. "No, I came to give you an update. I found Shannie's mother."

Hayley stilled. With her back turned, Jazzmine wondered what Hayley might be thinking. Would she be relieved? Scared? Or perhaps angry at the woman who'd raised a child in a homeless camp.

"Her name isn't Shannie, either."

Hayley dropped the knife with a clatter and whirled around. She spoke in a whisper. "Who is she?"

CHAPTER 10

"Could I make a cup of coffee?" Anything to put off the awful truth. At Hayley's nod, Jazzmine pulled a cup from the cupboard and dropped a Keurig pod into the machine. As the fragrant aroma of French roast filled the kitchen, Jazzmine formed her words.

"Her name is Dixie McNally. Her birth mother is in jail, scheduled to be released tomorrow."

A sob escaped Hayley's clamped lips.

"She'll go to rehab for three weeks."

"Then what happens?" Hayley turned. Her face was stiff and drained of color.

Jazzmine shrugged. "The court will decide if Shan, I mean, Dixie, will go back with her mom."

Hayley shook her head before Jazzmine finished the sentence. "No way can that happen."

Jazz laid her hand on Hayley's shoulder and squeezed. "You know how this works, sweetie. The court will decide what's in the best interest of the child."

"Best interest?" Hayley's words exploded. Shannie shrieked and scooted under the table. She lowered her voice. "How could it be in her best interest to go back to that—that—?"

"I know, I know," Jazzmine soothed. "The birth mother will have to prove she has a safe place for her and Dixie. She'll have to look for a job. You know this." Jazzmine dropped her hand and reached for the coffee mug.

Hayley went back to chopping vegetables with more force than necessary. She paused and turned to look at Jazzmine. "I can't let her go. Not now. We've made progress. She's almost potty trained." A tear glistened in the corner of her eye and trickled down her cheek. She used her arm to wipe it away. "I have a list. We haven't gotten through the list yet."

"List?"

"Yes. A list of things to accomplish. You know, like p-p-potty training..." Hayley's voice stuttered to a stop as she shook with silent sobs.

Jazzmine gathered her in her arms as if she was one of her boys. She rubbed Hayley's back, murmuring reassurances.

"It's gonna turn out all right. You'll see. God's eye is on the sparrow. Shh, now." If only all her foster parents were as concerned as Hayley. Many times, they were glad to see their little charges march out of their house, paper bag in hand. Especially the ones with behavior issues.

Hayley pulled away. She grabbed a paper towel and blew her nose. "Sorry. I don't usually lose it."

The control was back in place. This was the Hayley Jazz was used to. Jazzmine swallowed the last of her coffee and set the cup in the sink.

"Thanks for the brew, sweetie." She patted Hayley on the back. "Have faith. God is in this."

Hayley coughed up a laugh. "God. Right. How could I forget."

Jazzmine pushed herself away from the counter, gathered up her purse, and walked toward the table. She crouched down to Dixie's level. "Bye, little one. I'll see you soon."

She straightened and spoke to Hayley's back. "I sent you an email with the schedule for occupational therapy and psychologist meetings."

Hayley turned. "Thanks. For everything."

Jazzmine gave her a mock salute. "No prob. I'll be praying for you." As she strode out the door, she could hear Dixie wailing. Poor Hayley. Jazzmine's cell phone buzzed when she reached her car. Her supervisor had sent a text.

CARLA: Emergency placement. Call me ASAP!

Hayley dragged her feet as she approached the door to occupational therapy. The place smelled funky, like old gym clothes stuffed in a locker for a long weekend. She grabbed her last breath of fresh air before stepping inside the building in Midtown Sacramento.

"Come on, Sh-Dixie." She'd have to make more of an effort to use the girl's real name. Who named their daughter "Dixie," anyway? Contempt for Dixie's mother rose up in silent outrage. She gritted her teeth and led Dixie through the glass doors and into the reception area.

The pert receptionist looked up from her computer with a smile. "Mrs. Montgomery, good to see you. It's been a minute, hasn't it?"

Hayley attempted a smile. How could this thirty-something fashionista stand the smell, day after day?

"Hi, Madeline."

Madeline reached for the phone. "I'll let Doctor Yang know you're here."

Thirty seconds later, Dr. Yang appeared in the hallway, striding toward them. Her low-heeled pumps almost brought her to Hayley's height. The doctor wore what Hayley thought of as her uniform—khaki-colored skirt and collared polo. Golf clothes.

"Hayley, always a pleasure. And this must be little Dixie." Dr. Yang's smile was broad as she crouched down to see Dixie eye to eye. "What a beautiful child you are."

Dixie stared at her feet. Hayley had managed to wrestle a pair of sneakers on her—while the child had a meltdown, screaming and bucking. At the end of the struggle, Dixie finally fell limp onto the bedroom carpet. Maybe Hayley could count it toward her calorie goal. Kid wrestling, three hundred calories for ten minutes.

Dr. Yang straightened. "Come on back, ladies."

Hayley's stomach tightened. She had a plan, and she was going to go for a run, doctor or no doctor. "Uh, I have another appointment."

Dr. Yang's face tightened as she crossed her arms. "It's important for you to observe the therapy sessions so you can mimic them at home. You know the rules."

"I-I have an appointment. I'll be back. Twenty minutes."

Dr. Yang frowned. "If this isn't a convenient time for you, perhaps we should reschedule."

"N-no. Just, um, let me make a call."

Hayley slung her purse over her shoulder, dropped Dixie's hand, and raced out the door. She resisted the urge to rest her hands on her thighs and breathe in fresh air.

Tears sprang to her eyes. Hayley counted on this hour for herself. She could feel fat growing on her thighs. The scale she'd stepped on this morning had confirmed it. She was up two pounds from yesterday.

Straightening her shoulders, Hayley turned back toward the clinic, biting down hard on her bottom lip.

Madeline pointed Hayley down the hall to the playroom. Hayley knew the way by heart from the previous times she'd been here, bringing bruised and broken children for Dr. Yang to fix. Children of people who should never have been parents. *There should be some sort of test you had to pass in order to give birth. Amazing how screwed up kids could be in a few short years.*

Hayley crept through the door of the playroom and took a seat in the corner, partially hidden by a row of cubbies. Dr. Yang sat on a kid-sized chair, watching Dixie manipulate some wooden blocks.

What horrors had this beautiful little girl witnessed in her short life? The red insect bites on her arms had faded, but what internal scars did she still bear? How did Dixie's mother hide her from the world for five years? She'd never pass a motherhood readiness test.

Hayley set her mouth in a grim line. Her thoughts turned to her golden-haired little angel, now in heaven. Hayley would have failed the test too. Imagine letting your child run into the street because you weren't paying attention.

Maybe this time, with Dixie, she'd redeem herself. This was her chance, and Hayley wouldn't let her go. God demanded retribution, and by golly, she would give it to Him. Let Dixie's mother try to get her back. Hayley would fight like a mama bear. As she watched Dixie focus on the blocks, she mentally sharpened her claws.

God had extracted his payment for her sin, now she would earn her way back into his favor.

Outside Dr. Yang's office, Hayley could see a commotion a block away. Two groups of women on opposite sides of the street held signs and shouted. She froze as the words became clear.

"Leave our bodies alone!"

"Abortion kills!"

"Protect a woman's right to choose!"

"Abortion kills a beating heart!"

Hayley's breath caught as a few of the signs turned toward her. Photos of aborted babies. Sickened, she turned away, hustling Dixie toward the car. The pictures were a grisly reminder of what she'd done.

Hayley had been so sure of her decision. It seemed so easy. So convenient. Problem solved. No one had told her about the guilt she'd carry. The shame constantly weighing on her shoulders. Or the dreams she'd have about how the baby might have looked.

No one said a word about what God might think, or how his punishment would be extracted. Didn't the Bible say, "An eye for an eye"? *Well, God, I deserved it. You took Cynthia's life like I took an innocent baby's life.*

Were they even? Not quite.

Once Dixie was strapped in her car seat, Hayley did a mid-street U-turn to avoid the protesters and headed home.

They arrived back at the house a little after twelve. Hayley ignored her growling stomach. Those two pounds weren't going to go away without a fight. Hayley unstrapped the car seat, and Dixie slid out of the car. The shoes she'd fought to put on were on the floor. Dixie ran toward the door leading into the house. Hayley grabbed the shoes and followed her.

"I bet you're hungry, aren't you?" Hayley dropped the shoes inside the kitchen. "You worked hard today for Dr. Yang."

Dixie headed straight for the pantry.

"Oh, no you don't. No cookies until we have lunch. First, we potty."

"Potty."

Hayley froze. Did she hear correctly? This was the second word she'd heard Dixie say. First Mama, now potty. A thrill shot through her. Was she finally getting through to the child?

"That's right, sweet girl. Potty." She grabbed Dixie's hand and pulled her through the living room to the powder room by the front door. She pulled down Dixie's flowered shorts and pull-up and lifted her onto the toilet. The sound of tinkling soon filled the small room. Hayley used her finger to lift Dixie's chin so she could look her in the eye. "Good girl."

With her bladder empty, Dixie jumped off the toilet and bolted for the door. Hayley found her seconds later, in the kitchen, opening the pantry door.

"You're fast, little one." She pushed the pantry door closed with a grin. "Not so fast. Lunch first, dessert second."

Dixie howled in protest and threw herself on the floor.

"I'm impressed by your theatrics. Lunch first, cookies after." Hayley smiled. At least this was normal behavior. Her smile faded. Normal for a toddler, not a child of four. Would Dixie ever be caught up? Could she learn to talk, to exist in a world of regular people?

Hayley was flooded with a wave of protectiveness. She'd do it. She'd make sure Dixie had every opportunity to learn and grow into a normal child. That woman would not get her back, rehab or no rehab. Good thing Jazz hadn't said her name. Knowing the mother's name would have personalized her, and Hayley wanted her to remain faceless. Just another homeless addict. Not a mother with a child who depended on her.

Hayley's cell phone buzzed as she and Dixie sat on the sofa watching a *Little Einstein* video. Dixie sat mesmerized by the images on the screen. Leaning over, Hayley plucked the phone off the end table. Jason's picture filled the screen. Was he calling to give her more grief about Dixie? Should she even mention her real name?

"Hi."

"Hi. I'm on my way home."

"Okay." He rarely called before leaving work. "What's up?"

"How are things there?"

"Fine." She wrinkled her brow. "Why?"

His voice held a hint of humor. "Wondering if your wild child was under control."

Her wild child? Not *theirs*? A shaft of anger tightened her stomach. "We're watching a movie."

"Good." Pause. "Sorry about our argument."

What? Jason never apologized. What was up? Some of her anger dissipated. "Me too."

"What's for dinner?"

"I thought maybe you could barbeque some chicken when you get home."

"Oh, babe. Can you do it? I'm spent."

That was more like him.

"Sure." Whatever.

"I'll be home in twenty." He disconnected before she could respond. Classic Jason.

Hayley sighed and unwrapped herself from Dixie's side. She got to her feet, looking down at the child. "I'll be in the kitchen." No response. After this morning's word, Hayley hoped for something, anything, to indicate she'd broken through a wall. Disappointment weighed on her shoulders as she shuffled into the kitchen.

The tile floor chilled her bare feet. Mature oak trees on their property kept the worst of the late August heat from penetrating the house. Hayley ran her hand over the smooth granite countertop. She loved this house. She'd begged her parents for an advance against her trust to buy it. Jason had been thrilled to be able to pay cash for it.

"The last thing I need is to stress over a house payment," he'd said. His fledgling start-up hadn't generated much income when they were first married. Her monthly checks kept them from struggling while he and his partner grew their business.

"Good thing I married a rich wife," Jason told her. She wasn't rich. Not yet anyway. Grandpa Van Maren had left his offspring very well off. He'd sold several large undeveloped plots of land before he died. His legacy was the generous trust fund giving Hayley an allowance every month until she turned thirty. At thirty, she could do what she wanted with the money.

Hayley's plan was to let the funds continue to accrue interest. They didn't need a ton of money.

All she'd wanted to do after college was to get married and start a family. Jason had insisted they wait for a year or two. Almost two years to the day after their wedding, the home pregnancy test showed she was expecting.

Their beautiful, perfect Cynthia was the culmination of all Hayley's dreams. Until she'd ruined everything by one mistake. Jason said he forgave her. How could it be possible when she couldn't forgive herself? The abortion protesters she'd seen in the morning confirmed everything she thought about herself.

Murderer. Monster.

When would God be satisfied? The little girl curled up on her sofa might be the key to releasing his judgment against her. No one would take away her chance of ultimate forgiveness. Not Mother, not Dixie's birth mother, and not Jason.

With things settled in her mind, she set about preparing dinner. She pulled some chicken breasts from the Subzero fridge and set them on a plate. After sprinkling them with salt and pepper, she went to the door of the living room to peek at Dixie. The child sat entranced by the video.

Hayley strode back into the kitchen and out the French doors into the back yard to start up the gas barbeque. The afternoon wasn't too hot. Maybe they could eat outside. She'd like to get Dixie to sit at the table with them. Hayley tried at lunch, but Dixie couldn't seem to sit still. She'd slid off the chair and under the table.

One of these days. Maybe. First things first. Where had she left the list? Potty training was almost under control.

Her phone buzzed with a text from Zola.

ZOLA: Whatcha doin? Thot I heard you in the back

HAYLEY: Yup. BBQ chix maybe eat outside

ZOLA: Hubbs actually gonna be home 2nite. Making some vegetarian chicken pot pie

Hayley smiled despite herself. How do you make chicken pot pie vegetarian?

HAYLEY: think he'll like it?

ZOLA: He will if he knows what's good for him :-)

HAYLEY: :-)

What would she do without her wacky neighbor? A combination mother/best friend. Sometimes her God talk could be irritating, but all in all, Zola been a rock during those first few weeks after Cynthia's death.

All Hayley's college friends were on one of two tracks. Either they were career-minded, laser-focused women on a mission to break the glass ceiling, or they'd had one or two kids, moved to the suburbs, and sat in Starbucks with their baby tucked into a six-hundred-dollar stroller. No one her age lived in the Fabulous Forties neighborhood of Sacramento. Too expensive. Their neighbors' average age exceeded hers by at least thirty years.

Hayley focused on making a mixed green salad, then washed a potato and put it in the microwave, setting the timer for five minutes. The chicken she carried out to the barbeque and laid the breasts on the grill. Then she dashed back inside to check on Dixie. The video had ended, and still the girl stared at the blank screen.

"What are you thinking about, sweet girl?" Hayley sat on the edge of the sofa and rubbed Dixie's back. Sometimes the child seemed to fold into herself, sinking into some deep hole. Was she escaping some former terror?

The door from the garage opened and Jason called, "I'm home."

Dixie stiffened under Hayley's hand. "It's okay, sweetie. It's Mr. Jason. Remember? He lives here." She bent down and whispered into Dixie's ear. "He won't hurt you."

Jason stuck his head into the living room. "Dinner ready?"

With her hand firmly on Dixie's shoulder, Hayley got to her feet. "About ten minutes. I need to turn the chicken over."

With a nod, Jason disappeared into the kitchen. Hayley heard him drop his briefcase on the table. She started the video over.

"Stay here, little one, while I get dinner, okay?" No response. At least she hadn't scuttled behind the sofa at the sight of Jason. More progress.

Hayley hurried into the kitchen and gave Jason a quick peck on the lips. He grabbed her and gave her a warm hug. "I do love you, you know." He grinned down at her, tickling her forehead with his beard.

"I love you, too. Now let me go so I can feed you."

Instead of releasing her, he tightened his hold, forcing her face against his chest. "I see you got a text from our crazy next-door neighbor."

He'd snooped in her phone.

Hayley struggled against him. His voice rumbled in her ear. "I don't like you talking to her. That kind of crazy isn't the type of person you should have for a friend."

Hayley went limp, stumbling when he let his arms drop to his sides. "What type of person should I have as a friend?" Her voice was icy, matching the coldness seeping up her chest.

"Anyone other than her. She's overweight, and she dresses like a hippie."

Hayley swirled toward the back door before saying something she'd regret.

CHAPTER 11

Jazzmine pounded her hand on Rusty's steering wheel. "I've been holding for five minutes. I need information on Barbara McNally." The police department volunteer seemed unmoved by Jazzmine's frustration.

"I'm trying to reach Lieutenant Gonzales, ma'am. He isn't answering his cell."

"Can I leave a message?" Jazzmine wanted to say, *Another message*.

"Of course, ma'am. I'm sorry, what did you say your name was?"

"Jazzmine, two z's, Washington. My number is (916) 634-5219. Please have him call me ASAP regarding Barbara McNally."

Jazzmine disconnected, pulled out her ear buds, and tossed the phone on the passenger seat. It bounced off and landed on the bag of clothing headed to the dry cleaners. One more task left unaccomplished today. She pulled into the parking lot of a strip mall, leaving the car running.

"Think, Jazz, think." She tapped her forehead with a fist. Who else might know the whereabouts of Dixie's mom? All Jazzmine had been able to find out was she'd been released from jail the day before and was headed to rehab for three weeks.

Zeke's distinctive ring echoed from her cell. "Hi-ya, husband."

"Hey, baby. Called to say hi. How's my wife?"

"Frustrated. Frazzled. On my way home."

"Tell me all about it tonight?"

Jazzmine smiled. "After the kids go down."

"That works. In the meantime, hurry home. I need some sugar."

"Mmhmm. I like the sound of that."

"Drive safe, baby."

Jazzmine sat for a few minutes longer, savoring Zeke's words, sending up a quick prayer of thanks for Zeke's faithfulness, and for God's.

She smacked herself on her head.

"Why didn't I pray about finding Barbara before getting all worked up?" Her lips moved in the silent music of prayer.

God had been a part of her upbringing. Her parents attended a Baptist church in Reno and made sure Jazzmine and her brother went every Sunday morning and night, and to Bible study Wednesday evenings. It wasn't until graduation from college that she'd made a commitment to him.

Jazzmine put the car in reverse, backing out of the parking spot. Her thoughts travelled back to the incident after college which had thrown her world out of balance. One bad choice, one horrific night. She'd run to God and he'd gracefully pulled her through the trauma.

She'd met Ezekiel at church. He told anyone who'd listen that meeting her was like being struck by lightning. She'd been slower to commit, after ...

Jazzmine turned down the street to home, narrowly missing a child racing across the street on a bike. She slammed on her brakes, smacking her forehead on the steering wheel. The boy pulled around the back end of the car and up to her window. She rolled it down, ready to unleash fury.

"Hi, Mama." Marcus grinned at her.

Jazzmine felt heat rise to her head. "I almost hit you, child! What do you think you're doing riding like that?"

Marcus's smile faded. "Sorry, Mama." He put his feet back on the pedals, preparing to ride away.

Jazzmine called after him, "We're gonna talk about this with your Daddy."

Marcus hunched over his handlebars and pedaled quickly down the street. Away from her anger. Could she keep him alive long enough to discipline him?

Jazzmine pulled Rusty into the driveway, turned off the car and pulled the key out of the ignition. After stepping out, she made a mental note to call the prison chaplain first thing in the morning. Mindy would know what happened to Barbara.

Hayley stood in the shower and let the water wash the tears down her chest and down the drain. She held one hand clamped over her mouth to muffle the relentless sobs. The fight with Jason tonight had been the worst one yet. He'd been moody at dinner, hating the fact that she still couldn't coax Dixie to the table.

"This is ridiculous," he'd exploded. "Why can't you get her to eat like a normal kid?"

She'd tried to explain to him Dixie wasn't a "normal kid." She hadn't been raised in a home with furniture, with a stable place to sleep.

"I thought you were going to get rid of her." His callousness cut her already pummeled spirit. She'd waited until Dixie had been bathed and put to bed before confronting him. Somehow, he'd turned the situation around and made it her fault.

"Why can't you be like Chad's wife? She has her own kid, a job, and a normal life. You bring chaos home like you're trying to save the world."

"Chad's wife? She's a hot mess." Hayley tossed her flip flops into the bottom of the closet. "Have you seen their house? It's a disaster. And Brittany is too."

"Well, at least he has someone who meets his needs. You're doing a lousy job of it."

He did *not* just say that. *She* was a lousy wife? Hayley did everything he asked her to do. She checked off all the tasks on the lists he made practically every day. *Go to the*

THE GIRL IN THE CARDBOARD BOX

bank. *Pick up the dry cleaning. Get a bag of his favorite chips at the store. Call the yard service, the pool service, the pest control service.* On and on. Where did he get off telling her she didn't meet his needs? She told him this.

That's when things got ugly.

Hayley closed her eyes and let the water beat down on her head. trying to wash away Jason's harsh words seared on her spirit.

"If you'd kept a better eye on Cynthia, you wouldn't have this insane need to take care of other people's kids. What makes you think you'll do a better job with them than you did your own kid?"

How could she explain God had exacted his judgment against her? Jason knew nothing about Johann and the abortion. He thought he was the first. How much worse would it be if he knew the truth?

She'd stepped out of line one time and paid for it. Still paid.

Jason had tossed some clothes in his gym bag and headed out the bedroom door and down the stairs.

"Where are you going?" she'd demanded. When he didn't answer, Hayley followed him through the kitchen to the door leading into the garage, grasping at his arm. "Please, Jason. Don't go. I'm sorry. I'll do better. I promise."

He shook off her hand.

"Where are you going?" Hayley hated the shrillness of her voice. Hated her need to have him respond. "Talk to me. Please." Hayley tried to follow him into the garage. He closed the door in her face.

"I'm going to the office. I'll spend the night there."

The coolness of the tile floor in the kitchen seeped into Hayley's feet and up her legs. She stumbled back, eyes blurry from the tears already pooling there.

What had she done? She'd driven her husband away. Would he be back? What could she do to get him to come home?

Hayley dried off from the shower and dressed in a soft pair of shorty pajamas. She brushed out her wet hair, noting the need to touch up the highlights and lowlights. Yet another thing to do. She downed a couple of Tylenols and tiptoed into Dixie's room to check on her.

Not in the bed, of course. Hayley got down on her knees, bending over to peek under the bed. Two green eyes stared back at her, the light from the night light reflecting in Dixie's eyes.

"What are you doing still awake, sweet girl?"

Dixie crawled out from under the bed, blanket clutched in her bony fingers. She lunged at Hayley, throwing her arms around Hayley's neck. Hayley fell back, catching herself by stretching out her arms behind her. She regained her balance, returning the hug.

"Mama."

Hayley choked back a sob. "Oh, sweetie, how I wish that were true."

Dixie's breath was warm against Hayley's neck. Hayley felt Dixie's heart beating as fast as a hummingbird as they rocked together. This was the first time the child had initiated contact. Her spontaneous gesture hardened Hayley's resolve to keep her. No one would keep her from fighting for this little girl. No birth mother, no husband, and certainly not the system.

The girl's heart hurt. The man was mean to Mama. No, not Mama. Lee. She savored the word in her head, drawing it out. Leeeeee. She hoped the man would go away and never come back so she could have Lee all to herself.

Jason shoved the door to the garage closed with enough force to rattle the tools hanging on the garage wall. Why couldn't Hayley get it through her head? He was done with other people's kids. Especially that one. He swore under his breath as he punched the button to open the big garage door.

Three vehicles filled the cramped space. These older houses originally had space for one car. When they'd remodeled, they'd enlarged the garage, to the chagrin of the next-door neighbors. The side of the garage sat very close to their neighbor's bedroom. Not that Jason cared. He wanted space for his Miata, as well as his and Hayley's SUVs.

Jason shuddered as he glanced at the Miata, now covered with a shapeless tarp, like a shroud. He strode over to the car and tugged on the front corner of the tarp, ensuring none of the front bumper was exposed.

Jason remembered the last time he'd driven his prize possession. A year ago, he'd taken some potential clients to lunch, and they'd ordered a pitcher of margaritas to accompany their food at Zocalo. He should never have gotten behind the wheel. Why didn't he call for Uber or something? The one time he let loose of his carefully controlled world, he'd gotten buzzed, driven, and something bad had happened.

Jason climbed into his Escalade, revved the engine, and shoved the SUV into reverse. He backed down the driveway, bumping over the curb with teeth-jarring speed, screeching to a stop at the corner. He turned left to head to the freeway, needing speed and air to clear his head. At the stoplight before the entrance to Highway 50, he rolled down the windows.

Jason headed east on 50 toward Placerville, racing around anyone who might slow him down. His speedometer showed ninety miles an hour.

Anger burned against Hayley. How could she be so selfish? Didn't she know what kind of pressure he was under with work? He and Chad had big decisions to make. Should they sell or go public? The wrong decision could break his business, and his wife didn't seem to care. All she could think about was the feral kid who couldn't even use the bathroom by herself. Hayley was obsessed with these stupid foster kids, who came and went like they had a revolving door.

Jason needed to get her under control. They needed to have another kid. A baby would keep his wife at home where she should be. Not taking these messed-up kids to and from the shrink's office.

With the money from the business, and Hayley's trust fund, he'd be able to buy the yacht he'd been lusting after. They could spend six months of the year on land, and six months on the sea. He could buy another sports car and dump the Miata. Maybe buy a classic Corvette, restore it, and add it to a collection of cars. Maybe he and Jay Leno could connect and compare car collections. Two more years, and Hayley would have access to her trust fund. That's when their problems would be over.

Unless her parents got in the way.

Jason slowed the car down as he approached the little town of Placerville. Dusk settled over the historic bell tower as he turned left at Main Street and headed up the winding hill. It had been at least two years since he'd been up here, yet the car seemed to know the way. Turn right at Lilac Lane, continue uphill, left on Cold Springs Road.

Jason pulled to a stop outside a clapboard home, set back a hundred feet from the road. The picture window was barely visible through the trees covering the property. Directly in front of him at the beginning of the gravel driveway sat an old-fashioned mailbox, the kind with a red flag to signal the mailman you had outgoing mail. The address was written in black cursive letters, and above the numbers were the words, "United Friends."

Jason stared at the mailbox while the Cadillac's powerful engine purred beneath him. Darkness settled over the mountain town. The house porch light switched on, snapping him out of his trance.

He shifted into drive and rolled silently down the hill toward the town.

Hayley struggled to open her swollen eyes. Her head ached from a massive crying hangover, and for a moment she couldn't remember where she was. Clarity returned when she remembered she'd fallen asleep with Dixie in her arms. Sometime during the night, she'd pulled the blanket off the bed and covered them both up. Dixie had crawled back under the bed, huddled under her own blanket.

Hayley stretched, stiff from sleeping on the floor. After a jaw-cracking yawn, she stumbled down the stairs for a cup of life-giving coffee.

While the coffee maker heated up, she leaned against the counter, staring into the back yard. The early morning coolness beckoned. A breeze ruffled the canopy of trees hanging over the yard, calling for her to soothe her wounded spirit. Responsibility pulled harder, keeping her in the house. She couldn't leave Dixie alone. The last time she'd left her child for a moment, disaster struck. Lesson learned.

Maybe she'd take Dixie into the pool today. There was no "Jason list" sitting on the counter, and no occupational therapy appointments. Ah, sweet freedom.

A noise from upstairs interrupted her euphoria. She set her cup on the counter, spilling its contents, and broke into a run when she heard Dixie howling.

She skidded to a stop inside the bedroom door. Dixie stood in the middle of the room, head thrown back, as if she was howling at the moon. Hayley gagged at the smell. Brown semi solid goo ran down Dixie's legs and onto the floor.

"Oh—" Hayley grabbed her by the upper arms and carried her into the adjoining bathroom. It wasn't the first time one of her charges had diarrhea. It still didn't make the situation any easier. Holding her breath, she stood Dixie in the tub and turned on the water. While the water warmed, she pulled off the girl's pajamas, tossing them in the corner. Dixie continued to screech, even after Hayley turned on the shower and let the mess wash down the drain.

When Dixie was scrubbed clean, Hayley wrapped her in a towel and pulled her into a hug. Dixie stiffened in her arms.

"It's okay, sweetie. It's all right. We'll get through this." After Dixie was completely dry, Hayley released her. Dixie ran into the bedroom and grabbed her blanket. Hayley followed, wrestling the blanket away to examine it for any poop.

Dixie screamed, cried, and threw herself on the floor, arms flailing.

"No, sweet girl. This has to be washed." Hayley held the blanket by two fingers and carried it down the hall to the laundry room. She returned to the bedroom with a plastic bag. She gathered up the soiled pajamas and underwear, scooping them into the bag.

"These are going in the garbage. Not even going to try to wash them." With a grimace, she tossed the bag into the hall, returned to the bathroom, and washed her hands.

"Let's get you dressed," she said, over the sobs wracking Dixie's body.

Hayley pulled out a pink tee shirt with a kitten on the front, and a pair of matching shorts. Dixie squirmed away.

Hayley took a deep breath. "Patience," she muttered. Trying to dress a kid in the middle of a meltdown was more difficult than putting clothes on a cat. "Good thing I'm bigger than you."

Dixie's sobs turned to hiccups when Hayley finally got her dressed. Hayley pushed her hair out of her face, wondering when the situation would get easier. She'd thought, after the breakthrough the night before, Dixie might be on her way to a semblance of normalcy. Apparently not.

"I'm going to get dressed, little girl." Hayley stood, looking down at Dixie, curled in a ball on the floor. Hayley returned to the laundry room, threw the soiled blanket into the washer, and started it.

Face washed, hair pulled back into a clip, Hayley pulled on her favorite yoga pants and a tee shirt, leaving her feet and face bare. Why wear makeup if Jason wasn't home?

When she returned to Dixie's room, the girl still lay on the floor, picking at the carpet.

"C'mon, sweetie. Let's go get something to eat." If food didn't motivate her to move, nothing would.

Dixie jumped up and dashed down the stairs ahead of her.

After another battle over the pantry door, Hayley was finally able to make some oatmeal. She sat on the floor under the table, feeding Dixie spoonsful of the cereal.

In between bites, Dixie grabbed for the sippy cup, dribbling milk down her chin, wetting her tee shirt front.

"What am I going to do with you?" Hayley used a paper towel to wipe off Dixie's face.

Had this child never had enough food? Hayley noted with pleasure Dixie had gained a little weight in the past few days. Although the child was still skinny as a string bean, her legs had filled out a bit. Shorts no longer hung on her hip bones.

Hayley had to use her judgment on how much to feed Dixie. Otherwise, she'd keep eating until she vomited, stuffing everything into her mouth. Hayley's heart broke for the little girl who'd never had full meals on a regular basis. What a difference between Dixie's cardboard box childhood and the soft pink cocoon she had now.

And a stark contrast to Hayley's own upbringing. She and Hannah never thought about when they'd be able to eat next. Their biggest argument with Mother over food had been begging for Twinkies instead of an apple. Mother always won the argument.

"Eating junk food will make you fat," was Mother's mantra. "No one likes a fat girl."

Hayley spooned the last of the oatmeal into Dixie's mouth and crawled out from under the table to rinse out the bowl. The doorbell rang, interrupting the washing process. Hayley set the bowl in the sink, glancing at her watch. Already ten-thirty, and she hadn't had a chance to eat. Oh well. After a few days without working out, she'd better to watch her calorie intake, despite the protest coming from her stomach.

"Who could that be?" she said, crouching down to check on Dixie. "Maybe it's the UPS man with another box of goodies."

Hayley hurried to the front door and put her eye up to the peephole. Her stomach tightened into a knot, hunger gone.

Mother.

Hayley opened the door, stepping aside so her mother could enter. "Good morning." What did Mother want now?

Mother's black-and-white, low-heeled pumps clicked on the tile entry as she stepped past Hayley and into the living room.

"Good morning, Hayley. I thought I'd stop by on my way to my board meeting."

Her black pencil skirt and sleeveless white blouse looked as crisp as if she'd slipped them on before knocking on the door. The diamond and emerald necklace screamed "expensive." Mother's only concession was she never wore pantyhose in the summer. Even with bare legs, her mother looked like a model for AARP on how to age gracefully. In her mid-fifties, Mother kept her trim figure, staying in shape playing tennis, but Hayley couldn't ever remember seeing her mother break into a sweat.

"Would you like some coffee?" Hayley led the way into the kitchen. Out of the corner of her eye, she caught a glimpse of Dixie, still under the table, spinning the now-empty sippy cup around and around.

"Yes, please." Her mother pulled a chair out from the table and lowered herself into the seat. And gasped. "What—"

Dixie had reached out a hand and touched Mother's leg.

"This is Dixie." Hayley busied herself with the coffee machine.

"I thought you said her name was Shannon." Mother scooted her chair over to escape Dixie's hand.

"I didn't think you remembered."

Hayley didn't have to turn around to see her mother's expression. Her voice spoke volumes. "Of course, I remember. I'm interested in everything in your life, Hayley."

Perhaps too interested? Maybe she and Jason *should* move to the suburbs. Mother wouldn't be able to conveniently drop by to tell her what was wrong with her life.

Hayley finished preparing the two cups of coffee and carried them to the table. "Sorry, I'm all out of saucers."

"Don't be sarcastic. It's unbecoming." Her mother took a dainty sip of the hot liquid and set her mug down. "I came by to check on you. You and your sister never call any more. It's all texting, and you know I don't text."

"The phone works both ways, Mother."

"See? That's what I'm talking about. I'm worried about you, Hayley. All this anger, this sarcasm. What happened to my sweet, compliant girl?"

Hayley stiffened. For starters, she wasn't a girl. "Mother, what's this really about?"

Her mother steepled her fingers, inhaled deeply, and blew her breath out through perfectly lipsticked lips. "Your father and I are worried about you. And Jason."

Heat started in Hayley's chest and traveled up to her face. She clamped her lips together to keep from responding.

Her mother continued, tapping her manicured fingers together. "We think—"

Dixie took the moment to utter a high squeal. Her mother jumped to her feet. "What was that?"

Hayley bent over to look under the table. Dixie hurled the sippy cup at Hayley, narrowly missing her face. Hayley jerked, bumping her head on the table.

"Ow." She rubbed the side of her head.

Dixie scampered out from under the table and dashed into the living room.

Mother's skirt rustled as she returned to her seat. Her voice was full of reproach. "See? This is what I'm talking about. Your life is in shambles. We don't do shambles, Hayley. You should know that."

"You call taking in a broken little girl *shambles*?" Hayley shook her head. Unbelievable.

Mother reached her hand across the table to grasp one of Hayley's hands. "Hayley. Listen to me. You've stopped wearing makeup. You wear those ... those exercise clothes every day. You don't get out with friends anymore. And Jason, well, Jason said he didn't come home last night."

Hayley jerked her hand away. "You talked to Jason?"

Her mother had the decency to blush. "He called the house this morning, looking for your father."

"What did he want?"

"He wanted the number of your father's CPA."

Figured. It was always about him. His stupid company. Talk about being obsessed.

"You talked about me? Behind my back?"

"Of course not." Mother ran a hand over her blond hair. "I simply asked how you and he were doing."

"He told you all about our fight. Then what?"

"We talked about what you should do."

The burn that had begun when they first began to talk now erupted into a fire. "And?"

"Oh, Hayley, you know what you need to do. Stop this foster parent nonsense. Have your own children. Fill the house with kids if you must." Her mother gestured around the room. "Stop taking all this for granted. You have a wonderful life and a good husband. If you're not careful, you could lose everything."

Words she wanted to spew boiled up. Instead, Hayley stood. "It's time for you to go now, Mother. You'll be late for your meeting."

Her mother sighed, rising gracefully to her feet. She ran her hands down her sides, straightening her skirt. "Think about what I said, Lee." The childhood nickname sounded at odds with her mother's tone.

Hayley walked her mother to the front door, catching a whiff of her mother's signature fragrance as she leaned in for an air kiss. She leaned against the door frame, watching Mother stride to her white BMW sedan.

Hayley closed the front door and listened for noise. She followed a scratching sound and discovered Dixie behind the sofa, running her fingernails up and down the fabric on the back of the sofa.

"You can come out now. She's gone." And thank God.

Anger, frustration, and sadness raced through her in equal parts. In the kitchen, Hayley took out a block of cheese from the refrigerator, grabbed a knife, and retrieved a package of crackers from the pantry. The rustling of the cracker package was enough to bring Dixie racing into the kitchen.

"Tell you what, sweet girl. Sit here with me, and we'll both eat." Hayley brought the snack to the table, set everything down, and reached over for the child. She set her next to her, pulling the chair close. She cut a few small pieces off the block of cheese and doled them out. "One for you, one for me." All at once she felt exactly like Dixie. There wasn't enough food to satisfy the hole inside left by her mother's words.

"We'll both eat until we barf, eh, Dixie?"

The girl shoved the food in her mouth, anxious for the next bite. Now that the mean lady was gone, the air in the room was quiet.

By the time Jazzmine got to her office that day, there were already ten voice messages on her work phone and close to a dozen on the cell. She dropped her purse on the floor under her desk and logged on to the computer. Thirty-five unread emails. The morning's coffee burned in her stomach. The list of things to accomplish loomed, including three welfare checks and onboarding two new cases. She inhaled and blew out the breath through pursed lips.

The argument with Zeke this morning didn't help her state of mind, either. He thought she was too hard on Marcus, their oldest. She thought he was too lenient. The battle was ongoing. Jazz hated Marcus hanging around Xavier. Seemed like they were always up to something just short of dangerous. She'd been enraged at Zeke's comment, "Boys will be boys." Too many of those "boys" ended up in her case files.

Speaking of which ... She slung her messenger bag onto the desk. Files and papers spilled out, spreading onto the floor.

"Dang it all!" The words exploded from her mouth as she shot to her feet. Coworkers at neighboring desks looked up.

"Nothing to see here," Jazzmine said to the room, crouching down to gather up the mess, tossing the papers on the desk. She sank into her chair, cupping her face in her hands. Some days this job was too much.

With a sigh, she began to sort the papers, filing them in the correct folders. When the task was finished, Jazzmine set them aside and pulled a tablet toward her, then the desk phone. With a pen in one hand and the phone in the other, she dialed into her voice mail.

Message one: Uh, yeah. You're my daughter's case worker. That's what they told me. Anyway, I want to see my kid.

Message two: This is Barbara McNally, and my kid is Dixie. I wanna know where the (blankety-blank) she is. Call me back at this number. (530) 649-3279.

Jazzmine winced at the profanity. So, this was the feral child's mother. This ought to be interesting.

The rest of the messages were follow-ups from her own outgoing calls the day before. Nothing too dire. She made notes on the tablet, which would be transferred to the case files later.

The cell messages were another matter. Three messages from Zeke, each one more urgent. "Call me ASAP." Two from Marcus, his voice thick with tears. Four hang-ups, and three lengthy messages from other caseworkers, updating her on their progress. She wrote as quickly as possible, tamping down the terror as she prepared to call Zeke back. After putting off the call as long as possible, she finally pressed his name in her favorites list, wondering if life would ever be normal again.

Zeke answered within seconds. "Baby, are you sitting down?"

Jazzmine rubbed a hand over her face. "Yes."

"Marcus was arrested today."

CHAPTER 12

Hayley held the back door open, waiting for Dixie to walk through. She couldn't help smiling at the little girl, tugging at the back of her swimsuit. Dixie's ribs still stood out against the snug fabric, and her stick legs looked barely able to hold her up. Hayley wanted to eat her up—she was so adorable.

"C'mon, Dixie. Let's go to the pool and have some fun." After Mother's visit and a rough start to the day, a little fun was in order.

They walked across the patio to the fence surrounding the pool. The kid-proofed gate had a security lock high above the reach of little people. Hayley used both hands to snap open the lock, closing the gate behind them with a click.

"Let's get you into your little swimmers." Dixie's pull-up crackled as she moved. Hayley didn't trust her to keep from pooping in the pool. What a mess that would be. She'd already inflated the floaties for Dixie's arms, sliding them over Dixie's hands.

"Time to go in." Hayley stepped into the pool, motioning Dixie to follow her. Dixie took a tentative step into the water. The oblong shelf extended four feet into the pool, providing adequate room for the child to play without drifting into deeper water. Dixie sat in the water, mimicking Hayley's movements.

"See? It's like the bathtub, only bigger." She splashed some water in Dixie's direction. Dixie giggled and splashed back. Dixie slapped her hands on the water, blinking in surprise when the water got in her eyes.

"It's okay, sweetie. Just a little water. See?" Hayley splashed herself in response. "Look, I can put my face in the water, too." She lowered her face, blowing bubbles.

Dixie giggled again and tried, coming up sputtering and spitting.

"You aren't supposed to drink the water." Hayley patted her on the back, pulling Dixie into her arms.

"Let's go out into the pool." Dixie wrapped her legs around Hayley like an octopus, arms tight against Hayley's neck.

"Hey, not so tight. I can't breathe," Hayley said, gently loosened Dixie's grip while walking toward the deep end. She stopped midway between the deep and shallow ends. "I won't let go. Don't worry." She bounced up and down, wetting Dixie up to her shoulders.

After a few minutes, Hayley felt Dixie's grip relax. They bobbed in the water for a few more minutes. Hayley walked over and deposited Dixie back on the shelf. "Here you go. Let's play here for a bit."

Hayley leaned back against the side of the pool and stretched her legs out. Maybe she could get a little color in her fish-belly flesh. Dixie seemed content to flop on her stomach and thrash around in the water.

"Yoo-hoo! Neighbor." Zola's voice called from next door. Seconds later, her head appeared over the fence. "Looks like fun."

"Come on over," Hayley called.

Zola's laugh was deep. "Honey, I haven't been in a bathing suit since George W. Bush was president."

Hayley chuckled. "Well, come over and watch. We can get caught up."

Previous homeowners had installed a friendship gate in the fence between the two properties. Zola opened the creaky gate and made her way across the lawn to the pool. She unlatched the pool gate and stepped inside, closing it behind her. Zola held a colorful fan in her right hand. In the other, a plastic tumbler.

"It's hotter than Hades out here." Zola plopped down in a chair beneath a blue and yellow striped umbrella, fanning herself madly. "You sure you should be out here in this heat?"

"We're wearing sunscreen." Hayley realized she hadn't brought anything for them to drink. "Say, Zola, would you do me a favor?"

"Anything for you, *sheyn*."

"Would you run into the house and bring us a couple bottles of water?"

"Sure thing." Zola set her fan down on the table and waddled through the French doors and into the house. She appeared shortly with two bottles of water, dripping with condensation. "Here ya go."

Hayley stood and walked over to the edge of the pool, keeping one eye on Dixie. "Thanks."

Zola looked her over from head to toe.

"What?" Hayley asked.

"*Fraynd*, if I looked as good as you in a bathing suit, I'd never wear anything else."

Hayley chuckled as she unscrewed the top of one of the bottles. She held the water to Dixie, who guzzled a third of the bottle before pushing it away. Hayley set the water on the edge of the pool, unscrewed the other and drank deeply. "Thanks. Totally forgot to bring water out." Dixie went back to splashing happily.

Zola's fan fluttered like an angry wasp. "It's a sauna out here." She kicked off her sandals and stepped into the pool. The bottom of her dress fell below the surface. Zola leaned her bulk over to splash pool water onto her arms and face. "There, that's better," she said, stepping out and settling into the chair once again. "I saw your mom's car out front earlier."

"Zola, are you spying on me?" Hayley asked with mock horror.

"Not at all. I was taking some tomatoes over to Mack and Lindy and happened to see your mama walking up to your front door. Did you know Mack recently got out of the hospital?"

Hayley shook her head. "How do you know everything about everyone on the block?"

Zola tapped her temple with a finger. "I'm a keen observer of human nature. Plus the fact that my kitchen, unlike yours, looks out onto the street." She grinned. "So, I thought I'd take over some garden produce and get the scoop from Lindy."

Hayley ran her fingers over the surface of the pool. She used to know the neighbors. When they had first moved in, she'd organized a neighborhood watch group. They met at the house across the street, until those people moved. She'd gotten pregnant, and Jason insisted she drop all outside activities. "For the sake of our baby's health," he'd said.

Hayley didn't realize until that moment how isolated she'd become.

College friends stopped asking her to lunch or to any social gatherings. Since Cynthia's death, she hadn't felt comfortable with the moms' group. Jason said those women were shallow, anyway.

As soon as she got Shannie ... *Dixie* ... to a better space, she'd make some new friends. Ones Jason would approve of.

Her head shot up when she heard the door to the house open. A familiar voice called across to the pool.

"Well, isn't this a cozy scene." Jason stood in the doorway, a frown on his face.

Dixie scrambled across the pool shelf and crawled up the steps. She lunged across the hot concrete and planted herself behind Zola's long skirt.

"Hello, Jason. What a pleasant surprise." Zola's voice was droll.

Jason took a few steps forward and crossed his arms. "Hayley, it's too hot to be outside. You need to come in now."

Zola rolled her eyes. Hayley turned and spoke to Dixie. "Come on, Dixie. Let's go in the house." She took hold of Dixie's arm and pulled her gently toward the steps. Dixie planted her feet and shook her head in protest. Hayley's heart sped up. Jason watched her with his eyes narrowed.

Zola struggled to her feet. "Sounds like my invitation to go home. Later, my friend."

Hayley drew on the one thing she knew would motivate Dixie to leave the pool. She leaned down and whispered in her ear. "Let's go get you something to eat."

Dixie stopped struggling and allowed herself to be led up the steps and onto the patio. Hayley wrapped her in a towel and carried her to the gate. She adjusted Dixie on her hip and used her other hand to open the gate and grab her own towel. Jason stood and watched her. Irritation bloomed when he didn't offer to help. Hayley swept past him and into the house.

She set Dixie on a chair and retrieved a box of animal crackers from the pantry.

"Uh, uh, uh," Dixie grunted her approval.

"You didn't come home last night." Hayley dried herself off in between feeding Dixie one cracker at a time.

Jason closed the French door behind him. "What did you expect? You refuse to do what I want. You don't care one bit about the stress I'm under. You won't even talk to me about it."

Hayley bit down hard on her bottom lip. "You're right, Jason. I'm sorry. I'll try to be more sensitive." Her apology usually appeased him.

Jason leaned against the counter with his arms crossed, watching Hayley feed Dixie. "Lee, I only want what's best for us. We can't go on taking in foster kids instead of having our own family. We talked about this, remember? I'm not okay with this."

Hayley pinched her arm to keep from crying. Jason hated when she cried. "What do you want me to do?"

Jason dropped onto one of the chairs and pulled his satchel toward him. "I already told you. Let's have another baby. We'll move somewhere else if staying here is too painful. We have to move on from Cynthia's death." Jason pulled out his iPad. The conversation was over.

Hayley dried Dixie and removed her wet swimsuit and dressed her in a pair of soft cotton shorts and a tank. Dixie had practically fallen asleep before she was completely dressed. Hayley left her lying on the carpet, covered in her ratty, but clean, blanket.

Hayley changed into dry shorts and a tee and finger-combed her hair.

Remembering her mother's remark, she swept some lipstick across her mouth before heading down the stairs.

Jason was still engrossed in his iPad when Hayley walked into the kitchen.

"What do you want for dinner?" Hayley opened the fridge and spoke from its depths.

No answer.

"Jason?" No response. "Honey, what do you want for dinner?"

Her stomach tightened. She closed the refrigerator and walked around to the other side of the table, facing Jason.

"Are you still mad at me? I said I was sorry." She gripped her hands together, knuckles white.

"If you have to ask, it isn't worth my time to answer," He responded, not looking up.

"What did I do?" She spoke around the dread lodged in her throat, hating the whiny tone creeping into her voice.

Jason looked up, eyes cold. "You know what you did."

Hayley thought back over the time span since he'd appeared at the back door. Did she leave dishes in the sink? A dish cloth wadded on the counter? Did she take too long with Dixie, getting her changed?

"Are you mad because dinner isn't ready?"

Jason's fingers froze on the iPad keyboard. "I said, if you don't know, it isn't worth my time telling you."

"Please, Jason, tell me so I can fix it. I'm sorry."

She hated to beg, but sometimes it was the only way to get him to tell her.

"You're always sorry and nothing changes."

"I promise, I'll do better. Tell me."

A shriek sounded from upstairs. Jason's head shot up. He stood, grabbed his iPad, and headed for the door leading to the garage.

"Where are you going?" Hayley followed him, grabbing his shirt. He shook her off. "Jason?"

Before she could stop him, he stomped down the steps toward his car. Hayley ran to the passenger side and grabbed the door handle as he jumped in. He backed out of the garage, tearing the handle out of her grip.

"Jason! Come back! I'm sorry—" her words were drowned out by the screeching of his tires as he drove away.

Hayley clutched her arms across her stomach. He'd never left after one of their fights. He usually retreated to his upstairs office, slamming the door. This made twice in twenty-four hours he'd gone.

The neighbor across the street stared into the garage as he watered his lawn. Hayley's face burned with humiliation. She couldn't even keep her husband at home. She was a loser as a mother and a loser as a wife.

Slumped over, she shuffled to the door leading into the house, punched the garage door button, and watched it descend. Like her thoughts.

"You're making good progress." Dr. Yang sat next to Hayley as they watched Dixie together.

Dixie played on the floor of the occupational therapy room, which was no more than a large playroom. The carpet bore stains of indeterminate origin. By contrast, the room was cheery and well-lit. Colorful bins held wood blocks, puzzles, and stuffed animals. Plastic tubs full of crayons and coloring books sat atop two child-sized circular wood tables in the middle of the room.

"Look at how she's engaging with the crayons."

Dixie sat at one of the tables with her head resting on one arm, twirling a red crayon around and around on the tabletop.

"She's not coloring," Hayley observed. "Seems like she becomes super-focused on one thing."

"Give me an example." Dr. Yang's attention stayed on Dixie.

Hayley crossed one leg over the other. "Yesterday, or maybe the day before, we were in the back yard. She went from dandelion to dandelion, pulling them up."

"What did she do with them?"

Hayley shrugged. "Nothing. She pulled them out of the ground and tossed them aside and moved on to the next one. She had a melt-down when I brought her in the house for lunch." Hayley remembered the epic tantrum.

Dr. Yang tapped a finger on her chin. "That's actually normal childhood behavior. She's exerting her will, showing her frustration at being interrupted. However, it's more normal for a toddler than a child of five years."

"It's a good thing?" Hayley picked at a rough edge of a fingernail, her last manicure a distant memory.

"I've not had a lot of experience dealing with feral children. However, research shows children who are not given proper stimulation, nor have learned boundaries, are developmentally delayed. Add it to the autism spectrum, and you have behavior Dixie is exhibiting."

Hayley whirled her head around to face Dr. Yang. "You think she's autistic?" Another hurdle.

"It is within the realm of possibility. Notice how intensely she focuses on one thing. Her inability to maintain eye contact is also a sign." Dr. Yang sent Hayley a closed mouth smile. "More testing would need to be done to determine a diagnosis, of course."

"Of course." Hayley's stomach sank. She'd assumed Dixie would progress naturally into normal childhood behavior with Hayley's love and attention. And teaching her proper manners. She'd made a list. Things were supposed to go according to plan. This was a huge boulder dropped right in her path. She couldn't run around it, couldn't go through it. There had to be a way to go over it.

At home, she wrestled Dixie out of the car and guided her into the house. Dixie headed for the pantry, pulling at the door handle.

"Give me a moment, little girl," Hayley said as she dropped her purse on the counter. Snack time would be much easier if she could hand Dixie a bowl of crackers, or a couple of slices of apple. When would the child stop shoving everything in her mouth at once?

With a sigh, Hayley opened the fridge and pulled out an apple. She sliced it into thin slivers and sat at the table and fed them to Dixie, one by one. Hayley held the bowl out of Dixie's reach with one hand, while sending a one-handed text to Jazzmine.

HAYLEY: Hey—need to talk to you about Dr

The screen showed the message was delivered. She waited for a response, staring at the phone until Dixie howled in protest.

"Oops, sorry, baby girl. Here you go." She handed her another slice of apple. "Please chew it this time." Hayley took a piece and demonstrated by exaggerating the chewing motion.

Her cell dinged with an incoming text. Hayley sighed with relief, until she read Jazz's text.

JAZZ: Sorry. Can't talk. Taking a few days off. Family emergency.

What am I going to do? Hayley's first thought was of herself, then guilt for not feeling bad about whatever Jazzmine might be going through.

Distracted, she set the bowl of apple slices on the table. Before she could react, Dixie grabbed the bowl and was stuffing the remainder into her tiny mouth.

"No!" Hayley shouted. Dixie ran from the room and into the living room.

Hayley let her head drop into her hands. Two weeks into Dixie's placement, and she was ready to give up. Jason was mad at her, Mother and Daddy were disappointed, Hannah was mad, and now her one cheerleader was not available.

Hayley was drowning, and there was no life preserver. One time in high school, Hannah talked her into rafting down the American River with a bunch of kids. The raft rental place insisted everyone wear a life vest. They'd all complied, until they were around the first bend. Everyone had taken them off and tossed them in the bottom of the raft. Except Hayley, the rule follower. She'd been teased so cruelly she finally gave in and took hers off too.

The first set of rapids were mild compared to what was to come. The second rapids had twirled their raft around backwards, tossing Hayley into the icy cold river. Without a life jacket, she was pulled under and towed by the current downstream several hundred yards. When she finally popped to the surface, her lungs were close to bursting. If not for her lifeguard training and daily swimming in their pool, she might not have made it.

The guys hauled her into the raft, laughing and slapping her on the back.

"Way to go, Lee!" High fives were exchanged while Hayley sank onto the soggy raft bottom and tried not to cry.

"Are you okay?" Hannah had whispered.

Hayley shook her head, unable to speak.

The feeling of almost drowning overwhelmed her now. Dark, cold water, a deadly current, and no one to pull her back into the boat.

CHAPTER 13

Hayley woke slowly to the smell of ... What was that awful stench? She cracked open her eyes to see Dixie standing by the side of the bed. The hairs on the back of her neck prickled. How long had the child been standing there? Long enough to mess her pants. Hayley shot to a sitting position. Better get Dixie cleaned up before Jason woke. She slumped over, remembering he hadn't come home the night before. Again.

Relieved, yet guilty for her relief, Hayley slipped out of bed with a sigh.

"Come on, sweet girl. Let's get you cleaned up."

Bath, breakfast, and another bath after breakfast left Hayley as limp as the wet yoga pants she'd stripped off. Two more weeks of this emergency placement, and she'd be able to ... what, turn Dixie back over to the foster system for a more permanent home?

Two more weeks, and maybe she'd be able to restore her marriage. Two more weeks, and she could think about having another baby. Cynthia's face flashed before her eyes. Had she paid her debt to God yet by caring for kids no one wanted? Would God now be satisfied, his anger abated?

Hayley slid to the floor next to her bed and leaned back. Dixie stiffened as Hayley gathered her onto her lap.

"Shhh, little one. Relax." Hayley murmured reassurances into the child's ear until Dixie melted in her embrace.

Resting her chin on Dixie's head, Hayley let the fragrance from strawberry shampoo fill her nose. The sweet smell reminded her of Cynthia. For the first time since Cynthia died, the swift stab of grief was replaced by a memory. Hayley smiled, remembering the way her little girl loved to spin around in her princess dress. Would this little girl ever know the freedom of being loved unconditionally? Could Hayley be the one to show her? Would her marriage be sacrificed by doing so?

Dixie struggled in her embrace. Hayley let her arms drop to her sides as Dixie squirmed away. Her cell pinged with an incoming email. She pulled the annoying device off the nightstand to see who the email was from. Maybe Jazzmine had contacted her.

Not Jazzmine. Someone from Jazz's office.

"My name is Carla Jenkins, and I am taking your case while Jazzmine is on a leave of absence. I would like to set an appointment with you to evaluate your case. Are you available Thursday at 10:30 a.m. at your house? If so, please have your notes available as I will want to see what progress, if any, has been made. In addition, I need to set up a time for visitation with the child's biological mother. Please confirm via return email if this works for you."

Hayley reread the sterile, non-emotional email. Jazzmine's emails and texts always started the same way: *Hi-ya, Mama.* Jazz always ended with some encouraging note. "You're doing great!" "Thank you for what you're doing—it's important!"

This clinical note did nothing to warm Hayley's heart or make her feel like she was on the right track with Dixie.

And what was the deal about Dixie's biological mom? Jazz never mentioned she'd been released from jail. Or who she was and why Dixie was abandoned in a homeless camp. Plus the sexual abuse.

How could the system be so broken they'd let a little girl go back to a mother who would allow such things? A child deserved to be with someone who loved and cared for her. Protected her.

With a stab of guilt, Hayley realized she hadn't protected Cynthia. She'd raced in the house to grab some water when the car careened down the street, clipping Cynthia's trike, and throwing her in the air. Hayley had warned her not to go past the end of the driveway. Her little golden-haired daughter always pushed the boundaries. Was it her disobedience, or Hayley's inattention that had caused Cynthia to ride into the street?

If she'd only paid attention, she would have caught Cynthia before she had a chance to go past her boundary. None of the neighbors remembered seeing the car. Hayley couldn't have described the vehicle even under hypnosis. Her vision had narrowed down to a pinpoint on her daughter's body, limp on the black pavement. They'd never caught the driver.

Jason blamed her for Cynthia's death, using guilt to keep her more firmly under his thumb. Hayley accepted the blame, and the control, knowing God had exacted his punishment for her abortion.

She hoped by mothering these foster kids, she would earn her way back into God's favor. With this one, little Dixie, she might have failed yet again.

Hayley let her head drop back, resting it on the edge of the bed. She looked toward the ceiling.

"When will it be enough for you?"

The lady called Lee was crying again. She must have made Lee sad. Mama said it was all her fault. She should never have been born. What could she do to make Lee stop crying? Mama got medicine when she was sick. Maybe Lee had medicine too.

She ran to the bathroom and pulled open each drawer and cupboard, looking for the medicine Mama always stuck in her arm.

Hayley shot to her feet when Dixie made a mad dash into the bathroom. Before she could stop her, Dixie pulled out several drawers and dumped the contents on the floor.

"Stop! What are you doing?" Hayley reached for the child. Dixie dodged Hayley's outstretched hands. The contents of two more drawers were added to the mess. She wrapped her arms around the little girl. "What's got into you?"

Dixie squirmed and grunted, bucking against Hayley's embrace.

"Shhh. Shhh." Hayley crooned until Dixie relaxed. Hayley released her hold.

Dixie turned to face her. "Med-sin."

Goosebumps broke out on Hayley's arms. "Wh-what did you say?"

"Med-sin."

"Medicine?"

Dixie looked away and crouched down to pick through the pile of stuff spread out on the tile floor.

Why was Dixie looking for medicine? What was going on in that little brain of hers?

Hayley jumped when a male voice spoke from the doorway. "What the heck?"

Jason loomed in the door, resembling a Viking god. His red beard hadn't been trimmed in weeks, and his face was dark and menacing.

"Jason." Hayley pulled herself to her feet. "I was ... cleaning out the bathroom drawers."

"It's not what this looks like. And why is the kid digging through our stuff?"

Hayley glanced behind her. Dixie was on her haunches, picking up one item at a time and setting each item down.

"I don't know, but she actually said a word." Hayley couldn't contain her excitement, despite Jason's disapproval. "It's the third one she's uttered."

Jason crossed his arms. "Big flippin' deal. Normal kids have a full vocabulary by the time they're her age."

Hayley laid a hand on his arm. "Normal kids haven't been sexually abused at this age and weren't born to a drug-addicted mother."

Jason backed away from the chaos. "I came home to see if you were okay. You didn't answer my text."

"Oh. I must have missed it. When did you send it?"

Jason shrugged. "Doesn't matter. You're obviously still too busy with the kid to pay attention to your husband."

Hayley's stomach tightened. "I'm not too busy. What do you need?"

Jason grabbed a satchel from the top shelf of the closet and tossed it on the bed. "What I need is a wife who will ... oh, never mind. Help me pack."

"Where are you going?"

"Chad and I are flying to Los Angeles for a couple of days. He's changing his mind about the sale and may want to acquire another company. Cut down on the competition."

Hayley pulled open the top drawer of the dresser and took out tee shirts, underwear, and socks. She tucked them into Jason's overnight bag while keeping one eye on Dixie, still totally focused on the items in the bathroom.

"Can you guys afford to buy another company?"

Jason shrugged. "I'd rather sell the company and cut ties with Chad."

Hayley bit her lip. What happened to the Jason who'd won her over when she was in college? He'd been sweet and attentive. This Jason was a stranger. And a bully. What could she do to get the old Jason back?

After helping Jason pick out a couple of shirts and slacks, she scurried to the bathroom to retrieve what he'd need to pack in his shave kit. Dixie was still crouched, picking through the contents strewn across the floor from the vanity to the door.

With his shave kit in one hand, Hayley picked up each item Jason would need, all the time aware of his glare aimed at her back. Marriage wasn't supposed to be this hard, was it? Her parents had made their relationship look effortless. Hayley had never seen them argue. They never even disagreed. At least not in front of her and Hannah. Maybe it was because Mother's opinion was like a force of nature, and Daddy thought capitulation easier.

In any case, Hayley was stuck now in this relationship looking totally different from when they'd said their vows, and she wasn't about to break them. What kind of punishment would God extract if she told Jason she wanted a divorce?

Did she? Want a divorce? Would she be better off single than married to a man who criticized her every move?

Hayley finished filling his shave kit and tucked it into his suitcase with a sense of relief. At least she'd have a day or two while he was gone to mull over this new train of thought.

Who was she kidding? She'd never have the courage to ask Jason to leave.

"Do you need a ride to the airport?" Hayley stood on her tip toes to give Jason a peck on the lips.

"Nope. I'll leave the car in long-term parking."

A random thought popped into her head. "Are you taking the Miata?"

Jason stiffened. "No. Why?"

Hayley shrugged. "No reason. I haven't seen you drive it in, like, forever."

Jason loved the car. He used to take it to work every day.

"Uh, no, actually I'm thinking of selling it."

"Why?" Hayley looked up. Jason didn't meet her eyes. He was focused on the bathroom.

Jason slung his satchel over one shoulder. "Get the mess cleaned up. I'll see you in a couple of days. Maybe."

Hayley crossed her arms over her stomach. A wife shouldn't feel relief her husband was gone. She did.

The girl listened to the lady called Lee talk to the scary man. He was mad, like the other men Mama knew. When men got mad, they did bad things. The girl sat very still, pretending she was dead, so the man wouldn't see her. Maybe he would do bad things to the lady called Lee. What should she do? There was no one else here who could help her protect the lady called Lee.

The girl sank into herself. She would be invisible.

CHAPTER 14

Jazzmine rolled to a stop in front of her home. The driveway was cluttered with bikes and skateboards. With a *humph* of irritation, she parked on the street. "How many times have I told these kids not to leave their mess on the driveway ..." She muttered some additional motherly irritation, slamming Rusty's door with more force than was necessary.

She trudged to the front door, shoulders slumped. She and Zeke would have to deal with whatever mess Marcus had gotten himself into. Of the five, Marcus was the most trouble. But he'd never gotten into law trouble before.

"Mom's home," she called, pushing open the front door.

Jazzmine dropped her purse and keys on the entry table, glancing into the kitchen. She did a double take when she saw her second-oldest, Jerome, at the stove, stirring something in one of her soup pots. Beyond him the table was set, though it wasn't yet five o'clock.

"Hi, Mom." Jerome looked up at her, his face solemn.

"What's this?" Jazzmine indicated him, and the table.

"I thought you might be upset about Marcus and all, so I, you know, thought I'd start supper."

Jazzmine's throat closed with unshed tears. She grabbed Jerome, pulled him to her chest, and rubbed his head. "Thanks, baby." She sniffed.

Jerome pulled away with a shrug. "Don't go gettin' all 'motional."

"Well, thanks for all this."

Jerome shrugged again. "The twins set the table."

They always called Kito and Jamal "the twins" as they were almost the same age, and inseparable.

"Where is everybody?" Jazzmine opened a cupboard and pulled down a plastic tumbler. She dropped in some ice cubes and filled the tumbler with water.

"Hosea is in his room, the twins are out back, probably spraying each other with the hose. Marcus—" Jerome sent her a panicked look and gulped.

"I know, baby. Daddy is bringing him home." Jazz took a long drink of water. "Any idea what happened?"

Jerome set a lid on the soup pot and adjusted the temperature. "He said he was going to Max's house. On his bike. I thought it was okay." He shot a glance to her. His eyes filled with tears. "Was it okay, Mama?"

Jazzmine hugged him again, her own eyes tearing up. "Yes, baby, it was okay. He's gone there before. It's not your fault he got into some trouble."

Jazzmine let him go. He wiped his eyes, then disappeared around the corner into the family room.

The sound of Zeke's car pulling up drew her to the kitchen window. She watched him climb out of the van and waited for Marcus to get out. From her vantage, she could see Zeke's hand heavy on their son's shoulder.

Jazz strode threw the kitchen, threw open the front door, and stood with her arms crossed.

"You'd better have a very good explanation for this," Jazzmine said, her voice stern.

Zeke met her eyes, his expression grim. Marcus stared at his feet as he dragged himself toward the front door. Jazzmine moved to let them pass.

Hayley carried a sleeping Dixie from the garage into the house. She used her backside to shove the door closed and trudged through the kitchen and up the stairs. She laid the child on the bed, covering her with a light blanket.

She kicked her shoes toward the master bedroom as she passed. Her mind was set on one thing—a tall, frosted glass of iced tea. Nope, two things. Iced tea and a long rest on the sofa.

Her cell phone chirped as she took the first gulp of tea. A text from Zola.

ZOLA: What's up neighbor?

HAYLEY: Just got home from therapy with Dixie

ZOLA: Want company?

Hayley shrugged. Why not? Zola's cheerfulness usually dispelled any exhaustion on Hayley's part.

She typed a thumbs up emoji and went to the back door to wait. Thirty seconds later, Zola lumbered across the yard carrying a pastry bag. Hayley groaned. She still hadn't lost those pesky two pounds.

"What's in the bag?" she asked, pointing to the white bag in Zola's hand.

"Some afternoon delight for you."

"Huh." Hayley huffed. "You're my kryptonite, you know."

Zola laughed as Hayley pulled two plates from the cupboard.

"I'm trying to get you as fat as I am," Zola said, carrying the plates to the table. "This time I brought something from Ettore's. Fruit basket tarts."

Hayley's mouth watered. "I'll have one bite and that's it."

Zola settled on one of the kitchen chairs. "Sure. You keep telling yourself that, *sheyn*."

"*Sheyn*?" Hayley sat across from her and reached for the bag.

"It means beautiful."

Hayley felt her cheeks grow hot. Jason hadn't called her beautiful in ages. She hadn't felt beautiful either, just fat or out of shape. "How about some water? Or iced tea?" She turned toward the fridge so Zola couldn't see her face.

"No, thank you. Come, sit. Let's eat this wonderful, non-gluten-free, sugar-filled deliciousness."

Hayley laughed. "Let's do it." She'd sneak in a quick workout tomorrow while Dixie was at therapy. Maybe.

Zola took a bite of the tart and, with her fork, gestured toward the door to the garage. "Are you expecting hubby home soon? Maybe I should have brought one for him. You know, sweeten him up?" Zola's gentle smile took the sting from the truth of her words.

Hayley kept her gaze focused on a glazed strawberry. "I'm not sure when, or if, he's coming home." She glanced up to see Zola's eyebrows disappear into her bangs.

"Really? He seems to keep a pretty close eye on you, if you don't mind my saying so."

The need to vent overcame Hayley's natural reticence. She took a deep breath and held it for three counts.

"We had an argument. Another one. This time we argued about Dixie. He wants me to get rid of her. His words, not mine. He wants to have another baby." The words tumbled from her and trickled to a stop.

Hayley took a sip of tea, holding the glass with trembling hands. Guilt and relief fought in equal measure for control. She heard Mother's voice: *family business is nobody else's business.* And Jason, always putting up a happy front with her parents, even after he'd belittled her for some trifling thing.

Zola reached across the table and laid her hand over Hayley's. "I'm so sorry. What are you going to do?"

Hayley pushed away the plate of half-eaten tart, her appetite gone. "I don't know, Zola." Tears filled her eyes, blurring her vision.

"Do you mind if I pray for you?" Zola's hand, warm on hers, squeezed gently.

Hayley shrugged. "I guess so."

Zola's head bent and her eyes closed. "Father God, I come to you to intercede for my friend, Hayley."

Prickles of embarrassment shot down Hayley's spine. She tried to pay attention to Zola's words, but discomfort kept her mind zipping in a hundred directions. Would Jason burst in from the garage and order Zola out of the house and yell at her for keeping a friendship he'd expressly forbidden? Would her mother suddenly show up, pinching her lips together in disapproval? Church and God had always been a part of Hayley's growing up, but attendance was strictly a Sunday thing. Except for a hurried grace for Sunday dinner, prayer wasn't something they practiced. Especially out loud.

Her eyes flew open at Zola's amen.

Zola picked up her fork, using it as a pointer. "You need to pray for your husband, *sheyn*."

Pray? For Jason? Hayley almost laughed. She straightened her features into what she hoped looked neutral.

"Hm."

"I'm not kidding." Zola spoke around a bite of tart. "You'd be surprised what prayer can accomplish."

"Like what?" She hated that her voice sounded high-pitched.

Zola swept up some remaining crumbs onto her fork. "Do you have time for me to tell you a story?"

"I'll be right back." Hayley sprang to her feet and rushed up the stairs. Poking her head into the darkened bedroom, she saw Dixie curled up under the blanket, still asleep. On the bed, not under it. A feeling of satisfaction swept over her. Now *that* was progress.

Hayley paused on the stairs. What would Zola say now? She had no idea Zola was religious. She didn't wear a cross or say anything previously about going to church. She seemed proud of her and Sol's Jewish heritage. Could a Jew be a Christian?

The question piqued her interest.

"No peep from Dixie, so I guess I have time for your story."

Zola pushed her chair back and crossed her arms across her ample belly. "Sol was raised in a very traditional Jewish home. He was taught to strictly obey the Sabbath, the feasts and fasts, and all the rest. My parents were also Jewish, but we were raised as Americans. My dad wanted us to be normal kids, and not face some of the prejudice he and my mom had faced."

Hayley downed the last of her iced tea and set the glass back on the table. "Go on."

"When Sol and I met in college, and fell in love, there was a culture clash. He wanted us to be Orthodox, and I wanted to, well, be normal."

"What did you do?"

Zola laughed. "I broke up with him."

"You what?" Hayley's eyes widened.

"My roommate saw how grief-stricken I was over the breakup, so she invited me to a Bible study. I figured, why not?" Zola lifted her gray-streaked hair off her neck with one hand, her eyes far away as she continued. "At the Bible study, I met the most wonderful man ever. He was strong, kind, loving, and gentle."

Hayley slapped the table with her palm. "Wait a minute. Was this guy's name Sol too?"

Zola laughed again, letting her hair drop back down over her shoulders. "No. Jesus."

Jason punched the disconnect button on the screen of the Escalade's Bluetooth. He didn't need any more hassle from his partner about why he wasn't at the airport. His Apple watch showed he had plenty of time to arrive, park, and get through security to board their flight.

A drive in the privacy of his car would be the thing to clear his head after the mess he'd seen at the house. Hayley was out of control. What difference could she make in the kid's life? Hadn't she proved her lack of parental skills when she'd let their daughter ride into the street? He was still haunted by dreams of his daughter's lifeless body, lying in the street. Hayley needed a firm hand, and he was determined to bring her to her senses.

The car's powerful engine responded to his foot on the accelerator. Chilled air hit him in the face, cooling his head, doing nothing to calm the fire inside.

As if his car had a mind of its own, the SUV turned onto Highway 50. Jason knew where he was going and was powerless to change direction.

The midday sun showed details he hadn't noticed the last time he'd been here under cover of dusk. A couple of bicycles lay on the scraggly lawn. Two plastic patio chairs sat facing each other near the steps to the porch. Someone had made muddy handprints on the faded blue paint of the front of the house, under one of the bedroom windows. At least, Jason assumed they were bedrooms. He'd never been inside.

He turned the car off and slumped down in the seat. Waiting. For what, he didn't know. Without the air conditioning, the car gradually warmed. Jason buzzed down the driver's side window all the way.

Why this sudden compulsion to drive all the way up here, twice in a week? What did he hope to discover? Equal parts of guilt and revulsion filled his chest until he thought he'd burst. The Italian meatball sandwich he'd eaten for lunch threatened to make an encore appearance.

The front door of the house opened, and a few young men spilled out, down the porch steps, and across the lawn. A multi-passenger van sat in the driveway. Jason tried to focus on each of the faces as they ambled toward the van. A burly guy with a baseball cap unlocked the sliding van door and stood outside, offering a hand to each one as they struggled to climb in.

Two more people exited the house. Jason's heart leaped to his throat as one man, taller than the rest, picked his way down the front porch steps. Jason recognized his halting gait. His hair was a little longer, and he'd put on some weight. Jason would recognize him anywhere. His wrists were bent into almost a ninety-degree angle. His head leaned forward, as he dragged his feet along the concrete walkway toward the waiting van.

The man stopped, turning his gaze toward Jason's car. Jason stopped breathing, not daring to move. He'd slunk down in the seat, and he was sure he couldn't be seen, not from this far away.

"Come on, Danny. Hurry up." The burly guy beckoned. "We'll be late for the movie." He waved his hand in an impatient gesture.

The guy called Danny turned his head toward the van and lurched toward it. Only when he was safely inside the van did Jason dare to breathe.

Danny. His older brother.

CHAPTER 15

"Dude, where's your head at?" Jason's business partner, Chad, stroked his soul patch, that annoying little hair growth just below his lip, while staring down at Jason's closed laptop, perched on the airplane's tray table. Why didn't the man have a proper beard?

Jason pulled his thoughts back to Chad. With a guilty start, he opened the laptop, watching as the computer purred to life. "Sorry, bro. Mama drama."

Chad leaned toward him, his Birkenstocks squeaking as he arranged his feet underneath him. "I need you here, buddy. This deal is way too important for you to be distracted."

Jason rubbed his head. "I know, I know." He entered his password at the computer prompt and leaned back in his seat. "I'm thinking of staying a few extra days in LA, so I can concentrate." Or until the kid was gone.

Chad's hazel eyes bored into Jason's. He bobbed his head. "Okay, whatever's clever. Let's not blow this." He straightened. "Eyes on the prize, bro, eyes on the prize."

After this looming acquisition, he'd be glad to have a break from his partner's incessant clichés.

Chad settled back against his seat. "Don't forget what will happen if you don't follow through."

A cold chill followed by sweat spread over Jason's torso. He never should have confided in his business partner. They'd never been friends, nor would they ever be. For one thing, Jason couldn't stand Chad's all-kinds-of-crazy wife. At least she stayed home and watched their two kids. No foster kids in their world.

The one time Jason confided in Chad, it had come back to bite him. Not blackmail, exactly. Subtle digs he knew something that could potentially cause a problem with him and Hayley. And her parents. Especially good old Mother and Daddy. No way could he take the chance on losing all that money. Hayley's trust fund was an added bonus to their marriage. He never dreamed when he fell in love with Hayley's unrelenting cheerfulness, she was also heir to what he considered a fortune. With a stab of guilt, he remembered her tear-stained face as he stormed out after their last argument.

Note to self: order flowers for Hayley.

While Chad's eyes were closed, Jason went to his favorite bookmarked page. Luxury Yachts For Sale. He whispered into his Apple Watch. "Set timer for ten minutes." He'd allow himself a few minutes to daydream before reviewing the spreadsheets one more time.

A squawk from upstairs kept Hayley from allowing Zola into more of her story. "I'll be right back." She jumped up from the table and sprinted up the stairs, hoping to get Dixie on the potty before any more accidents.

She pushed open the door and peered into the darkened bedroom. Dixie sat on the floor, turning pages of a children's storybook.

"Hi, Dixie." Hayley's voice was soft, but loud enough to startle the child. Dixie sprang to her feet. The book dropped from her fingers.

"It's okay, sweet girl. You can read any books you want. Come on, let's go use the bathroom."

Dixie's unfocused eyes stared at the wall behind Hayley. Hayley touched her shoulder. Trembling began from her head, travelling down to her legs. Silent tears ran down Dixie's face, dripping off her cheeks. Her mouth was open, and no sound emerged.

Goosebumps rose on Hayley's arms. "What did your mother do to you?" Dixie allowed herself to be led into the bathroom, where Hayley set her on the toilet. The child was practically catatonic as she did her business on the potty.

As they washed their hands, Hayley wracked her brain, trying to figure out what might have caused Dixie's distress. Did the girl's mother hit her with a book? Was she scared because she wasn't allowed to read? Maybe it was Hayley's fault. Dixie had startled when Hayley came into the room.

With a sigh, she gently urged Dixie down the stairs to the kitchen. Zola was gone. A hastily scratched note sat on the now empty table.

Had to run. Finish our conversation later. Zola.

Disappointed, she let Dixie crawl under the table while she prepared their dinner. Dixie sprawled on her stomach on the floor, stretched out her arms and slapped the floor with open palms. Smack, smack, smack. If she continued, her hands would be bloody by the time Hayley fixed dinner.

Hayley stooped to peer under the table. "Hey, Dixie."

No response.

"Dixie, stop."

No response. She tried holding Dixie's arm down. Dixie shook off her hand and kept going.

"Dixie! Stop!" Hayley's sharp reprimand wasn't enough to penetrate the child's state.

Hayley sank onto her bottom. Maybe Jason was right. She was in over her head.

The girl sank into the dark place inside. The place where she went when men hurt her. She was a tiny little bug, and no one could see her. She imagined herself shrinking, shrinking, shrinking until she was almost invisible.

Hayley brushed the hair back from her sweaty face. She'd tried everything to break through the zombie-like Dixie. As a last resort, she'd tried bribing her with food. No response. Dixie had finally exhausted herself and was asleep on the cool tile floor under the table.

Head in hands, Hayley exhaled with an audible sigh. If Zola was praying for her, she'd better pray harder. How weird to think of someone praying for her. Mother made sure they attended services when she and Hannah lived at home. Her parents still attended the Lutheran church downtown. Jason had never expressed an interest in church, and she hadn't pressed, despite subtle pressure from her mom. Growing up, they'd never talked about God. Hayley and Hannah were expected to be in church each Sunday, dressed in their most impressive best. God was someone up in heaven, waiting to judge anyone who dared step out of line.

Why would Zola think God would be interested in doing anything for her?

What did Zola mean about meeting a man who fulfilled all her ideals? Jesus? She'd definitely have to get more information. In the meantime, she'd call Jazzmine in the morning and make arrangements for the end of the thirty-day placement—to have Dixie taken to a home where someone could care for her.

No, she'd talk to Carla, Jazz's replacement, when she came for the evaluation. Wonder what was going on with Jazzmine? Hayley had been so focused on her own drama she hadn't given much thought to Jazz. She should be a better friend. Why did she always fail? Jason, her parents, her baby girl, Jazz, and now Dixie. Hayley couldn't fix her, not even close. Maybe it was time to give up and give in to Jason's pressure to have another baby. Start over. Maybe he'd return to the way he was when they were first married.

With a pang, she realized she'd miss Dixie like crazy. Her occasional smiles lit up Hayley's heart. Her grunts of pleasure as she ate fresh strawberries. The way her little hands moved gracefully as she played some imaginary game in her head.

A crack was opened in Hayley's bruised heart, and Dixie had slipped in. Although she'd grieve Cynthia for the rest of her life, she was able to allow this cardboard box girl to help her heal.

Jazzmine hoisted her messenger bag over one shoulder. "I'm heading back to work," she said to the five dark-haired boys in various slouched positions in the cluttered family room. "Your Auntie Mays will be over in about half an hour. I've left a list of chores on the fridge. No playing outside until chores are done. Daddy will be home after his meeting."

"What about me?" Marcus, her oldest, folded his arms across his chest.

"You are not to leave the house. Remember, you are on house arrest until further notice."

"That's not fair!" His eyes shot fire as only a twelve-year-old's could.

Jazzmine sighed. "Life's not fair. And actions have consequences. Next time you're tempted to shoplift, remember how it feels to be stuck in the house for six weeks."

"Whatever."

"Longer if you don't change your attitude, mister," Jazzmine warned.

"That's harsh." He slumped in his chair, chin to his chest.

Jazzmine glanced at the clock on the stove. "I have to go. We'll go over the details of your mandatory stay-at-home order tonight. Again." She gathered up her purse and headed out the front door to Trusty Rusty.

For once, he started on the first try. While she'd been on leave, Zeke had washed and detailed her car. She smiled at the fragrance 'tree' hanging from the rear-view mirror. What a blessing her man was.

In the office, Jazzmine tossed her purse under the desk and laid the messenger bag on the shelf behind her desk. Once the computer was powered up, she logged on.

Carla spoke from behind her. "I see you're back."

Jazzmine swung around. "Yes. Thank you for the time off. We needed to regroup as a family." She'd told her supervisor only the basics. How humiliating to have your son picked up for shoplifting.

Carla clutched a pile of file folders. "While you were gone, I reassigned most of your cases. Here are some new ones." She dropped the pile onto Jazzmine's battered desk.

Jazzmine inhaled. "You what?"

"Reassigned. Your cases." Carla tapped her foot.

"B-what about my homeless child case? Dixie McNally?"

Carla turned to leave. "I kept that one. After a thorough evaluation, I'm recommending permanent placement."

Jazzmine's hands closed into fists. Anger bubbled from her stomach, up her throat, hot and raw. "I don't understand," she choked out.

Carla stopped, turned back, and spoke in a condescending tone. "The McNally case is going to the county for parallel rehabilitation. We've done all we can for the child. It's obvious the emergency placement with the foster mother isn't producing results. Permanent placement with a family better able to help is the best option." Carla spun on her low-heeled pumps and strode into her office, closing the door with a snap.

Jazzmine crossed her arms over her stomach and leaned forward. What had happened in the few days she'd been gone? Hayley had seemed to have made progress with Dixie. She glanced over her shoulder toward Carla's office. Pulling her phone close, she sent a quick text to Hayley.

JAZZ: Hi ya, Mama. How ya doing?

While she waited for a response, Jazzmine started the process of winnowing out junk emails from ones needing to be dealt with.

With only half a mind to the task at hand, Jazzmine's mind wandered to Hayley and Dixie. The thirty-day emergency placement was just that. An emergency. Temporary. Now Dixie's mother had been located, supervised visits needed to be set up. Sounded like Carla had started the process already.

The best option for a child was to be reunited with a mom or dad whenever possible. With Dixie's mom in rehab, she should be able to regain custody in about six months. In the meantime, regular supervised visits were crucial to the re-bonding process.

Jazzmine knew the system. The county would swarm in with all sorts of therapy. They'd work with the foster mother and the bio mom to be sure Dixie became as functional as possible, given her lack of, well, any kind of normal life prior to being found in the homeless camp.

They'd coach Dixie's mom, help her with parenting skills. After rehab, she'd move to a temporary group home where she'd receive drug and alcohol counseling assistance with life skills, with the goal of reuniting the two permanently.

Did Hayley even know plans were in place to move Dixie?

CHAPTER 16

Jason stretched out onto the king-sized hotel bed. He plumped the pillows behind his back and reached for the remote. After surfing through the hotel's selection of channels, he settled on a soccer game.

He and Chad had received a surprise when the men and women they met with turned the tables, offering to purchase *their* small business.

The meeting had gone well. At least he thought so. Chad's parting comment as they exited the elevator echoed in his ears.

"Thought they'd offer us more," he'd said.

Jason thought the offer was more than generous, given they'd only showed a profit in the prior two years. The more he thought about it, the more eager he was to sell. He'd finally be able to break away from his eight-year business relationship with Chad. Now that Chad knew his secret, he used it to keep Jason in line. Like the famous line from *Dirty Dancing*, "No one puts Jason in a corner."

Jason would be in control. Of his life, his marriage, his finances. As long as he could keep all the pieces together, life would be fine. Chad would fade into the distance as Jason, Hayley, and their new baby sailed off on the beautiful yacht he'd buy with some of Hayley's trust.

Hayley would never find out what he'd managed to keep hidden for over a year.

Speaking of keeping things hidden, his finger hovered over the voice mail he'd received earlier in the day. His mother's voice quavered, whether from emotion or age, he didn't know.

"Jason, this is Mom. Please call me back. Your dad is sick. Um, okay, well, bye."

Jason hadn't spoken to his parents since he'd left for college. As if they'd noticed. Everything was about Danny. Danny's therapy, Danny's special diet, Danny's need for quiet. Don't pick on your brother, he's fragile.

Jason snorted. *Fragile, my behind.* When Dan was in full melt-down mode, he could land a punch that could give you a busted lip.

Jason had given up trying to get his parents' attention. He left for college and literally shook the dust of Bakersfield off his feet. He'd never again try to gain anyone's attention or affection by being anything other than himself. He was an only child and an orphan. That was his story. He might as well have been an orphan, for the amount of attention his mom and dad had paid him.

Enough. He was through being bitter. So what if his dad was sick. He didn't care.

A little voice inside whispered, "If you don't care, why not delete the voice mail, huh?"

"Shut up!" Jason said aloud. He turned up the volume on the soccer game to drown out any more attempts at pricking his conscience. He couldn't afford to go down the road of contacting his family now. Hayley would ask too many questions.

There were things a wife didn't need to know. How he had a special-needs brother.

And why he never drove the Miata anymore.

Today would be a good day. Hayley felt it the moment her eyes popped open. Today, she'd finally get Dixie to use the bathroom without food bribery. Today, she'd teach Dixie how to eat more slowly.

With Jason gone, there'd be no additional stress to cause Dixie to withdraw. She thought back to Carla's evaluation the week before. The hour had gone well, she thought. Even though Carla showed no emotion, Dixie had behaved well. Except for the one incident sending her scurrying behind the sofa. Who knew the sound of the doorbell would still freak her out?

Carla read through all Hayley's detailed notes and had asked for a copy. Hayley had been meticulous in recording all the activities with the play therapist both in Dr. Yang's office and in Hayley's home. She'd also kept a copy of the psych evaluation and notes on Dixie's height and weight on an almost daily basis. Which was a challenge—getting her onto the scale needed lots of prompting and bites of a granola bar. Same with getting her to stand still against the wall so Hayley could mark her height.

Carla had said she'd get back to Hayley this week. Maybe even today. Hayley couldn't wait to check her email. She'd told Carla she wanted to keep Dixie on a more permanent basis.

Carla had frowned and reminded her Dixie's mom would be on a parallel track of therapy, rehab, and counseling, with the goal of reuniting the two.

Hayley wouldn't think about that now. She and Dixie had had a wonderful weekend swimming and hanging out with Zola. Nothing would spoil her mood on this gorgeous Monday morning. Even the weather seemed to cooperate. The heat spell that had settled over the valley had blown away in the night. Hayley opened the bedroom window to let in the cool morning breeze.

After a quick peek to see Dixie still sleeping, Hayley took a quick shower and dressed in denim shorts and a tank. She fumbled with the button on the shorts. Seems those two pounds had invited all their friends to settle on her waistline. With all the therapy sessions, Hayley hadn't been able to work out as regularly as she should. Maybe she could slip out during today's play session and get in a three-mile run.

If only Jason were here. He could easily watch Dixie for thirty minutes or so.

"Ha," she said aloud. Jason avoided Dixie like an illness he might catch if he got too close.

Hayley gathered her hair into a damp ponytail. The first time they'd fostered an infant, Jason had been super supportive. The second time, they'd been placed with two little girls. By that time, Jason had already lost interest in fostering. That's when he'd started pressuring her to get pregnant.

Jason would never understand how much she needed to redeem herself for Cynthia's death. Even though Jason said he'd forgiven her, she doubted it. Surely, he hated her as much as she hated herself. What about God? She hadn't done enough to appease him. Hayley wasn't sure he'd ever be satisfied. Maybe Zola would know. She seemed more in touch with the Man Upstairs.

Hayley sat on the edge of the bed and pulled off the shorts. Better stick with running shorts today. The cheese and crackers Dixie loved, and she loved, refused to go anywhere except around her middle. Jason would freak out if she got fat.

Jason wouldn't be home until later in the day, and there was all day to work with Dixie.

Her cell phone pinged as she pulled the comforter up to make the bed.

JAZZ: Hi ya, Mama. How ya doing?

Hayley smiled. She sent a quick text back to Jazz.

HAYLEY: Good! Are you back?

Without waiting for a response, she finished straightening the bed, looked around the room to be sure nothing was out of place and headed across the hall to check on Dixie.

Hayley found her sitting on the floor, holding a doll. The doll was naked, and Dixie was doing something horrific to it.

Hayley raced to her bathroom and barely made it in time to dry heave into the toilet.

"How is Miss Dixie today?" The play therapist eased her long legs into a sitting position. Hayley always thought she resembled a stork, with her skinny legs and round torso. Today she wore capris and sandals with colorful stones on the straps. Dixie seemed entranced by the woman's shoes.

Hayley pulled a chair out of the way and sat on the floor near them. From her vantage point, she could see the film of dust on the dark mahogany of the coffee table. One more thing to add to her 'to do' list. They'd had a cleaning lady once a week when Cynthia was born. Jason let her go. He didn't like the idea of a stranger in the house, cleaning up their mess. Hayley had never been bothered—they'd had a maid and a cook during her entire childhood.

She pulled her attention back to Myra, the play therapist.

"I thought we'd try some play with dolls and stuffed animals today," Myra said, rummaging through her backpack.

"No!" A shot of adrenaline had Hayley back on her feet, remembering the doll incident from the morning.

Myra's head shot up. "What?"

Hayley inhaled and blew the breath out through pursed lips. "I mean, let's do a stuffed animal." She crossed her legs and sank back down to sit.

Myra shrugged. "Okay." Myra pulled a bear from the backpack. "Dixie, this is Brown Bear. Can you say hi?" Myra held the bear in one hand, shaking it back and forth near Dixie's face. Dixie reached out a finger and touched one of the stones on Myra's sandal.

Both women watched. The silence grew as Dixie concentrated on touching each of the stones, one by one.

Myra looked over and met Hayley's eyes. "Guess I'd better not wear these again," she said with a smile.

Hayley studied the back of Dixie's head. She'd pulled Dixie's thick, dark hair into a ponytail, tumbling down to the middle of her back. She'd dressed her in a pair of pink shorts and a matching striped top.

She looked like any other normal little girl. But inside her little head swirled memories of the evil done around her and to her.

Hayley's heart swelled with a mama bear protectiveness. No wonder Dixie behaved the way she did. Who wouldn't, given the terror she'd been incubated in. A drug-addicted mom, who'd do anything to get her next hit. Even if it meant sacrificing the body of her child. Hayley mentally shook her head. No, not a mom. A monster.

A bit like you. The words came from a dark recess in Hayley's soul. *You killed your own baby.*

Monster.

Hayley was no different than Dixie's birth mother. Neither one had protected their little girls. Hayley bit her lip to hide her distress.

Myra touched Dixie's hand. Dixie yanked her hand away from Myra's sandals. While her concentration was momentarily broken, Myra used the opportunity to wiggle Brown Bear in front of her.

"Look, Brown Bear is sad. He needs someone to hold him. Can you hold him, Dixie?"

Dixie stared at the beige living room carpet.

Myra chewed on her lip while alternately holding out the bear and encouraging Dixie to take him. After a few minutes, she dropped her hands into her lap. "Let's try something different. Go along with me, okay?"

Hayley nodded.

Myra held Brown Bear out to Hayley. "Look, Hayley, Brown Bear is sad. He needs someone to hold him. Can you hold him for me?"

"Sure." Hayley took the bear and cuddled him to her shoulder. "Good bear. Don't be sad." She murmured reassuring words, hoping they got through to the child.

After a few minutes of this with no response from Dixie, Myra got to her feet. "You keep Brown Bear, okay? And continue trying to engage." Myra sat on the sofa and pulled an iPad from her backpack. "I'm going to make a few notes before I go."

Hayley watched Dixie run her fingers back and forth over the tight weave of the carpet. If she could channel Dixie's concentration onto something different ...

Hayley glanced around the room, remembering how much fun she and Jason had picking out the furniture and the decor when they'd first moved in. The result was a mix of modern and traditional. The overstuffed sofa oozed comfort, while the wing chairs were all business. She'd inherited a few antiques from her grandparents. The china hutch and etagere completed the look of casual elegance.

In the early days of their marriage, she and Jason had agreed on everything. Every shopping trip was an adventure.

They hadn't had that much fun since Cynthia ...

"I'm all done." Myra's voice interrupted her train of thought. Myra stood and slung her pack over one skinny shoulder. "I'll see you again on Wednesday. Is this time okay with you?"

Hayley nodded and stood to walk her out.

As Myra stepped onto the porch, she turned. "I still think you should try using a doll instead of the bear."

Bile rose again from Hayley's stomach, burning her throat. Unable to answer, she nodded again and closed the door, leaning her forehead against it. There would be no doll play today. Or maybe ever.

The lady Hayley was sad. She was sad most of the time. Did the girl make her sad? Probably. Mama said she was the reason Mama was sad. The lady called her 'Dixie' and 'sweet girl.' The girl only thought of herself as 'girl.'

She rolled the word "Dixie" around in her head. She decided she liked it. She was Dixie.

CHAPTER 17

Hayley sat on the edge of the pool moving her feet back and forth in the water. Dixie splashed happily on the wide, shallow ledge. They'd already eaten dinner. Hayley had joined Dixie on the floor under the table, unable to coax the child onto a chair. Even though she tried to bribe her with food, all Dixie did was grab for the plate before scuttling back under the table.

Time enough for that tomorrow. They'd made good progress in the potty-training area. Hayley mentally ran through the list she'd made:

1. Potty training
2. Eating slowly
3. Using utensils
4. Dressing herself
5. Talking???

Maybe she was expecting too much too soon. Only about two and a half weeks had passed. *Relax*.

"Ha," she said out loud. When was relaxing an option? The one time she'd strayed over the double yellow lines, look what had happened. She'd committed the unforgivable sin—murder of her own child. God's revenge had almost taken her life as well.

Hayley looked up at the darkening sky. "When will you be satisfied?" Her voice sounded weak to her own ears. This new challenge, nurturing this little girl, was her chance for redemption. Her mind took her far into the future, where

Dixie was a growing teenager. She'd go to dances like a normal girl, graduate high school, and maybe even attend college. All because Hayley took the time and energy to love her and protect her.

"Hayley!" Jason's sharp voice cut through her imaginings. "It's getting dark. Why are you still outside?"

Hayley jumped to her feet. "I-I guess I lost track of time." She squatted down and spoke into Dixie's ear. "Time to go in the house, little one." For once, Dixie let herself be led out of the pool.

"I didn't expect you home yet." Hayley wrapped a towel around Dixie and lifted her to one hip.

"That's obvious." Jason held the door open and closed it behind them. Hayley heard the lock click and the whisper as he lowered the fabric blind.

"I'm starved. What's there to eat?" Jason opened the fridge and stuck his head in.

"Give me a couple minutes to get Dixie to bed and I'll fix you a sandwich or something."

"Sounds good." Jason leaned in to kiss her. Dixie stiffened in her arms, turning her head into Hayley's shoulder. Hayley received his peck, turned, and carried the girl up the stairs.

When she returned to the kitchen after putting Dixie to bed, Jason had opened a package of crackers. Crumbs covered the counter where he'd laid the opened sleeve.

"I have some lunchmeat and cheese. How does that sound?" Hayley waited for his answer, her hand on the door to the fridge.

"Sure." Jason had his laptop open and was scrolling through an Excel spreadsheet.

"How was your meeting?" Hayley assembled the sandwich and cut it in half crossways, the way Jason liked it.

Jason leaned back in the chair and stretched his arms over his head. "It went okay. They actually offered to buy us out. Go figure. Chad thinks they low-balled their offer."

Hayley sat across from him. "What do you think?"

Jason shrugged. "I think it's generous, since we barely showed a profit last year. We're on target to do a hundred and fifty percent more this year. I think they're mainly interested in our customer base, not in our actual business."

Hayley's stomach, which had been in knots since Jason's arrival, finally relaxed. They hadn't had a normal conversation in weeks.

"What are you and Chad going to do?" If they sold their business, he'd be underfoot all day, every day. Maybe he'd start something new. Ever since they'd met, Jason had said he never wanted to work for someone else. He wanted to be his own boss, call the shots, make the decisions. Like a slow-moving oil spill, his need for control had gradually spread into their marriage. Every day he gave her a list of things to do, as if she was his personal administrative assistant.

Jason inhaled, blowing out through pursed lips. "I don't know. As soon as we have the offer on paper, we'll hash it out." He scraped the chair back and stood. "Right now, I'm going upstairs to shower."

Jason walked around the table, pulled Hayley to her feet, and wrapped her in a warm embrace. "Thanks for the sandwich." His breath was warm in her ear. "Don't stay down here too long. I missed you."

Tears sprang to her eyes. He hadn't been this tender for a long time. She'd hurry and clean up the kitchen and head upstairs to bed.

Jason's phone rang as Hayley finished wiping the last crumb from the black granite countertop. His phone rarely left his possession. Hayley looked at the screen to see if it was Jason's partner, Chad. The screen read a 415-area code—the Bay Area, where Jason was from.

"Hello?" Hayley answered.

A tremulous woman's voice on the other end. "Hello? Jason?"

"No, this is Hayley."

A pause. "Is Jason there?" Hayley guessed the woman was older. Why was an older woman calling her husband at nine o'clock at night?

"He's here. He can't come to the phone. Is there something I can help you with?" Hayley kept one eye on the stairs in case

Jason decided to return to the kitchen. He wouldn't want her to touch his phone.

Another pause. "Are you ... Jason's friend?"

Hayley wrinkled her brow. "I'm his wife."

There was a gasp on the other end. "His wife? Oh. I didn't know he was married."

"Who is this?" Hayley's stomach tightened. Did she really want to know? She was filled with a sudden premonition her life was about to change.

"This is his mother."

Hayley grabbed the counter with her free hand to keep herself upright. Her knees had suddenly turned to jelly. His mother? Jason had told her his parents died when he was sixteen.

"No. That isn't possible. Jason is an orphan."

Hayley heard a sob on the other end.

"Is that what he told you?"

"What is this about?" Hayley's brain swirled like she'd spun in a circle too many times.

"You tell Jason his father had a stroke. He's asking to see his son."

"His father." Hayley repeated the words, unable to process them. Jason had a mother and a father out there? Why? How?

"Yes. Please ask him to call me. Promise me you will."

"Uh, okay." Hayley agreed, her brain still in crash mode.

"And one more thing." The woman's voice quavered. "Tell him Danny says hi."

Before Hayley could ask who Danny was, the call was disconnected.

She sank onto one of the padded kitchen chairs and dropped the phone on the counter. Everything she knew to be true about Jason had shifted. First, why would he tell her his parents were dead? He'd said he'd been in a foster home for two years until he turned eighteen. He'd gotten a scholarship to UC Santa Barbara for baseball. Was that a lie too?

Second, if he did have parents out there, why lie about it? Pretty obvious he hadn't spoken to them in at least five years, since they didn't know he'd gotten married.

Third, what to do with this new knowledge?

With a sinking feeling, Hayley knew she had to confront him. With one last look around the kitchen, she stood, turned off the light, and headed upstairs for what would surely be an ugly scene.

Jason wore a pair of boxers as he exited the bathroom. "There's my beautiful wife. What took you so long?" Hayley hesitated at the warmth of his smile. He'd been so tender this evening, like the old Jason. Should she mention the call now? Or wait until tomorrow? She chewed her lip, suddenly unsure.

His mother's voice had sounded distraught. Mentally girding herself up for what would become a battle, Hayley sat on the end of the bed. "Your mom called."

Jason practically skidded to a stop in front of her. "What did you say?"

Hayley met his blue eyes, which had turned angry and dark. "Your mother. She called while you were in the shower."

Jason hesitated before going on the offense. "Why were you answering my phone? I told you—"

"No. Not this time, Jason. You won't blame this on me." With inner strength she didn't know she had, Hayley stood and faced him. "Why didn't you tell me your parents were still living? That's cruel."

Jason turned to the dresser and grabbed a tee shirt, pulling it over his head with force. "My parents." He spat out the words. "They're not my parents. Yes, they gave me life, but they aren't worthy of the title." He jammed his hands on his hips. "This is none of your business, Hayley."

Jason only used her full name when he was angry with her. A bit of her wanted to capitulate and let it go. Unfortunately, ignoring the lie would be like ignoring the last bit of crumbs on the kitchen counter. She couldn't let it go, couldn't ignore it.

Hayley laid a hand on his arm. Jason shook it off.

"It *is* my business, Jason. I can't believe you let me think your parents were dead. They could have come to our wedding. Do they even know about Cynthia?" Her challenge hung in the air for a moment.

"No. And better they don't." His mouth formed a sneer. "Would you want them to know you let your baby girl get hit by a car?"

Hayley's breath whooshed like she'd been punched in her solar plexus. Tears filled her eyes as she crossed her arms over her stomach. "No," she whispered.

Jason's words continued to hammer her. "Better they don't know you, and you don't know them."

Hayley sank onto the bed again. "Who's Danny?"

"Jeez!" Jason exploded. "Stop with the third degree."

"Who is he, Jason?" Hayley insisted. She needed to know. What else did Jason keep hidden from her?

Jason's voice raised to a shout. "He's my brother, okay? My older, stupid, mentally challenged brother." He used air quotes around *mentally challenged*. "There, are you happy?"

Pieces of a puzzle clicked into place in Hayley's head. Not the entire picture—enough to realize Jason's disdain for Dixie. The girl represented everything he hated about his brother. Special needs, developmentally delayed, outbursts of emotion—things Jason must have experienced first-hand. Knowing his need to control things, Dixie's behavior must have driven him crazy. Hayley was tempted to give him a little grace, but the lie was too big to forgive yet.

"Why did you lie about them, Jason? Don't you think we could have talked about them back when we first started dating?" Hayley leaned back on the bed, resting her weight on her arms.

Jason was already shaking his head before she finished. "No. I left home to go to school and never looked back. They are dead to me."

Hayley studied him, willing herself to understand things from his perspective. She'd had such a good family life, she couldn't imagine disowning her parents. They'd provided everything she and Hannah needed and almost everything they wanted. They'd shown their love in their own way, her mother by taking them shopping, to dance lessons, ensuring they had enough cultural education. Daddy, when he was home, was more effusive in his affection. He cuddled his girls, hugged them, and took every opportunity to touch them.

What had Jason's parents done to cause him to consider them dead?

Something occurred to her, something dropped into her heart. Something she had to ask.

"Jason, what else have you lied about?"

Jason was up and out of the house before Hayley stirred in the bed next to him. He'd slept horribly, his dreams filled with bizarre images. What had happened to his sweet, compliant wife? She'd turned on him like Bellatrix Lestrange from Harry Potter. Why did she think she had a right to know his reasons for declaring himself free from his mother and father?

Jason padded through the dark kitchen and let himself into the garage. The shroud-covered Miata mocked him. How long before he could rid himself of the constant reminder of his carelessness? He'd had a business lunch and had indulged in a couple of drinks with the potential clients. They'd ordered a pitcher of margaritas to go with their tacos, and he'd been a little buzzed. The Miata's speed had gotten away from him. He could still hear the sound of impact.

He shook off the feeling and climbed into his SUV. The garage door slid up and he backed into their quiet street. The only light showing was their next-door neighbor's. He could barely make out Zola's outline in the kitchen. That was one relationship he'd have to quash. Zola was much too nosy. When the police investigated Cynthia's hit and run, she'd been the only one to offer any kind of description of the vehicle. After more than a year, the driver still hadn't been found.

Now, instead of his beautiful little golden-haired princess, he was stuck with Hayley's latest project. Dixie. Who named their kid Dixie, anyway? His lip curled in derision, both for

Dixie's druggie mother, and for Dixie herself. She brought too many memories of his brother.

During his childhood, all the attention was on the neediest. Jason's parents had done everything to help his brother, Daniel. The best autism workers, the best physical and emotional stimulation, the best special needs school. Everything for Danny.

"Don't upset Danny or he'll have a meltdown. No, we can't go to your baseball game, Danny has a session."

Jason slammed his closed fist on the steering wheel. Exactly like his parents, Hayley was consumed with this child. So what if she was raised in a homeless camp in a cardboard box? So what if her mother was a drug addict? What about him? What about his needs?

Hayley should finish up this thirty-day placement and get pregnant. He'd sell his and Chad's business and buy the boat he'd lusted after. He, Hayley, and his son (he hoped) would travel the world via the ocean. Hayley could home school. They'd be a little family and live happily ever after. They'd need no one else.

Hayley would turn her attention back to him.

A dog ran into the street. Jason slammed on his brakes as the seatbelt locked. The dog stopped, looked at the SUV, and trotted to the other side of the street.

Jason took a minute to let his heart slow down to a more normal pace. Stupid animal. Stupider owners, letting their dog run free. He didn't need to be reminded of the sound made when you hit a living thing.

CHAPTER 18

Hayley squeezed her eyes shut as Jason slipped out of bed at five the next morning. She'd slept in snatches, flopping from side to side like a fish on dry land.

"What else have you lied about, Jason?" He'd exploded again at her question.

"A wife should trust her husband," had been his answer. Niggling doubt kept her awake throughout the night. Why hadn't he answered the question? What else could there be?

A thousand scenarios played out in her imagination. Did he have another wife and child somewhere? Was he divorced? Widowed? Did he have a prison record?

Jason was hiding something, and Hayley was determined to find out what it was. Even if it cost her marriage.

The door from the kitchen to the garage closed with a slam. Hayley climbed out bed and padded across the hall to check on Dixie, who was asleep in her usual place, under the bed.

After a quick shower, Hayley made her way down to the kitchen for the first of several cups of coffee she'd need after a sleep-deprived night.

Her calendar showed an appointment with Dr. Yang. She'd need to get Dixie up, dressed, and fed before nine o'clock to get to Dr. Yang's office by ten. Hayley would need thirty minutes' leeway in case of any melt down.

Over the second cup of coffee, Hayley thought back to her fight with Jason. He used her inattention to Cynthia to continue to drive the stake further into her already broken heart. When would he let it go? For that matter, when would she?

As soon as God was satisfied. Maybe she should talk to Zola about it. Zola would know about God's vengeance. Wasn't there a verse in the Bible about that?

Vengeance is mine, I will repay, saith the Lord.

Hayley took another sip of coffee, and immediately regretted it. The now-cold brew hit her stomach like a dose of bleach. She took a couple of deep breaths to settle her tummy, then grabbed a piece of bread and shoved it in the toaster.

All this stress with Jason and Dixie was messing with her system. *Note to self: eat better today.*

Hayley ate the toast dry, chasing the moistureless bites with a bottle of water. She made her way upstairs to start the process of readying Dixie to face the day.

Potty, clean clothes, wrestle Dixie's hair into submission, eat breakfast. Exhausting even on a day when she'd slept soundly.

Hayley found Dixie sitting on the floor, the stuffed bear in her lap. "Good morning, sweet girl. I see you've found Brown Bear."

Dixie kept her eyes down, using her index finger to poke the bear's stomach. At least there wasn't a replay of the doll incident.

"Let's take Brown Bear to the potty. I'll bet he needs to go after sleeping all night."

Hayley was gratified to find Dixie's pull-up dry. Brown Bear sat on the counter while she finished her business.

After she was dressed, Hayley led Dixie downstairs to have breakfast. "Let's try to sit on the chair, okay?" She lifted the child onto one of the chairs. Dixie slithered off and plopped onto the floor.

"Let's try again. Stay up here, and I'll get you some breakfast." Hayley lifted her up and set her on the chair for the second time. Still no go. Dixie slid off, crawled under the table, and opened her mouth like a baby bird.

Hayley pursed her lips. "Hm. Maybe I should let you go hungry until you sit up here." She shook her head and busied herself making scrambled eggs for the two of them.

She carried the plate of eggs to the table, blowing on them to cool them. "Just right. Ready?" Hayley took a bite, sat down, and bent over to peer at Dixie.

Dixie held the stuffed bear in one hand, and with the other, smacked Brown Bear across the face. "Shut up!" Dixie shouted.

Hayley dropped the fork from limp fingers. Dixie struck Brown Bear again, and repeated the words, "Shut up!"

Hayley slid off the chair onto the floor. Goosebumps broke out on her arms. Not only was Dixie speaking, but she exhibited more emotion than Hayley had seen out of her.

Why hit the bear? What nightmare had this child lived so the only words she spoke were violent? Dixie continued to shout and hit the bear, until she finally flung the toy away from her.

"Bad!"

Dixie's legs began to quiver. The shaking moved up her torso to her arms. She opened her mouth and screamed. The hair on the back of Hayley's neck prickled as Dixie threw herself backward onto the floor and began to kick her legs and wave her arms.

Dixie was in full-on meltdown and Hayley had no idea what to do.

The bear was very, very bad, so the girl slapped him. He refused to obey Mama when she wanted him to go with the ugly man. He knew what would happen if he went, so he lay down on the ground and refused to budge. Slap, slap, slap. Next time he would do what Mama said. Or else.

The girl felt her legs move, as if someone had grabbed her by the ankles and was trying to shake her. Her body shook, and she was thrown back. She kicked and yelled. She wouldn't go, not with the man. Not him. Not again.

Jazzmine stepped into the bustling office of Love's Agency. A glance at Carla's closed door meant one of two things. Either her boss was working and didn't want to be interrupted, or she was out on a visitation. Either way, Jazz relaxed. There wouldn't be any interaction with her boss. A private conversation with Hayley was in order, and it wouldn't happen with Carla's bat-like hearing.

Jazzmine stowed her bag under the desk and glanced around the room before sitting. Most of her coworkers had a phone pressed against their ears. Jazzmine sank onto her chair and scrolled through her contacts until she found Hayley's name.

"Hello." Hayley's strained voice answered.

"Hi-ya, Mama. How are things?"

A muffled sob before Hayley answered. "Not good."

Oh, dear. That was what Jazzmine feared. She hadn't been there to support Hayley, and now things were going south. Carla was a great administrator. However, she lacked the warm fuzziness most foster parents needed from their social worker.

"Talk to me." Jazz glanced up to be sure Carla's door was still closed.

"Oh, Jazz, you wouldn't believe what happened. Dixie had an outburst and started hitting a stuffed bear. She was yelling, too. 'Shut up' over and over as she slapped him. When she was done, she had a complete and total meltdown. Jazz, I'm terrified."

Jazzmine rubbed a hand across her closely clipped hair. She spoke, choosing her words carefully. "Can you think of anything that precipitated the outburst?"

"N-no. I mean, I don't think so. We got up, got dressed, and came downstairs. The usual."

"What about in the past couple of days?" Jazz twirled a pen around in her fingers.

There was silence for almost a minute.

"There was an incident with a doll." Hayley's voice was strained.

Jazzmine's head started to pound as Hayley described the incident. Unfortunately, Dixie's behavior was not out of the ordinary. Most children who'd been subjected to physical and sexual abuse acted out similarly. This was the part of the job she hated. Seeing the aftermath of destruction wreaked by parents who struggled with drug addiction.

At least Dixie's mom, Barbara, was getting help. Before she'd taken the days off to deal with Marcus, Jazzmine had followed Barbara's progression from jail to the rehab center. A few more weeks sober and she'd be moved to a halfway house for six months. When she completed her program, including supervised visits with Dixie, they'd be reunited. Jazzmine hoped for a better outcome. In the meantime, Hayley was doing what she could.

Jazz murmured assurances as Hayley sobbed into the phone.

"Where is Dixie now?" Jazzmine asked.

"Under the table, asleep."

Jazzmine spied Carla striding through the front door of the building. Oops. Carla's territoriality was legendary in their office.

"Look, Mama, I have to go. Hang in there. You're doing great. This is normal behavior. Well, normal in the context of what Dixie has been through."

Carla paused outside the door to her office, leveling a look at Jazzmine.

"Okay, talk to you later." Jazzmine ended the call and turned toward her computer.

"Everything all right?" Carla had made her way to Jazzmine's cubicle and now spoke over the top.

Jazz swiveled her chair around. "Yes. All's good." Did her face show guilt?

Carla stared for a moment longer before turning toward her office, her heels tapping on the wood floor.

Jazzmine slumped back in her chair. *Dodged a bullet, girlfriend.*

Hayley gathered a sleeping Dixie into her lap and hugged her close. Dixie never would have allowed such close contact if she were awake. Hayley rocked back and forth on the floor, rubbing the child's back.

What kind of parent repeatedly slaps their kid? A bad one, she told herself. Hayley never raised a hand to Cynthia, and her parents had never even spanked her or Hannah. Although Hannah probably needed to be spanked a few times.

Hayley ran through the morning in her mind, wondering if she had done something to cause Dixie's outburst. The only good thing that had come about was Hayley knew Dixie could speak. The words she'd uttered so far were Mama, medicine, bad, and now shut up. Not much to go on, but it was a start.

An idea that had been a tiny seed germinated into life. She'd talk to Jazzmine about extending her time with Dixie, beyond the thirty-day emergency placement. If she could keep her for a few months, Hayley was sure she'd make more progress. Perhaps God would be satisfied, and maybe even happy with her. Maybe it was the key to his forgiveness.

What about Jason? The voice inside her head gave her pause.

What about him? Anger boiled inside as she remembered how he'd lied. Betrayal burned like acid. *I don't need to consider you, Jason. This is something I want, no—have to—do.*

Dixie stirred in her arms. Her beautiful green eyes opened, and Hayley was amazed again at their color. "Good morning, sweet girl. Let's get you cleaned up."

They arrived at Dr. Yang's office fifteen minutes late. Madeline showed them right into the playroom where Dr. Yang waited.

"Sorry we're late." Hayley's breath came in small puffs. She really needed to get back into her morning running routine. Out of shape and flabby, she had to catch her breath after heaving Dixie out of the car and carrying her from the parking garage to the office.

"Tough morning?" Dr. Yang's look was sympathetic.

Hayley looked down at her rumpled tee shirt and shorts bearing dried remains of Dixie's scrambled egg. This was no way to go out in public. Her mother's voice whispered, *you're a mess. You can't go out in public wearing that. What would people think?*

Hayley felt her face grow warm. "Yes."

"Come on, let's get started."

Hayley watched Dr. Yang's attempts to engage Dixie in play. Until Hayley got down on the floor next to her, Dixie showed no response.

"Talk her through what you're doing," Dr. Yang urged.

Hayley pulled a pile of wooden blocks toward her. "Look, Dixie, I'm going to put this red block on top of the blue one." Hayley demonstrated how to make a stack of blocks.

"Here, you try." Hayley put a block into Dixie's limp hand. "Look, you're holding the yellow block. Let's put the block on top of the stack." She guided Dixie's hand.

"No." Dixie shook off Hayley's hand.

Hayley met Dr. Yang's eyes with raised eyebrows.

"I do it." Dixie's voice was gravelly from non-use. Hayley didn't care. It was music to hear her speak more than one word.

Dixie set the block on top of the stack. The blocks teetered and fell into a noisy pile. Hayley clapped her hands. "Good girl!"

She tried to get Dixie to repeat the move, but the girl had retreated into herself.

Dr. Yang smiled. "You've made such good progress with her."

High praise from someone who rarely gave compliments.

"Thank you." Hayley thought back to the morning's meltdown. "Not nearly enough."

Dr. Yang smoothed the legs of her khaki pants and stood. "I'm impressed. Dixie is thriving in your care. Too bad she's being moved to a more permanent home."

"Wh-what?" Hayley felt as if she'd stepped on a trap door and was sliding down into darkness.

"I thought you knew," Dr. Yang continued. "This will be our last session together. The child is going into a foster home which has agreed to keep her until the birth mother completes her rehab. Six plus months."

Hayley struggled to her feet. "No, I wasn't informed of this." Now she was channeling her mother in a different way. "Why wasn't I informed?" She drew herself up and glared at the psychologist.

"You'll need to discuss the decision with the child's case worker." Dr. Yang returned to her professional persona. "I only mentioned it because I thought you knew."

"I didn't know. And I will be discussing this with *Dixie's* case worker."

Hayley gathered her purse and strode out of the room, Dixie trailing behind like a baby duck.

Outside the building, she stood for a moment in the bright sunlight. No way would she let Dixie go. Not yet.

CHAPTER 19

Jason disconnected the call and leaned back in his leather office chair with a sigh of satisfaction. Three more days and Dixie would be gone. Moved to another foster home more suited to a long-term stay.

His conversation with the new case worker, Carla, had gone better than he expected. She'd told him a move was already in the works. Jazzmine had been relieved of their case, and she, Carla, would be handling Dixie's oversight.

Jason placed his hands behind his head and stretched. Sometimes things worked out the way they should. Now he needed to regain Hayley's trust, and they'd go back to being the way they were. They'd have another baby, and she'd be tied to him forever. And in two years, all that money would be his.

Jason remembered when he'd first become aware of Hayley. There'd been some college girl chatter about "Miss Trust Fund." They'd mocked her perfect hair, flawless complexion, and expensive clothes. At the time, he thought they were simply jealous.

The first time Jason saw Hayley, he'd been bowled over by her beauty and the way she seemed a bit sad. Almost as if life was too difficult. Jason made it his mission to make her smile. His strategy worked. They'd begun a friendly relationship that moved into love, at least on his part. Jason used all his powers of persuasion to convince Hayley he was the one.

When Hayley told him about the trust fund that would be hers when she turned thirty, he could hardly contain himself. His life was finally going to change for the better. He'd scored the Trifecta: the girl, the incredible wealth, and a bright future.

Everything changed with the death of their daughter. After Cynthia, a dark cloud seemed to cover him and Hayley. The only bright spot was the money Hayley would receive in two years. Maybe when the money was theirs, they could escape from the sadness.

Now if he could figure out what to do about his mother's incessant calls. How did Mom get his number, anyway? Chad must have told her. He and Chad had known each other since before college. Although they'd never been what Jason would call friends, their mutual interest in software creation had made them partners. Chad didn't know Jason despised him. Chad's quirks irritated him every day. His scraggly soul patch, the pretentious man bun, his sock-wearing Birkenstock-clad feet.

Jason shuddered. Why couldn't the guy dress like a normal human being? Was he trying to be a cliché of how a software developer should look?

Jason leaned over and wiped a speck of dust off his Italian leather shoe. He'd be glad to sell the business and be done with Chad forever.

With a touch of his finger, his laptop sprang to life. Jason settled in to work on updating their projections.

"Dude!" Chad burst through the door of his office. As usual, he didn't bother to knock.

"What?" Jason said, fixing his gaze on Chad's sweaty face, trying not to sneer.

"We've gotta go back down to Los Angeles for another round of talks with the Miller Group."

Jason groaned. How was he supposed to work his way back into Hayley's good graces if he was three hundred miles away? "Can't you go without me?"

Chad shook his head. "No way, man. There is no 'I' in team. We both have to go." More clichés.

"When?" Jason pulled at the cuffs of his shirt, straightening the diamond cuff links.

"Saturday." Chad shot him an apologetic look. "Sorry to mess with your weekend, amigo."

"Why can't we do this over the phone—or Zoom?"

Chad half-sat on the edge of Jason's desk. Jason resisted the urge to shove him off. "Let me unpack this for you, partner." Chad's hands waved as he spewed out more empty words. Jason stopped listening, instead waiting for Chad to wind down so he could ask about how his mom managed to pry Jason's phone number from him.

"You see, J-man, we both have to go. Guns loaded. Take no prisoners."

Jason wanted to gag. "Can I ask you something?"

Chad slipped off the edge of Jason's desk and bounced on the balls of his feet. "Anything."

"Did you give my mother my cell number?" Jason gritted his teeth, waiting.

"Well, yeah. She called me a few weeks ago. Dude, I thought it was okay." Chad turned to leave, stopped. "Why don't your parents know how to contact you, anyway?"

Jason mumbled something that must have convinced his business partner.

"Later, bro." Chad raised a hand in a quick wave and disappeared through the door.

Jason rested his elbows on his desk, chin on his fists. His parents. Danny. Why couldn't they disappear? Of course, Chad wouldn't understand. He and his parents were close. His family celebrated Thanksgiving, Christmas, and every holiday together. Chad didn't have a special-needs sibling who robbed all the attention. From what he could tell, Chad had a solid middle-class upbringing. He'd played soccer, learned to drive in his mother's minivan, and earned his Eagle ranking in Boy Scouts.

Jason's parents could never afford soccer. Danny's care was too expensive. They wouldn't have had time to attend a game anyway. They'd missed every milestone of Jason's life because of some medical emergency.

Still, it was difficult to hate his brother. His parents, yes. Danny, no. Danny had always looked up to him. Before his condition worsened, they'd played silly games together. Jason smiled, remembering his failed attempts at getting Danny to understand the concept of hide and seek.

Jason sat back in his chair and rubbed a hand over his heart, erasing the shame he felt over having a brother who needed to be hidden.

Before he returned to his work, Jason had one more thing to do. He pulled up his search engine and typed in "sell my car." The Miata had to go. The sports car was one more reminder of something he'd rather forget. His parents, his brother, and anyone or anything standing in his way, had to go.

By the time Hayley arrived home, she'd already left two voice messages for Jazzmine and one for Carla. Where was everybody? Someone needed to tell her what was going on.

Dixie dozed in her car seat. Hayley bundled her into the house and trudged up the stairs to the bedroom. She looked down at the sleeping child, dwarfed by the canopy over the bed. Her heart swelled with fierce love.

No child deserved to be raised in a homeless camp. Dixie deserved the same chances in life as any other kid.

Hayley padded back downstairs and poured herself a glass of ice water. Her stomach growled at the cold liquid. When had she last eaten? She'd fed Dixie some watermelon, one piece at a time, stretching her arm into the back seat. Dixie grabbed each piece and jammed it in her mouth, barely chewing before swallowing and grunting for more. When there was no more, Dixie fell asleep.

Hayley put a hand over her tummy. What could she eat that wouldn't pack on any more pounds? The scale that morning read a gain of three ugly pounds. After grabbing an apple from the fridge, she munched on it, carrying the apple and her phone into the living room. Plopping down on the sofa, Hayley scrolled through her recent calls, looking for Carla's number.

As she was pushing the 'call' button, the phone leapt to life in her hands. Finally, Carla was returning her call.

"Hello." Hayley set the apple on a coaster on the coffee table, trying to keep her voice neutral. She wanted to scream and yell and the injustice of the system. Why would they move Dixie to another home, when she'd already had too much upset in her little life?

"Ms. Montgomery, I am returning your call."

"Thank you." *It's about time.* "I was calling about Dixie. I understand you plan to move her?"

Carla sounded hurried. "That's right. As I told your husband, she'll be going to a semi-permanent home until the biological mother is released from rehab."

Hayley shook her head. "Wait. You talked to my husband."

"Correct. He explained his unwillingness to take on any more responsibility regarding the child. It is in the child's best interest to be with a family, preferably with siblings, who can better nurture her."

Hayley pulled the band off her ponytail and shook her hair around her shoulders.

"I—"

"If there isn't anything else, I really must go. I have a meeting in ten minutes, and I'm already running late. A case worker will be by on Friday to pick the child up from your home."

Hayley fell back against the sofa cushions as Carla disconnected. Jason's betrayal fueled the anger that had been smoldering deep inside, to an out-of-control fire.

"How dare he." Hayley flung herself to her feet and paced the living room. All the slights and snide remarks he'd made came to her mind. All the ways he tried to control her, choose her friends, spend *her* money. Every time he'd made her feel small and insignificant. The times he'd punished her with cold silence when she'd made some error. How he insisted she have every speck off the kitchen counters, every dish in the dishwasher, and nothing out of place. How he found ways to make her feel guilty over Cynthia's death. As if she needed more guilt. She'd never forgive herself for not watching her toddler as she rode her trike into the street.

The police never found the driver of the vehicle that hit her. He or she never slowed down. Hayley had a dim memory of a dark sports car, similar to Jason's Miata. When the accident happened, her attention had been on Cynthia's body, sprawled on the road. She'd never realized how rough asphalt was. From the safety of her front yard, the street looked smooth. Small rocks dug into her knees as she'd thrown herself down to pick up her precious baby. Ugly scrapes bled onto her tee shirt as she'd cuddled Cynthia's limp form. Hayley shuddered, remembering how the paramedics had to pry Cynthia away to take her to the hospital.

Every call to Jason went to voice mail. When he'd finally met her at the hospital, his breath smelled like alcohol.

"How could you let this happen?" he'd demanded.

All Hayley wanted was to be held. He didn't even offer a morsel of comfort.

At this moment, Hayley needed a place to direct this anger before she exploded. The anger that had grown for the past five years. How dare Jason talk to Carla behind her back. How dare he undermine Dixie's placement with them.

Maybe she could get someone to stay while Dixie slept. She'd be down for at least an hour. Dr. Yang's sessions always exhausted the poor little thing.

Nope, not possible. Hayley could lose her foster license if she left Dixie with anyone not on Sacramento County's list of respite workers.

There was always the treadmill they kept folded up in the spare bedroom used as their office. Not her first choice.

Ten minutes later, her feet pounded the treadmill, imagining she was running through their mature neighborhood. August was almost finished dishing out furnace-temperature heat. The trees, planted in the early twentieth century, created a shade canopy, reaching across the street to meet in the middle. Every house in these old Sacramento neighborhoods was different. Built at the turn of the century, the Fabulous Forties were considered suburbia. The homes exuded old money and wealth. Some upstarts had purchased a home here and there and added a second story or had torn down the house and started over. Most homes remained untouched except for a new coat of paint, new windows, and up-to-date roofing. They had maintained their class for more than a century.

Hayley mentally sprinted past the homes on her street, realizing she knew none of her neighbors except for Zola and Sol. Was that the reason no one had stepped forward when questioned about the car that had struck her daughter?

She envied Zola's easy way with people. Zola knew every story of every person on the block. Hayley had once been at least friendly with their neighbors. Until Jason had pulled her back.

"They aren't like us," he'd said. At the time, she'd been too involved with decorating the house, remodeling the kitchen, and caring for their infant, to notice how completely Jason had shut her off from outside contact.

Except for Zola. Her persistence at making friends with Hayley had broken down Hayley's reticence. She'd continued to advance despite Jason's obvious dislike.

Thank God for Zola.

God. How could she thank a God who was such a harsh judge? Hayley used her sleeve to wipe sweat from her forehead. She was *this close* to finally feeling she'd done enough penitence to appease his anger. Maybe now she could finally forgive herself.

The baby she'd aborted haunted her dreams. She'd named him Luke. He came to her as a little boy, always asking "Why?" Hayley always woke before she could answer. Which was a relief. How could she tell him the truth?

"Being pregnant was inconvenient. You were not supposed to happen." She'd been selfish and stupid. Would her world have come to an end if she'd given birth to him?

The questions buzzed around her head.

Hayley focused on her breathing as the treadmill increased in speed. Her timing was off, from lack of exercise. Or stress. She was close to losing control, and losing control couldn't be tolerated.

Why would Jason call Carla and undermine what she was doing with Dixie? How could he be so cold? So cruel? He didn't understand her need to nurture and protect Dixie. Maybe if she explained ... no, he'd never get it. She'd let him believe she was a virgin when they got married. What would he do when he found out she'd lied to him?

Jason had lied to her too. He'd told her his parents were dead and he was an only child.

Had their entire marriage been built on lies? What else had he lied about? Did he even love her? Did she love him?

Hayley halted the treadmill, resting her hands on her thighs. Her lungs burned with the effort to breathe.

Hayley finished packing Dixie's things into a cute pink suitcase. She closed the case with a snap, surveying the room to see if she'd forgotten anything. Dixie sat on the floor, Brown Bear in her lap. Hayley touched Dixie's head, gently ruffling her hair. Dixie looked up and smiled.

Hayley's heart swelled. The child had a beautiful smile. Hayley had hoped to see her smile more and more, but the County of Sacramento had a different plan. Dixie needed to be in a permanent place until her birth mother could get straightened out.

Hayley's head understood. Her heart didn't. Maybe she wasn't cut out for this fostering thing. She'd become too attached. Like the two girls before her, she'd let Dixie into her heart.

Maybe Jason was right about having another child of their own. One she'd watch every moment.

Or maybe it was time to rethink everything. Her marriage, her career, her life. Who was she, now that she'd let everyone else tell her what to do, what to think, who to hang around with? She should become more like her sister Hannah, the wild one.

Who was she kidding? She'd never be like Hannah. And she'd probably never have the courage to leave Jason, even if she wanted to.

With a sigh, she pulled up the suitcase handle.

"Come on, sweet girl. Let's go downstairs for a snack."

Dixie jumped to her feet and raced down the stairs ahead of her.

Hayley dragged the suitcase down the stairs and sent a text to Zola.

HAYLEY: Can you come over? I don't think I can do this alone

Zola's answer was immediate:

ZOLA: Of course, sheyn. Five minutes.

Taking a deep breath, Hayley stepped into the kitchen, trying to find words to tell Dixie she was leaving.

Her bare feet slid to a stop. Dixie sat on a chair at the kitchen table, like any other normal child, waiting for a snack. Tears sprang to Hayley's eyes, and she wiped them away with the back of her hand.

How far Dixie had come. Even though sitting at the table hadn't been on Hayley's list, it was another step in the right direction. How far would Dixie regress when placed in another home?

Or was Hayley overreacting? Perhaps Dixie would be further along with brothers and sisters to show her how to behave.

Hayley sliced an apple into tiny pieces and put them on a plate. She sat at the table next to Dixie, feeding her piece by piece. Dixie grabbed for the plate, but Hayley kept the plate out of reach.

"No, little one. One bite at a time, remember?" Dixie grunted as she barely chewed. Swallowing quickly, she continued to lunge for the uneaten pieces.

They both looked up at Zola's appearance at the back door. Hayley motioned for her to come in. Jason preferred the doors to be locked all the time. Hayley triumphed in this little bit of rebellion against Jason's rules.

"I came as fast as I could." With a whoosh, Zola settled onto a chair across from Hayley. "I see I'm not too late."

Hayley rubbed a hand across her face. "I don't know how I'm going to let her go."

Zola reached across the table and laid a hand on Hayley's arm. "God has this. Trust him."

Hayley resisted the urge to laugh. Where was God? This was supposed to be her ticket back into his favor. Instead, her last chance at redemption was being ripped from her life.

What more did he want? Her baby—gone. Her marriage—full of falseness. Now Dixie was being pulled out of her care and sent away. What chance did she have against all the walls God had thrown up in her path? She was doomed.

Zola squeezed Hayley's arm. "What time will the social worker be here?"

"They said around ten," Hayley replied, glancing at the digital display on the microwave.

"It's almost ten now." Zola picked up the now empty plate and carried it to the sink. "Where's Jason?" Zola asked, glancing over her shoulder.

Hayley shrugged, feigning indifference. "Work."

"Shouldn't he be here with you instead of me?" Zola said the words Hayley silently thought.

Hayley didn't respond. Instead, she pulled Dixie close to whisper in her ear.

"I love you, sweet girl. You're going to be fine with your new family." Hayley felt the child stiffen. Dixie looked up into Hayley's eyes, slid off the chair, and dashed from the kitchen. Hayley heard rather than saw Dixie slither behind the sofa. How would she get Dixie out when the social worker arrived?

Zola sank onto the chair Dixie had vacated. "Come on, honey. Let's pray."

Hayley bowed her head, fixing her gaze on Zola's big hand covering hers, biting her bottom lip to keep from screaming. Why would Zola's prayers make any difference to God? No amount of praying on Zola's part could possibly quench his anger.

Zola murmured, "Amen." She stood. "Come on, let's wait in the living room."

Hayley couldn't sit. She paced the room while Zola rested on the sofa.

"Too bad your kitchen doesn't face the street," Zola commented. "You'd be amazed at how much you can observe while cooking or doing the dishes."

Hayley let Zola's words go by without responding.

"I see practically everything that goes on."

Hayley stepped to the front door and peered through one of the side windows. "Too bad you didn't see the driver who hit Cynthia." Without a witness, the police said the case was unsolvable. Whoever hit her little girl would forever go unpunished.

Hayley turned and met Zola's eyes.

A shadow passed over the older woman's face. "Would you want to know who the driver was? Wouldn't knowing make it harder to move on?"

Hayley crossed her arms. Was Zola holding something back? If so, what?

Hayley's cell phone rang. She pulled the phone from the back pocket of her shorts. "Hello?"

"This is Carla. Dixie's social worker."

She knew who Carla was. Hayley pictured her perfect hair, polished nails, and severe expression. "Yes?"

"There's been a change. The family who was to take the child had an emergency."

"Oh? What kind of emergency?" A sliver of hope pierced Hayley's heart.

"One of their children was in a skateboarding accident. They are unable to take the child now. I will update you as soon as I have another family lined up."

"You mean ... Dixie is staying here?" Hayley stepped closer to Zola, phone to her ear. Zola grinned.

"For the time being."

"Oh. Okay, well—"

"I'll be in touch." Carla ended the call.

Hayley pulled the phone away from her ear, suppressing the urge to laugh hysterically. She held her breath for a moment. "She's staying here."

Zola lumbered to her feet and grabbed Hayley in a bear hug. "Praise Jesus!" She rocked back and forth with Hayley in her arms. "He answered our prayers."

"Your prayers." Hayley pulled away. "Thank you." She burst into tears and was embraced again.

Zola held her at arms-length. "What's wrong? You're a thousand miles away."

Hayley shook her head to clear it. "I'm fine. Not sure what to think."

"Let's have some coffee and talk. I might have some cookies in my satchel."

At the word "cookies" Dixie materialized in the kitchen door. "That's right, *zis kind*. Cookies." Zola chuckled as Dixie scurried into the kitchen.

Hayley stood still, wondering about what had happened.

The girl followed the big lady into the kitchen. The big lady said pretty words. The girl knew everything would be okay. She would stay here in this house. Lee was crying. Again. This time she sounded different. She was laughing too. The big lady, Zola, laughed. She said a name Dixie had heard before. Jesus. Mama said Jesus Christ when she was mad. Zola sounded happy when she said the name. Maybe Jesus told Hayley not to send her away.

CHAPTER 20

Hayley stepped out of the bathroom after her shower to find Dixie sitting on the bedroom floor.

"Hello, sweet girl. Did you wake up from your nap?" She didn't expect an answer. "I'm glad you're staying here longer. What would I do without my sweet girl to take care of?"

Hayley leaned over to rub a towel across her hair. She desperately needed a trim. When could she go?

"I'll put my hair up in a ponytail and we can go find a snack. I bet you're hungry, aren't you?"

Hayley tossed the towel across the shower door, ran a comb through her hair, and slapped a band around her hair.

The cell phone buzzed on the dresser.

"Hello, Mother." The dopamine she felt from the time on the treadmill dissipated with her mother's voice.

"Hayley, I have wonderful news!"

What on earth could it be? She and Daddy were leaving for Europe? She'd found a great bargain on a pair of designer shoes?

"What is it?"

"Well, you know how I'm on the American Heart Association board."

"Uh-huh."

"One of our volunteers retired, and there's a board opening."

"Okay." What did this have to do with her?

"So, I nominated you for the open board position, and the vote was unanimous! Oh, my goodness, I'm excited we'll be able to serve together. There's so much we can accomplish."

"But—"

Mother was a tsunami, and Hayley was swept up in the wave.

"Now your little feral child is gone, you'll have all this time on your hands. We'll have so much fun."

Hayley sank onto the end of the bed. Before she could form a coherent response, Mother continued.

"I talked to Jason, and he agrees this will be the thing to help get you out of the house."

Hayley clenched her fist. "You talked to Jason?"

"Yes, he told me the social worker said they were moving the child to a more permanent home. I can't tell you how happy this makes me. Mother, daughter, helping women who have heart conditions. Think of all the good we can do." Mother's enthusiasm oozed through the phone, filling Hayley's brain with dread.

Hayley took a deep breath, exhaling with a whoosh. "First of all, Mother, Dixie is still here. The other family had an emergency, and they couldn't take her. Second, you never asked me if I wanted to be on the board of the heart, whatever."

In the silence on the other end, Hayley pictured her mother gathering up every weapon to use to bend Hayley to her will.

"I don't know what to say, Hayley. Surely you and Jason have discussed this."

"Actually, we haven't."

Mother's voice turned hard. "I'm disappointed in you. I thought you wanted to help the community. Serve on a board that actually makes a difference in people's lives."

"I am doing something that makes a difference, Mother. In one person's life. A little girl named Dixie. Besides, you never asked me what I wanted to do. You decided all this before discussing it with me." Hayley chewed on her lips, waiting for Mother's response.

"I can't even talk to you right now. I will call you later when you've decided to be reasonable."

Mother disconnected. What did that even mean—when Hayley decided to be reasonable? Reasonable meant falling in with Mother's plans to run her life. As usual.

A tiny bit of fear rippled through her. How would she stand up to the pressure from Mother and Jason? How could she keep from going along with them as usual, to keep the peace? She rocked back and forth, imagining the worst.

A tiny hand touched her cheek, shocking her out of her runaway thoughts. Dixie stood in front of Hayley.

"Sad," Dixie said.

Hayley grasped Dixie's hand, pressing it to her cheek. "Yes. And scared."

Dixie's green eyes stared up into Hayley's. "No sad."

Tears sprang to Hayley's eyes. "Okay, sweet girl. No sad."

A door opened downstairs. Dixie startled, then dashed into her bedroom as Jason's voice yelled from downstairs.

"I'm home!"

Zola's text that morning came early. Hayley grabbed her phone and carried it into the bathroom before Jason awoke.

ZOLA: Can you come over this afternoon? My nephew is in town.

Hayley glanced over her shoulder to where Jason slept. He hated to be disturbed on Saturday mornings. "It's my only day to sleep in." Hayley did her best to creep around until he finally stirred, usually around ten.

Taking a deep breath, she tapped out her answer.

HAYLEY: Sure. What time?

Zola's answer appeared within ten seconds.

ZOLA: Three. Want you to meet David. Bring Dixie. And Jason.

Hayley chewed her lip as she answered.

HAYLEY: Okay.

What choice did she have? Where she went, Dixie went. Especially because Jason refused to be involved in her care.

The bigger question was whether Jason would want to go with them. She hoped not.

He'd arrived home the night before in a great mood. Hayley didn't know what surprised her more, his smile or the bouquet of flowers he held out to her.

His mood had turned ugly the moment he saw Dixie sitting on the living room floor, a pile of colorful wood blocks strewn out in front of her.

"What the—" Jason exploded. "She was supposed to be gone!" He'd flung the flowers on the counter and stalked to the sink with a scowl on his face.

Hayley had felt an unusual sense of grim satisfaction. "Apparently, she is not. Gone." Hayley swallowed the words threatening to spew out of her mouth, refusing to be drawn into another argument. "Plans have changed. The family that was supposed to take her had an emergency."

For once, Jason was speechless. Hayley wanted to rail at him, challenge his interference, and condemn his lack of understanding. She took a calming breath.

"What do you want for dinner?" Hayley pulled a vase from a cabinet and filled it with water.

"Not hungry," Jason had grunted. Hayley sagged with relief against the counter when he headed upstairs. The door to the office slammed.

What resistance would he throw out to keep her from going to Zola's house that afternoon? Zola was the only person who was immune to Jason's not-so-subtle hints that she wasn't welcome. Hayley's few college friends got the message loud and clear and stopped calling. Hayley hadn't realized until her treadmill time yesterday how much she missed social involvement. In high school, she'd led student council. In college, she'd volunteered at a day care center, reading to children. Though she'd had few friends, she'd kept busy with campus clubs and social activities. How had she let Jason gradually enclose her in a cocoon? She'd gone along with him for the sake of keeping peace. It was easier to agree with him. If not, he'd badger her, pout, or use the silent treatment until she was crazy with the need of his approval.

When had she lost herself? Was Cynthia's death the turning point? Hayley wracked her brain for what life was like before. She couldn't remember. Maybe that was when the balance of power shifted to Jason. Hayley was so consumed with guilt she agreed with everything Jason said, everything he wanted.

Until now. The little girl upstairs needed her. And she wouldn't let Jason or anyone get between them.

Jason clomped down the stairs and into the kitchen, dragging his overnight case behind him. The laptop case dangled from one hand.

"Where are you going?" Alarmed, Hayley advanced toward him. Did he intend to leave her again?

"Chad and I have to head for LA again." With a quick peck on her lips, Jason headed for the door leading into the garage.

"When will you be back?"

Jason shrugged. "Tomorrow or Monday. I'm not sure."

Hayley watched him leave with a mixture of guilt and relief. The problem of Zola's invitation was solved by Jason's departure.

Hayley examined herself in the mirror after changing clothes three times. What did one wear to a neighbor's house in the middle of the afternoon? Mother would say to wear a skirt, low-heeled sandals, and a nice blouse.

In defiance, Hayley dressed in a pair of khaki shorts and a tee shirt before changing her mind.

Too casual.

Hayley donned a mid-length flowered skirt, then discarded it for what she now wore. A sun dress in a bold geometric pattern. She slid her feet into a pair of flip flops and headed to Dixie's room to make sure she was still dressed in her own sun dress. As usual, Dixie had discarded the sandals. She sat in the same place Hayley had left her twenty minutes before.

Hayley observed her from the door. Dixie seemed captivated by Brown Bear, the only thing in the toy box she'd become attached to. There had been no more slapping incidents.

The air in the house was calm since Jason had left.

Except for telling her he was going out of town, Jason hadn't spoken a single word to her since he'd gotten home from work the night before. He stayed in the office until after she'd gone to bed. A month—no, a week—ago, his silence would have driven her crazy. She would have pounded on the door, demanding he talk to her. She'd dissolve into tears, begging him to come out. When he felt she'd groveled enough, he'd allow her to apologize some more.

Not anymore. Something fierce rose in her when she looked at Dixie. Hayley was a lioness. And this was her cub.

Dixie looked up and met her eyes. "Come on, sweet girl. Let's go see Zola."

They walked down the stairs, out the back door, and across the lawn to the gate separating their two back yards.

Hayley halted before walking all the way through. Should she have gone to the front door? After all, this an invitation to meet Zola's family. She stood with one hand on the gate latch, the other hanging loose by her side.

"Yoo-hoo!" Zola's voice called out from the sliding glass door. "Come on over. We're waiting for you."

With a quick glance down at her outfit, Hayley motioned Dixie to follow, and stepped into Zola and Sol's back yard.

Evidence of Zola's big personality was everywhere. Raised beds exploded with color—peonies, roses, marigolds, all growing together. A sago palm spread its scissor-like fronds from a huge Mexican pot on the edge of Zola's porch.

So different from her own carefully cultivated beds and neat rows of flowers.

"Come on out of the heat," Zola urged, waving her hand at them.

Hayley's stomach clenched as she stepped onto the raised wood porch. Though they'd lived next door to each other for five years, she'd never been inside Zola's home.

"Goodness, it's a pizza oven out here." Zola slid the door closed as Hayley and Dixie brushed past her to enter the dim coolness of Zola's living room. Like hers, Zola's living room faced the back of the house. There the similarity ended. Hayley's home was filled with expensive and mostly uncomfortable furniture. When she and Jason shopped for their home, he'd insisted on the best of everything. Designer fabric, stiff upholstery, and elaborate wood.

The sofa in Zola's room looked like you could sink into it for a long nap. The dual recliners were well worn, and the coffee table bore the scars of well-used furniture.

"Is Jason coming?" Zola asked.

"Um, no, he had to go out of town. For business." Sweat prickled under Hayley's arms. Thank goodness Zola let it go.

"Well, come on, let me introduce you to our nephew, David. David, this is my neighbor, Hayley."

Hayley held out her hand as David stood. He was barely taller than she, and his eyes were a chocolate shade of brown. He wore his black, curly hair close cropped, with a yarmulke in varying shades of blue.

His hand was warm. "Nice to meet you."

"Nice to meet you, too."

David crouched down to Dixie's level. "And who is this pretty little miss?"

Dixie scooted around Hayley's legs.

"This is my foster daughter. Her name is Dixie." Hayley lowered her voice to a whisper. "She's not used to being around people." At least Dixie hadn't screamed and dashed for a place to hide.

David straightened. "It's okay."

Sol embraced Hayley in a quick hug. "Come, sit." He waved toward the sofa.

Zola disappeared into the kitchen. "I'll be right back."

Hayley lowered herself onto the sofa, as she'd been taught. Never drop into a chair like a bag of potatoes. You sink gracefully, like a feather.

Before Hayley could speak, Zola appeared, bearing a tray of glasses filled with iced tea, and a plate of cookies which she set on the coffee table.

Hayley opened her mouth to warn Zola. Too late. Dixie launched herself at the tray, grabbing as many cookies as she could with both hands.

Sol and David's mouths dropped open.

"I'm sorry!" Hayley sprang to her feet, wrestling the food away.

Zola boomed out a laugh. "I'm the one who should be sorry. I forgot about the food issue." She gathered up the plate and broken pieces of cookie and carried them back into the kitchen, returning with a wad of damp paper towels, handing them to Hayley.

As Hayley cleaned up a howling Dixie, she tried to explain to the two men. "She's been food-deprived for much of her life. She reacts to any kind of nourishment. I'm sorry. I should have warned you." Hayley was breathless by the time she was done apologizing and wiping Dixie's face. "We should probably go."

"Oh no, you don't. You just got here. Sit." Zola pointed to the sofa.

Hayley opened her mouth to argue. Closed it and sat.

David reached for a glass of tea. "Aunt Zola tells me you're a runner."

Zola coaxed Dixie to her side with a piece of cookie. The wailing stopped.

Hayley pulled her attention to the conversation.

"Uh, yes. I run." Was she so unused to being around people she'd lost the art of small talk?

Sol crossed one leg over the other. "Too much work for these old knees. Now if I were younger ..."

Zola chuckled. "You wouldn't run if you were being chased by a rabid dog."

"Not so, my sweet," he protested. They bantered back and forth for a moment.

"I run as well," David said. "Perhaps I could go with you sometime. You can show me where to go and help me get back here."

"That's right," Zola interjected. "David has the worst sense of direction of anyone I know."

"True, true," Sol said with a laugh. "He gets lost going around the block."

"No, Uncle, I think that's an exaggeration."

Hayley watched the interchange, marveling at their easy way with each other. There were no hidden currents, no sly backhanded compliments. The three obviously adored each other. Were they the norm?

172

Zola continued to feed small bits of cookie to Dixie. Hayley took advantage of the lull to rejoin the conversation.

"How long are you staying, David?"

"I've moved here," he said. "I'll be here for at least six months, maybe longer."

Zola's voice was full of pride. "David is finishing up his residency at Sutter Hospital."

"Oh, you're a doctor. What field will you specialize in?" Hayley's charm school training finally kicked in. She could make small talk with the best of them. Mother would be proud.

David looked at his Uncle Sol. "I thought I'd follow in my uncle's footsteps and go into reconstructive surgery. There's something about helping someone who's suffered a traumatic accident or been burned in a fire restored back to how they looked before."

Hayley watched with interest while David and Sol discussed various techniques. The words whistled by her ears, but her concentration was on David's hands. They were slender with long fingers. He gestured with emphasis on some point of procedure. Passion for his work poured from him. Hayley nodded as his intense eyes pinned her.

She felt herself flush. David was a very attractive man.

Jazzmine stepped through the open front door of her house, dropped her bag on the floor, and shoved the door closed.

"Why is the front door wide open?" she asked to no one in particular. Open doors, toy-strewn floors, and general chaos was part of raising boys.

She glanced in the living room and saw all five of her brood, curled up like puppies, watching a movie. Zeke sat at the kitchen table, pounding away at his laptop.

"Can I quit my job?" she asked, sinking down onto the chair next to him.

Zeke glanced up, eyebrows raised. "Huh?"

"You know. Quit. My job." Jazzmine knew quitting was impossible but asked anyway. Since almost everyone's adoption was final, they no longer received county assistance as foster parents. Zeke made good money as a consultant, and her meager salary as a social worker in a private foster agency helped stretch the budget. One of the boys always needed something. Soccer shoes, braces, and food. Jazz shuddered to think how expensive things would be when the boys were teenagers.

"Tough day?" Zeke closed the laptop to give her his full attention.

How she adored that man. "Another one, yes. Carla shifted most of my cases to Ami and Shermila—however, she kept my favorite. You know the one."

"And it's a problem, why?"

Jazzmine shoved back her chair and walked to the refrigerator. She pulled out the pitcher of iced tea and poured herself a glass. "You know how I feel about her." She shrugged. "I think in a different life we would have been friends."

A laugh rumbled up from Zeke's belly and out his mouth. "Really, baby? She's from serious money. Lives up there in a million-dollar home, surrounded by surgeons, attorneys, and such. We live in Rancho Cordova. Our neighbors are machinists. Construction workers."

Jazzmine ran her fingers over the condensation of the glass. "Not to mention the silver spoon." She sat down at the table.

"Silver spoon?"

Jazzmine sent her husband a skeptical look. "Don't tell me you've never heard the phrase, 'born with a silver spoon in her mouth'?"

"Nope."

"It means she was born with everything. Money, looks, brains. All that and a bag of Doritos."

Zeke laughed again and shoved his chair back. Leaning in to kiss her cheek, he murmured, "Well if she was born with a silver spoon, you were born with a diamond."

Jazzmine smiled up at him.

"Still, I'm concerned about her and Dixie." She swiveled in her chair to watch Zeke start dinner preparations. "Carla doesn't even want me to contact her. I don't know what to do. I mean, the foster mom keeps calling and texting me. Oh, and Carla's planning to remove Dixie from her care and place her with a more permanent family."

Zeke threw some hamburger in a pan. "Why is that a bad thing? Didn't you all go into it as an emergency placement?"

"Yes, but ... the foster mom's become attached. And Dixie's making progress. I still read the reports. I think if the child is moved, it could set her back."

Zeke filled a large pot with water and set it on a burner. "Talk to Carla, honey. If she stands her ground, you've got to let it go."

Jazzmine slumped over the table, resting her head in her hands. "I know." Could she let it go? Was there a way she could influence the outcome without going head-on to Carla?

This would require some serious prayer. She and Hayley had discussed religion in some of their talks. Jazz shook her head. That girl had some messed-up beliefs about their Heavenly Father. Hayley saw him as judge, jury, and jailer. Jazz had tried to show her God's mercy and grace. Somehow Hayley couldn't conceive of a God who forgave without extracting payment for wrongdoing.

God, I need more time with her.

During the flight home, Jason took the opportunity to map out a plan. The plane was full, and he and Chad sat at opposite ends. Thank God for small favors.

The buyer of his Miata would meet him tomorrow at the house to do a test drive, and hopefully drive away in the car that held too many memories.

Although it pained him to do so, Jason would send a fat check to his mother, with the caveat she never contact him again.

He'd work on getting Hayley back under control. First, how to get rid of the kid? As soon as they landed, he'd make another call to Carla. Once they were rid of her, he'd make sure Hayley got pregnant again so they could be the family he envisioned. Heck, maybe this time they'd have a boy.

A son. He was filled with a flush of pride, thinking about teaching his boy to play football. Or soccer. Any sport, really. Any of the things he'd been denied as a kid due to lack of money. Or time. Or because of Danny's incessant needs.

Jason bit his lip, remembering.

"Going home?" The guy in the next seat interrupted his musings.

"Huh?"

"Going home or going somewhere else?"

Jason sighed. He wasn't in the mood for small talk. "Heading home."

"Oh, that's nice. So am I." Jason took notice of the clerical collar hugging the guy's neck.

"I'm Ben." He stuck out his hand in an awkward position in the cramped plane.

"Jason." How could he shut this guy down?

"I've been gone for a month. This is my last leg to get home."

"Hm." He refused to be drawn into a conversation with a minister.

"I've been overseas, delivering Bibles to remote tribes in Uganda. You'd have thought our team had brought diamonds instead of Bibles. The people held those books as if they were the most precious thing in the world."

"Wow." Jason tried to look uninterested, but the guy refused to get the hint.

"Anyway, I can't wait to get home to my wife and kids. Do you have kids?"

"Uh, yes, well, no."

Ben laughed. "Which is it, yes or no?"

Jason felt himself grow hot. This guy was too nosy. He opened his mouth, and words tumbled out. "My wife and I had a little girl. She died about a year ago. We're caring for a foster child."

Ben nodded. "I'm sorry for your loss. Losing a child is a parent's worst nightmare. We lost a child, a toddler, several years ago." Ben picked at a snag in his dark slacks. "Sometimes

176

it feels as if you never get over it. The guilt, wondering if there wasn't something we could have done differently."

Jason's chest swelled as his heart thudded painfully in his chest. He needed to get up, get away from this guy. He was trapped in the dreaded middle seat. Memories of his little daughter, twirling and dancing, filled his head.

Ben's brown eyes met Jason's. "How did she die, if you don't mind my asking."

Something like a fist closed around Jason's throat. "Hit by a car." He had a sudden image of Cynthia's little body, flung in the air and landing on the black asphalt.

Ben's words continued to pierce him. "How tragic. When our little one was diagnosed with leukemia, I had a real crisis of my faith." He tugged at the black and white collar. "Hard to believe a man of the cloth could question God, right? I wondered how a merciful and loving God could let an innocent child, my child, suffer from such a disease." He shook his head, running a hand across his unshaven cheek. The sound grated on Jason's already frayed nerves.

Jason believed God wasn't much interested in his people down here on Earth. He neither planned nor caused illness, death, accidents. He existed far, far away. Jason preferred to think of him that way. His faith was in himself—in his own abilities. God was a baby in a manger at Christmas. End of story.

Ben finally ran out of steam. Jason pulled his phone out of his shirt pocket, hoping the guy would get the message he was done talking.

He didn't. "How wonderful you're taking care of a foster child. Boy or girl?"

Jason had a sudden image of Dixie, screeching and diving behind the sofa. "Girl." A memory of his brother, Danny, falling to the floor in a meltdown, in much the same way.

Ben smiled. "Great. How old is she?"

Make it stop, Jason pleaded to the universe. A quick glance at his Rolex showed there was still another thirty minutes left of the flight. "Um—" He wracked his brain for any scrap of information Hayley may have dropped about the kid. "They think she's around five years old."

Ben turned his shoulders to more fully face him. "Think?"

Jason nodded. He remembered bits and pieces from Hayley's incessant chatter. "She was found in a homeless camp. She doesn't talk, so the social workers didn't know anything about her." Jason willed himself to stop. Words kept pouring from him. "She's been abused and neglected. You can't leave even one scrap of food around her, or she'll gorge herself until she throws up. My wife has done a really good job with her so far." Like the sun filling the plane's window as they banked for landing, Jason realized Hayley really had done a phenomenal job with the kid in the short time they'd had her. What else had he missed? Did she still grieve for Cynthia? They never talked about her. Jason couldn't even mention her name. What he'd done haunted his dreams. The one time he'd lost control, it cost him dearly.

He and Chad had been courting a new client. They'd met for lunch at Zocalo, a midtown Mexican restaurant. The clients ordered a pitcher of margaritas. And another. Lunch stretched late into the afternoon. He should have called for an Uber. In his supreme self-confidence, he figured he could navigate the few blocks between the restaurant and his home.

He'd meant to slow down when he reached his driveway, when his foot slipped off the brake and onto the gas pedal. The sound of the car hitting his little girl's body echoed in his guilty conscience.

"Are you okay?" Ben's voice brought him back to the present. "You look a little green."

Jason scrambled for the seat belt, releasing it. "I need to use the restroom."

Ben stood to let him out. Jason dashed for the restroom. Leaning his weight on his hands, resting on the counter, he looked at himself in the mirror. His face was pale and his eyes red with unshed tears. He'd never be able to forgive himself. Instead, he shifted the blame onto Hayley. If only she'd paid more attention to Cynthia's whereabouts. If only she hadn't run into the house for something.

Only he and Chad knew what he'd done. If Hayley found out, she'd never forgive him. His dream of sailing away from everything would be consumed by fire. She'd divorce him and he'd have nothing. No family, no money, no home. He'd be in prison, condemned by his own recklessness.

Jason splashed his face with water, drying it with the stiff paper towel, and headed back to his seat with dragging steps.

Ben stood to let him back into the middle seat.

"You look like you had some bad sushi," he commented.

"Something like that." Jason rubbed a hand across his mouth, smoothing his beard.

Ben's silence now irritated him. First the guy asks a thousand questions, then ignores me. Jason pulled out his cell to play Solitaire. Anything to take his mind off the thoughts pinging in his brain. How could he get everything back under control?

As the plane nosed into the terminal, Ben laid a hand on Jason's arm. "I'll be praying for you."

Jason nodded, unsure of how to answer. He'd prefer God stay far away from him. He was pretty sure God had some special punishment for fathers who killed their own children. Accident or not.

CHAPTER 21

Monday morning, Hayley woke to the sound of the shower. Jason was up early. She slipped out of bed and padded to Dixie's room. After peeking under the bed to assure the child was still sleeping, she descended the stairs to the kitchen. Maybe the weighted blanket she'd ordered online would arrive today. The reviews indicated the extra weight was a good way to help calm a nervous child or an anxious adult. Maybe this would help Dixie sleep all night in the bed.

Hayley finished her first cup of coffee, sitting at the table and watching sparrows flit from branch to branch in the Japanese maples lining the back fence. To be that free. No worries or concerns, flying through blue skies. She was that free once. Before Johann, before Jason, before Cynthia. High school was a blur of social activities in her private, all-girls' school. Student council, volunteer work at a special-needs preschool, and parties. All within the confines of what Mother and Daddy considered acceptable. Everything planned, no detail left out. Mother groomed her to take her place in Sacramento society. After college, even after marriage, Hayley had a lane to stay in. And she had. Until Cynthia's death.

Her death was the dividing line in Hayley's life. Everything before was colors. Everything since was grays and sepia tones.

Until Dixie. She was the key to gaining forgiveness from God. A tiny bit of color around the edges of Hayley's life began when Dixie entered her life.

No one would take her away. She needed Dixie. And Dixie needed her.

"Good morning. Got any coffee for your man?" Jason's form filled the kitchen door.

Hayley sprang up out of habit and threw a pod in the Keurig machine while Jason rummaged in the fridge. He turned to the table, setting down a jug of milk.

"Grab me a bowl while you're over there." He opened the pantry door and pulled out a box of cereal. "And a spoon."

Hayley complied, carrying the items to the table.

Jason grabbed her wrist. "Thanks." He smiled up into her eyes. This was the Jason she remembered from their dating days. Charming.

Hayley fixed herself a second cup and sat across from him. "Are you heading to work this morning?"

Jason nodded, chewing. "I wanted to talk with you about something first."

Hayley's stomach knotted. The coffee in her stomach turned to acid. Would this be another fight about Dixie?

Jason took a sit of coffee, set the mug down, turning it in circles. "I'm thinking of selling the Miata."

Hayley frowned. "Why?"

Jason shrugged, keeping his eyes on the swirling mug. "I don't drive it anymore and I want more space in the garage."

"Why don't you drive it?"

"It's impractical. I think I bought it on a whim. It isn't practical for a growing family. If, I mean, when, we have another baby, I'll need to have a car seat." A red flush worked up from Jason's beard, coloring his face.

Hayley stood and walked to the sink, dumping out her undrunk coffee. "Do whatever. Yours is the only name on the title." Which had been another slap in her face. He'd bought the car with her money. He hadn't consulted her, just showed up at the house with a big grin, as if he'd won the Super Lotto or something.

"Well, I wanted to make sure you were okay with it."

Jason would do whatever he wanted anyway.

"Why wouldn't I be?" Hayley swallowed, hoping to keep from vomiting up the roiling liquid in her stomach.

Hayley and Dixie arrived home after a busy morning. They'd had another session with Dr. Yang. Afterward, Hayley dared to stop at Target on the way home. Dixie sat in the cart, eyes wide open at all the sights. Hayley sped through the aisles, grabbing paper towels, tea bags, and shampoo, plus a few other items she'd forgotten from her online Walmart order.

She and Dixie had finished lunch when the doorbell rang. "Oh, good, maybe it's the blanket I ordered for you."

Hayley strode to the front door, Dixie on her heels. She expected to find a delivery box on the front porch. Instead, two uniformed police officers filled the small space.

Dixie screeched and dashed for the sofa, wedging herself behind it.

"What the—" said one of the officers.

Hayley gripped the edge of the door, knuckles white. "Sorry. She's scared of men. And police too, I guess." Hayley shrugged. "What's this about?"

"Ma'am, I'm Sergeant Fechter and this is Officer Wilcox."

The sergeant appeared to be in his forties, dark skinned and well built. Wilcox looked to be about her age, slightly doughy and pale. He shifted from one foot to the other as if he'd rather be any place except on her front porch.

"Are you Hayley Montgomery?"

Hayley nodded, her mind whirling. Was this about the driver who hit Cynthia? No witnesses had ever come forward, like the entire block of neighbors was gone that day. No one saw or heard a thing.

"We were wondering if we could speak with your husband, Jason."

"Jason?"

"Yes, ma'am," said Officer Wilcox. "Is he at home?"

"N-no. He's at work." Hayley looked behind her in the direction of the sofa. No movement. "Is this about my daughter?"

The two officers exchanged a look. Sergeant Fechter reached into his pocket for a business card. "Would you let Mr. Montgomery know we were here? Ask him to call me?"

"Why?"

The men turned to go. "Thank you."

Hayley watched their backs as they walked down her driveway and got into a parked patrol car. If this was about Cynthia, she had a right to know. Why did they want to talk to Jason?

If this wasn't about Cynthia, then what? She turned the business card over and over. What had Jason done?

"Hey, man, I'm leaving early." Jason poked his head into Chad's office.

His partner looked up from his computer screen. "'Sup?"

"I have someone coming to the house to look at the car I'm selling."

Chad stroked his soul patch with a thoughtful look. "Yeah? Good idea."

"I'll work on those numbers at home tonight." Jason hated the feeling he was explaining himself to his idiot partner.

"Sit down for a mo." Chad motioned to one of the chairs facing his desk.

Jason dropped his computer case on the floor and sat. He also hated that Chad was the only one who knew what had happened that day. Jason had panicked and returned to the office. Chad was there, downing some aspirin with a bottle of water. He hadn't drunk as much as Jason had, enough to give him a headache.

Jason remembered pacing Chad's office, unable to stop the words pouring out. He'd told Chad everything, from the drinks to the fuzziness, to the sound of his car hitting Cynthia's trike.

Chad agreed to keep silent. For a price. Jason was his minion.

Chad ran a hand across his head, loosening the man bun perched there. "I don't feel good about this, bro. You need to, like, confess or something."

"Confess?" Not now. Not ever.

"Yeah, dude. I could, like, be an accomplice or something. I don't want to go to jail. Now that we've got another kid on the way, I need to be sure I'm around to see him grow up. Comprendo?"

Adrenaline surged through Jason's veins as panic set in. Would his partner betray him? He couldn't let that happen. He couldn't lose everything because of one mistake. One mistake with serious consequences. Haley would never forgive him. He couldn't forgive himself, either. Easier to place the blame on Hayley. If she'd only kept a better eye on their little girl, this wouldn't have happened.

"Got it. Look, once I dump the car, no one will ever have to know. After all, there were no witnesses." Jason stood. "Besides, you need me to help you finish with the sale. You better not say anything." He leaned down to retrieve his computer case. "To anyone." He pointed a finger at Chad's chest. "Comprendo?"

Jazzmine pulled Rusty to a shuddering stop in her normal parking spot outside the building where the private foster agency was housed. There were no signs on the gray stucco walls to indicate the business that was done behind closed doors.

Jazz rested her clasped hands in her lap and whispered a prayer. "Please, Lord. Let her say yes."

Today was the day Jazzmine would ask Carla to return Hayley's case to her. Jazzmine didn't hold out much hope Carla would say yes, although sometimes God surprised her.

The car door creaked as she pushed it open and stepped onto the warm asphalt. Cooler weather couldn't come soon enough. Sacramento in August and September saw temps in the high nineties.

Jazzmine was so done with sweating.

The old building's air conditioning was already at work, doing its best to keep the occupants if not cool, at least slightly comfortable.

"Good morning," she called out to the few coworkers scattered among the cubicles. Dropping her messenger bag on the desk, she booted up her computer. While waiting, she checked her phone for voice mails.

Moments later, Carla swept into the building, the heels of her shoes tapping on the cracked linoleum.

"Jazzmine, when you get a moment, may I see you in my office?" Carla didn't wait for her response.

"Okay, Lord, this is it," Jazzmine whispered. She gave her boss a few minutes to get settled before knocking on the open door of Carla's office. "Ready for me?"

Carla nodded. "Sit, please." She pulled a stack of files toward her.

Jazzmine waited, her heart a jackhammer against her ribcage.

Carla lowered her reading glasses, regarding Jazzmine over the black rims. "I have a favor to ask you."

"Favor?" Carla never asked favors. She demanded.

"As you know, Marci's daughter is pregnant."

Of course, Jazzmine knew. Marci had danced around the office a few months ago when her daughter had finally conceived after months of trying. Marci regularly brought in ultrasound pictures documenting the baby's in uteri growth.

"Because of Marci's daughter's age, it's considered a high-risk pregnancy. There have been some complications, and she is now on bed rest until the birth."

Jazzmine nodded. Poor Marci. She must be devastated. This would be her first, and possibly only, grandchild. But what did this have to do with her?

"Marci is going to take a few weeks off to be with her daughter. I'm going to spread her cases around to everyone."

Jazzmine was used to this. Someone always had family issues come up.

"I want to give you a couple of her cases."

"Of course. Not a problem. Will Marci be here today to get me up to speed on them?"

"Good. I knew I could count on you." Carla pulled off her glasses and set them on the files. "I'm also reassigning the McNally case back to you. I find I'm much too busy to give this one the attention it needs."

Jazzmine bit her lip to keep from grinning. She was getting Hayley and Dixie back!

Carla continued, "Find another, more permanent home for the child. Make this a priority. The husband does not want the child. As you know ..."

Jazzmine's thoughts raced as Carla droned on. Jason didn't want Dixie? When did this happen? She thought they'd both been on board. Had she been so wrapped up in her own family's drama she didn't pay attention to the clues? A visit to Hayley was in order as soon as she could clear her calendar.

"Oh, by the way," Carla concluded. "Supervised visitation with the birth mother begins on Thursday. Please let Ms. Montgomery know."

Peachy.

Jazz returned to her desk with thoughts whirling through her head. Adding more cases to her already full load meant extra work and extra hours doing welfare checks and getting up to speed on the case files. Not to mention the counseling appointments she and Zeke had scheduled with Marcus. How could she squeeze any more room onto her overflowing plate?

I asked for Dixie's case back, God, not a ton more work.

There was no response from heaven.

Hayley fed Dixie lunch before settling her down for a nap. After the visit from the police, Hayley hadn't been able to eat a thing. Which was probably a good thing. Lack of exercise and snacking with Dixie twice a day made her feel fat as a bear in hibernation. She needed to get back into a routine of running at least thirty minutes a day. Keeping her routine hadn't been this difficult with the prior foster girls. Jason watched them when he returned from work, or first thing in the morning. This time, he wouldn't even look at Dixie.

Hayley remembered him saying he had a special needs brother. Things must have been bad for him to make him so uncomfortable around Dixie. A momentary flash of sympathy was quashed by his lies about his family. What was his mother like? His dad? Would they ever meet each other?

His mother sounded vulnerable on the phone. Not at all like her own mother. Mother was always in control. Always put together. Always about the rules, not the relationship.

Thank goodness for Grandma Van Maren. Hayley and Hannah had spent many weekends with Grandma and Grandpa before she died. Making cookies, learning to sew, snuggling on the sofa watching movies. Grandma's rules were simple: have fun, stay up late, sleep in. She always pictured Daddy's parents as soft bean bag chairs, while her own parents were the wooden, straight-back type.

Hayley powered up her laptop in the office. While it booted up, she picked at the polish on her fingernails. She was in desperate need of a manicure. If Mother could see her hands, she'd press her lips together and shake her head. Disgraceful.

Hayley made a mental note to remove the rest of the polish before Dixie got up. When the home screen popped up, she opened the documents file, searching for the one labeled "Police Report."

She'd scanned and saved every bit of information from the accident that had taken her little girl. Precious little was contained in the file. The gruesome autopsy report showed Cynthia had died from massive internal injuries. No skid marks on the street indicated the car hadn't slowed before or after impact. There were no witnesses.

Hayley tried for the millionth time to remember any details about the vehicle. At the time, she'd even considered hypnotism to see if she could recall any detail of the accident or the car. Jason had said, "Why bother? Nothing will bring her back, Lee. Focus on your grief."

Should she have ignored him and done it anyway? Was Jason trying to hide something? Maybe he knew who drove the car.

That must be it! He knew something, and the police wanted to question him about the driver. Who was he trying to protect? His partner, Chad? Someone else?

The alternative was too terrible to consider.

Hayley closed the computer and stood. She checked on Dixie, pausing at the top of the stairs. Who could she talk to? Someone to pour out her heart to. Her head was fuzzy, confused.

Stomach rumbling, she descended the stairs and headed for the kitchen. A piece of toast would ease the beast in her tummy. While the bread toasted, Hayley tapped her fingers on the counter. Why would the police come to the house, asking for Jason? Why not tell her if it was about the accident? If not the accident, what could it be?

Hayley pulled out her phone and tapped on the location app Jason had insisted they install. Each of them could be located by the other by a tap on the screen. Jason said he was concerned for her safety. But the locater was another way for him to control her every move.

"Jason has been located," the screen said. His icon was motionless at his work address. She huffed out a breath as the toast popped.

After slathering the toast with peanut butter and agave nectar, she downed it in a few bites. *I guess I was hungrier than I thought.* Her phone rang as she reached for the loaf of bread.

Jazzmine's smiling face appeared on the screen. "Hi ya, Mama."

"Oh, Jazz, I'm so glad to talk to you."

"Why? What's up?"

Hayley sank onto a chair, mentally switching gears to talk about Dixie. "So much has happened."

"I heard. The good news is, I'm back on your case."

"Wonderful! Dixie is doing so well. She's gained five pounds, and we've mastered the potty training. I even got her to sit at the table with me." Hayley's words gushed from her, excited to have someone to share with.

"Awesome. I knew you could do it."

Hayley took a breath. Before she could continue, Jazzmine interrupted.

"There is some other news. I won't call the news bad. It's not what I expected to happen so soon."

Alarm bells sounded in Hayley's head and the toast she'd eaten rumbled in protest. "What is it?"

Jazzmine paused. "Supervised visitation with Dixie's mom starts this week. I've scheduled the first one for Thursday afternoon."

Hayley pressed her lips together and swallowed hard. The food in her stomach threatened to come up. Must be the stress of the past few weeks. Food didn't want to stay in her stomach. Hayley focused on Jazz's words.

"You can bring Dixie to my office and drop her off."

Hayley let her head fall, resting her chin on one hand. Visitation already? She hoped Dixie seeing her mom would go well, for the child's sake.

Jazzmine's voice dropped. "I know how hard this is. Dixie's mom has been sober, and she wants to see her daughter. You know our ultimate goal is reuniting families."

Hayley's head knew it. Her heart refused to agree. There was so much more to be done with Dixie. How could Dixie's mother pick up where Hayley dropped off? Besides, Hayley still needed confirmation she'd worked hard enough to get back into God's favor. Redemption was still out of reach.

Hayley heard Jazz's quick intake of breath. "And I have to talk to you about removing Dixie from your care."

"What? Why?"

"Carla said Jason told her he didn't want her there. As you know, his reluctance creates a problem. When both parents aren't on board, the placement isn't in the best interest of the child."

To Hayley's ears, Jazz was reading out of a textbook. *Best interest of the child?* Dixie's improvement had been because of *her* work. *Her* nurturing. What did Jason have to do with it?

"I'm sure you understand."

No, Hayley didn't. She kept her lips clenched together to keep from saying something she'd regret.

The girl woke slowly to the darkened room. She snuggled for another few moments, savoring the feel of the heavy blanket covering her.

Here within the pink walls of the bedroom, she was safe from bad people. Safe from Mama yelling. Safe from the men who ... no. She wouldn't think about that. She would think about the food Lee gave her.

Her stomach rumbled. Pushing the blanket away, she swung her legs over the side of the bed and slid to the floor. The soft carpet tickled her bare feet.

Hayley would smile when she used the toilet after her nap.

When finished, she tiptoed down the stairs to the kitchen where she heard Hayley talking.

What was visitation? Was it the same as Mama taking her to a place where a man waited? Her heart thudded against her ribs. Maybe she wasn't safe here.

CHAPTER 22

Jason pulled into the garage and threw the car into park. He fixed his gaze on the tarp-covered sports car he'd enjoyed so much. Hopefully the car would be gone tonight, and with it, the memory evoked every time he pulled into the garage.

His hands gripped the steering wheel with white knuckles. Self-loathing rose inside him.

Think, Jason. There must be a way to make this work out. *Confess.*

Where did that come from? Jason released his grip on the steering wheel and glanced around the garage to assure himself he was alone. He shook his head. He must be losing it. Confessing was the one thing he could not do.

He'd lose everything he'd worked so hard for.

Jason reached for the computer bag on the passenger seat, pulling it onto his lap before climbing out of the vehicle.

Confess. Ha. To what? To whom? If there was a God, he was tucked away in a manger. A little baby, helpless to do any good here. If God existed, why didn't he spare Cynthia's life? If only Hayley had paid more attention. If only he hadn't had so many margaritas. If only...

The door opened with an annoying squeak. Jason frowned. Hadn't he told Hayley to oil it? Did he have to do everything himself?

Hayley spun around, knife in her hand. "Oh, you're home."

"Is that any way to greet your husband?" Jason flung the computer bag on the table. Dixie scuttled from behind the counter and sprinted into the living room.

"Good grief, Lee. Why does she do that?"

Hayley shrugged. "Dixie's afraid of you. Of men."

"I'm gonna go up and change into some shorts. A guy is coming over in about an hour to look at the Miata." His shirt was halfway unbuttoned when Hayley spoke.

"Two police officers were here today, asking for you."

Jason froze. "W-what?" Sweat broke out on his forehead. "Did they say what they wanted?"

Hayley set the knife down and leaned both arms on the counter. "What could they have wanted, Jason?" Her eyes bored into his. This was a Hayley he'd never seen before. Time to take back control.

"Whatever they wanted it isn't something you need to be concerned about."

"When police come to my door, it is something I'm concerned about."

Jason moved to the counter to stand across from her. He leaned in, using his height to make her look up. "First of all, it's *our* door. Second, I'll deal with the police. If they were asking for me, their visit wasn't anything to do with you." He saw the first flicker of doubt in her eyes. Lowering his voice, he said, "I'm going upstairs to change. End of discussion."

In the master bedroom, he removed his shirt and wadded it into a ball, heaving the shirt toward the closet door. Why were the police at his house? What did they want? And what was he going to do about it?

Jason went into the bathroom and splashed his face, letting the cool water drip from his beard onto the counter. Things were slipping out of his control. Hayley, Chad, and his mother's constant calling, wanting him to see his dad. Now this.

Could Chad have said something? No, they'd talked a couple hours ago. What time did the cops show up? He grabbed a towel and scrubbed what was left of the water off his face. Dropping the towel on the floor, he returned to the bedroom to change clothes.

There was no way they could know what really happened that day. No one had come forward for months. Their appearance must be about something else. Maybe Chad had done something illegal, and they needed him to testify.

Whatever it was, he'd deal with it. Like he always did.

A blast of cool air hit Jazzmine's sweaty face as she pushed through the door to Love's Family Foster Agency. The 'o' in Loves was a red heart. The logo hadn't changed, even though the agency's founders, John and Melissa Love, had been retired for over ten years. Their generous donations helped keep the private foster/adoption agency going year after year.

At least once a year, Zeke pressed her to work for a state or county agency. Usually when the announcement was made there would be no salary increases again. Jazzmine knew she'd make more money working for the county, but she couldn't bear to leave the nest she'd created for herself. Her coworkers were close friends.

Except for Carla. Since Carla had become supervisor, things were different. Perhaps it was time to make a change.

Her desk phone rang as her computer booted up.

"Good morning. Love's Family, Jazzmine speaking."

"Hey, Jazz. It's Marta Gonzales, McNally's case worker. Checking to be sure we're good for this afternoon's visitation."

Jazzmine sighed. "Yes. We're good. The foster mom will drop Dixie off at 2:45."

"I will see you at 3:00, *chica*."

Jazz smiled for the first time that day. Marta's unrelenting cheerfulness was a bright spot in an otherwise difficult world. Jazz tried to count the number of cases they'd worked on together. The tapping of Carla's heels snapped her out of her reverie.

"I have some updates for you," Carla said, holding out a few sheets of yellow lined paper.

Jazzmine inwardly grimaced while keeping her face neutral. "Okay. Thanks."

"What do you have scheduled today?" In the past, Carla's question would have been a friendly one. Now, however, her micro-managing nosiness got on Jazz's last nerve.

"I'm following up on a few cases before heading to the children's home. I'll be back here at 2:30 to wait for Hayley Montgomery to bring Dixie in for visitation with her birth mother."

Carla nodded. "Good. Give me a report when you're done." Carla turned and headed to the next cubicle to grill another employee.

After the visit to the children's home and a quick lunch, Jazzmine was back at her desk. An unusual wave of nerves washed over her as she thought about the upcoming visit between Dixie and her mom, Barbara. When had this case become personal? Jazz was always able to take supervised visitation in stride. Were her nerves because she and Hayley had become friends?

The goal was to reunite children with their biological parents. In this case, however, Hayley had made a lot of progress. She'd hate to see Dixie regress because of a difficult meeting with her mother.

Supervised visitations *were* stressful for both the parent and the child. Aware someone was watching, their actions were stilted and unnatural. Children were often confused at how to respond to a parent who was suddenly loving, when in the past they'd been verbally or physically abusive.

A glance at the time showed her Hayley was due any minute. Jazzmine stood and took a couple of calming breaths. She watched as Hayley herded Dixie through the glass doors with a gentle touch on the girl's back. Jazzmine marveled again at the change in Dixie. The child had filled out, and her cheeks had the rosy glow of health. Hayley had brushed Dixie's hair until it hung in dark waves over the shoulders of her flowered sun dress. Her feet were bare. Jazzmine smiled.

"Still can't get her in shoes, can you?" Jazz asked, approaching the pair.

Hayley shook her head with a smile barely curving her lips. While Dixie's physical appearance had improved, her care had taken its toll on Hayley. Her blond hair was pulled back into a messy ponytail. Hayley's face was devoid of makeup, and dark circles accentuated her blue eyes. Jazzmine noticed her normally manicured nails were chipped and uneven, the polish dull.

Jazz moved toward her for a hug. "You holding up okay?" She felt Hayley nod against her shoulder.

"I know this is difficult," Jazzmine said. "Remember, it's for Dixie's sake."

Hayley started to speak, stopped, and bit back what she was about to say. "When should I be back?"

Jazzmine glanced at the clock on the wall over the door, mentally calculating the time for the visit and time for Marta to take Barbara back to the rehab center. "Three forty-five."

Hayley bent down and spoke to Dixie in a low voice. "Okay, sweet girl. I'm leaving you here with Miss Jazz. I'll be back soon, okay? You're going to see your mama."

"Mama," Dixie repeated.

"That's right," Jazzmine said. "We'll have a nice time with your mama."

Hayley straightened, wiped her eyes, and looked at Jazzmine. "All right. See you later." Before she turned to go, she spoke to Dixie once more. "Bye, bye, Dixie."

Dixie continued to stare at the floor without responding.

The girl's heart thudded in her chest. Why did Lee say bye? Would she come back? Why was Lee scared? The girl was scared too.

Hayley pushed through the glass door of Jazzmine's office, stopped around the corner, and leaned against the brick building. She fumbled in her purse and brought a tissue to her face with a shuddering breath.

You need to compose yourself before you get back to the car.

She'd asked Zola to accompany her to Jazz's office, someone to lend moral support for the first of many difficult visits. If Dixie stayed with her. That was a very big IF.

Zola dragged David along, saying they could all go for a cold beverage while waiting.

"No use driving all the way back home," Zola had said. "David and I will both come with you."

Hayley hurried to where the car was parked, anxious to not come face to face with Dixie's so-called mother. Lunging for the woman who'd left her sweet girl in a box and scratching her eyes out wouldn't go well with Love's Agency. What kind of a monster let her baby girl be used so she could indulge in her addiction?

The same kind of monster who lets her little girl ride into the street, came the accusing voice. Hayley shuddered. She was no different than Dixie's mother. She'd failed to protect her baby girl, resulting in her daughter's death. Not only had she failed to protect her, she'd set Cynthia up because of her one rebellious act. When would her torture end? When would the angry God be done punishing her?

She'd done her best to be the good daughter her mother expected her to be. She'd done her best to be a good wife to Jason, whose demands had become unreasonable. Hayley's attempt to be a good foster parent might be the only thing she could say she'd succeeded at. Dixie's progress so far had been remarkable. Maybe this time she'd prove she could care for a child.

"I'm sorry I was gone so long," Hayley said as she climbed into the driver's seat. The windows were down in a vain attempt by Zola and David to stay cool while they waited. The oak tree she'd parked under gave small respite from the late summer heat.

Zola waved a colorful fan in front of her moist face. "Not to worry, *sheyn.* David and I have had a nice chat." Zola glanced over the seat with a smile to her handsome nephew. "Now, let's go get some iced tea and a sweet."

Hayley smiled despite herself. "Zola, you have the sweetest sweet tooth of anyone I've ever known."

Zola's laugh boomed. "You might try eating more sweets yourself. A few pounds on your skinny body wouldn't hurt."

Hayley glanced in the rearview mirror as she backed out. David's face had reddened, the blush spreading up from his neck to hairline. She should have at least slapped on a little lipstick when Zola told her David would be joining them. *I look terrible.*

They pulled up to a deli a few blocks away from Jazz's office, advertising European pastries. "How's this?" Hayley asked as she parallel parked the SUV.

Zola patted her belly. "Perfect. I've always wanted to try this place. My stomach is jumping up and down already."

When they'd ordered, Hayley put on her best hostess impression. "You're awfully quiet today, David," she said, hoping to draw him out. He was a mystery, with his traditional Jewish yarmulke white dress shirt and black slacks. He wore the same thing on the three occasions she'd seen him. Was he an Orthodox Jew, or more like Zola and Sol?

"I apologize," David said. His voice was low and well-modulated. "I am thinking about my upcoming residency."

"My David takes his medical training very seriously," Zola said with an affectionate pat on David's shoulder.

Hayley tried to remember if her mother had ever touched her so casually. Or Jason, for that matter. Not for a long time.

"Let's talk about you," Zola continued. "How do you think today will go with little Dixie? Isn't this the first time she's seen her mother since she was found in that dreadful homeless camp?"

Hayley swallowed her sip of tea and pushed her dessert away with a nod. "I'm worried," she said, resting her chin on her palm.

Zola reached across the table and laid her hand on Hayley's arm. "I don't blame you for being concerned. It's bound to be difficult for both of them. I've been praying nonstop ever since you told me they'd been scheduled for visits."

"I have been praying also," David added. His dark eyes bored into hers. "I believe I have a word from the Lord for you."

Hayley's heart clenched, fearful, yet curious as to what David would say. What did he mean, "a word from the Lord"? More condemnation? She dropped her hands into her lap and clasped them together.

Zola's face wore a look of concern. "*Sheyn*, David sometimes hears from God. Not necessarily in an audible voice. More like an impression. I've found his words to be correct. You'd best listen carefully."

Hayley braced herself for what was to come. Would her secret be laid bare in front of David and Zola? Would she be stripped down to her very core, naked and bleeding on the table in front of them? If Zola knew she'd had an abortion, would she withdraw her friendship? Her love?

Sol and Zola had struggled for years to have children. Zola had shared her heartbreak only once, but it was enough to know they still grieved over their empty home.

David cleared his throat. "I believe the Lord wants you to know ..."

All the noise in the deli faded as Hayley concentrated on David's face.

"... he loves you. Seek Him first and His righteousness. He offers hope to all who seek him."

Hayley almost laughed. Hope? What hope did she have when she'd sinned so badly God had to take revenge? She'd realized a long time ago God was like her mother. Be a good girl and you'll be loved and accepted. Step out of line, disappoint, and you'll pay the price.

"There's more," David said, closing his eyes. Zola leaned forward, her bulk pressing against the edge of the table. "What you seek is not what you need." David's forehead wrinkled in concentration. There was silence for a few beats. David's eyes slowly opened.

"Is that it?" Zola asked, waving one hand in front of his face.

David sighed. "It's all I have."

"What does it mean?" Zola insisted.

"That's for Mrs. Montgomery to determine," David answered, glancing Hayley's way.

"Call me Hayley," she said absently. What in the world was that all about? 'What she sought was not what she needed?' She shook her head. "I don't get it."

Zola pursed her lips. "I'd advise you to meditate on everything David said. Write it down, pray about it. I'm sure his words will become clear."

Hayley glanced up at the clock on the wall. "Oh, my, it's time to go!" She stood, gathering their empty cups.

"You didn't finish your pastry," Zola said. "Want me to box it up for you?"

Hayley shook her head, appetite gone. "No, thank you."

They finished clearing the table before heading outside in the heat. Hayley cranked up the air conditioner when they'd climbed back into the car. When they'd left the house, she wondered at the wisdom of letting David sit in the back, next to Dixie. She'd shown fear around most men. Even Sol. David didn't have that affect. Must be his almost Zen-like demeanor.

On the drive back to the agency, David's words pounded in her aching head. She'd do what Zola said, write down the words, but there was no way to comprehend what they meant. God loved her? She only knew one kind of love. Conditional. Even Jason approved when she followed his rules, catered to his needs. If not, his words belittled and wore her down until she did what he wanted.

Hayley pulled into the parking lot outside Jazzmine's office. "I'll leave the car running," she said. "I'll try not to be too long."

Hayley took a deep breath to calm her nerves. How would Dixie respond to seeing her mother? Mouth dry, Hayley approached the building.

A car was pulling out of the parking lot as she approached the door. A dark-skinned woman maneuvered a sedan. Hayley and the woman in the passenger seat locked eyes. The woman was pale with mousy brown hair. The resemblance to Dixie was unmistakable. Hayley gasped. Dixie's mother! Hayley froze until the sedan pulled into traffic and drove away.

Trembling, she pushed through the door, wondering how the visit had gone.

"Hi-ya, little mama," Jazz greeted her.

"How was it? How did she do?" Questioned tumbled from Hayley's lips as her eyes looked Dixie up and down, as if to see any physical damage.

Dixie sat on the floor of Jazzmine's cubicle, idly picking at the gray carpet. Hayley made a face. How many dirty feet had walked on that very spot? Hand sanitizer would be the first thing the minute they got into the car.

"It was fine, for a first visit. Let me know how it goes when you get home." Jazzmine made the sign of a phone with her thumb and pinky. "I'll call you later, okay?"

"Sure. Yes. Thanks." Hayley was filled with a sudden urge to grab Dixie, throw her in the car, and get home to safety. She touched Dixie's shoulder. "Come on, little one, let's go."

Dixie stood without any more urging. When they reached the door, Hayley half-turned. "Thank you, Jazz." Jazzmine's intentions were to reunite Dixie with her birth mom, and at the moment Hayley resented her for it.

They drove home in silence. Dixie dozed in the car seat. Even Zola was subdued, as if overtaken by the seriousness of the day's events.

Hayley pulled over in front of Zola's house to let her and David out.

"Bye, neighbor," Zola called as they walked toward their front door. David didn't say anything, and he didn't acknowledge his aunt or her. Disappointed, Hayley pulled forward and into her own garage.

She hefted a sleepy Dixie out of the car. When Hayley opened the door from the garage to the kitchen, Dixie collapsed on the floor and burst into tears. Jumping up, she dashed for the pantry, yanking the door open.

Too late, Hayley realized she'd forgotten to lock it. Before she could react, Dixie had gotten into a package of crackers and shoved a fistful into her mouth, still sobbing like she'd been beaten.

Dixie sprawled on the floor, tears pouring down her face. Mama looked different. Smelled different. Her voice was the same. She'd waited for Mama to yell at her. She didn't. Mama kept looking at the lady who was in the room. Where was the lady named Hayley? All she wanted was to crawl under the bed with Brown Bear.

CHAPTER 23

Hayley blew out a breath through puffed cheeks. Dealing with Dixie's meltdown had taken every energy reserve she'd had. She stumbled into the master bedroom and collapsed onto the bed, asleep within moments.

Her eyes flew open an hour later when her cell chirped with an incoming text.

JASON: How was the visit with the mother?

Hayley stared at the text for several moments. As if he cared. He didn't even mention Dixie's name.

She struggled to a sitting position, fingers poised over the phone, inclined to ignore the text. Knowing Jason, he'd keep texting until she answered. Or he'd call. She wasn't up to talking to him yet. The police visit scared her.

Standing, she grabbed for the nightstand as she was hit with a sudden wave of lightheadedness.

Guess I'd better eat something.

A peek into the pink bedroom showed Dixie fast asleep. With a smile of satisfaction, Hayley noted the child was still in the bed. Small steps. Would it all be for nothing if Dixie went back to her mother?

Downstairs, Hayley stared into the refrigerator. Nothing looked or sounded appealing. With a sigh, she closed the door and headed to the pantry.

A knock on the French door leading to the back yard made her spin around in alarm.

"Hi, neighbor!" Zola's friendly greeting brought a smile to Hayley's face.

Hurrying, she opened the door, and Zola swept in carrying a pan of rich-smelling brownies.

"Brought you some sustenance," Zola said, setting the pan on the counter with a flourish.

Zola had pulled her gray hair up into a messy bun. Even with her hair up, she looked every bit the Earth Mother.

Hayley's mouth watered. "I'll get a knife."

"Got milk?" Zola asked with a grin.

Hayley waved toward the fridge. "Grab a glass for both of us."

While Hayley served generous pieces of brownie onto silver-rimmed plates, Zola poured two glasses of milk.

"How's the wild child?" Zola bit into a brownie and moaned with pleasure.

Hayley did the same. When she'd washed down her bit with some milk, she answered, "She had a massive meltdown the minute we walked through the door. I expected it, though. The last two little girls did the same every time they saw their dad."

"Breaks your heart, doesn't it?" Zola pinched off another bite.

Hayley nodded. "Makes me wonder what will happen when her mother gets custody back."

"How long will that take?"

Hayley rubbed a hand across her forehead. "Not for a while. She'll have to get out of rehab, stay clean, and prove she has a stable home environment."

"So, not a cardboard box?"

Hayley pursed her lips and shook her head. "Definitely not a cardboard box in a homeless camp."

Zola reached across the table and rested her hand on Hayley's. "This is a good thing you're doing. I have to ask why?" Zola released her hold and waved her arm. "You have all this. Beautiful home, husband, and the ability to have your own children."

Zola's eyes focused on her with laser intensity.

How could she put her motives into words Zola would understand? Zola's God seemed to be one of forgiveness.

"Let me go check on Dixie." She was stalling and she knew it. Hayley dashed up the stairs and peeked in on the sleeping child, taking a moment to gather her thoughts before padding back downstairs. How much should she tell Zola? The need to confess to someone, anyone, urged her into the kitchen.

Zola had cut another brownie for both. "I know I shouldn't," Zola said, patting her protruding belly. "We need comfort food right now."

Hayley sank onto the chair facing Zola without making eye contact. "You wanted to know why I decided to become a foster parent." Out of the corner of her eye she saw Zola nod. "When I was in college, I met a man. His name was Johann. I fell head over heels for him. I thought he felt the same. I did something I knew was wrong. After he graduated and returned to South Africa without me, I discovered I was pregnant."

Hayley paused, remembering the devastation of his casual goodbye.

I had fun, Sissie. I will have a hard time forgetting you.

She'd begged him to stay, begged him to take her with him. Away from her mother's control. He'd waved goodbye, climbed into a taxi, and was gone.

"Oh, no," Zola said. "What did you do? Did you tell him? Was Cynthia—"

"No, Cynthia was Jason's." Hayley picked at a loose thread in the place mat. *Here it goes.* "I had an abortion." She waited for Zola's intake of breath, her disgust. Her disappointment. The brownie she'd eaten threatened to make its way back up to her throat. She quickly raised her eyes to Zola's.

"I'm sorry, dearie." Zola's eyes filled with tears. "How desperate you must have been. I wish I had been there to help you through that time."

Tears that burned the corners of Hayley's eyes pushed their way out and down her cheeks. "I murdered my child," she said with a wail. "And God took Cynthia as punishment."

Jason glanced at his phone for the seventh time in the previous ten minutes. He'd sent a text to Hayley, asking about the kid and hoping his text would placate her for the time being. The screen was blank. No return text. Was she still mad? Probably. This was a new side of her he hadn't seen before. Hayley was usually malleable as a marshmallow, easy to direct.

Jason rubbed the back of his neck with one hand. What did he need to do? Maybe send her some flowers. That usually worked. He logged on to a local florist's website and used his company credit card to order a dozen red roses. He gritted his teeth and paid the extra money for same-day delivery.

Tapping his fingers on the desk, he checked his phone again. Still no response. He thought about calling before dismissing the idea. His wife should come to him. After everything he'd done for her, she should be grateful. He'd agreed to the whole foster thing to stop her nagging. Her misguided idea she somehow needed to make amends for Cynthia's death haunted her. They needed to have their own kids. He needed another child to fill the hole left in his heart since Cynthia ...

No use going down that path. He shoved the guilt down into the dark cellar where it belonged. Besides, it was Hayley's fault. If she hadn't gone back into the house for a bottle of water, Cynthia wouldn't have ridden into the street. Ten, no, five minutes later and nothing would have happened.

Jason smacked his fist down on the desk and stood, shoving his chair back. He paced the small office.

Jason had never raised a hand to Hayley or anyone, although he'd come close that day. He cursed the fates that had pushed him to drive after drinking over his limit. He cursed the car that was too easy to accelerate. He cursed his wife for not being a better mother. Finally, he cursed himself.

The knock on his office door pulled him out of his dark thoughts. Chad never knocked. Jason strode to the door and grabbed the handle, pulling it open with a jerk.

Two men in dark suits stood in the hall, Chad crowding their backs.

"Jason Montgomery?" one of them asked.

Jason nodded, feeling the blood rush to his head.

"We'd like you to come down to the station so we can ask you a few questions."

Jazzmine tossed her bag onto Rusty's passenger seat and climbed in. She started the car and turned the air conditioner on full blast. Her first call was to her husband, Ezekiel. His voice mail let her know he was unavailable and to leave a message.

"Hi, baby. Wanted to let you know I'm on my way home. Can't wait to see you."

The next call was to Hayley.

"Hello?" Hayley's muffled voice sounded as if she'd been crying.

"Hi-ya, mama. Calling to check in."

Hayley sniffed. "Hi, Jazz."

Jazzmine placed an earpiece in her ear and switched the phone to hands-free as she pulled out of the foster agency parking lot. "What's wrong?"

"Oh, Jazz. It's, well, everything."

"Talk to me, sweetie."

Hayley breathed against the phone. "Dixie had a huge meltdown when we got home. My neighbor came over with brownies, and I ate too many and threw up. My husband sent me flowers. And I don't even like red roses!"

Jazzmine suppressed the urge to laugh. "Meltdowns are expected. It's difficult for kids, especially ones like Dixie, to process the visitations with a birth parent."

"I know," Hayley wailed. "It's ..."

"Go on," urged Jazzmine. What wasn't Hayley telling her?

"My neighbor, Zola, I think you've met her. She asked me why I was fostering."

There was a pause and Jazzmine resisted the urge to interject.

"I—I'm wondering if I've made a huge mistake." Hayley sniffled again.

I need wisdom, Lord. What should she say? Hayley and Jason had been thoroughly vetted through the licensing process. Though she'd only talked to Jason once or twice, he seemed committed. Hayley's degree in early childhood development and her minor in psychology made her a perfect fit. She'd seemed to be handling her daughter's death with a normal amount of grief. Why was she now questioning the decision to foster parent?

Jazzmine maneuvered the car onto the freeway, merging into the afternoon commute. "You're doing such a great job with little Dixie. She seems to be flourishing under your care. Is there something else bothering you?"

Hayley sighed into the phone. "I don't know. It's so … difficult."

"Of course it is," Jazzmine said. "Dixie has been through stuff we'll never be able to understand. Oh—before I forget—I found out how Dixie got her name. You'll get a kick out of this." Maybe this would distract Hayley from her funk.

"Really?" Hayley asked with a bit more energy in her voice.

"I asked Dixie's mom about her name. She told me after she delivered the baby, the nurse asked what she was going to name her. The mom was thirsty, so she asked for a drink of water. They brought her a Dixie cup filled with ice water. And that's where she got her name."

"You've got to be kidding."

"Nope. You have to laugh, or you'll cry. Imagine carrying a baby for nine months and never once thinking about what to name her." Jazzmine couldn't conceive of the notion. She'd had the names picked out for all the kids she'd planned to have. When life handed her three foster kids after Marcus was born, she accepted she'd never have another natural baby. Until Hosea. He was her miracle baby. Her only regret was not having a little girl to dress up.

"It's kind of sad," Hayley said. "We named Cynthia after my grandmother's middle name. It seemed to fit her."

Jazzmine murmured her agreement. "If there's something else you want to talk about, let me know."

"I think I'll be okay. I needed a moment. It's been a long day."

"Okay, sweetie. Tell Jason hi from me."

There was a long pause before Hayley answered. "Okay."

A feeling of dread settled in the pit of Jazzmine's stomach. Something was wrong in the Montgomery house. Behind the beautifully carved front door simmered an undercurrent. She felt the urge to pray. For what, she didn't know. The Spirit knew. Jazzmine obeyed.

Zola's visit left Hayley unsettled. She'd thrown up the brownies, drunk another glass of milk to wash away the yucky taste in her mouth. Dixie sat under the table, pushing a block back and forth, Brown Bear in her lap.

Hayley cut up some cheese and put some crackers on a plate, all the while keeping one eye on Dixie, lest she jump up and try to grab the food. She was sneaky that way. And quick. Hayley had to be two steps ahead when it came to anything edible.

After filling a sippy cup with juice, Hayley sank onto the floor across from Dixie. She set an empty plate on the floor, putting one chunk of cheese on it. Dixie abandoned the block and plucked the cheese off the plate, shoving a piece into her mouth, bouncing up and down on her bottom while she devoured the treat.

Hayley did the same thing with one cracker. When would Dixie trust her enough to know food in this house would always be available? Hayley went through the motions of feeding the child, her mind elsewhere.

Zola had talked about God's forgiveness. About grace. She'd said God wasn't in the business of taking a child simply because a woman had an abortion. Zola mentioned all the hundreds of thousands of women who'd done the same thing since Roe vs. Wade. Did all those women have another baby God killed?

Hayley couldn't argue with Zola's logic.

The grace thing had her baffled. If she couldn't do anything to please God on her own, why try? Wasn't that what she was doing by fostering?

"Come on, little one. Let's see if we can get you to eat at the table." Hayley stood, plate of food in her hand.

"No more food until you come out from under the table." Hayley beckoned to Dixie, waving the plate.

Dixie's face scrunched into a scowl. "More," she said.

"That's right. You can have more. Come on out."

"More," Dixie demanded, her voice rising.

Hayley smiled. This was normal childhood behavior, a battle of wills. Cynthia had tried her patience many times.

Her phone chirped with a text.

JASON: Call me!

Jason. Hayley shoved the phone away. He could wait.

"Come on, sweet girl. Let's finish your snack up here."

Hayley coaxed again and again while Dixie grew angrier, trying to reach the plate.

With a sigh, Dixie stood.

"Good girl. Now sit here." Hayley pulled a chair near her own, patting the seat. After a few minutes of wrangling Dixie into the seat while keeping the cheese and crackers away, she had Dixie settled.

"Whew." Hayley exhaled with relief. Her phone rang. "Not again," she said, expecting Jason. Instead the caller was Hannah.

"Hello, sister mine," Hannah greeted her. "I need your help."

Hayley swallowed back a sarcastic response. This was Hannah's typical MO. No niceties like *hi, how are you? What's going on in your world*. Straight to her own needs.

Hannah didn't wait for a response. "I want you to be my maid of honor. Let's go dress shopping Saturday. Mom wants to go, of course."

Hayley looked at Dixie, happily eating her snack. The last thing she wanted to do was go wedding dress shopping with Hannah and Mother. She pictured Hannah as Bridezilla, piling drama upon drama, with Mother calling the shots.

Hayley would much rather be here, working with this sweet little girl. Her heart swelled with pride at how far Dixie had come.

Please, God, let me keep her a little longer.

Wait, had she uttered a prayer?

Hayley sat back, the crackers and cheese momentarily forgotten. She hadn't prayed since, well, she couldn't remember the last time.

Hannah's voice interrupted her train of thought. "Are you still there? Sheesh, Hayley, can you pay attention to someone other than yourself for one minute?"

"I'm sorry. What were you saying?" Hayley blocked Dixie's lunge for the plate of food.

Hannah's sigh echoed through the phone. "I said, we'll meet at eleven o'clock at Mom and Dad's, grab some brunch, then go to the bridal shop."

"Oh, well, I have to see if I can get respite care for Dixie."

"What about Jason? Can't he do it?" Hannah snapped.

Hayley froze. What about Jason? No, that wouldn't work. Dixie was clearly afraid of him. Of all men. Except Zola's nephew, David.

"I don't think so." Hayley stood, carrying the empty plate to the sink.

"I thought I could count on you, Hayley. After all, you got the big wedding, and now it's my turn. Can you not be selfish and get someone to watch her so we can have a little fun? Don't you want to be my maid of honor?" Hannah sniffed.

A knife-thrust of guilt slid between Hayley's ribs. She was always letting someone down. Jason, her mother, Hannah, Cynthia. Especially Cynthia. Not Dixie. This time she'd get things right.

"I'll see what I can do," Hayley said with a sigh.

"Good. I'll see you Saturday." Hannah disconnected.

Hayley leaned back against the kitchen counter, eying Dixie sitting at the table. "Come on, sweet girl. Let's go watch a video."

Dixie slid off the chair and headed into the living room. While the Dora video played, Hayley replayed the conversation with Zola.

"God didn't take Cynthia because you had an abortion. He doesn't work that way, *khaverte.*"

Was it possible God had already forgiven her? According to Zola, Jesus had paid the price for everyone's sin—past, present, and future. Hayley remembered a prayer she'd said at summer camp when she was sixteen. She'd asked Jesus into her heart, and somehow the commitment had been forgotten.

After a few months of attending youth group at the church they attended, she'd stopped going. She didn't fit in. With her designer clothes and BMW sports car, the other girls shunned her as too good for them.

Which was why Johann's attention captured her, making her vulnerable to his need of physical intimacy. Along came Jason, with his persistence wearing her down. Mother approved of him, and her not-so-gentle shoves toward marriage made Hayley acquiesce. The way she always did.

With a start, she remembered Jason's text. He'd be furious by now at her lack of response. With a sweaty hand, she punched his number from her list of favorites.

Hayley sighed with relief when her call went straight to voice mail. He probably thought he was punishing her by not answering. Not the first time he'd done it.

This time, Hayley would stand up to him. She had Dixie to consider first.

Her phone rang again. This time Zola's face filled the screen.

"Hi, *mishpocheh,* I thought I'd call to see how you were doing."

"*Mishpocheh*?"

Zola laughed. "It means family. Am I going to have to get you a Yiddish dictionary?"

Hayley crossed her legs under her on the sofa. "Perhaps. Or you could stick to English."

"Ah, *sheyn*, that's not possible."

Hayley knew the English translation for *sheyn* was "beautiful." At this moment, she felt anything but. When she'd vomited earlier, she'd gotten some on her green workout shirt. Greasy marks on her yoga pants were evidence she'd wiped her hands on them more than once. Any makeup she'd applied in the morning was long gone.

"How is little Dixie?" Zola asked.

Hayley glanced at the little girl before answering. Dixie had her thumb in her mouth. The other hand clutched Brown Bear. "She's doing well. I got her to sit at the table."

"That's huge! Good for you. Did you tell Jason the news?"

"Uh, not yet. He didn't answer his phone."

"*Feh*, he's probably busy."

Zola continued, "How are you doing after our conversation?"

Hayley absently stroked Dixie's hair while pondering her answer. "You've certainly given me a lot to think about." Her brain whirled with all the events of the past few hours. Dixie's first supervised visit with her mother, the confession to Zola about her abortion, Jason's attempt to make up by sending flowers. She still hadn't told anyone about the visit from the two policemen.

Jason had yet to explain why he'd told her he was an only child, and his parents were dead. His convoluted story about his special-needs brother didn't add up. Who was the man she'd married?

"Zola, have you ever wondered if you made a mistake marrying Sol?" Hayley held her breath, waiting for Zola's answer.

Zola chuckled. "Only about twice a month."

Hayley heard the ding of Zola's microwave in the background. "Really?"

"Oh, *khaverte*, every woman feels that way from time to time. We look at our husbands and wonder if we could have done better. I have to remind myself God brought us together. Who am I to question His will?"

Hayley stood and walked to the window overlooking the back yard. Yellow dandelions stood in bright contrast against the green lawn. She'd forgotten to call the landscape service. Again. Another thing to reap Jason's annoyance.

"But, what if ... what if God didn't bring people together?"

"Are you talking about you and Jason?"

Hayley pressed her forehead against the glass. "Maybe."

Zola was silent for a few moments. Hayley pictured her setting out food for Sol and her nephew. What would her life have been if she'd married someone like David? Handsome, gentle David.

Instead, she'd married someone who was becoming more and more a stranger. He hadn't been truthful about his past.

Neither have you. Ouch. She'd never told Jason about Johann and her pregnancy. He thought she was a virgin when they married, and she never corrected him. Would he have married her if he'd known?

Zola answered, "The question is, do you think you've made a mistake?"

Did she? Lately, it seemed she couldn't determine where Jason ended, and she began. She used to be confident, assured of her place. Or was she? Maybe once the onion of herself was peeled back, there was nothing in the center. Jason used to make her feel like she belonged, unconditionally loved. Slowly, like the proverbial frog in the pot of water, she'd allowed Jason to control her every move, her every thought.

"I-I'm not sure." Hayley cringed, remembering how she'd rush to change out of her workout clothes into crisp shorts and a top before Jason got home from work. How she'd freshen up her lipstick and do a quick run-through of the house to be sure everything was neat and tidy.

"He expects a lot from you, doesn't he?" Zola asked.

Hayley hesitated, warring between wanting to say yes, and being loyal to her husband. "Sometimes."

Hayley heard the crackle of popcorn being dumped into a bowl. Her mouth watered, imagining the smell. Too bad her stomach didn't share the feeling. All the stress was wreaking havoc on her appetite. At least she didn't need to worry about those few pounds added to her waist.

"Have you thought about counseling?" Zola's voice was muffled, as if she carried the phone between her ear and shoulder.

Hayley huffed out a laugh. "Jason would never agree to it." As far as she could tell, the only two people besides her Jason talked to were his partner Chad and her mom. Sometimes she believed her mother loved Jason more than her. He never seemed to disappoint Mother.

"I'm sorry, *sheyn*, I have to go. Sol just walked through the door. I will pray for you, my dear."

Hayley disconnected and tossed the phone on the sofa. "Come on, sweet girl. Let's go jump in the pool until it's time to fix dinner."

With no call or text from Jason, there was no telling when he'd be home. At this point, Hayley didn't care.

Jason strode to his car, the stench from the police station clinging to his clothes. His fists clenched and unclenched, remembering how they'd made him wait in the cramped room until he could call his attorney. The two officers tried to intimidate him into answering questions, but he'd shown them who was in control.

"I want my lawyer." The words echoed in the tiny interrogation room, no bigger than his walk-in closet at home.

He jammed the key into the ignition and the SUV roared to life. While waiting for the air conditioning to cool the car's interior, he powered up his phone. Hayley must be frantic by now. His one phone call had been to Thomas Chao, his and Chad's business attorney.

Only one text from Hayley.

HAYLEY: Where are you?

He quickly speed-dialed Chad. The call went directly to Chad's voice mail.

No need to call his wife. He'd be home in less than twenty minutes. What to tell her?

Jason pulled out of the parking lot and headed toward the freeway on ramp. His eye was caught by a business card, stuck in the sun visor. With one eye on the road, he pulled the card out. It was from the talkative guy on the plane. Pastor Ben. He tossed the card on the passenger seat. He didn't need spiritual guidance. What he needed was a good alibi.

Thirty minutes later, the familiar sight of his home came into view. He tapped his fingers on the steering wheel while waiting for the garage door to lift.

The door to the kitchen flew open before he could turn the car off.

"Where have you been, Jason?" Hayley's arms were crossed, and she looked a combination of angry and worried.

"At least let me get into the house before you start." Jason slammed the door with enough force to rock the SUV back and forth.

Hayley stepped out of the way as he pushed past her into the house, squinting against the brightness. Was every light in the house on?

"Where were you? I was worried. Why didn't you answer my text?" Hayley's voice pierced his aching head.

"Give me a minute, will you?" Jason strode to the refrigerator and pulled out a bottled iced tea. What he wouldn't give for a shot of whiskey right now. Not an option. Alcohol was what got him into this situation in the first place.

He downed half the bottle, setting the remainder on the counter. Looking around the kitchen, he noticed an open loaf of bread, a jar of peanut butter, two dirty plates, and a sippy cup.

"The kitchen is a mess."

"You're four hours late coming home and all you can say is 'the kitchen is a mess'?" Hayley's hair swung around her face as she shook her head.

This was not the Hayley he'd married. The old Hayley would have scurried to clean up, eager to please. Acquiescent. He didn't like this new Hayley. Jason's mind raced to come up with an appropriate response.

"Did you get my flowers?" He held his breath, waiting for her rush of thanks for his thoughtful extravagance.

Hayley rubbed her face with both hands. "Oh, Jason. You don't get me, do you?"

He took a step closer. "I want to get you. Really." He reached for her. She took a step away.

"First of all," she ticked up one finger. "I hate roses. Second, you're home late, and I've been crazy with worry." Another finger. "Third, you can't even give me an explanation for why."

"I was at the police station," he blurted.

"Where?" Hayley leaned toward him, her face a mask of confusion. "Why?"

"They think I had something to do with Cynthia's death." There. He'd said it. Out loud.

The silence in the kitchen was broken by the sound of ice dropping into the freezer from the ice maker.

Hayley's voice was barely above a whisper.

"Did you?"

A Grand Canyon-sized chasm opened between him and his wife. The need to confess everything was hindered by the knowledge his answer would change his world. He opened his mouth to speak. Nothing could get past the guilt lodged in his throat.

The silence lengthened.

Hayley's face turned white. With a strangled cry, she dashed out of the kitchen and up the stairs.

"Hayley, wait. I can explain." Could he?

His heart pounded as he ran up the stairs. The door to the master bedroom was closed. Leaning, Jason let his head rest against the door. With shaking hands, he pushed down on the door handle and slowly stepped into the room. Hayley had collapsed on the floor, sobbing. One fist pounded the carpet. Jason leaned over and laid a hand on her back.

She whirled around. "Don't touch me!" Her eyes were filled with hatred. "You killed our baby! All this time, you made me think her death was my fault. It was you."

Jason sank onto the bed, head down. "It wasn't my fault. I had too much to drink. Chad should have made me ride with him." Words poured from him. He wasn't sure Hayley heard, so he kept speaking. "I didn't even see her. She was so little. So beautiful. I—" A sob burst from him. "They're probably going to arrest me. I'll go to prison."

Bile rose in his throat. His beautifully crafted life crumbled. The family he'd created, his dream of sailing away from everything, all the money, gone. At that moment, he wished he'd never been born. This was a mess not fixable with money, power, or force of will.

He had a sudden vision of Pastor Ben, talking to him on the plane.

"I wondered how a merciful and loving God could let an innocent child suffer. I reminded myself God is in control, even when things look the darkest. That's when I cried out to Him for peace. And believe it or not, He gave me peace."

At the time, Jason thought his words sounded trite. Now he wasn't sure. He'd made a mess of his life and he was the only one to blame. Not Hayley, not Chad, not his parents. Tears filled his eyes, overflowing down his cheeks, hot and burning. He collapsed on the floor next to his wife.

"I'm sorry. I'm so sorry." A new feeling filled him. Remorse. "I've blown it. Please forgive me." Jason wasn't sure if he was talking to Hayley or to God. "Help me make this right. Take the miserable mess I've made of my life. It's yours."

At that moment, he knew he was talking to God.

CHAPTER 24

Dixie stood in the shadow of the hallway, listening to the sound of crying. The man was on his knees next to the bed. Her heart pounded hard in her chest, so hard she was afraid the sound would carry into the bedroom.

The carpet tickled her bare feet as she crept toward them. She focused her attention on the man, no longer scary. She felt his fear. What was he afraid of? His sadness filled the room and spilled onto her. Words poured from him like the water pouring from his eyes.

Dixie placed her hand on the man's back. Heat radiated from him. She kept her hand on him until he stilled under her touch.

She crept back to the pink bedroom.

An unfamiliar sound from the baby monitor roused Hayley from the sleep that had finally claimed her aching body. She rolled to her side and pushed herself into a sitting position. What was Dixie up to?

Grabbing the sports bottle sitting on the nightstand, she swallowed some water to soothe her aching throat. Jason's side of the bed was empty, his pillow cold. After his failed attempt to comfort her when they were both in bed, he'd turned on his side, away from her, and scooted to the far side of the bed.

Fresh grief filled her burning eyes with more tears. How could she have not known Jason was at fault all this time? The times he'd deflected her comments about not driving the Miata. His unwillingness to speculate on who might have driven the car that killed their baby. Shouldn't her mother's intuition have kicked in, suspecting something wasn't quite right?

Or had she been so used to acquiescing to her husband she let him brush her questions away? How dare he let her take the blame. Resolve strengthened her backbone as she stood, ready for battle. First, what Dixie was doing?

Hayley paused in the doorway of Dixie's bedroom. "What in the world?"

Dixie had pulled out every drawer in the dresser and scattered the contents all over the room. Dixie stood in the middle of the mess wearing a mismatched outfit of striped shorts and a flowered shirt.

Hayley couldn't help smiling despite the grief resting on her shoulders.

"You look awfully proud of yourself, missy."

Her heart swelled with motherly pride at Dixie's normal childhood behavior. "Let's go get some breakfast."

"Brock-foss," Dixie repeated.

"That's right, sweet girl. Breakfast. We're going to eat breakfast." Hayley's stomach growled. The thought of food brought bile up into the back of her throat.

They padded down the stairs together. Hayley froze at the door to the kitchen. Her husband sat at the table, iPad propped up next to a steaming cup of coffee. A glance toward the Keurig machine showed three empty pods on the counter. Did he seriously expect her to clean up after him? After what he'd done?

Hot anger replaced the queasiness in her stomach. Anger turned to surprise when Dixie pushed past her and trotted to the table, taking a seat across from Jason. He glanced at the child, at her, and back down to his iPad.

Pancakes were on the agenda this morning, but her arms were like ten-pound weights. Last night's revelation and subsequent crying jag had her weak and shaky. Brushing past the back of Jason's chair, she headed for the fridge and pulled out a package of frozen waffles kept on hand for emergencies.

Jamming one into the toaster, she leaned her back against the counter, arms crossed, and observed her husband tapping away on his iPad as if nothing had happened. As if he wasn't guilty of murdering their little girl.

"I'll call the landscapers today," he said.

"Really, Jason? That's all you have to say?" What did she expect? An apology? As if "I'm sorry" would make everything right.

Head down, he spoke again. "I've made a list of everything I have to do before—"

"Before what?"

Jason continued as if she hadn't spoken. "I wrote out all the online passwords for banking and stuff. It's next to my laptop upstairs."

What alternate world had she woken to, where Jason responded with eerie calm, and Dixie sat unafraid of him across the table?

His eyes held a mixture of guilt and grief when they caught hers. How dare he sit there like he hadn't shattered their world.

"I'm going to visit my dad today. He's in the hospital." Jason rubbed his hands on his jean-clad thigh. "I should have gone when my mom first called, but—"

"You mean the parents you told me were dead?" The words shot toward him with laser intensity. Hayley needed him to respond with his normal way of making her the one at fault. She'd capitulate, grovel, and the world would return to normal.

Jason nodded. "I should have told you." He took a deep breath and blew it out. The chair scraped across the tile floor as he stood. "Hayley, I—"

The toaster sprang up with a pop. "Whatever you're going to say, Jason, don't. There's nothing you can say or do to make this right." She buttered the waffle with savage gestures, hoping to hurt him as much as he'd hurt her. How could he stand there and act as if this was any other day?

Stifling a sob, she cut the waffle into tiny pieces and began to feed them to Dixie, one at a time.

For once, Dixie accepted each piece as it was set in front of her without grabbing for the plate. What was happening? Hayley was the only one in this weird play without a script. Jason was calm, Dixie was calm, and she was roiling with rage and grief.

Glaring at him, she said with force, "Get out." Her eyes dared him to argue.

Jason sighed. His eyes searched the room, and Hayley waited for the criticism she knew was coming. He insisted the counters be free of clutter, the floor spotless, and the blinds closed.

He grabbed his iPad and clutched it to his chest. "I'm leaving in a few minutes. As I said, I'm going to visit my dad. After that, I'm going to turn myself in."

"What?" Hayley dropped the piece of waffle she'd been holding.

Jason's voice wavered. "I'm going to the police station and turn myself in."

Hayley sprang to her feet. "No."

"I have to, Lee. They're probably going to arrest me for hit and run. Vehicular manslaughter, whatever." That sounded more like the old Jason. Sarcastic. Deflecting blame.

"What am I going to do if you go to jail?" A thousand scenarios flooded her brain. What would she tell her parents? Zola? What about Jazzmine? Would they take Dixie away from her?

Jason rubbed his head with one hand. "Would you rather I go myself to the police station or wait for them to drag me away in handcuffs? How would that look to all the neighbors?"

That was pure Jason, worried about looking good.

He shrugged. "I know it's too little, too late. I'm sorry. Sorry about everything. I messed up, Lee. I know you'll never look at me the same, and it kills me. I wish ..." He shrugged again and shuffled out of the kitchen. At the door, he turned around. "I'm sorry I didn't help you with Dixie."

Tears sprang to Hayley's eyes as she filled a sippy cup with milk and set it in front of Dixie. She sank onto the chair where Jason had sat and rested her head on the table. This was too much to take in. Everything had changed in the space of a few hours. The truth about Cynthia's death was enough to break her already-bruised heart. How dare he blame her all this time? She'd gone down the self-hate road for so long she feared never finding the way back. Jason kept his secret for almost a year. How could he?

A tiny niggle of conscience wormed its way into her aching head. You kept a secret too. The words accused, bit. *You killed your baby, like he did. You're both guilty of murder.*

Jason surveyed the bedroom where he and Hayley had fought, made up, and fought some more. The carpet at the end of the bed was still tamped down from where they had both collapsed the night before. Something happened last night. He still remembered the feeling of peace that had overwhelmed him when he'd prayed. This morning, the world looked different. Brighter. How could that be when confronted with the awful thing he'd done?

The truth shall set you free.

Where did that come from? Some long-forgotten Sunday school verse? Or one of the motivational posters his partner, Chad, insisted on hanging in their office? He'd never really be free, not from the guilt of killing his own little girl. Nor from lying to Hayley about his past. Or from all the times he'd made Hayley feel lesser, to make himself feel better.

Jason's eyes were caught by a stuffed animal sitting on one of the chairs in front of the window. He strode over and picked it up. A bear. Cynthia used to have a similar toy. Brown Bear.

Holding the bear to his chest, he sank onto the chair and took another look around the room. The jail cell wouldn't be at all like this. There wouldn't be a walk-in closet for his designer clothes. No mini fridge to keep bottled water cold so he wouldn't have to go downstairs. Or make Hayley go down to fetch him one. The next thought made him wince. No private bathroom big enough to hold twenty people.

He stood up, dropped the bear, and slapped his thighs. No use waiting any longer. Grabbing his wallet and car keys, he strode out of the bedroom with a sense of resolve.

First to the hospital. Afterward, head to the police station.

In the kitchen, Hayley sat at the table, feeding Dixie small bits of apple, avoiding Jason's gaze.

"I'm taking off now. If you need anything, let Chad know."

"Why would I ask Chad for help?" Hayley's mouth twisted into a sneer. "I haven't divorced myself from *my* parents."

Jason pressed his lips together to hold back a nasty response. "You're right. Call your mom or dad." The keys jingled as he removed the house keys from the ring. "I'll make arrangements for my car to be picked up and brought back here."

What else was there to say? Goodbye hardly seemed fitting. It wasn't as if he was dying, though what was in his future might be worse than death. Too many words and still there was no way to make things right.

"Well, I guess that's it. I'll try to keep you posted."

Hayley spoke as he reached for the door.

"I hate you."

He paused. "I know." He stepped into the garage and pulled the door closed behind him.

While waiting for the big garage door to open, his eyes rested on the Miata, still shrouded by a tan cover. He approached the car as if it was a rabid dog. With shaking fingers, he pulled back the cover. Barely an indent marred the perfect black bumper. Tears burned his eyes as his shoulders sagged with the weight of guilt.

The third margarita was what tipped him over the edge. Or was it the fourth? One do-over and things would be different.

The big SUV roared to life. Before he pulled out of the garage, a white piece of paper caught his eye. The business card he'd casually tossed on the passenger seat the night before. He tucked the card in his shirt pocket for later.

"Siri, call Mom." The sound of a phone ringing filled the speakers.

"Jason? Is it really you?"

"Yes, Mom, it's really me."

"It's good to hear your voice. I have Dad here. I know he'd love to talk to you." Garbled sounds came through the car's speakers. "Jason, tell your father hello."

"Hi, Dad. How are you?"

Silence.

His mom whispered, "He can't talk since the stroke."

More guilt. He should have been there for his mother. How long had it been since he'd seen his parents, much less talked to them? Way before he and Hayley got married.

"Tell Dad I'm on my way to the hospital. Tell him we can talk when I get there, okay?"

"Okay." She choked back a sob, disconnected.

Jason tried to recall the feeling he'd had the night before when he'd fallen on his knees. So much peace. Maybe even forgiveness. Was that possible?

Pulling out the business card, he dialed the number listed.

"Hello?"

"Hi, um, this is Jason Montgomery. We met last week on the flight from Los Angeles to Sacramento."

"I remember." Pastor Ben's voice revealed nothing.

"I need to talk to you."

"Okay. When?"

Jason pressed his lips together. After a moment, he said, "Can you meet me at the Sacramento Police Department in, say, about an hour and a half?"

"Police?"

Jason's heart thudded hard against his rib cage. When was the last time he'd asked for help from anyone? He'd always been the one with the answers. The expert in his field. Even Chad was awed at times. Was this guy going to make him grovel?

"I have to do something, and I'd appreciate if you could be there. If you can, that is." He held his breath for Pastor Ben's answer.

He heard shuffling papers. "I can rearrange some things. Shall we meet in the parking lot?

Jason squeezed his eyes shut. "Sure. How about I call you when I get there."

"Sounds good. Can you tell me what this is about?"

How much should he say? "Well, I..." He, what? Was about to go to jail and needed someone to hold his hand. Fat chance. That wasn't him. Asking for help showed weakness, and he never wanted to be that person.

Maybe he should forget the idea of having this Ben guy come and babysit him. The thought of showing up at the police department turned the coffee in his stomach to acid.

He wiped a sweaty palm down his pants. "Look, I probably shouldn't have called you—"

"No, it's fine," Ben said. "You can explain when I get there."

"Fine." Jason gripped the steering wheel with white knuckles as he neared the hospital. Guilt tore through him at the thought of his dad being so close to him physically, yet miles apart emotionally. He'd blamed them for too long.

Now it was time to man up.

Or was it? Maybe he should keep driving, away from everything and everybody. The urge to escape overpowered rational thought.

Stop at the bank, withdraw every last dollar, and keep driving. The voice shouted inside his head. You could disappear in Mexico. Or central America. Live like a king on the beach. You don't want to go to jail. You're not a bad guy. You made one mistake. It shouldn't cost you your freedom.

Jason banged his fist on the steering wheel, then shot across two lanes of traffic to merge onto the freeway. Away from the hospital.

Two exits later, he slowed, took the offramp, and coasted to a stop at the signal. No, he would face his parents and face the crime. Maybe he'd be out of jail by the time Hayley turned thirty, and they could still live out his dream of buying a yacht and sailing around the world. This would be a blip, a speed bump in their marriage. He'd figure out a way to make it work. He always did.

Making a U-turn in the street, he headed back toward the hospital and pulled into the parking garage. He turned the car off and sat, hands on the steering wheel.

"Dear God." How were you supposed to pray? "I, um, need your help." What did that even mean? What a lame prayer.

Would his parents hate him for avoiding them for so long? Had they turned his brother, Danny, against him? Did they know about Cynthia?

His stomach churned with an uncomfortable feeling. Remorse. Sweat beaded on his forehead as he sat in the gradually warming car. Probably not a good idea to park on the top level in full-on Sacramento sun.

Best get this over with quickly. He jogged down the concrete steps, strode through the walkway and into the air-conditioned hospital.

"Sign in, sir, and get your visitor badge," instructed the young front desk volunteer. "And I'll need to see your ID."

Jason fished his driver's license out of his wallet. How much longer would he be able to identify himself with a driver's license instead of an inmate number?

He exchanged his father's name for a visitor badge which he stuck to his shirt.

"Room 403b."

"Thanks."

The elevator ride didn't give him enough time to plan what he'd say. Before he knew it, Jason was standing at the door to his dad's room.

"Gomorrah." Garbled words came from his dad's mouth as he pointed to Jason.

"Jason!" squealed his mom, rushing to him and wrapping her arms around him in a warm hug. Pulling away, she placed her hands on his arms and gazed into his face. "It is wonderful to see you, Jason." Her eyes filled with tears.

"Don't cry, Mom, please." At least not yet. Not until he'd told her everything.

"Look who's here, honey," Mom said, leading Jason by the hand to his dad.

His dad raised up his arm, which shook with the effort. Jason grasped his dad's cool hand in his warm one. "Dad."

Tears coursed down his father's cheeks. Pretty soon he'd need a tissue himself.

"The doctor said the stroke may cause your father to be more emotional than usual. We expect him to regain full speech, don't we honey?" His mom's voice sounded forcefully cheerful. "He should be released tomorrow, to a rehab facility where he'll get some hands-on care." Her face fell. "I'm not sure how we're going to pay for it, though."

Jason felt the spear of guilt thrust into his heart. He and Hayley had more than enough money to pay for the best care that could be provided for his dad. Would Hayley even talk to him about helping? He'd tried to call her from the car, but the call went straight to voice mail. Even if the rehab cost several hundred thousand dollars, they could do it. He winced, thinking about how stingy he'd been about spending money on anything except his own wants. He wouldn't be able to enjoy any of the things he'd bought once he was locked up. Another unfamiliar emotion—generosity.

"Mom, Dad, Hayley and I might be able to help. I'll talk to her."

Mom covered her mouth with her hands. "We could never ask you to do that, Jason."

"I know, Mom. I want to help. We want to." He emphasized the *we*, hoping he was right about Hayley feeling the same. Her monthly income from the trust was enough to take care of all their household needs. Though his income would go away, Hayley would still be fine. And in two years, she'd inherit more than they'd need for the rest of their lives.

After a few minutes, Jason could tell his dad was getting tired. He said his goodbyes.

"When will you be able to come back?" His mom gripped his arm as he tried to leave.

"I'm not sure," he said with a shrug. How much should he lay on them? Not too much, with his dad lying in bed, helpless to respond. "I have to go away for a bit. I'll try to be in touch."

"Please tell your wife to come by. I'd love to meet her."

Jason pursed his lips and nodded.

"I forgot to ask, son, do you have any children?"

Another heart-stab. "No. We're taking care of a foster child." A stretch of the truth, and he knew it. How to explain his behavior. The truth would only bring her and Dad pain to know he'd hated the sight of Dixie because she reminded him of Danny and their favoring his brother over him.

"Oh, wonderful," Mom said with a sweet smile. "Well, I'm sure you'll have your own children soon."

Not for a while. Not if he was put in prison for what he'd done. Jason froze.

What if Hayley divorces me?

CHAPTER 25

Dixie slid off the chair and crawled behind the island. Hayley heard one of the drawers open.

"What are you doing in there, sweet girl?" Hayley reached across the table for Dixie's empty plate. She stood on unsteady legs and surveyed the mess in the kitchen. The empty waffle box, Jason's cereal bowl with a gelatinous mess congealed on the bottom, his half-full mug of cold coffee, discarded Keurig pods. The kitchen needed to be cleaned, but her body ached. Sobbing for hours burned a lot of calories, and crying sucked out the energy needed to face the day.

Setting the plate in the sink, she saw with dismay Dixie had emptied the contents of one drawer and had started on another.

"What's with the drawer emptying thing?" Dixie didn't answer, and Hayley didn't expect her to.

What if I don't clean right now? The mutinous thought came out of nowhere, filling her mind with doubt. Jason freaked out if even one glass was left out. He'd been known to fly into a rage if there were crumbs on the counter she'd missed during her final sweep before going to bed.

Jason wouldn't be home, not for a while. What was he doing right now? Was he at the police station?

Maybe he was being handcuffed. The thought filled her with satisfaction. He needed to be punished. Not for running their daughter down in the street. For blaming her all this time. No hell was too good for him. Hayley wanted—no— *needed* him to suffer.

How could he respond calmly? Like someone had taken her husband and replaced him with a Zen master. The old Jason would have lashed back at her, somehow turning his mistake into her fault.

Forgiveness was not an option. He'd lied about too many things. His parents, his background, his brother, and now this. Had he ever loved her, or was that a lie too?

The thought squeezed her heart. Maybe this was part of God's wrath, his payment for her abortion. Cynthia's death, at the hands of Jason, whom she was now bound to by marriage.

"When will you be satisfied?" Her shout made Dixie skitter across the floor and under the table. Hayley sank to the floor, crawled under the table, and burst into tears.

Dixie's touch was light on Hayley's shoulder. She patted Hayley's back until her sobs turned into hiccups.

"All my life, all I've wanted to do was make people happy." Hayley's hoarse voice barely carried to the sitting child. "My parents, teachers, and always my h-husband." Hayley could barely utter the word without wanting to throw up. "I thought God was happy with me. I was a good girl." Dixie's hair was warm under her touch as she stroked Dixie's head. "At least I thought I was. Until Johann. I blew it. Big time. Now, I'll never stop paying the price." She shrugged. "Or maybe this is it. Maybe Jason and I are even. I killed my child, he killed ours." The thought sent her to her feet. She bolted for the sink, heaving up bile.

A knock on the back door sounded as Hayley splashed her face with cold water.

Zola. Exactly the person she needed to see. Maybe Zola could help her make sense of the past twenty-four hours.

Zola swept into the kitchen, the scent of cinnamon and cloves wafting from the plate in her hand.

"I made some vegan muffins. They aren't bad, if I do say so myself." She skidded to a stop. "Forgive my bluntness. You look terrible. Are you sick?" She glanced around at the mess before her gaze settled on Hayley.

"I've been better." Hayley closed the door. "Do you want coffee?" Even the thought of her favorite beverage made her stomach clench. "I'm going to have some peppermint tea." Maybe tea would help calm her stomach.

Zola wrinkled her nose. "I'll stick to coffee." She pointed to the table, where Dixie peered up at them from underneath. "You sit. I'll get my own. Where's the tea?"

Hayley slumped onto the chair she'd vacated a few moments earlier and indicated the cupboard over the coffee maker. "In there. Cups too." She rested her chin on one hand, waiting for the nausea to pass.

The microwave dinged and Zola handed her a steaming mug of fragrant tea. "Better put the muffins up in the cupboard, or you-know-who will get to them."

Zola complied, settled herself across the table, and wrapped her large hands around a mug. "Are you sick, *khaverte*? I haven't seen you look this bad since you ate bad Thai food last year. Which is why I never eat out." She wagged a finger in Hayley's direction.

Hayley sighed. Where to begin? How could she put into words the horror of what she'd learned about Cynthia's death? Tears burned her eyes. How many tears could one person cry before they ran out?

"I'm not sure where to start. I guess I should have known something wasn't right when two police officers showed up at my door the other day."

Zola's eyes narrowed. "What day was it?"

Hayley tried to think through the fog clouding her brain. "I don't know. Monday? Tuesday? Anyway, Jason blew me off as usual, when I questioned him. Last night ..." Had only a few hours passed since her carefully planned life unraveled?

Zola's question cut through her thoughts. "Where is he? Jason, I mean?" She looked up as if expecting him to walk through the door.

"I-I'm not sure. He said something about going to visit his dad in the hospital."

Zola set her cup down hard, sloshing the contents onto the table. "I thought you said his parents were dead." Zola stood and went to grab a paper towel.

Hayley rubbed her hands down her thighs, realizing she was still in her pajamas. If Mother could see her now. She'd shake her head and with one look, make Hayley scurry to change. She was the poster child for people-pleasing. How pathetic.

Zola's voice brought her back again. "So?"

Hayley frowned. "Apparently it was a lie. He hated his parents and wished they were dead. He has a mentally disabled brother who demanded all their time. He resented them so much, he basically divorced them. To him, they were dead."

Zola tossed the damp paper towel onto the counter and returned to her seat. "That explains a lot."

Hayley rubbed her aching temples. "Have you ever played Jenga?"

"No. What is it?"

"It's this game where you stack blocks on top of each other, and each person removes a block until the whole thing crashes down."

"Okay, I'm getting a picture of it." Zola took a sip from her mug.

Hayley paused. How much should she tell her friend? Zola already knew her deepest and darkest secret. What would she say when she found out the rest?

Dixie took that moment to come out from under the table. Glad for the distraction, Hayley touched the child's shoulder. "What is it, Dixie?"

Dixie laid a hand on Hayley's arm. After two quick pats, she scooted around the island. Hayley heard another drawer open. Hayley sighed. More mess. What did it matter now, anyway? All her tidying up, obsessive cleaning, never made Jason happy.

Overwhelming need to tell someone everything welled up inside. "Zola, I don't even know how to say this." A sob caught in her throat. "Jason's car was the one that hit our daughter. He is the one who killed her."

When Zola didn't respond, Hayley raised her eyes to her neighbor's. Something flickered there before disappearing.

"I know." Zola dropped her gaze, turning her mug in circles on the table. "I was the one who saw it."

"You?" An electric current of shock ran down Hayley's arms, making her fingers tingle. "You knew all this time and said nothing?"

Zola nodded. "I kept hoping he would tell you. I kept the secret inside, terrified of ruining your life. When I couldn't stand it anymore, I talked to Sol and he told me I *had* to call the police. He's worried I'll be liable for withholding information about a crime." Zola ran a hand over her hair. "I'm sorry, *sheyn*."

Hayley struggled to speak through her dry mouth. "Why?"

"Don't you see? You were so consumed by guilt over your abortion you blamed yourself for Cynthia's death. You blamed God for taking her as payment for your sin. All this time, and you've been trying to work your way back into God's favor." Zola pointed in the direction beyond the island counter. "Not that God doesn't have a plan for you and the little one. What you need to realize is, you can't possibly earn God's forgiveness because it's already been given."

"W-what about Jason?" Hayley's mind whirled with this new information. She wanted to scream and shout at Zola for betraying their friendship. At the same time, it was a relief to know she, herself, hadn't been one hundred percent at fault.

Besides, Jason needed to pay for what he'd done. Hatred for him turned her heart to a piece of concrete.

Zola shrugged. "I don't know about Jason. All I know is you can't continue to blame yourself for what you did in college. Forgiveness is yours. You only have to ask for it."

"I'll never forgive Jason." Hayley clamped her lips together.

Zola stood. "Remember, *khaverte*, holding hatred in your heart is the same as drinking poison and expecting the other person to die." She carried her mug to the sink. "Do you want some help straightening up before I go?"

Hayley shook her head. "Leave it. I don't care."

"I'll check on you later."

Zola let herself out the back door. Hayley watched her cross the lawn and disappear through the gate into her own backyard.

Jazzmine struggled to carry her laptop bag, lunch, purse, and travel mug from her car to the office.

"Thank God, it's Friday," she muttered. Maybe she'd be able to leave a little early and head to the community pool to watch the boys swim before dinner. First things first, though. She set the mug on her desk, letting the laptop case slide off her shoulder while mentally reviewing her to-do list.

1. Check on Dixie's mom
2. Call Hayley and schedule a welfare check
3. Follow up on the two new placements received yesterday
4. Start on the paperwork for Carla

Paperwork, so much paperwork. The bane of her existence. If only there was a paperwork fairy to do all the mundane stuff so she could concentrate on the best part of her job, helping kids in crisis.

"Good morning!" Jazzmine called over the cubicle walls. A few muffled "good mornings" greeted her in return.

Time to settle in and get to work. First, email cleanup. Words blurred as a nagging worry expanded the headache forming behind her eyes. The Spirit seemed to be calling her to pray. For whom? Hayley's husband, Jason, came to mind.

Jason? Really? He was likely the last person she'd think of praying for. He always seemed distant during their visits. Not warm and welcoming like Hayley. Jazzmine assumed he was super busy and anxious to get back to his iPad or laptop, or whichever electronic device he had in front of him. Hayley always made excuses for him, mentioning his work, his demanding schedule in a small, two-man business. Jazz had taken it at face value, anxious for this young couple to be successful in their foster parenting journey.

Perhaps she should have dug deeper. Jazz wracked her brain for any indication Dixie might have been abused by him. Nothing came to mind, except for the urgency to pray. For him. Specifically.

Jazzmine obeyed.

Hayley sat on the broad bench in the shallow end of the pool and watched Dixie splash. The water cooled her body, but her anger burned so hot she was sure it would raise the water temperature a couple of degrees.

Over and over, Hayley recalled the times she had jumped to do his bidding. All the times she'd walked on eggshells around him, afraid to make him angry. The friends he'd made her drop. How he'd even tried to chase Zola away.

Zola. The thought of her motherly, Jewish Christian neighbor ached like an unfilled cavity. Zola had called the police. She'd seen the accident that took her daughter's life, and yet stayed silent all these months.

Fresh grief for her little girl brought more tears to her tired eyes. Pain, betrayal, and anger roiled inside. Everyone she'd relied on, everyone she'd loved, had deceived her. Made her think they loved her.

Maybe she was unworthy of anyone's real, unconditional love. It was exhausting trying to keep everyone happy. Slumping down, she let the water cover her shoulders. Dixie played with a plastic ball, batting it back and forth on the bench.

"Careful, little girl. Don't go too far." Hayley kept her eyes focused on Dixie. This time, she wouldn't make a mistake. This time she'd get it right.

Her eye caught a movement at the French doors leading from the kitchen.

"Hello, Hayley," called Mother, stepping through onto the patio.

"Mother?" Even though the demure one-piece bathing suit covered everything it should, Hayley had the urge to cross her arms over her body.

Mother's tan capris still held a sharp crease down the center of the legs, despite the midday heat. The flowered top had cap sleeves and the coral color matched her low-heeled sandals. Even Mother's toenails were painted the same shade.

She picked her way across the grass to the fence surrounding the pool. "I was on my way home and thought I'd stop by."

"Why?" Mother was the last person Hayley wanted to see.

"To confirm tomorrow's shopping." Mother unlatched the gate and stepped into the pool enclosure. "You really shouldn't be outside on such a hot day, pool or no pool. You and the child can get sunstroke."

Hayley didn't answer. What could she say? She forgot about wedding dress shopping because her lying husband was on his way to jail for killing their daughter. Not likely.

Mother's voice took on a tone of disapproval. "Don't tell me you've forgotten about it. Hannah will be devastated."

"Well, I—"

"Hannah said you promised to get someone to watch the child. She said you were ecstatic about being her bridesmaid." Mother perched on the edge of a lounge chair, far enough away to keep from being splashed. "It's a big responsibility, you know, being maid of honor." She flicked an imaginary piece of lint from her slacks.

Hayley squinted up at her mother. "How did you get in the house?"

Mother laughed. "Jason gave me a key eons ago. Just in case, he said."

"Oh." Typical Jason. Not bothering to ask her or even tell her after the fact. Assuming she was fine with giving her mother carte blanc to come and go in their house whenever she pleased.

"After shopping, we'll go back to the house. Your father bought a new barbecue, one of those filled with pellets," Mother shrugged and sighed. "Anyway, he's anxious to put it to use. You and Jason, Hannah and Keith, we'll have a little party."

Mother stood, as if everything was settled. Hayley pulled Dixie away from the edge of the bench to keep her from floating into the deep end.

"That isn't going to work." Hayley bit down on her lip, waiting for Mother's rebuttal.

"What do you mean? It's all settled." Mother crossed her arms and frowned, tapping one sandaled foot.

Hayley battled with the urge to burst her mother's bubble about how wonderful Jason was by telling her the truth, and her need to protect her mother's image of them as the perfect replica of her parents.

Maybe if she dived down deep enough into the pool, when she emerged, she'd find this was all a bad dream. Cynthia would be alive, Jason wouldn't try to control her every move, Mother would approve of her. Or perhaps she should go under the water and never come back up. Surely drowning would be less painful than her current reality.

Dixie paddled to her. "Okay?" Hayley looked down at Dixie's little brown face, hair plastered to her head like a baby seal, and smiled.

"Okay." How could she think of leaving this precious little one?

"Hayley?" Mother's voice cut through her moment with Dixie.

Hayley stood, water dripping down her torso. Time to stand up to her mother, maybe for the first time. "Mother, Jason is unable to watch Dixie on Saturday. I won't be able to go with you and Hannah to shop for wedding dresses."

"Why not? Where is Jason?" Mother frowned, revealing the wrinkles developing on her forehead.

Hayley chewed on her lip before answering. "I'm not sure how to tell you this." So tempting to make something up, something to protect her fantasy about Jason being the perfect husband and father.

"Tell me what? Spit it out, for goodness' sake, Hayley."

Fine. She'd spit it out. Why even think of trying to protect Jason and his reputation? He deserved no mercy for his lies and deception.

"Jason is on his way to jail. He's the one who killed Cynthia. He was drunk, Mother. He hit our baby and lied all this time."

Mother's face drained of color. She gasped and grabbed hold of the back of the lounger to steady herself.

"I don't believe it!"

"Believe it, Mother. You could ask him yourself, but he's probably in a cell by now. Oh, wait. He was first going to see his parents. The ones he said were killed when he was sixteen."

Mother's eyes filled with tears. She shook her head. "No." She turned, fumbled with the gate, and practically ran toward the house.

Hayley looked down at Dixie, who'd climbed out of the pool and now clung to her leg.

"What are we going to do, sweet girl?"

What would happen to them now? Jazzmine would have to be told. Would they demand Dixie be removed from her home? Would Jason have to stay in jail? Would there be a trial?

Too many questions, and no answers. One thing she did know. She'd never forgive her husband.

Dixie was finally down for a nap. Hayley surveyed the mess in the kitchen with a weary eye. Her mind automatically started a list of things to do to clean as quickly as possible, before Jason got home and went ballistic.

Wait. Jason wouldn't be home. The thought brought both relief and fear. Relief she wasn't under constant scrutiny. Fear because her nice, comfortable life was in shambles. What would everyone think when they found out Jason was in jail because he ran down their little girl? Would they wonder how she could have married him? That was the same question she'd asked herself more than once.

What began as gentle coaxing from him to get her out of her shell, had turned into climbing into a gilded cage. She couldn't go anywhere or do anything without him demanding to know.

Who did you talk to?

What did you talk about?

Why are you hanging around with her?

He'd chased off the few friends she had from college, even alienated her own sister. Only Mother still thought he walked on water.

Well, not anymore. With a sweep of her hand, she brushed crumbs from the counter and onto the floor. *Take that, Jason!*

An unfamiliar emotion started in her legs and crawled up her spine. Jason wasn't coming home, and she was ecstatic.

A laugh bubbled up from her belly. She was free.

Jason wasn't coming home.

The kitchen was forgotten as she bounded up the stairs and into the master bedroom.

Her cell phone buzzed with an incoming call. Jazzmine's face appeared on the screen. The euphoria she'd felt dribbled away.

"Hello?" Hayley collapsed on the bed and laid her head back on the decorative pillows.

"Hi ya, mama. How are you?"

How to answer? Honor dictated she tell Jazzmine the truth about Jason. What about Dixie?

"I'm good. A little tired. I didn't sleep well last night." *Because my husband had confessed he'd run over our baby.*

"I'm sorry to hear it. I know it's been super busy for you, all the doctor visits, speech therapy sessions, and now visitation with Dixie's mom."

"Yeah." Hayley pulled a pillow onto her lap with one hand. "What else?"

Count on Jazz to cut to the chase.

Curse you, Jason! If you hadn't gotten drunk, if you had only told the truth, all this could have been resolved months ago.

Hayley struggled to a sitting position. She'd managed a few bites of the sandwich she'd made for Dixie's lunch, and now the food threatened to come back up.

"Something happened. I-I'm not even sure how to put this."

Jazz was silent. Apparently, she wasn't going to make this easier.

"So, remember when we first started getting licensed for foster care?"

Jazz's voice was guarded. "Yes, I remember."

"One of the questions was if either of us had committed a felony?"

"Yes."

"Well, uh, Jason turned himself in to the police today. He was the one who drove the car that killed our daughter. He was drunk." Speaking the words filled her mouth with saliva. She was going to barf. "Hold on." Hayley tossed the phone on the bed and bolted to the bathroom.

When her stomach was empty and her face splashed with cool water, she picked up the phone. "Are you still there?"

"Yes, I'm here." Jazzmine's voice was distant. "This changes things."

Hayley bit back a sob. "I know." Jason had ruined everything.

"Will he be released on bail? If so, when?"

"I don't know."

"Mama, you need to find out. If he is allowed out on bail, and he comes home, we'll have to immediately remove Dixie from your care."

Jazz's words slammed Hayley's chest. Her breaths came in small puffs.

"Get the details, please, and let me know." Jazz was in full-on social worker mode. No more friendly banter. This was all about Dixie now, and how to protect her.

Hayley understood. It hurt, nonetheless. "I'll see what I can find out."

They disconnected. Hayley leaned back against the pillows and tried Jason's cell. The call went straight to voice mail. Chad's phone also went to voice mail. With a groan of frustration, she tossed the phone down.

"Think, Lee. Think." With a sudden flash of inspiration, she grabbed the phone again and dialed.

Daddy would know what to do.

Several hours later, after she and Dixie had eaten, Daddy's number flashed on her cell. She answered, keeping an eye on Dixie as she played in the back yard.

"I finally got some answers for you, Princess. I did a lot of calling and asking for favors."

Hayley's thighs quivered as she waited.

"Your Jason went to the Sacramento Police Department around three o'clock. He had a friend with him."

"Chad?"

"No, someone named Ben."

Ben? Hayley bounced a knuckle against her lips. Who was Ben?

"He was processed and declined to make any calls, not even to an attorney."

"What does 'processed' mean?"

"Fingerprinted, mug shot, strip-searched, and put in a cell."

Horrible as it sounded, a tiny part of her was glad. He deserved it—and more.

Daddy continued. "I have our family attorney going to see him tomorrow, although he doesn't practice criminal law. His specialties are estate planning and real estate. He'll find someone to represent your husband."

Hayley swallowed the saliva pooling in her mouth. "What happens next?"

"He'll be held over the weekend, most likely arraigned Monday morning. It'll be up to a judge as to whether or not he'll be released."

Hayley gasped. A whole weekend to wait.

Daddy continued, "Princess, what happened? Is it true what he did? Your mother came home in tears. I've never seen her so broken."

"Oh, Daddy," Hayley sobbed. "It's true. Jason was drunk and he hit Cynthia."

"And he hid it all this time? Incredible. Something about that boy isn't right. Have you considered divorce?"

Had she? Maybe in some dark recess of her mind. During one of their arguments, she might have wanted to blurt, *I want a divorce*. Other days, when he was attentive, she wondered how she could have considered leaving him. Plus, there was always the question of whether he'd let her go.

Hayley swallowed her tears. "I don't know, Daddy. I'm confused right now. He dropped this on me yesterday. I'm still processing."

"Of course. I shouldn't have brought up the subject. I want to protect my little girl."

"Thanks, Daddy. I love you."

"You, too, Princess. Let us know if we can do anything else for you."

There wasn't anything anyone could do. She was stuck in a mess she wasn't prepared for. Fresh grief over her little girl rolled in like a tsunami.

Visions of Cynthia, laughing the way only children could laugh when Jason tossed her in the air. Her sweet strawberry blonde hair fanned around her head on her pillow. Warm hugs and wet kisses. Chubby hands holding hers as they walked around the block.

All Hayley's dreams turned to ashes when Jason's car struck their baby. She was losing Cynthia all over again. The wound she'd stitched closed had reopened and sorrow she'd been careful to tuck away was back in her face.

God must hate her.

The feeling was mutual.

Jazzmine sighed as she disconnected the phone. The conversation with Hayley had taken the last bit of her energy after a long week. Next on her to-do list, power down the laptop, pack up her things, and head home. Smiling, she pictured the scene. Zeke would have fed the kids, and he'd be waiting for her with a cold glass of lemonade. They'd watch the boys play outside, sitting in webbed lawn chairs on the driveway. Someone would invariably get hurt and would need a hug and kiss before returning to the fray.

How many times had she envied Hayley and her seemingly perfect life? The beautiful house in one of the oldest and most refined neighborhoods in Sacramento. The perfect lawn, stunning wardrobe, huge diamond wedding ring. The appearance of wealth. Hayley had even seemed to bounce back from her daughter's death, after going through grief counseling.

Now, to find out her husband was the one responsible, well it was too much to process. Jazzmine looked heavenward as she trudged out to her car.

"Why did you have me pray for Jason?" she asked God, not expecting a voice from heaven to answer. Hayley was the one who needed prayer.

And Dixie. What would become of her? Dixie's mom, Barbara, was only a few weeks from being able to have unsupervised visits. As long as Barbara could show she had a stable place to live, Dixie would go back with her. As the child should.

Jazzmine stopped by her car, keys in hand. She stared at the ground, thoughts racing. Could she find another place for Dixie if Jason was released? How would a move affect the progress Hayley had made? How would it affect Hayley if Dixie was removed? Would Hayley and Jason's marriage survive this?

Jazz shook her head, jammed the key into the door lock, and yanked open the car door. Too many questions and no answers.

Maybe Zeke would be able to shed some light.

Jason had never been so humiliated. He sat in the jail cell, back against the concrete block wall, thinking about his life. He remembered the time he'd been out to dinner with his parents and his brother, when Danny had thrown food at him because he didn't like what he was eating. Some kids from his school were there, and they'd laughed about him at school the next day. They'd called his brother a retard. That humiliation was minuscule compared to being patted down, forced into an orange jumpsuit, and locked up like a common criminal. The guards' contempt was evident in the way they'd eyed him.

At least he'd been able to see Ben afterward, before being thrown into a ten-by-ten cell.

"How are you doing?" Ben had asked.

Jason shrugged. "Okay."

"Is there anything I can do?" Ben leaned forward against the stainless-steel table separating them.

"Call my wife. Let her know what's happening." If she cared. Her parting words echoed in his brain. *I hate you.*

He hated himself. Despite what Ben had told him about God's forgiveness, what he'd done was the unforgivable sin.

Noises echoed through the jail, men yelling and cursing, the harsh voices of the guards, the sounds of desperation. The smell of fear permeated every crack in the rough walls of his cell.

Ben had told him to pray. Jason didn't know how. "Talk to God," he'd said.

Jason opened his mouth. No sound escaped. He squirmed on the bunk, the rough fabric of his jumpsuit making him itch. Entirely different from the soft designer golf shirts, or the crisp white dress shirts he wore to client meetings. The hard rubber slippers he'd been issued were in stark contrast to his Italian leather loafers.

He should have followed his instinct, gathered all his money, and fled the country.

What then? He'd be running the rest of his life. A fugitive, exactly like the Harrison Ford movie.

What was Hayley doing right now? Jason had no idea what the time was. Could be midnight or noon. No natural light came through the door. Was she putting Dixie to bed? Did she think about him and where he was?

Shaking his head, Jason went back to Ben's encouragement to pray.

"God," he whispered. "I'm scared." Goosebumps broke out on his arms. He'd never admitted to anyone he was afraid. "I don't know what's going to happen to me. I'm sorry." More goosebumps. Sorry was not a word in his vocabulary. His arrogance had gotten him into this situation, and now he was sitting in jail, praying. The irony didn't escape him. If he wasn't careful, he'd be blubbering in a minute.

"Please help." As he uttered the words, the cell door clanked open and a guard with an evil grin appeared.

"Montgomery, we got a roomie for you."

A skinny guy of indeterminate age was shoved into the cell. Jason first noticed his smell. He reeked like he'd slept in a Porta potty for a month. His hair was long and matted and his beard hung below his collar.

Jason recoiled as the man bared his teeth and growled.

"Enjoy your new BFF," the guard said with a laugh.

CHAPTER 26

Evening was fast approaching, yet Hayley couldn't make herself move off the lounge chair. The mature valley oak trees created a canopy over the backyard, shielding their home from the relentless summer heat. This was her favorite time of day. The Delta Breeze would blow in, making the leaves sing overhead. Goosebumps rose on Hayley's arms, reminding her to go inside before the temperature dropped and they both were chilled.

Dragging herself to a sitting position, she called Dixie. "Come on, little one. Let's go inside for dinner."

That got Dixie's attention. Any mention of food, and she was close by. Poor thing. She still hadn't figured out she wouldn't go hungry here.

Dixie trotted ahead of Hayley into the house.

Hayley's heart sped up at the sight of the still-messy kitchen. She tried to take a few calming breaths. The disaster had to be dealt with.

"Let's have eggs and toast for dinner," Hayley said to the waiting child. "Breakfast for dinner." Hayley kept a running patter while preparing their food. Perhaps by talking, she'd eventually get Dixie to speak more than one or two words. The speech therapist said there wasn't anything functionally wrong, but Dixie hadn't ever been encouraged to talk. Or Dixie refused to.

The mind is a mystery. As she buttered toast and scrambled eggs, Hayley thought about what could have been in Jason's mind when he hid his dark secret for almost a year. She'd held her own secret. The one she'd blurted to Zola. Not even Jason knew. She'd gone to the clinic by herself and had taken Uber back to the dorm, telling her roommate she had the flu to explain why she was curled in bed with a heating pad around her middle.

Cynthia's birth had filled the hole left by the baby she'd aborted. Now her little girl was gone too, and the nightmare would begin again. Only this time, Jason was the monster, not her.

By the time she got Dixie to bed, Hayley's limbs felt like she'd run two 10k races. The kitchen and the bedroom called to her in equal parts. With a deep, shuddering sigh, she knew she'd never sleep with the kitchen so messy, Jason or no Jason.

Why was he continually in her thoughts? Who cared if he was locked up, having to eat horrible jail food, and sleeping on a grimy mattress? He deserved all of it for what he'd done.

What do you deserve? The question came from nowhere, bringing her sliding to a stop inside the kitchen. Until last night, she thought she deserved being responsible for Cynthia's death. Now?

Her heart closed. She was done feeling guilty. She'd committed murder of her unborn child, and in retaliation, God had allowed Jason to kill their daughter, while she watched. That was cruelty at its most horrific.

She'd hoped to earn forgiveness, redemption even, by helping foster kids. Even that would probably be ripped from her. If Jason was released to come home, Dixie would be yanked out of their home. To go ... where? Another family? Back with her mother?

Hayley swept through the kitchen, tossing Keurig cups into the trash, jamming dishes into the dishwasher, and shoving jars into the refrigerator. She scrubbed the counters as if she was trying to rub off the mottled design of the granite.

"I'm tired of trying," she said aloud. "I'm done. You've taken everything from me. From now on, I—"

Her cell phone vibrated on the counter with a number she didn't recognize. Who would be calling this late?

"Hello?"

"Is this Hayley Montgomery?"

"Yes. Who is this?" If he was a telemarketer, she'd give him a piece of her mind.

"My name is Ben Landis. I'm a pastor here in Sacramento."

Hayley tossed the rag she'd been using into the sink. *Get to the point or I'm hanging up.*

"I was with your husband earlier today. Can you talk for a minute?"

Hayley clenched her teeth. Did she really want to hear this? Who was this guy anyway, and how did he know Jason? Why would Jason be talking with a pastor?

Hayley walked into the living room and sank onto the sofa with legs too weary to hold her a minute longer. "Yeah, I have a minute." While she wanted to know the answers to her questions, part of her simply didn't care anymore. Jason had done everything in his power to hurt and humiliate her, making her the villain in every single way. Until last night.

Ben's gentle voice continued. "First of all, I am sorry for your loss. I've lost a child too, and it's the worst kind of pain a parent has to endure." He paused. "I met Jason on a plane a couple of days ago. He shared a little of your story with me. He's proud of you, you know."

Hayley suppressed a snort of derision.

"He told me what you're doing with your little foster girl."

Hayley sprang to her feet. "What does this have to do with anything? Did he tell you what he did? How he hit our daughter with his car, drove away, leaving her in the street? Did he explain how he'd shown up at the hospital, alcohol on his breath, acting as if he'd just found out? How about this, Pastor Ben. Did he tell you how he's blamed me for the past year for letting our daughter, Cynthia, play in the front yard. How I took my eyes off her for one minute—one tiny minute—and she rode her trike into the street? How I've blamed myself all this time, too? Did he tell you any of that?"

"Yes, he did."

Ben's soft answer abruptly stopped Hayley's torrent of words. Her mind reeled, wondering why Jason would have told this stranger everything. What had happened to her husband? The man who shed blame like a snake. She gathered her hair up in one hand, letting it fall.

"I don't understand." Sinking onto one of the kitchen chairs, she let her head drop onto her chest.

"You and Jason should probably have a long talk. I'm happy to help walk you through this difficult time."

"I'm done talking," Hayley said, exhaling with a sigh.

"I won't keep you any longer. Jason asked me to call you and let you know what's happening. He is at the Sacramento City Jail. I can text you the address if you want to see him. He'll be arraigned on Monday, and the judge will decide whether to keep him or to release him on bail. You'll need to post bond."

Hayley waved her hand before realizing Ben couldn't see. "I know all this. My dad already told me."

Ben was silent for a moment. "Oh. Okay. I'm going to see him tomorrow."

"Why?" Who was this guy, anyway? Some random person Jason met on a plane and now they were best friends? Jason had no friends. He never hung out with other men, not even his partner, Chad. He went to work, came home, and did the same thing every day. He never thought anyone was good enough to hang out with.

"This is what I do," Ben said. "I'm a pastor. I help people in trouble. Your husband asked for help."

Hayley pursed her lips. Jason, asking for help. That was a new one.

"Don't be taken in by him," she warned. "He'll use you to gain sympathy, and when he's done with you, well, you'll never hear from him again."

"I don't think so, Mrs. Montgomery. Something happened to your husband which changed him—"

Hayley laughed. "Something happened all right. He got caught." She stood. "Look, I have to go. Thanks for the call." She disconnected without waiting for Ben's response.

Jason hadn't changed. If he had, the change was temporary. He'd manipulate Ben and anyone else around him to get what he wanted. In this case, freedom.

After one last look to make sure Dixie was asleep, Hayley undressed and collapsed into bed.

What a mess. She'd taken on the responsibility for Dixie, and now was in danger of losing her. All because of Jason. His pillow provided a convenient punching bag.

(Punch) *Why did I marry him?*

(Punch) *Why did I let myself get lost in his demands?*

(Punch) *What happened to me?*

Letting her hand drop, she pondered the last question. Who was she, anyway? Wife, mother, daughter. Always connected to someone else. Where was the real Hayley? The one who had dreams and desires? What happened to the Hayley who wanted to be a kindergarten teacher?

Jason had discouraged her dream, saying she should raise their own kids. "Why be around a bunch of runny-nosed kids," he'd said. "Isn't our own family more important to you?"

Of course, Mother had sided with him. "You don't need to work, Hayley. Why take a job from someone who really needs it?"

She'd put away the job applications, gotten pregnant with Cynthia, and let the dream gather dust.

Now she had no daughter, her husband was in jail, she was in danger of losing the one thing connecting her to children, and she'd never get back on God's good side again.

Jazzmine gave final kisses to her youngest, tucking him in with special care. "I love you, Mommy," Hosea said.

"I love you too, little man." She watched as his eyes closed and tiptoed out of the room he shared with Jamal and Kito.

Zeke handed her a frosty glass of iced tea. "Come on, baby, let's go sit outside."

Jazzmine sank onto a chair with a sigh. "Please tell me bedtime will get easier."

Zeke's laugh rumbled in his chest. "Bedtime will get easier."

"You're saying that to make me feel better," she responded with a smile.

"You know it, baby. I needed to see your smile. Now, talk to me."

Jazzmine sighed. "I don't even know where to begin." She took a long sip of the tea. "Remember Hayley?"

"Trust fund Hayley?"

Jazzmine nodded. "She called me today. This is heartbreaking." She wiped condensation from the glass with a finger. "Remember how I told you her little girl was killed by a hit-and-run driver?"

"Sure, baby. How could I forget? That's why I'm always yelling at the boys to be careful when they're riding in the street."

She took a breath and blew it out. "Apparently her husband was the driver."

"What? You've got to be kidding."

"Nope. He confessed to her yesterday. Today he went down to Sac PD and turned himself in."

Zeke gave a low whistle. "That's the worst thing you've told me in a long time. He killed his own daughter and never said a thing? All this time?" Zeke shook his head. "Unbelievable."

"I know. It gets worse. The thing is, if he is released on bond, and he goes home, I'll have to remove Dixie from Hayley's care."

Zeke grabbed her hand and gave it a squeeze. "Rough."

"It's bad all the way around. Dixie will lose the stability of a home and someone she's come to trust, Hayley will be heartbroken, and she'll have to live with the knowledge her husband not only killed their daughter but kept it a secret all this time."

"Talk about reopening a wound."

"I know, right? Half of me hopes he stays in jail until trial."

"What about the other half?"

Jazzmine rubbed a hand over her face, shrugging. "I don't know. I wish I could see a way out of this for everyone."

Zeke took the glass of tea from her hand and set the glass on the deck. Taking both of her hands in his, he said, "Let's pray."

Hayley woke with a start from a dream filled with disturbing images of children running from men wearing ski masks. Her breaths came in shallow gasps as her heart pounded against her ribs.

The bedside clock glowed the time, 12:33. A little over two hours of sleep. Today was now Saturday, the day she was supposed to shop with Hannah and her mother. That wasn't going to happen.

No sound came from the baby monitor on the nightstand. Her thoughts turned to Dixie. What would become of her? How would she adapt to a new home if Jazzmine was forced to take her away? Would she be able to go back to her birth mother?

Too many questions with no answers.

In the few short weeks since Dixie's arrival, everything in Hayley's world had turned upside down. What she once thought of as a strong partnership with Jason had been revealed as fragile as a piece of silk against a flame. Even Zola's friendship was in question. What kind of a friend would keep a secret that huge for all those months? All her God talk was just talk.

Hayley remembered David's words to her in the pastry shop. "What you seek is not what you need."

What did she seek? Forgiveness. Relief from constant nagging guilt. How could he say she didn't need those things?

Turning on her side, she tucked her knees into her chest and hugged them. *What you seek is not what you need.* She played the words over and over in her head. Was he saying she needed something different? Like freedom from her husband?

The thought germinated into a thorny weed. She could divorce Jason, take Dixie far away, and start over. She'd be a single mom, able to support herself on her small trust allowance. In two years, the trust would be hers to do with what she wanted.

What do I want? What do I want? Freedom. Happiness. To put all this behind her and do what she wanted to do. Finally.

Jason bolted upright at the sound of the cell door clanking open.

"Montgomery, you have a visitor."

Jason ducked out from the bottom bunk, to avoid hitting his head. "Who is it?"

The guard shrugged. "I don't know. I open the door, you walk out ahead of me."

Jason was handcuffed and led down the row of cells to the visitor room. Ben sat at one of the metal tables, hands clasped in front of him. He looked up as Jason approached.

"Remember, no physical contact," the guard warned.

Jason sank onto the metal bench across from Ben. "It's good to see you, man."

Ben pointed to Jason's eye. "What happened?"

Jason shrugged and glanced furtively at the guard. Lowering his voice to a whisper, he answered, "Crazy roommate."

"That looks bad. Did you have it looked at?"

Jason shook his head. "Too much trouble. It's healing okay."

"You'll have a scar."

Jason's lips curved up into a slight smile. "It'll give me some character."

Ben leaned in. "Other than getting belted by your roommate, how are you doing?"

"Okay. I have a lot of time to think."

"Is that a good thing?"

"I guess. I'm regretting a lot of stuff." The handcuffs clanked on the table, a reminder of how far he'd fallen. "Did you talk to Hayley?"

What must she be thinking right now? Her parting words echoed in his brain. *I hate you.* Regret sat like a stone on his chest.

Ben's eyes shifted left. "Yes, I spoke with her last night."

"What did she say?" Was he prepared for the answer? He'd lain awake the night before, afraid to sleep lest his roommate decide to attack him again. He'd imagined scenarios where Hayley forgave him, and they went back to the way things were before. Reality crashed in, and he knew he'd lost everything.

Ben licked his lips. "She's hurt and angry, Jason. You need to give her time."

Jason laughed without humor. "Once I'm sentenced, she'll have all the time in the world."

"You don't know that. Maybe the judge will put you on house arrest or something."

"Sure. And I'm the tooth fairy." Jason scratched his nose with one hand, the other dangling uselessly from the cuffs. "I deserve to go to prison." Talons of fear dug into him as he said the words. His eyes filled with tears. "I'm scared," he whispered.

Ben nodded wordlessly.

"Could you call her again? Please? Tell her I'm sorry." The last word was choked out on a sob.

"Sure, man. Anything."

The guard spoke from where he stood watch by the door. "Montgomery. Five minutes."

Ben's gaze shifted to the guard and back at Jason. "Look, you need to know something. You have been forgiven. For everything. The prayer you prayed? It was directly to God. The minute you did it, everything changed. You're a new person, Jason. Never forget it." Ben leaned forward. "Ask for a Bible and start reading in the book of John in the New Testament."

Jason rubbed the tears from his eyes, embarrassed by his emotions. "Okay."

"I mean it. God has already forgiven you. Give Hayley time to forgive you too."

Jason meditated on Ben's words on the short walk back to his cell.

"Can I get a Bible?" Jason asked as the guard removed his handcuffs.

"Jail house conversion, Richie Rich?"

Jason didn't bother to answer. The door clanked shut, rousing his roommate.

"Hey, shut up!" The guy sat up, swinging his legs over the side of the top bunk. Jason tried to dodge the guy's skinny legs, instead was kicked. A blow landed on his shoulder.

Jason backed up, hands up in the surrender position. "I only want to sit on my bed."

The other man started flailing his arms and yelling. "Get them away from me! They have scales!"

He threw himself back against the concrete wall and batted his hands against some unseen enemy.

The hairs on the back of Jason's neck prickled. Diving into his bunk, he huddled against the wall as his roommate writhed and screamed.

Was this how he was going to die? At the hands of some drug-crazed dude?

What seemed like hours later, two guards burst into the room and marched the crazy guy out. A few minutes later, a Bible was tossed through the slot in the door.

Jason grabbed it like a lifeline, holding the book to his chest.

CHAPTER 27

Monday morning dawned with the usual sound of chirping robins who made their nests in the oak trees surrounding the homes in Hayley's neighborhood. On any other day, she would have taken a moment to enjoy their song. After another night of tossing and turning, she resented the interruption to a brief bit of restless sleep.

Sliding her legs from the bed, she mentally checked off the tasks needing to be accomplished before heading to the courthouse for Jason's arraignment. Everyone expected her to be present, to be the supportive wife. "Stand by your man," and all that rubbish.

Today would be like living through the accident again, only worse.

Jazzmine had arranged for respite to arrive at nine. Three hours to whip the house into shape, shower, dress, and ready Dixie for the day.

Why couldn't she make herself move from the bed? Exhaustion tugged on all four limbs, sucking her into the mattress. Even the thought of a boost of caffeine couldn't make her budge. How had her life gone from smooth to bumpy to head-on collision in a few short weeks?

With a sigh of resignation, Hayley forced herself to stand and go through the motions of caring what would happen to her husband.

Hayley ran a sweaty hand down her skirt as she glanced around the courtroom. What was the proper dress code for the event of your husband's arraignment? Would pants be more appropriate than the dark skirt and cream silk blouse? Jazzmine wore her usual khaki pants and collared shirt with the agency's logo embroidered on the left pocket.

Jazzmine grabbed her hand and squeezed it.

Hayley squeezed back. "Thanks for being here. I don't know if I would have made it if you hadn't offered to pick me up."

"Anything for you, little Mama."

Hayley was grateful for Jazz's support, even though if Jason was released, Dixie would have to go. Everyone assumed she wanted him released.

A rustle in the aisle grabbed her attention.

"Mother! Daddy." What were they doing here?

Mother looked her up and down and nodded. She'd passed inspection.

Standing, her mother embraced her in a stiff hug. Daddy pulled her to him.

"We're here for you, Princess," he said, his lip warm against her ear.

Pulling away, she quickly introduced them to Jazzmine, who stood and shook their hands.

They sat in unison, and stood again when the bailiff announced the entrance of the judge. Once they were seated, Daddy leaned around Mother.

"I arranged for an attorney for Jason," he whispered. "He's one of the best."

"Thanks, Daddy." They didn't need an attorney. They needed a miracle. Something to turn back the calendar to before any of this. When she and Jason had been happy.

Or had they?

Nerves skittered up her spine as they waited for the judge to call Jason's name. She'd managed to choke down a cup of peppermint tea, forgoing the usual two or three cups of coffee. Even the dry toast was a rock in her stomach.

She was going to be sick. There was no time to run to the restroom as her husband appeared in the doorway to the courtroom.

Jason wore an orange jumpsuit as he entered the room, guided by a beefy officer. He glanced her way before looking at his rubber-soled shoes.

Mother stiffened and clutched Daddy's arm. Jazz's lips moved as if in silent prayer.

Loneliness engulfed her. Between her parents—two people who were as different as night and day, yet somehow making their marriage work—and Jazzmine and her God, what outcome could be hoped for? If Jason came home, Dixie would be removed from her care and she'd have her husband. If Jason stayed in jail, she'd have Dixie and no husband.

When had the line become blurred between who she was before Jason, and who she was now? Was this the way marriage worked?

Pay attention, Lee. The judge had addressed the attorney, and she'd missed what he'd said. The attorney now spoke to the judge.

"Your honor, we are asking the court to release Mr. Montgomery on his own recognizance until sentencing. He poses no flight risk. He is employed and has a family. He needs the time between now and sentencing to tie up his business and personal affairs."

The judge looked down like Hayley imagined God would look. As if she were a crawling bug who dared appear in his presence.

"Your honor." The prosecuting attorney spoke. "This man has committed a heinous crime resulting in his own child's death."

"Allegedly!" shouted Jason's attorney.

The judge shot him a stern look before turning back to the prosecutor. "Go on."

"We believe he should stay in jail until he is sentenced."

People in the row behind her stirred. A moment later, a hand tapped her shoulder. Turning, she saw a dark-haired man wearing a black suit and clerical collar.

He leaned forward to whisper, "Sorry I'm late. I'm Pastor Ben. We spoke on the phone."

Hayley nodded, turning her attention back to the drama unfolding in front. The two attorneys addressed the judge. After some back and forth, the judge held up a hand.

"Gentlemen, since Mr. Montgomery has entered a guilty plea ..."

This was it. The judge's next words would be the difference between keeping Dixie or losing her. All because of Jason. He now stood between her and God's forgiveness. He was the cause of the grief that still ambushed her.

What more do you want, God? You've taken everything away. My child, my husband, my identity ...

Time stretched like a rubber band until it snapped.

"I am releasing Mr. Montgomery on one hundred thousand dollars bail. He will wear an ankle monitor until sentencing, which will be in the next ten days."

His gavel banged, echoing in the courtroom. Hayley sagged against the hard wooden seat, watching as her husband conferred with the attorney. The bailiff led Jason through a side door, his attorney following.

Daddy stood and held out a hand to Mother, helping her to stand. Standing, Hayley grabbed the seat in front as the room spun. Jazz grabbed one arm, Daddy the other, as they led her out of the courtroom and into the hall.

"Get her some water," Daddy barked as Hayley lowered her head between her knees.

A hand shoved a bottle of water under her nose. "I'm fine," she said, waving the bottle away.

Mother and Daddy hovered, while Jazz retreated to the end of the hall, cell phone against her ear. Would Dixie be gone by the time she arrived home from court?

"Take her to the car," Daddy instructed. "I'm going to see if I can find out when Jason will be released. And post bail." He patted the breast pocket of his jacket.

With one last look at Jazzmine, Hayley followed Mother out of the building. Pastor Ben caught up with them at the bottom of the concrete steps.

"Hi. I wanted to catch you real quick before you take off." His brown eyes held sincerity and sympathy. "I'm going to wait for your husband."

A slight breeze ruffled his light brown hair.

"And you are?" asked Mother, fixing him with an icy stare.

"I apologize. I'm Pastor Ben, a friend of Jason's." He held out a hand. "And you must be Hayley's mother. The resemblance is unmistakable."

Mother extended her hand for a weak handshake. "I wasn't aware Jason had a friend in the clergy."

Ben's look turned serious. "We've recently become friends. I want to help him, and his family, through this difficult time." Ben reached in his pocket and pulled out a business card. "Please, take my card. My cell phone is on there. Don't hesitate to call me any time."

Mother took the proffered card and wordlessly examined the information before handing it to Hayley.

Hayley tucked the card in her purse and murmured her thanks.

Hayley couldn't remember how she got home, only that she stood in her own living room, saying goodbye to the respite worker. Mother and Daddy dropped her off, promising to call later to check in. Daddy had said Jason would be home sometime that afternoon or evening.

As soon as the front door closed behind the worker, Hayley's cell buzzed.

"Hi, Jazz."

"Hi-ya, little Mama. I'm sorry things turned out this way. I have to remove Dixie from your home."

Some aspects of her job stank like the boys' athletic shoes. Jazzmine shoved away from the desk and stood, rolling her shoulders to loosen the tension knotting the muscles into two bricks.

After a few phone calls and a conference with Carla, they'd located another foster home for Dixie. The situation wasn't ideal, but the law was the law. A child couldn't stay placed in a home where a—what was Jason anyway? He hadn't been sentenced, but he'd pleaded guilty to the charge of vehicular manslaughter. The law stated a federal conviction meant automatic disqualification and revoking of a foster care license.

Had she been too hasty in her decision to move Dixie? Her job was to do what was best for the children in her care. What if Dixie were allowed to stay at Hayley's for the next ten days, until Jason was actually sentenced? By then, Dixie's mother might be released from detox and perhaps find a place for them to live.

Stop second-guessing yourself. Jazzmine rubbed a hand across her face. In her experience, mothers coming out of rehab were rarely able to take back full responsibility for their children. Unless there was a set of grandparents out there, Barbara McNally had a lot of work to do before regaining custody of her little girl.

At the end of the day, Jazzmine's responsibility had to be to do the best for the child. Why did doing the right thing hurt so much?

Watching Dixie climb into the car with the chubby older woman felt like losing Cynthia over again. Sadness weighed her down until she felt as if she'd collapse there on the front porch.

Clinging to one of the pillars, she raised her hand to wave goodbye. Dixie's face pressed against the car window, tears making wet streaks down the glass. Hayley choked back a sob.

"Goodbye, sweet girl," she mouthed to the departing car.

Stumbling into the house when the car disappeared out of sight, she pushed the door closed, slid to the floor, and wept.

Sobs wracked her body as she wailed her grief into the empty house.

Alone again. Everything had been taken. Her unborn child. Cynthia. Jason. And now, Dixie.

Raising her head, she shouted, "Are you happy now?"

The words echoed in the air, settling like dust. Why should she expect God to answer?

The wood floor cooled her hot cheek. Struggling to her feet, she stumbled into the kitchen to ease the gnawing hunger.

One of Zola's brownies sat in the fridge, wrapped in clear wrap. Just the thing to give a bit of comfort. Warmed in the microwave and topped with vanilla bean ice cream.

Jason's favorite.

Would she ever be free of him?

The brownie and ice cream went down but refused to stay in her stomach. She dashed for the sink, gagging and retching until her stomach was empty once again.

Using both hands as support, she leaned against the counter, panting. The only other time she'd thrown up this much was when ... no. She couldn't be.

Taking the stairs two at a time, Hayley dashed up, pausing a moment outside the pink bedroom as tears filled her eyes again.

In the bathroom, under the sink, she spied the familiar rectangular box. She ripped the box open with shaking hands.

Should she? What if? Would the result make things better ... or worse?

Perhaps she'd feel better if she changed out of the skirt and blouse, and into something more comfortable. She quickly stripped down, tossing the clothes onto the unmade bed with a grim smile. Jason would never have allowed the bed to stay unmade.

Hayley pulled on a pair of flowered yoga pants and a white tee shirt before using the bathroom to activate the test results.

"Hayley! Where are you?"

"Are you sure you want to do this?" Jason jiggled the keys up and down as Ben pulled up to Jason's house.

"The bigger question is, do you still want to stay with me?"

Jason looked down at the worn floor mat beneath his feet. Ben's sensible sedan was a far cry from Jason's top-of-the-line luxury SUV. The cloth seats smelled of old French fries. If his car was any indication, Ben's house would be a lot simpler than his and Hayley's.

Hayley. Would she divorce him now that he would be going to jail? Could there a chance he might win her back?

"Earth to Jason." Ben's voice cut into his thoughts.

"Oh, sorry. Yeah, I appreciate the offer of staying at your place until sentencing. I doubt Hayley will want me within two feet of her."

Ben released his seat belt with a snap. Leaning over, he clapped Jason on the shoulder. "Have some faith. This will all work out in God's timing."

Jason nodded. "God's timing. Right." *I don't even know what that means.*

His newfound faith was tenuous at best. What had he committed himself to? Or to whom?

He took a deep breath and blew it out. "Guess I'd better go in and pack my bag."

Ben sent him a smile, meant to encourage. "I'll be waiting."

"Sure you don't want to come in? Grab something cold to drink?"

"Stop procrastinating."

Jason grabbed the handle and swung the car door open. The door creaked, grating on his already-frayed nerves. Which Hayley would greet him? Cold as ice Hayley, or screaming angry Hayley? Was it too much to hope compliant Hayley might still exist?

The key slid easily into the lock and the door swung open. Would this be the last time he could call this place home? He breathed in the familiar scent of fresh lavender, the indoor plant Hayley nurtured from a tiny seedling. She was good at nurturing. A good mother, even opening her heart to foster kids after Cynthia ...

Regret was an angry ocean wave, washing over him. He staggered up the stairs, gripping the handrail. Hayley wasn't in the bedroom.

"Hayley?"

She stood in the bathroom, whipping around with a start when she saw him. What did she hold in her hand? A thermometer? Whatever she held, it was hidden behind her back.

"I didn't hear you come in," she said.

"I'm here to pack some stuff. I'm staying with Ben," he said, moving to the closet. "I thought, well, I wasn't sure ..."

"N-no. It's okay." She walked into the bedroom and perched on the edge of one of the chairs in front of the window.

Jason swung a soft-sided leather suitcase from the closet shelf and tossed it on the bed. He opened his mouth to say something about the unmade bed. The old Jason would have insisted the bed be neat, corners tucked in tight, pillows exactly placed. According to Ben, the old Jason died, and he was now a new creation in Christ. Whatever that meant. All he knew was he still loved his wife, even though she hated his guts.

Jason tossed underwear, socks, tee shirts and jeans haphazardly into the bag. On every other occasion when he'd had to go out of town, Hayley had packed for him. Everything neatly folded and organized.

He was an idiot. He'd made a huge mess of things and the price was so great as to be unbearable. Tears filled his eyes, burning. Unfamiliar.

"Hayley, I—"

"No, Jason. Don't. Don't tell me you're sorry. I. Don't. Care." She emphasized the words with her closed fist, pounding on her thigh. "Between you and God, you've taken everything from me."

He paused, hand stilled on the opened suitcase. "Hayley, God can—"

Hayley sprang to her feet. "Don't you dare talk to me about God."

"You're right. I'm sorry. It's only in these past few days, I've realized—"

She put her hands over her ears. "Stop."

"Okay. You win." He zipped the bag closed, slinging it over one shoulder. Reaching into his shirt pocket, he pulled out a business card. "Here's Ben's card. His cell number is on it. That's where I'll be."

He stopped short of the bedroom door. Turning back, he said, "Where's the k—Dixie?"

Hayley barked out a laugh. "She's gone, Jason. She couldn't stay here because of you."

Guilt settled heavy on his shoulders. He had no way to fix it. And no one to blame except himself. "Oh, baby, I'm s—"

"No more 'I'm sorry's.'" She advanced toward him, arm raised as if to slap his face.

He backed into the hall and fled down the stairs.

The sound of the front door closing echoed in the downstairs entry. Hayley slumped onto the end of the bed, head bowed. Now what? Unbearable sorrow. Her heart betrayed her when Jason appeared in the doorway. She still loved him, though she didn't want to. His was the unforgivable sin. He'd killed their child.

A tiny voice whispered in her ear, "So did you." Yes, she'd deliberately killed her unborn baby because being pregnant would be inconvenient during her final year of college.

Jason had been drunk, careless, and mostly unaware of what he'd done. Should his sin be more easily forgiven?

The more pressing question, did he see the test she'd tossed on the bathroom counter? Springing up, she strode into the bathroom and snatched up the test.

"I'm afraid to look." Biting her lip, she slowly turned the wand over.

+Yes.

She was pregnant. No wonder she'd barfed every day. Not from the stress. Morning sickness. Placing her hand on her still-flat belly, she made a promise.

"I will protect you, little one, the best I can."

A frisson of excitement rose from the tips of her toes. Where had they stored the crib they'd packed away when Cynthia outgrew it? Jason would know.

Jason. Did he have a right to know about this child? Would her being pregnant change anything? How could she raise a child whose father was in jail?

What a mess.

Her cell phone chirped with an incoming text.

ZOLA: How did court go? Do you want some company?

Hayley tapped the phone against her lips. Did she want company? Zola was on her list of people she didn't want to see. If Zola had only kept her mouth closed, no one would have known Jason was at fault. They could have gone on about their lives.

Jason would have known. The guilt which turned him into a control freak would have only increased until ...

Until he left? Or worse, until he became physical?

HAYLEY: I'm a little tired. Maybe later.

ZOLA: okay. Worried about you.

She started to type "You should have thought about that before ..."

She backspaced to delete.

Hayley collapsed on the bed, scrunching the pillow under her head. What was Dixie doing right now? Was she crying, wondering why she'd been taken to a stranger's house? Was she hiding behind the sofa or under the bed? Did she understand Hayley didn't want her to go?

"I didn't get to complete my list," Hayley said aloud. Could God be giving her another chance with this baby inside her?

If so, what about Jason? Her eyes closed, picturing Cynthia as an infant, held in Jason's big hands.

When Hayley woke, early evening sunlight bathed the room with a soft glow. She pulled the cell phone close. Seven o'clock, plus three more Zola texts and a missed call from Hannah.

Her stomach growled, a good sign. Perhaps she could keep down some decent food before facing Zola, Hannah, and anyone else's insatiable curiosity about her well-being.

Hayley washed her face and headed downstairs, turning on lights. Pausing in the living room, she flicked on the television for background white noise.

As soon as she turned on the kitchen light, a face appeared at the window of the French door. She jumped with a gasp.

"Zola! You scared me!" she said, though Zola couldn't possibly hear her through the dual-paned window.

As soon as she unlocked the door, Zola burst in carrying a bag smelling of something fragrant.

"I've been worried about you, Hayley! Every two minutes I've checked to see if your lights are on. As soon as I saw the upstairs light go on, I couldn't wait a minute longer to see how you're doing."

Zola set the bag on the counter while Hayley closed the door.

"Oh, listen to me with all my *plapleray*. How are you, *sheyn*?" Zola grabbed her in a smothering hug against her ample chest. A sob worked its way up from Hayley's throat.

"It was awful, Zola," she sniffed.

"Tsk. Let me unpack this bag and you can tell me all about it." Zola bustled about the kitchen, grabbing a bowl and spoon and setting them on the table. "Sit, sit. I brought soup. Everything will look better after a bowl of chicken soup."

Hayley settled onto a chair, the growling in her stomach becoming louder.

Zola chuckled. "I bet you haven't eaten all day."

Hayley shook her head, then nodded. "Well, I ate, but I threw up." She didn't mention what she'd eaten was one of Zola's famous vegan brownies which had gone into Sacramento's sewer system.

The fragrant smell of chicken soup soon permeated the kitchen. Hayley took a tentative spoonful. When her stomach didn't react, she dug into it. Zola watched with a smile.

"Let me butter a biscuit for you, too." Zola dug into the bag to reveal another treasure. Homemade drop biscuits. Hayley had to stop herself from grabbing one out of Zola's hand, like Dixie would have done. Dixie. A wave of sadness washed over her. Was Dixie eating dinner? Did her new family know how to cut her food into tiny pieces so she wouldn't choke?

Zola handed her a biscuit dripping with melted butter. Perhaps she wouldn't stay mad at Zola. How easily she gave forgiveness when food was involved.

When Hayley scraped the last bit of chicken from the bowl, and licked butter off her fingers, Zola crossed her arms, leaned on the table, and said, "Tell me everything."

CHAPTER 28

The girl craned her neck to peer out the window as the car pulled away from the big house where Lee lived. Tears poured down the girl's cheeks, not because she was leaving, but because something in Lee had changed. She didn't understand the change and her heart hurt.

Jason stretched out on the hard futon, feet dangling over the edge. This was a far cry from his six-thousand-dollar memory foam mattress at home. He'd best get used to trying to sleep on something akin to two pieces of cardboard glued together.

After they'd arrived at Ben's house, he'd done a quick online search of the sentencing requirements for vehicular manslaughter. At best, he'd be locked up for one year in county jail. Worst case scenario, a prison term for as long as six years.

His stomach churned at the thought of being in prison, shoulder to shoulder with gangbangers and murderers.

Wait. He was one of those. A murderer. Of his own child.

Curling on his side, he pulled a pillow over his head to drown out the cheerful sounds of Ben's three kids playing in the back yard. Would he and Hayley be able to get past this? Have their own kids, laughing in the yard, splashing in the pool, or cuddling up on the sofa?

Dear God, what a mess I've made.

Sometime later, Ben tapped on the door. "Jason? Krista has dinner ready."

Jason groaned and rolled onto his back. "I must have fallen asleep. I'll be there in a minute."

Ben left the door open a crack. Delicious aromas wafted in from the kitchen. Stomach growling, he struggled up from the low futon and made his way into the kitchen.

"Hi, you must be Jason." A petite blond approached, one hand extended, the other covered by an oven mitt. "I'm Krista. And these are my kids."

Three expectant faces peered up at him from their place at the table.

"Hi," Jason said, shaking Krista's hand.

"Adam is the oldest, Aaron is in the middle, Brianna is our youngest."

Ben entered the kitchen, rubbing his hands together. "I see you've met my tribe." He kissed Krista on the cheek. "Smells wonderful, honey."

Jason's jaw clenched at the easy way Ben and Krista had around each other. Had he and Lee ever been that casually affectionate? And the kids. Really cute. Although he'd been content with Cynthia, the warmth around the table as they held hands to pray made him rethink having more than one child.

"Are you staying with us?" Adam asked.

Jason nodded, taking a bite of steaming lasagna.

Brianna, sitting next to him, asked, "How long?"

Krista quickly interjected, "Bree, it's rude to ask someone how long they're staying."

"Why, Mommy?"

Krista set her fork down. "Because asking when they're going implies you want them to leave quickly."

"What's 'imply'?"

Ben laughed and ruffled her hair. "Never mind, Cupcake. Jason will be here for about a week and a half."

"That long?" asked Aaron.

"Aaron! Mind your manners," Krista said.

"I have to sleep in Adam's room, and he stinks!"

"Do not."

"Do too."

Ben crossed his arms. "Okay, guys. We're going to eat in silence for five minutes. No exceptions."

Jason's pulse quickened. Ten days to wait until he found out his fate. The ankle monitor irritated both his skin and his spirit. Did they really think he'd try to run?

Didn't you? A little voice inside pricked his conscience. What would he do for the next ten days? Work only filled so many hours. Coming back to Ben's house every night would be a reminder of how badly he'd messed things up with Lee. With Cynthia. With his parents. And hers.

Krista laid a hand on his arm. "We're happy to have you, Jason."

"Thanks." Perhaps he should find a hotel to stay in. Sooner rather than later. All this family happiness was driving him deeper into depression.

Hayley sank onto the bed, unable to raise enough energy to undress. She'd managed to keep down the soup Zola brought. They'd talked about Jason's arraignment and sentencing—and about Dixie's sudden departure. The only thing Hayley kept from Zola was the positive pregnancy test. She'd keep that secret to herself for now.

The next morning, Hayley opened her eyes and glanced at the clock. Ten o'clock and Dixie hadn't awakened? Panicked, Hayley shot up and bolted into Dixie's bedroom.

"Oh!" The realization hit when she saw the bed neatly made. Dixie was gone. Hayley hugged herself as tears filled her eyes.

"Sweet girl, what are you doing today? Do you miss me?"

The thought of Dixie crying for her was too much to bear. Hayley padded back into the master bedroom and crawled back into bed, wetting the pillow with her tears.

Two days later, Hayley had only been out of bed to splash water on her face and force down a dry piece of toast chased with peppermint tea. When she finally turned her phone back on, it blew up with texts and calls from Zola, Mother, Pastor Ben, and Jazz. Hayley couldn't bear to talk to any of them.

Two days turned into three, three into four. On the fifth day, Hayley dragged herself into the bathroom. Her reflection showed dark circles under bloodshot eyes. Her hair hung limp and tangled down to her shoulders.

"Ugh." She made a face.

Fierce pounding on the back door startled her out of her reverie.

She made her way down the stairs, holding onto the handrail for balance. Zola stood at the back door, face pressed against the glass. In one hand she held a bag. The other she used to cup around her eyes to see into the darkened house.

Hayley sighed and stepped to the door to let Zola in.

Zola bustled past her, setting the bag on the counter. "I thought you were dead. You didn't answer my calls or texts. What's going on?" Without waiting for an answer, she gathered Hayley into a motherly hug.

"Let's get some food into you," Zola said, releasing her. She pointed Hayley toward the table with a gentle shove.

Zola reached into the bag and brought out several plastic containers. "Fruit salad, potato salad, green salad. Homemade rolls, some lunchmeat, and even potato chips. Now, what sounds good?"

Hayley raised her lips in a wan smile. "Some fruit, I guess."

Zola dished some fruit salad onto a plate, setting the food in front of Hayley. "I'm going to make you a sandwich while you eat."

When Hayley started to protest, Zola stopped her. "No arguments. You need to feed the baby you're growing inside you."

Hayley's mouth dropped open, then closed with a snap. "How did you know?"

Zola laughed. "Women's intuition. I've been pregnant enough times to know how a woman looks when she's expecting."

Tears filled Hayley's eyes. "I'm sorry you never got to have your own baby."

Zola shrugged and turned back to the counter. "Adonai gives and Adonai takes away. Blessed be the name of Yahweh."

Hayley had taken her first bite of sandwich when she was startled by the sound of a key in the lock of the front door. Could it be Jason? In a reflexive movement, she glanced around the kitchen, noting the containers on the counter, crumbs left from the sandwich, and a general feeling of messiness.

Zola moved to a defensive position near the kitchen doorway. Hayley held her breath, waiting.

"Hayley?" Mother's voice broke the stillness.

"Mother? What are you doing here?" Hayley reached for her head in a vain attempt to smooth her hair.

"Oh, my dear Hayley. I've been trying to phone you." Mother swept into the kitchen, tossing her purse on the table. She grabbed Hayley in a hug. Stress vibrated off her.

Hayley pulled back, alarmed. "What's going on?"

Mother clasped one hand around Hayley's arm. "Jason's sentencing was moved up to today. That's why I've been trying to get hold of you. Your father too."

Hayley took a breath and sat back at the table and reached for her sandwich with shaking hands. "And this concerns me, why?"

Mother's voice rose an octave. "Because he's being sent to prison tonight! In Colorado."

Hayley's eyes shifted between Zola, who stood like a sentry, and Mother, who quivered with outrage. Mother's blouse was rumpled, and she had lipstick on her teeth. "Sit down, both of you. You're making me nervous," Hayley said.

"I don't see how you can remain calm, Hayley." Mother moved toward the table and rested her manicured hand on the back of a chair.

Zola stacked the containers she'd brought and carried them to the refrigerator.

Hayley set the sandwich down and glared at her mother. "I'm glad he's going to prison. I hope he dies there."

Mother gasped. "You can't mean that!"

"I'll never forgive him for what he did. Never." She pushed the plate away, appetite gone.

Mother grasped her head with both hands. "This is awful," she moaned.

Hayley stood. "I know this upsets your idea of what our perfect family appears to your friends. You'll have to spin the story in a way to keep your social standing. You wouldn't want to be kicked out of the Sutter Club."

"Oh, Hayley." Mother's eyes filled with tears. "That's not it at all. I'm worried about you."

"Why, because I haven't fixed my hair, put on makeup, dressed for success?"

Mother skirted the table to stand in front of her. She grasped both of Hayley's upper arms. "I know I don't always show love in the way you want, but I care about you. I love you."

Love? Hayley's heart turned to stone. She shook off her mother's hands. "You need to go. I'm fine. I don't need Jason, and I certainly don't need you telling me about him." She turned away to avoid looking at the effect of her words. She heard Mother sniff.

"At least answer your phone so I know you're all right," she said.

Hayley heard the front door close and turned to face Zola.

"That was awkward," Zola said.

"I'm sorry to draw you into my family drama."

"*Sheyn*, every family has drama. Your mother is certainly a force of nature. When are you going to tell her you're pregnant?"

Hayley sank down onto a chair with a shrug. "I don't know. For now, I want to keep my pregnancy a secret. My secret."

Zola pulled out a chair across the table and sat down with a sigh. "You've told me a little about your mother's high expectations, but she really does love you."

Hayley snorted. "I'm surprised she didn't mention my appearance." She rested her chin in her hand. "I'm so tired of disappointing everyone. I wish everyone would leave me alone."

Zola shoved herself to her feet. "On that note, I'll go home. You should get some rest."

"I didn't mean—" Hayley began. Zola cut her off.

"*Feh*, you're tired. Have a nice bath, crawl into bed, and things will look better tomorrow."

I doubt it.

Later, after she'd forced herself to shower, Hayley sat on the edge of the bed, drying her hair with a towel. On one hand, she was glad to be left by herself. The stillness of the house without Dixie's constant motion filled her with melancholy.

"I'm scared," she whispered. Scared the baby she now carried might be taken from her too. She hadn't been able to follow through with her commitment to Dixie. Would God let it go? Not possible.

What made her think there would ever be a way to appease an angry God? Zola could talk all she wanted about forgiveness and reconciliation. Hayley knew better. Hadn't Mother and Daddy taught actions had consequences?

She tossed the towel on the floor (take that, Jason) and pulled open the nightstand drawer to grab her phone and turn it on.

Five texts from Jazz, each more strident than the last.

JAZZ: CALL ME, MAMA!

Missed calls from Mother, Hannah, Zola, and several from an unknown caller. More texts from Zola.

Hayley let the phone drop into her lap. Clenching her fists, she recalled each person and how she didn't want to see or speak to any of them. Hannah, for being self-centered. Mother for her constant need of perfection. Jazz, for letting Dixie be taken away. And finally, Zola. She'd seen the accident, seen Jason's car careen into Cynthia, yet she kept silent for *over a year*. What kind of friend did that?

How easily Hayley let Zola slide back into her kitchen, all because she brought food. The little bit Hayley had eaten threatened to come up as she dwelt on how wronged she'd been. By everyone.

Hayley slid down in the bed and pulled the covers up to her neck.

"It's going to be you and me, little one," she said, patting her still-flat tummy.

She'd sell the house, move somewhere far away where Jason, her parents, and so-called friends couldn't find her.

CHAPTER 29

Jason sat on a bus several degrees above boiling with six other inmates. They were handcuffed with their legs shackled to a ring on the floor. All wore orange jumpsuits courtesy of Sacramento County Jail. They'd made him cut off his beard, all the while watching to be sure he didn't try to harm himself with the razor. Jason scratched his naked face, wondering if Hayley would recognize him without the facial hair he'd had since they'd met.

Hayley. The thought of her brought an ache to his chest. What was she doing right now? Did she think about him with anything except hate? Would she ever forgive him?

Jason had hours to think about his mistakes while lying in the jail cell. He'd hidden the scars caused by his parents' neglect. Looking back, he could forgive them for focusing so much attention on his big brother. Going into his relationship with Hayley, he'd demanded from her something she couldn't give—one hundred percent devotion. Because he hadn't told her about this childhood, she couldn't understand his need.

Cynthia's death had been the catalyst to reveal the fissures in their relationship. The harder he pushed to control, the more he pushed her away.

Had their marriage been doomed from the start because of him?

A burly guard climbed into the bus and turned in his seat to face the inmates. "Y'all ready for a road trip?" He didn't wait for an answer.

One of the men sitting across from Jason spoke. "Get prepared to be Greyhounded."

"Huh?" Jason asked.

The guy leaned forward. "We're supposed to go straight to Colorado. Should take about two, maybe three days max. These guys," he indicated the driver and the guard with an elbow. "They'll drive us around the country for days. Better get used to eating cold bologna sandwiches for breakfast and dinner. No lunch." The guy laughed. "Oh, yeah. Don't drink too much water. They only let us out twice a day to use the bathroom."

Jason's heart kicked up a notch. "Can they do that?"

The guy shook his head in disgust while a couple of the others snickered. "Yeah, newbie. They can."

The bus rumbled as the driver started it up. Soon, barely cool air began to circulate in the interior. Jason grabbed at the neck of his jumpsuit to loosen the pressure as he began to sweat from the heat and the terror filling him.

He should have run when he had the chance. Why turn himself in when he had the means to disappear for a good, long time?

Because you are a new person. Pastor Ben's words echoed in his brain. Good old Pastor Ben. The only light in this dark dungeon. A true friend. Not like his partner, Chad. He'd closed their business account to remove Jason's authority to withdraw money. Jason's attorney tried to block Chad from shutting Jason off, but he'd been too late. Chad had dissolved the partnership and opened a brand-new business with himself as the sole owner. Last Jason had heard, Chad was selling to the group in Los Angeles. Jason's share of the sale: zero.

He tried to keep from being bitter. Ben told him his situation was in God's hands. Jason had a hard time believing it. "Trust God," Ben said. Difficult to do when his sentencing had been moved up, and now, he was headed for a very long trip to a federal prison. He wiped his sweaty hands on his orange-clad thighs. *Dear God, help me.*

There was a sudden commotion outside the bus. The men inside craned their necks to see. A dark-skinned man wearing a suit seemed to be in an argument with a uniformed guard. The bus driver climbed down to enter the fray. The suited man pulled a sheaf of papers from inside his coat and waved them at the guard. Their conversation lasted several minutes.

Jason's bus-mates began to speculate on what was going down.

"Someone's gonna get water-boarded."

"One of us is really a woman and they just found out." This brought on some snickers and not-too-gentle elbow nudges.

"Someone's heading for death row." This comment quieted the noise.

Everyone held their breath as the driver opened the door and stuck his head in. "Montgomery. You're outta here."

Jason's stomach sank as he was hit with a jolt of adrenaline.

A guard climbed in and released his legs from the shackles holding him to the floor. "Get out," he commanded.

Jason climbed awkwardly over two men and was helped out of the bus.

"Good luck, newbie," called the guy across from him.

The dark-skinned man took Jason's arm and led him to an unmarked police car. His jacket flapped open and Jason saw the guy's police department badge.

"Where are we going?" Jason asked. He felt sweat dampen his chest and back.

"Get in," the officer said, holding open the car door. He slammed the door shut after Jason climbed in.

Was this the end? Would this guy take him out somewhere and kill him? Gossip in jail travelled faster than a high school locker room. How sometimes cops "lost" inmates. Would this be the day he'd die?

Hayley woke as the first rays of light peeked through the oak trees shading the house. She stretched, then swung her legs over the side of the bed. Today would be the day she'd make some life changes. She'd Google a realtor, set an appointment, and talk about selling the house. With the money she'd get from the sale, she'd move someplace more temperate. Hawaii, maybe. Or San Diego.

She was hit with a sudden wave of queasiness as she stood to walk to the bathroom. Feeling warmth between her legs, Hayley looked down and gasped. Bright red blood trickled down her legs and pooled on the carpet.

"Oh, God, no." Panic filled her as she grabbed her phone with shaky fingers, dialing the one person who could get there the fastest. Zola.

Jason's heart hammered against his rib cage. The officer climbed into the sedan and started the car. Within moments, icy cold air blasted from the vents, chilling Jason's sweaty face. With a mouth dry as cotton, Jason asked, "C-can I ask where we're going?"

"Thought we'd swing into Starbucks so I could order you a mocha Frappuccino and maybe a scone." The guy burst into laughter. "Just kidding. Sometimes I crack myself up."

Jason had a sudden urge to grab the guy around the neck and shake him. Good thing he was handcuffed and separated from the front seat by a mesh screen.

"I'm taking you to California State Prison, Sacramento. Commonly known as Folsom Prison. Some yay-hoo messed up on your paperwork. You were never supposed to go to Colorado."

"Why Folsom?" Weird. Or was this an excuse to dump him off the Rainbow Bridge and let him drown in the river?

The officer shrugged. "Folsom has a bed available with your name on it."

Jason let the words sink in. The lack of control, of information, drove him crazy. He'd always been the one calling the shots. In his business, his marriage, his life. Now he was at the mercy of some very unsympathetic public servants. His every move was controlled by someone else. When to eat, sleep, use the bathroom, was all on someone else's schedule.

"I'm Sergeant Smith, and yes, it's my real name." He directed the car onto the freeway. "So, did you hear the one about the restaurant on the moon? Great food, no atmosphere."

Jason's chin dropped to his chest. Who was this guy?

"What do you call cheese that isn't yours? Nacho cheese." Sergeant Smith guffawed. "Here's one more. What is the first car mentioned in the Bible? Want to guess?"

Jason shook his head.

"A Honda. Because all of the disciples were in one accord."

Jason groaned. This was getting weirder and weirder.

Smith caught his eye in the rearview mirror. His voice turned serious. "You read the Bible?"

Jason shrugged. "A little." Pastor Ben told him to read the Gospel of John. He'd gotten through the whole book, reading it again before his belongings were bagged up and taken who-knew-where.

"You should read the Bible a lot. It'll help you while you're locked up. Maybe when you get out, you won't be inclined to get arrested again. Know what I mean?"

Yeah, Jason knew what he meant. When he got out, he'd never touch another drop of alcohol and he'd never drive over the speed limit. He'd thought the guilt he'd carried over Cynthia's death was bad. This was a thousand times worse.

"So, what's your story, big man?" Sergeant Smith asked.

Jason stared out the window at the passing landscape. Travelling west on Highway 50, they'd passed downtown Sacramento and were travelling through the bleak industrial landscape on either side of the highway.

His gut churned as he considered his response. This cop probably knew what he was being incarcerated for, maybe not the details. He'd give Smith the bare minimum of information.

"Hit and run. Vehicular manslaughter."

Smith nodded. "Why'd you run?"

Jason squirmed on the seat. "I'd had too much to drink."

"You must have been scared."

Scared didn't even begin to describe his feelings at the time. Horror at what he'd done. Fear for his reputation, his business, his marriage. Everything was about him. Guilt. Remorse. Shame. Turning things back on to Hayley to shove the guilt from his shoulders onto hers. She hadn't been able to carry it. She'd begun to crumble under the weight. The strong, confident woman he'd married melted like a candle left in the sun.

Jason met Smith's eyes in the rearview mirror. "I was a jerk."

"Was?" Smith raised an eyebrow.

Jason looked away. How to explain what happened the night he confessed to Hayley? Pastor Ben's explanation hadn't taken root yet.

Smith took a different tack. "You married?"

"Yes. No. I'm not sure."

Smith laughed, a deep, booming sound. He was getting on Jason's last nerve with all the questions. Why couldn't they ride in silence?

"Let me guess," Smith said. "Your wife isn't sure she wants to stay married to you, now you've been convicted. Am I right?"

Jason nodded. He hadn't spoken to Hayley since the day he'd left for the police station to turn himself in. He assumed she was making plans to divorce him. With good reason. What he'd done went beyond her ability to forgive.

"Let me give you some advice, from someone who's been married a long time. Write her a letter. Tell her you're sorry and you'll do anything to make things better. Got it?"

"Sure." Jason very much doubted a letter would make any difference.

CHAPTER 30

Hayley lay flat on the hospital bed, staring at the ceiling. Beeping from the heart rate monitor reminded her of being in the birthing room, waiting for Cynthia to be born. She'd been happy. Jason had hovered, bringing ice chips and rubbing her feet. This time, Zola gripped her hand.

"Are you sure you don't want me to call your mother?" Zola asked for the fifth time.

Hayley shook her head. "Not yet." Not until after the ultrasound. Not until after she found out if she was losing this baby. Her eyes filled with tears.

Zola murmured assurances. "I'm sure you'll be fine."

"You can't know that," Hayley exclaimed. "It's another way for God to punish me!" Tears overflowed and poured down her cheeks.

Zola sighed. "*Sheyn*, I've told you that's not how He works."

Hayley's sobs grew. "Why ..." Before she could finish, a technician pushing a cart shoved aside the emergency room curtain.

She observed Hayley over the half-glasses sitting precariously on her nose. "Hello, dear. I'm here to do your ultrasound. How are you feeling?"

"How do you think she's feeling?" Zola asked with uncharacteristic sarcasm. "She's lying in a hospital bed, bleeding, and scared to death she's miscarrying." Zola mumbled something under her breath that sounded like *idyot*. Hayley smothered a half-sob, half-laugh.

"Let's begin." The tech squeezed cold gel on Hayley's barely round tummy.

The machine hummed as the tech spread the gel around with the wand. Hayley gripped Zola's hand until her knuckles turned white.

"Hm. Hm." The tech's noises did nothing to assure Hayley her baby was still viable. She'd counted backward from when she thought she might have conceived, trying to remember when she'd last had a menstrual cycle. Life had been chaotic with Dixie and she couldn't remember.

After a few minutes, the tech removed the wand and handed Hayley a towel to wipe off the gel. "I'll let the doctor know we're done," she said.

"What about the results?" Hayley struggled to half-sit, anxious to see the screen. Zola gently pushed her back.

"The doctor will go over all the results with you," the tech said as she swept out of the room.

Her bad mood left a pall in the tiny cubicle. Hayley sniffled. Zola's mouth moved in what Hayley assumed was a silent prayer. Good. She needed all the good thoughts she could get. She *had* to keep this baby.

"Hello, I'm Doctor Cohen. You must be Mrs. Montgomery." The doctor approached the bed to shake Hayley's hand. Her handshake was firm, and she oozed competency.

"How is my baby?" Hayley asked. "The tech told us nothing."

Dr. Cohen turned to Zola. "Are you the grandmother?"

Hayley answered before Zola could open her mouth. "This is my neighbor, Zola Rubenstein."

The doctor consulted her notes. "Before we talk, I need your verbal permission to discuss your condition in front of someone who is not family."

Zola straightened, looking outraged. "I'm the one who called 9-1-1. I rode in the ambulance with her. I have a right—"

"Relax, ma'am. HIPPA laws require me to ask. I didn't mean to *baleydikung* you."

Zola smiled. "No offense taken."

"So, Mrs. Montgomery, do I have your permission to discuss your condition in front of Mrs. Rubenstein?"

"Of course," Hayley answered. *Get on with it, already.*

Hayley was surprised when Dr. Cohen squeezed more gel on her tummy. She moved the wand around without the annoying humming.

"Is everything okay?" Hayley asked.

Dr. Cohen grabbed the monitor to turn the screen around. "Yes. Your babies are fine."

Hayley gasped. "Babies?" The monitor was turned so she could see the black and white ultrasound image of two fetuses. Both little hearts beat as one.

"Looks like you're having twins." Dr. Cohen beamed at her before becoming all business. "Based on the babies' size, I'd say you're about twelve weeks along. My concern is the bleeding you experienced. I'm going to recommend four weeks of complete bed rest. In the meantime, I want you to see your OB/GYN for a follow up."

Hayley barely heard the rest of the doctor's instructions. Twins? How was it possible? Multiple births didn't run in their family. Two babies? Two? Her mind repeated the words over and over. She still couldn't grasp it.

"Here's a printout of the ultrasound," Dr. Cohen said, handing her a four-by-four piece of paper. "I'm sending you home. Good luck!" With that, she was gone, pulling the curtain closed.

Hayley looked at Zola, who started to chuckle, beginning with a low rumble, moving up her ample chest, before bursting into a full laugh. "Oh, *sheyn*. This is wonderful news. The Lord has given you a double portion of blessing!" She clapped her hands as if she, herself was pregnant.

Hayley hugged the ultrasound picture to her chest. Was this a sign she was forgiven?

When they arrived at Hayley's house, Zola helped Hayley into bed, making her promise to call or text if she needed anything.

"I'll be over later with some chicken soup." Zola grinned. "Nothing a little chicken soup can't fix."

Hayley grabbed Zola's hand. "Thank you. For everything."

Zola grabbed her in a fierce hug. "I'm sorry I didn't tell you about Jason sooner. Please forgive me."

Hayley's eyes filled with tears. "I'm sorry, too. I shouldn't have been angry at you. Jason's the one who deserves what he got."

Zola sank onto the bed next to Hayley. "Sheyn, every one of us deserves punishment. That's why Jesus came. Remember, he offers grace to anyone who asks. You, me, Jason. Please think about it. Promise?"

Hayley nodded. "Promise."

After Zola left, Hayley reached for her phone and dialed a familiar number.

"Hello, Mother. I have some wonderful news for you." Hayley explained to her mother the results of the ultrasound and the doctor's orders.

"Let me help you. Please, Hayley. May I come over?" Mother sounded anxious—a new experience.

Hayley paused before answering. After all this time, Mother was now asking permission. Hayley reflected on Zola's words about grace. Perhaps it was time to extend grace to Mother, Zola, and Jazzmine, since God had extended grace to her.

"Sure. That would be nice," Hayley said.

They disconnected. Hayley lay back on the fluffy pillows, resting her hand on her tummy. Were these babies God's way of showing his forgiveness? Could it be that easy?

If what Zola said was true, it didn't matter how much she tried to earn God's favor—it was already there.

"God, I've been blind, deaf, and dumb. Thank you for these two little lives. I'm sorry I was so wrong about how you work. Help me forgive all those who I thought were out to hurt me. Zola, Jazz, Mom, even ..." Hayley gulped back a sob. "Even Jason."

Peace spread from the soles of her feet, ending in a tingling on her scalp. *So that's what Zola meant.*

Later, Zola let herself in. Hayley woke to the sound of Zola huffing up the stairs.

"Good, you're awake," Zola said. "I brought some warm soup. Do you want me to stay while you eat it?"

Hayley nodded with a smile. "Thanks, my friend. For *everything.*"

Zola quirked an eyebrow. "Anything you want to tell me? You look different."

"I finally understand, in here," Hayley patted her chest. "What you meant about how God works. I've been doing it all wrong, expecting to get him to forgive me for the abortion, when I had his forgiveness all along."

Zola grinned, then sobered. "What about Jason?"

Hayley took a deep breath. "I'm working on that."

Zola took her hand. "I understand. Forgiveness can sometimes be a process. Now, about that soup."

CHAPTER 31

FIVE WEEKS LATER

Hayley shifted her weight on the brand-new recliner. She could only take so much lying in bed before going stir-crazy. She'd had the stiff white chairs removed from the living room and the recliner delivered, against the protests of her mother. "That kind of chair doesn't match your décor!" Eventually she'd agreed and had even helped Hayley pick one out online.

In true Mother fashion, she'd arranged a cleaning service to come three times a week to dust, vacuum, clean the bathrooms and kitchen, and change the sheets. Hayley thought three times a week overkill, but to argue with Mother once she was in motion was useless. In addition, Mother hired a personal chef. Perry came three days a week as well, bringing meals that only needed to be heated in the oven or microwave. Plus a variety of fresh fruit and vegetable salads.

The babies were especially active today. Hayley sighed. At least four more months of being kicked all hours of the day—and especially the night. Cynthia had never been this active. Hayley rubbed her tummy. Identical twin boys. Closing her eyes, she pictured them dressed the same, wondering how she'd tell them apart.

Her cell phone pinged with an incoming text.

JAZZ: Hiya Mama. Want to get out of the house?

HAYLEY: YES!

JAZZ: Great. Pick you up in 30 min?

HAYLEY: (thumbs up emoji)

How great to go somewhere other than to a doctor's appointment. Wonder what Jazz had in mind? They'd spoken a few times since Dixie had been moved. At first, Hayley struggled with renewing their friendship, but Jazz eventually wore her down with unrelenting friendliness. The hand-made plaque finally broke through Hayley's resistance. "With God all things are possible" was stenciled on a smooth piece of wood, painted soft blue. There were tiny hand and footprints around the edge in white. Jazz told her she'd taken up a new hobby, and the plaque was her first attempt. Hayley thought it beautiful, and she burst into tears when she opened the gift bag.

Grace extended and grace received.

Hayley locked the front door behind her and sat on the porch step to wait for Jazz. The Indian summer sun warmed her shoulders as it peeked through the leaves of the fruitless mulberry tree. About half of the leaves had already turned yellow and lay on the ground. Hayley imagined raking them into a big pile while the boys jumped in, laughing and playing.

Jazz pulled into the driveway with a quick toot of the horn. Hayley pushed herself to her feet and headed toward the car.

"Where are we going?" she asked.

Jazz grinned. "Nice to see you too!"

"Nice to see you, Jazzmine. Now, where are we going?"

"You'll see." She put the car in reverse as Hayley buckled her seatbelt. "You look good," she said, glancing at Hayley's bulging tummy."

"Huh. I'm as big as the state of Vermont."

Jazz laughed. "Sorry to tell you this, Mama, but you're going to get bigger."

"For sure."

"I like your new haircut," Jazz said with a sideways glance.

Hayley ran her hand through her pixie haircut, resting a hand on her bare neck. "I'm not entirely used to it yet."

"Easier when the babies come."

Hayley murmured her agreement.

They chatted while Jazz negotiated the Midtown traffic. A few minutes later, they pulled up to a park.

"We're here." Jazz unlatched her seatbelt and climbed out of the car. Puzzled, Hayley did the same.

Jazz pointed to a bench. "Let's sit there."

What was this about? Did Jazz get her out of the house to sit in a park? If she did, well, Hayley would enjoy the outing. Jazz rarely did anything without an agenda.

"How are you feeling?" Jazz asked when they were seated.

Hayley shrugged. "I'm okay. No more bleeding. I'm super tired most of the time. And hungry. All. The. Time." With a pang, she remembered how Dixie never seemed to get enough to eat.

Before Hayley could ask about the child, Jazz continued. "Is someone helping you with meals?"

Hayley rolled her eyes. "Mother hired a personal chef to take care of food." Since Hayley's stay in the hospital, her relationship with her mother had subtly shifted. Mother rarely criticized Hayley's clothing choice. She turned her overbearing tendencies toward making sure Hayley's every need was met.

"Of course she did," Jazz said. "Your mother is a human tsunami."

"Don't I know it. Now that Hannah and Keith have broken up, and Hannah moved home, Mother has someone else's life to control. You should see them. Hannah is Mother's Mini Me. They go to all these fund-raising events together. Mother even recruited my wild sister to be on the board of the heart association." Hayley shook her head. That was a train wreck she'd avoided.

Jazz reached over to lay her hand on Hayley's arm. "I wanted to let you know I've given notice at Love's. I'm doing some consulting work, helping families navigate the system of foster/adopting."

"Wow. What a change. What brought that on?"

Jazz's face clouded. "I need to be home more for my boys. Zeke and I are attending counseling with Marcus. He's been acting out more."

"I'm sorry."

A moment passed. Jazz looked across the park. "See the van over there?" A gray minivan pulled to a stop and four kids tumbled out and ran to the swings and play structure. "That's one of the families I'm helping."

Did Jazz bring her all the way to this park merely to show her a family she was helping? Hayley watched as the two littlest girls swung on their bellies, pushing themselves back and forth with their feet. The girl with long dark hair jumped off the swing and climbed to the top of the slide. Hayley watched as the girl looked across the expanse of lawn and saw Hayley looking at her. The girl smiled. Hayley gasped.

The girl, no, she was Dixie. Not the girl anymore. Dixie climbed to the top of the slide and saw Jazzmine with another lady, someone with very short hair. The lady saw her and smiled. Hayley. The lady who loved her first.

"Dixie," she whispered.

"Yes." Jazz patted Hayley's arm. "The family wants to adopt her. Dixie's mother disappeared again, so I'm helping them have her parental rights terminated."

The girl slid down the slide, ran around, and climbed again. Hayley wiped the tears from her eyes with her fingers.

Jazz handed her a tissue. "Dixie is doing great. She wouldn't have come this far if you hadn't given her the chance to experience what it means to be loved and cared for."

Hayley nodded and wiped her eyes.

"I know you think Dixie was some sort of test from God," Jazz continued. "I hope you realize such a little girl couldn't carry that burden for you."

"Zola's been talking to me a lot about forgiveness and grace. I always thought forgiveness was something I had to earn."

"And now?"

Hayley shifted on the hard, wooden bench. The babies pressed down on her bladder. They'd have to leave soon, or she'd be looking for a restroom. "She's helping me see things differently."

"Speaking of forgiveness, have you heard from Jason?" Jazz stood to leave, helping pull Hayley to her feet.

"He sent me a letter."

"Oh?"

"I haven't opened it."

They climbed back into Jazzmine's Honda. "Why not?"

Hayley made a face. "I don't know." She *did* know. Zola said forgiveness can sometimes be a process. Forgiving Jason something she was still working on. "I'll read it. Sometime."

When they arrived at Hayley's house, Jazz got out of the car to embrace Hayley in a tight squeeze. "Let's do this again soon, okay?" As she climbed back into her car, Jazz said, "Read the letter, Mama."

Hayley dragged herself into the house and up the stairs. She sank onto the bed and fell into a deep sleep.

Two hours later, after lunch, she took Jason's letter from where it had sat on the kitchen counter and carried it outside into the afternoon sun. The padded lounger sat in the perfect spot, half-shaded by the giant oak tree hanging over the yard. The landscapers had been by while she was with Jazz. The intoxicating smell of freshly mowed lawn filled the air. Hayley inhaled deeply, then exhaled with a *whoosh* as she settled into the lounger, dropping the letter in her disappearing lap.

A few minutes later, Zola's nephew David appeared at the gate. "Can I come in?"

"Of course."

293

David approached, kneeling next to her. He took Hayley's wrist in his hand, resting two fingers on her pulse.

"How are you feeling? Any pain? Any more bleeding?"

Hayley smiled. "Are you sure you aren't studying to be an obstetrician? You ask me the same thing every time I see you."

David released her, then grabbed another chair. "Actually, things have changed for me. I'm leaving the residency program to go overseas."

"What? That's different."

"I'm going back to Israel. I feel God is calling me to be a missionary for Yeshua to my people."

Hayley studied his handsome face. What he was going to do felt right. She'd miss him, but he was doing a good thing. She told him so.

"When do you leave?"

"Next week. I won't be here for the babies' birth. I'm sure Aunt Zola will send me lots of pictures." They smiled at each other. He glanced down at the envelope in her lap. "Letter from your husband?"

"How can you tell?"

"I have the uncanny ability to read upside down. I can see the return address is from Folsom prison. Just a guess, of course."

Hayley picked up the letter and slapped it against her thigh. "His letter came a few days ago. I haven't read it yet."

David stood. "I'll give you some privacy."

Hayley watched his back as he strode across the lawn and through the gate into Zola's yard. Using her thumbnail to pry open the envelope, she pulled out the pages and began to read.

CHAPTER 32

Dear Hayley,

I've started writing this letter about a hundred times. It's difficult to say in a letter what I want to say in person. Obviously, that's impossible right now. Pastor Ben convinced me to write. You remember Ben, right? He's become a good friend. My only friend. He visits me about once a week.

So, what I want to say is this. I hope you can someday forgive me for everything. When Cynthia died, I was so ashamed I couldn't handle the guilt, so I threw it on you. I was wrong. I've been wrong about a lot of things.

When we got married, I thought I'd won the lottery. I was the luckiest guy in the world—I got the prettiest girl in school. I thought I was all that. I paid my own way through college, started a successful business, and managed to convince a gorgeous woman to marry me. You can see there are a lot of 'I's' in those statements. Everything was all about me and what I wanted.

I did something horrendous and lost everything. The pedestal I'd set myself up on was high, and the subsequent fall was painful. I've had a lot of time to think while I've been here. I wish I could have a do-over, and I guess it's up to you.

As it turns out, I'm being released early. The prison here is overcrowded and they need to make room for more violent criminals. I'll be wearing an ankle monitor for the rest of my time. The date of release is November 3. I've asked Ben to drop me off at our house. I'll ring the front doorbell. If you don't answer, I'll know you don't want to see me. I hope you open the door.

Love,
Jason

Hayley read the letter through twice before setting it on her legs. Jason didn't have a clue she was pregnant. Did she have the right to keep the information from him? Did forgiving him mean she had to let him back in her life?

November 3 was tomorrow. Not enough time to know what to do. She briefly thought about calling Zola or her mother to get their advice before deciding against it. This was a decision she needed to make.

Hayley spent the night tossing and turning. Jason had called her gorgeous. He still loved her. She loved him, she knew that, but what he'd done to Cynthia, to her ... could she forgive him? That was the big hurdle. He'd asked for her forgiveness. Could she withhold forgiveness from him?

She'd finally understood God hadn't punished her for the abortion by taking Cynthia. Her death was a tragic accident, not retribution. She'd been stupid and selfish.

With sudden clarity, she realized Jason had also been stupid and selfish. He'd lied about so many things. Hadn't she lied by omission by not telling him everything?

The next morning, she sat in the recliner, feeling the babies move under her hands.

Waiting for the ring of the doorbell.

She must have dozed off. The sound of the bell made her jump. Hayley launched herself out of the chair and waddled to the front door, resting her head against the wood, still undecided.

Taking a deep breath, she reached for the knob and slowly opened the door.

The End

ABOUT THE AUTHOR

Jane is an author/speaker/teacher based in Oregon. She has served on the boards of Inspire Christian Writers as well as West Coast Christian Writers and regularly teaches the craft of writing at workshops and conferences up and down the west coast.

An award-winning author, Jane's first two books, *Because of Grace* (Hallway Publishing, 2015) and *The Caregiving Season: Finding Grace to Honor Your Aging Parent* (Focus on the Family, 2016) established her as a moving nonfiction voice.

Jane navigates all genres effortlessly, having written articles, essays, flash fiction, and a regular blog. She is nearing completion on two novels-in-progress and has been anthologized in several publications.

When not teaching, speaking about, or practicing writing, Jane can be found in the financial district, where she's the Branch Officer at a community bank.

To everyone who has read and recommended this book—thank you! The best way to help me is to leave a review on Amazon, Goodreads, and Barnes and Noble.

You can sign up for my newsletter at www.janeSdaly. com. Follow me on Facebook, Twitter, Instagram, MeWe, and Parler. Whew—that's a lot of social media.

If you've enjoyed *The Girl in the Cardboard Box*, you'll love *Broken* ... Chapter One follows for your reading pleasure.

CHAPTER 1

Worst. Night. Ever. She stank like the inside of a Porta-Potty; human misery baked to perfection in ninety-degree heat. Spending a night in jail will do that.

Jinxi Lansing shoved open the door to the Sacramento City Courthouse and squinted in the August morning. She gingerly crossed the concrete porch, careful of the stiletto-grabbing cracks in the pavement. No wonder they were called ankle-breakers.

Sweat dripped down her back in the blistering heat. Was she really in Sacramento, or had she been transported back home to Bakersfield sometime in the hours between lockup and release?

The door to the courthouse slammed open behind her. Jinxi swiveled her head. Were armed police officers coming out to haul her back inside? Was she sprung by mistake? She released a deep breath as a group of women in heavy makeup crowded through the door. Everyone wanted outta there. Including her.

A couple of the women bumped her off balance.

"Geez, am I invisible," Jinxi muttered with a curse. She tugged the hot-pink mini skirt to cover what needed to be covered. At least in broad daylight.

Now, which way to go. The corner street signs read 7th and I Streets. Totally meaningless. She pulled the gold stud in her bottom lip against her front teeth and clicked it back and forth. Where was the bus station? She took a chance and started down the sidewalk next to the street with the most traffic.

Broken

Plan A: She'd collect her backpack from the bus station locker, change out of these ridiculous clothes, and grab a shower at the YWCA.

Plan B: If the Y was full, she'd—bam! A cop with his head down, texting, nearly bowled her over. Stupid jerk.

"My bad. Didn't see you." He held out a hand as she lost her balance and regained it.

He looked her up and down. But not in a creepy way. Weird, considering how she was dressed.

"What're you looking at?" Jinxi demanded, hand on her hip.

"Sorry."

She flicked her fingers at him. "Move along. Nothing to see here." Was it okay to tell a cop to get lost?

When he didn't move, she raised her eyebrows and gave him the stink eye. What the—Why was he still staring? He didn't look creepy. More like some guy on a TV cop show. Dark buzzed hair, the shadow of a beard—all clean-cut and American. Still, his cop stare creeped her out.

He spoke at last. "You hungry?"

"Why do you care?" Was he trying to trap her like the cop last night?

"I'm heading up the street to grab some breakfast. You look like you could use something to eat after ... you know." He lifted his arm in the general direction of the jail.

Jinxi narrowed her eyes. "And you get what, exactly, for buying me breakfast." There had to be a catch. There always was.

The cop shrugged. "Nothing. Hey, it's no biggie to me. Eat or don't eat. Your choice." He turned toward I Street and started walking.

Jinxi's stomach growled. Dang, she was hungry. Maybe it wouldn't hurt to let him buy breakfast. If this was another setup, at least she'd have food in her.

"Hey, wait up." Jinxi tripped, struggling to catch up. Stupid shoes. Why had she ever listened to Shana? 'An easy way to make money,' she'd said. Yeah, right. Who was lamer, Shana, or Jinxi for believing her.

At least the cop had the decency to slow down until she reached him. "How far is it?" she huffed.

"Couple of blocks."

"Hold up. Let me take these off." Jinxi slipped off the shoes, wincing.

They walked the two blocks in silence. Jinxi's bare feet slammed onto the hot concrete as she scrambled to keep up with his longer strides. At the diner's entrance, she shoved her aching toes back into the shoes.

Delicious aromas wafted out. Coffee. Bacon. Her stomach took that moment to growl again. Loud.

The cop grinned at her. "See. I knew you looked hungry."

He held the door to let her enter first before heading toward a booth in the back. He took the bench on the side facing the front. Jinxi hesitated. Could this be another in a string of bad decisions? With a sigh, she tossed her purse on the cracked plastic-covered bench. As soon as she was seated, the waitress dropped two mugs on the table and sloshed coffee into each.

"Mornin', Dean. Who's your friend?" She motioned to Jinxi with the pot.

Before Jinxi could protest that they weren't friends, the cop answered, "Well, Mindy, I'm about to find out." He smiled at the older woman. Mindy chuckled as she strolled to the next booth.

So, his name was Dean. Figured. It suited him. All muscular and jock-like. Not much older than her. But seriously, what kind of a guy was a regular at a dump diner like this.

"If I'm going to buy your breakfast, I guess I should know your name."

Jinxi watched him ruin his coffee by adding two creamers and three sugars. Disgusting.

She looked up to find him staring at her.

"Huh?"

"Name." He pointed his spoon at himself. "Dean." At her. "You."

"Oh, uh, Jinxi." She picked at the black nail polish on her thumb. Wait for it, wait for it.

"Is that a nickname?"

Bam. This guy was right on point. "Yup."

Broken

She took a swig of pure, unadulterated coffee, waiting for the caffeine to kick in. She'd need it if this guy was a talker.

"What's your real name?"

Yeah, he was a talker. "Jeanette Xaviera." Now maybe he'd leave her alone.

"I'm Dean Rafferty. Nice to meet you."

She shifted on the bench. Her skirt stuck to the Naugahyde, trapping her legs in a pink sheath.

Really. Nice to meet someone your guys arrested. Nice to meet some loser who spent the night in jail. Where did this guy come from, Sesame Street?

"Could it get any hotter?" asked the waitress as she sidled up to their table. She had a pencil tucked behind her ear, apparently forgotten as she dug around in her apron pocket, order pad in one hand.

"Makes me glad I work nights," the cop answered.

Jinxi grimaced. Yeah, she tried to work nights, too. That didn't go so well.

"What'll it be today." All business once she found the missing pencil.

Jinxi scanned the one-page, laminated menu, searching for the plate with the most food.

"Ladies first," the cop said.

"I'll have the Big Breakfast."

"Same for me," the cop said.

"Bacon or sausage."

"Bacon," they answered in unison.

"Pancakes or French toast."

"Pancakes." Again, they answered at the same time.

"All-righty, I'll be back to warm up your coffees."

Not soon enough.

What would happen if she laid her head down on the table and took a nap until the food came. Jinxi sighed as the cop spoke.

"So, Jinxi, what do you do for fun?"

Was he serious? What kind of a dumb question was that.

"Well, I love hanging out at the tattoo parlor, especially when drunk college girls come in. They squeal like pigs the first time the needle hits 'em. It's totally hilarious." She drained her coffee. The waitress breezed by their table, and Jinxi stuck out her empty cup for a refill.

Dean stared at Jinxi's bare arm, mouth slightly open.

She turned both arms up, laying them on the table. Might as well give him a good look. Most of the scars had faded into a white mosaic, evidence of her brokenness.

Color darkened his face.

"What's the matter? Never seen a cutter before?"

He rubbed the back of his neck with one hand. "Uh, yeah."

Jinxi put her hands in her lap. "Lucky you. Now you got to see it up close and personal." She should never have agreed to breakfast. Her thoughts turned to the knife in her backpack. How long until she could get out of here, locate the bus station, and find release.

At least he'd stopped talking for, like, ten seconds.

"I was watching this cool video on YouTube the other day, about how these guys train their dogs."

What the... Where did that train of thought come from? This guy was too much.

"They put a dog biscuit on the dog's nose. The dogs are trained to stay still until the owner says, 'go,' or something. The dogs throw the treat up off their nose and grab it in midair."

Despite herself, she answered, "Sounds mean. Making the dogs wait. Like animal abuse."

"Hmm. I never thought of it that way. I guess if someone told me to put a Twinkie on my nose and not eat it until they said to, I'd have a hard time with that."

"A Twinkie, no. That wouldn't do it for me. But a Taco Bell Burrito Supreme, yeah, that'd be tough." Go figure. She was having a conversation with a cop.

Dean laughed. "Oh, yeah. Definitely couldn't wait for a Burrito Supreme."

"Looks like you've known lots of Burrito Supremes." Oh, great. Did she tell this cop he looked fat? That had to be against the law.

Broken

Jinxi looked up to see his face as red as if he'd been sissy-slapped. He was blushing.

"It's the Kevlar vest," he said. "It adds twenty pounds."

Wow. The cop was embarrassed about his weight. Priceless. Jinxi took a sip of coffee to keep from smiling.

Their food arrived, and she was saved from having to continue. Her thoughts returned to the cop's story about the YouTube video. It'd be nice to have a dog. Or a cat. Or any pet. Maybe someday when she settled down somewhere. Like that'd ever happen. She had five bucks, half a pack of cigarettes, and two changes of clothes to her name. Her nerves frayed like a too-long pair of jeans. Who was she kidding? There wasn't a Plan B. Living on the street sucked.

The cop mowed through his breakfast as if he hadn't eaten in a week. His masculinity filled the small booth, suffocating her. The guy was massive, intimidating. Appetite gone, she shoved her plate away.

After he'd sopped up every bit of syrup and eaten every piece of egg, he drained his coffee cup. He leaned back and rubbed his stomach. "You done?" He indicated her half-eaten breakfast with a wave of his hand. Before she could answer, he reached across the table and grabbed a piece of bacon off her plate. Yup, done now.

Jinxi followed him to the register while he paid. They stepped outside the diner. The sky had turned a dirty gray while they'd been inside.

Dean sniffed. "Smells like a fire somewhere."

A fire. Jinxi's hand flew to her mouth. Images of a house in flames threatened to make her hurl. She needed to get away. Ripping off the shoes, she strode back the way they'd come.

"Thanks for breakfast," she called over her shoulder. But the cop was right behind her. She startled and dropped her shoes. "Dude. Are you trying to give me a heart attack? What do you want?"

"Do you need a ride somewhere?"

So that's what this was all about. Here's where the guy gets you into his car and expects payment for breakfast.

She clicked the lip stud back and forth against her teeth and shrugged. Might as well get it over with. If she said no, he'd probably find a way to arrest her. Ten minutes. She could put up with anything for ten minutes. Maybe he'd drop her at the bus station after.

"Sure. Whatever. Drop me at Greyhound."

"All right. My truck is parked at the police station." He turned and started back toward the jail as she doubled-stepped alongside.

Dean ducked his head as they passed by the police station. When they reached the parking lot, he hit the remote to unlock his truck while they were still four or five cars away. He opened the passenger door and hustled her in. The truck's cab was as clean as a new penny and smelled similar to the furniture polish they used at the Girl's Ranch. Yuck.

Dean swung around to the driver's side. Jumping in, he shoved the key into the ignition and pulled out of the parking spot with a jerk. They bounced over the curb and into the street as he gunned the accelerator.

"Geez, what's the rush?" Was he that desperate. Jinxi gripped the armrest, wondering where he would take her. "Mind if I smoke?" A cigarette would calm her jangling nerves.

"As a matter of fact, I do."

Figured. Jinxi pulled down the sun visor and flipped open the mirror. And gasped. "Why didn't you tell me I had black stuff smeared around my eyes?" The streaks of mascara created a macabre mask. Out of the corner of her eye, Jinxi saw him shrug.

"I thought it was all part of the, you know, Goth thing."

Jinxi muttered a curse. "You got a tissue or anything in here?" She pulled open the glove box and found some crumpled fast-food napkins. She licked one to moisten it and went to work on the mess.

Satisfied she'd gotten the worst of it, she finger-combed her hair.

"That your natural color?" Dean asked.

Are you always this nosy? "Nope." He didn't need to know she dyed her hair black to cover up the white-blonde mane she'd been cursed with, making her look even younger than her twenty-one years.

Maybe if she faced the passenger window, he'd shut up. They turned into a residential street in the downtown area. Seemed every other house was under construction. Prominent Victorians with wraparound porches and square pillars sandwiched between smaller homes, vying for position. She pictured families eating breakfast together, children getting ready for school, cozy and happy. A foreign country. A secret language with no translation.

"What are you thinking about?"

Geez, this guy was relentless. Jinxi glared at him. "I thought you could give me fifty bucks for a hotel room."

"What?" His head rotated between her and the windshield. Twice.

"Fifty bucks. Hotel room. Isn't that where we're going? So you can get paid back for breakfast? You get a little something extra, and I get something extra." The words rolled out from a dark place. A place where everything had its price, and nobody expected something for nothing.

Dean maneuvered the truck around a slow-moving cab. "All right. I see how it is. How 'bout I offer you something better than fifty bucks and a hotel room?"

This situation was getting weirder by the minute. Maybe the cop was a perv. Jinxi put her hand into her purse and wrapped her hand around the cold canister of pepper spray. The cop was going down. He just didn't know it yet.